Masterfully composed, with a steady pace, a stunning plot, and characters I am going to remember for a long time. This is a haunting story that has been deftly woven together with care, to encourage the reader to peek behind the curtain and view a world that needs help from us – the instruments of God. Remarkable read, and highly recommended.
—**International Review of Books**

When it is late at night, you have no electricity, and the only light is from your cellphone, but you can't stop reading, then you know this is one of the best books you have ever read. Paige Abernathy is a great role model, a character that young girls can look up to. The topics discussed within these pages are something this generation needs to consider, now more than ever.
—**Antoinette Wessels, Readers' Favorite**

The Samaritan's Patient reminds us of the power of love and forgiveness. It is a touching story that is also filled with mystery and suspense. Who wants to kill Paige, and can she ever recover from the scandal? To find out the answers, pick up a copy of Chevron Ross's latest book. You won't be disappointed.
—**Entrada Publishing**

Chevron Ross presents a gripping tale that delves deep into the twisted underbelly of our online world. This book is a must-read for anyone looking to understand the dangers of our digital age. This thought-provoking and emotionally charged novel shows the risks social media can have on our lives.
—**Suzie Housley, Midwest Book Review**

With strong pacing and a cast of memorable characters, this is the sort of novel that's perfect for a reading group; the sort of book you'll want to discuss at length, that might even take you out of your comfort zone. And that is its strength.
—A 'Wishing Shelf' Book Review

Chevron Ross's *The Samaritan's Patient* is a veritable treasure chest of storytelling. The author fuses the issues of teenage suicide and homelessness together with many other social concerns. There is a current of mystery that will keep you on the page, wanting to know who the anonymous donor was. Readers will want to read more from this author.
—**Linda Wood Rondeau, author of *Ghosts of Trumbull Mansion*.**

The author evokes strong emotions about fairness, justice, and God's sovereignty in our lives. Paige's resourcefulness and courage are traits to be admired in this heroine. I especially enjoyed the interrelationship of the main and secondary characters at the conclusion of the story.
—**Patti, Shene, author of *Cathy's Christmas Confession***

The Samaritan's Patient will grip a reader's emotions from beginning to end due to its highly adrenalizing plot, and will leave many wondering just how much misery from the world one can be able to endure when the tables turn, and offer lemons as a reward for noble work.
—**Ephantus M., Pacific Book Review**

Tightly written and briskly paced, *The Samaritan's Patient* is packed with memorable characters, credible dialogue, and a razor-sharp plot that will keep you turning pages into the wee hours (don't ask how I know that). I especially loved the way the author ties each main character's story together, weaving a rich tapestry of shared experiences and understanding.
   —Kristine L., Reedsy Discovery

Gripping from the start, *The Samaritan's Patient* tells the story of Paige Abernathy, a teenager who sets up a website where unhappy youngsters can talk about their problems. With the ultimate message being one of hope and redemption, The Samaritan's Patient is a book to ponder on.
   —Barbara Scott Emmett, author of *Delirium*

The Samaritan's Patient is a thoughtful and well-developed novel that explores the pitfalls and dangers of social media, particularly when it comes to sites designed for individuals with suicidal ideation. Readers will relish the complexity of Paige's character as she pieces together her identity and faces the accusations being thrown against her.
   —BookLife Prize

The Samaritan's Patient

Chevron Ross

AIA PUBLISHING

Also by this author

Weapons of Remorse
The Seven-Day Resurrection

Contents

Author Note

Chevron Ross is a pseudonym for this novel's typist. Its author is God, the author of love and salvation.

Foreword

PART ONE:

Broken

Princess

Three young men ambled up the roadway toward the Bustamante Bridge. A girl stood at the apex, her eyes fixed on the horizon. Gripping the guardrail with both hands, she leaned forward, watching the evening sun settle over the Texas plain.

Her view was impressive despite the abandoned shacks, tumbleweed piles, and pyramids of junk cars at either end of the crossing. The road beneath her arched high above a set of railroad tracks extending as far as she could see.

At first glance, one might think the young woman had stopped there on her way to a formal occasion. A diamond tiara graced her hair. Her pale blue gown fluttered in the breeze above her silver dance shoes. Violet clouds flanked the sun like royal escorts, complementing the girl's regalia.

The boys gathered around her. "Hey, girl. What's up?" The speaker was tall and bony. The other two, short and squat, might have been twins except for their noses, one flat, the other narrow and bent to the left, perhaps from a blow struck in anger. All three wore black T-shirts with purple gang logos.

The girl didn't seem to notice them. Far below, the tracks

ran westward in a straight line. Had a train passed beneath her at that moment, the girl could have watched the sun swallow the engine, boxcars, and flatcars one by one.

"Hey, Mona Lisa. Whatcha doin' out here?" Their eyes crawled over her willowy figure. "What's with the crown? You Princess Kate or somethin'?"

The girl seemed oblivious. She kept a tight grip on the rail and her eyes locked on the sun, its glow marred by buzzards scouting for a late evening snack.

"Hey, girl! Ain't you got no tongue?" Tall Boy snapped his fingers in her face. "Whatcha doin' here, sweet face? This ain't no place for honky debutantes." His companions giggled. The girl remained silent.

"You got any money, honey?" Flat Nose asked.

"Use your head, dude!" Tall Boy shoved him with a bony hand. "How's she gonna have money without no purse?"

"Maybe she's got it hid in that sexy dress," Bent Nose leered.

"How about that, Jordyn Jones?" Tall Boy leaned closer. "You got a secret hidin' place?"

"Got your money in them fancy shoes?" Flat Nose added. "Tucked inside your undies?"

Their grins faded as the girl watched the sun dip below the horizon.

"I'm talkin' to you, girl!" Tall Boy said. "Ain't you got no manners?"

"Yeah! This bridge is our hood," said Bent Nose. "We ain't invited no blondies."

Flat Nose passed a hand across her face. "I think we got her so scared she can't talk."

"How about that, Taylor Swift? You scared of us?"

"You think we're gonna just go away if you ignore us?"

The girl maintained focus, her fingertips white from

gripping the rail.

"I think she's just teasin' us," Tall Boy said.

"Yeah, she's a tease," Flat Nose echoed.

"She ain't gonna tell us nothin'."

"She sure ain't gonna give us nothin'."

"Naw! She's gonna make us look for it."

A gleam appeared in Tall Boy's eyes. "Let's have a treasure hunt!" He yanked her hands loose and spun her around. "Hoo, ain't she pretty?"

"She's fine!" Flat Nose frisked her roughly. "She ain't got no money, though."

"She's got somethin' better than money!"

"Let's see what you've got." Tall Boy's fingers probed for zippers. "How do you get this thing off, Baby Cheeks?"

The girl's eyes cleared. A moan of terror rose from her throat. Her hands flailed at him.

"Now we've got her attention." Tall Boy laughed, seizing her wrists. "Hold still." From behind, Bent Nose grabbed the bodice and ripped it open. "Whoa! She's juicy under this thing!"

"She's about to get juicier!"

"You're gonna give it up, girl!"

"No! No!" She yanked one arm free and slashed at Tall Boy, her nails tearing four deep gashes in his cheek.

"Wha . . ." His fingers came away with blood. "She cut me! She tore my face!" Furious, he backhanded her, slamming her head against the rail. The others tore into her with fists, kicks, and curses.

Twin beams of light pierced the scene. The trio spun around to face them.

"Let's get outta here!" Tall Boy cried, blood oozing from his face. He ripped the tiara from the girl's hair and sprinted in pursuit of his friends. They vanished into the sanctuary of dead automobiles and empty hovels.

The car stopped beside the unconscious victim.

"Keep going, Stan. That's none of our business."

"Betty, that girl's hurt bad! Look at her!"

"Keep going, I said!"

"Shouldn't we at least call 911?"

"And stay in the police station all night, answering questions? We're fifteen minutes late as it is!" The vehicle sped over the archway and into the twilight.

Several minutes passed. Long shadows from the fading sun crept over the girl's body.

A bicyclist came along and paused beside her. He looked around uncertainly, then pedaled down the slope into the encroaching night.

By now the horizon was a deep blue. The buzzards were gone. Trickles of blood ran from the girl's nose and mouth, staining her blond hair.

As darkness fell a second car roared up the incline, stopping with a screech of tires. Now the only sounds were the chirping of crickets and a persistent *ding* as a door clicked open.

Little White Dove

https://serenityshare.com

Welcome to SerenityShare
A haven for the troubled and weary

Greetings everyone! My name is Little White Dove. I created this website for people seeking peace amidst life's challenges.

There's a lot to explore in my drop-down menus: Psalms, poetry, songs, essays, and videos. Best of all, SerenityShare is a forum where you can express your thoughts and feelings.

To access the Sharing Menu, you must first create your user account. Use the link at the top right corner of the screen.

Keep in mind that visitors to this site are people in pain and in search of help, so please make your comments constructive.

FORUM

APRIL 4
FROM BARRENWASTE
Dear Little White Dove,
I'm so lonely. Please talk to me.

FROM LITTLE WHITE DOVE
I am here. How can I help you?

FROM BARRENWASTE
Dear Little White Dove,
Guess I should introduce myself. My given name's Tony, but I chose BarrenWaste because that's what my life is.

Lately, I've become so isolated. Many of my closest friends have moved on, and I can't really blame them. I've lost a lot of the social confidence I used to have. Late last year I had to move back in with my parents because I can't afford to be on my own. A month ago, my girlfriend of over three years left me, and it's been tearing me apart. She was the one part of my life that still felt stable. I thought she was going to be my friend for the rest of my life.

Sometimes things seem to get better, but then they get worse. I'm just so exhausted from the cycle of loving and losing.

FROM LITTLE WHITE DOVE
I know exactly what you mean. My mother X'd my boyfriend and I didn't do anything to deserve it. Life can be so unfair. But I find comfort in scriptures like Proverbs 3: "Trust in the Lord with all your heart and lean not on your own understanding."

APRIL 10
FROM LEFTBEHIND

I can't remember myself ever having much energy. I have never really wanted to live and I have always struggled to cope with life. Life is mostly just meaningless suffering. It is a pointless experience that we go through for the sake of it.

FROM LITTLE WHITE DOVE

I feel that way too sometimes. Sadness just drains all the energy out of you. Please know that there are others like me on this site who understand and sympathize. Tell us about your suffering. Where does it come from?

FROM LEFTBEHIND

The more I see someone especially my age who has done a lot of things, I feel envious. Maybe it's vain, but I really am struggling right now so when I connect with people online and learn how much better are their positions in life compared to me I can't help being envious. I think it's mainly because I tied my self-worth to my grades, but studying to appease my parents doesn't work anymore. A lot of people I meet online are relatively well-adjusted, they're relatively normal, so it's hard to talk to them. I get that there's high functioning depressed people, but in comparison I'm just ashamed to be uselessly alive. Then I start to avoid them. Then I get lonely all over again.

FROM LITTLE WHITE DOVE

Have you spoken to anyone about this?

FROM LEFTBEHIND

None of them would understand. If I see a therapist I'll just pretend I'm getting better when that's not the case. I feel clueless. I'm tired. I want to die but I'm a coward. I think it's too late now.

MAY 1
FROM GONEFORGOOD

Thanks for this thread, Little White Dove. I'm going to use it as a way to document my efforts to CTB. My first try, cutting my wrist, was messy and didn't work. My second, ——— poisoning, nearly landed me on an oxygen tank in the ER. But this time will be different. This time I'll be using my dad's Ruger 9mm.

Cinderella

The admitting clerk bent over the gurney. "Is that who I think it is?"

"Looks like her," said the orderly. "Or what's left of her."

Observers in the waiting area rose from their chairs and gathered around. Some pushed forward, aiming their cell phone cameras.

"What's wrong with you people?" barked a man in a business suit. "This isn't a circus!" Placing his jacket over the girl's face, he stared the intruders back to their seats.

"What happened to her?" asked the clerk, recovering her aplomb.

"Some kind of mugging. I found her on the Bustamante Bridge."

"Are you a relative, sir?"

"No, I, uh . . . just happened along."

"Did she have any ID with her? An insurance card maybe?"

"I didn't find anything."

"Okay." The clerk tapped at her keyboard. "I can admit her as a Jane Doe, but I'll need some contact information. Will you please fill out this form and include your name, address, and phone number?" She handed him a clipboard.

"I thought you said you recognized her."

"I said I thought I did. With her face like that, it's hard to be sure."

The orderly wheeled the patient away. The suited man donned his jacket, checked his watch, and took a seat.

A woman beside him whispered, "Is that the girl who—"

"Please! Let me finish this. I've got a plane to catch." He scribbled rapidly.

The woman turned to her companion. "I think it's really her!" A chain of whispers ran through the room. "It is! Here's her picture on Facebook!"

Returning to the desk, the suit found a line of people ahead of him. A stout man in a wheelchair coughed harshly into his ventilator mask. Next was a weary-looking mother with a howling infant on her shoulder. Behind them stood two boys in basketball trunks, one holding a bloody sock to his elbow.

The suit pushed past them. "Here's your paperwork," he told the clerk. "I've got to get going."

"Sir, will you be taking responsibility for this patient?"

"What do you mean?"

"I'm asking because I'll have to admit her as indigent. But the computer needs a billing address. Can I use yours?"

He checked his watch again. "I can't wait any longer or I'll miss my plane."

"Sir, all patients require a billing status."

He produced a credit card, then hesitated. Digging through his wallet, he offered the clerk a wad of bills. "Here's two hundred dollars. That's all I've got on me."

"I'm sorry, the minimum for initial visits is—"

"Please, just take it! I'll be back to check on her in a

few days."

The clerk logged the payment. "Sir, are you sure you want to do this? She's not even a relative, and everybody knows what she's done."

"It's the Christian thing to do. Please, I'm in a hurry!" The clerk handed him a receipt. The suit dashed for the exit. "Call me if she needs anything," he yelled over his shoulder. "Anything at all."

The clerk watched him disappear into the night. "The Christian thing?" she muttered. "Crucifixion's too good for her. Next, please!"

"Rough night at the ball, Cinderella?"

The girl's eyes flew open. For a moment she was back on the bridge. She thrashed and kicked at the sheet covering her body.

"Whoa, take it easy!" Strong hands seized her wrists. "Shh, shh. Calm down, you're safe. You're in the hospital." She groped at the frozen lumps on her face. "Those are ice packs," the doctor said gently, "to keep the swelling down."

A nurse approached the gurney with a blanket. "Here, this will keep you warm."

The girl's breathing slowed. Through blurry eyes she made out two shadows surrounded by artificial light. "Warm?" Slowly, she relaxed beneath the blanket. "Warm," she purred. "Warm."

"Careful now. Looks like you've got a couple of fractures in that left hand. Try not to move it until we get you down to X-ray."

"X-ray," she babbled. "B-blanket. Warm."

"I'm Dr. Wingate. You're in Frazier emergency. Can you tell me your name?"

"Name?"

"What's your name?"

The nurse whispered, "Doctor, I think that's—"

"Shh! I want to make sure she knows." He turned back to the patient. "Miss, who are your parents? Is there someone we can call for you?" No answer. "What's your name, sweetheart?"

"P-P-P . . ." The girl's face went blank. Her eyelids fluttered.

"Never mind. You just lie there and rest. You're in good hands."

"Hands," she mumbled. "G-g-good . . . hands . . . p-people."

He chuckled. "That's pretty close, but it's Wingate, not Allstate. Dr. Wingate." He aimed a penlight at her eyes. "That's some outfit you were wearing, Cinderella. If I'd known you were going to a ball, I'd have volunteered to be your escort." He paused. "How do you feel?"

"G-good . . . hands. Warm-gate. Blanket." She drifted off.

The doctor frowned. "Looks like brain trauma. Let's put her in ICU, at least overnight. I'll notify radiology and neurology." Leaving, he paused to examine the ruined dress on the floor. "What a shame. She must have been beautiful in it."

Discouraging Words

MAY 18
FROM UNHAPPY UNBIRTHDAY

I've been nothing but a mistake my whole life. Every single thing I've done is wrong. I also worry/hate myself for the words I wrote on here. Afraid they're not good enough. That even on this forum, I am also failing. Maybe showing too much or too little or being way too vulnerable and not smart enough. Never enough.

FROM LITTLE WHITE DOVE

Here's a quote from C. S. Lewis that you may find useful: "You can't go back and change the beginning, but you can start where you are and change the ending." Don't give up, my birthday friend. You're as good as anybody else.

MAY 20
FROM HELLHOLE

Today is very depressing and miserable, I don't feel like doing much. I just want to sleep.

FROM LITTLE WHITE DOVE

Sleep can make depression worse. Do something constructive, even if it's something simple, like cleaning your room. And try prayer. That always makes me feel better.

FROM HELLHOLE

Pray to who? If there was a God, the world wouldn't be like this.

MAY 24
FROM DEAD ZONE

Whenever I start to draw or write, I often think to myself, "Is this how I'm going to spend my last year alive? Doing something I only do as a substitute for the validation I never got as a child? Something I hate doing?"

I don't really have any other hobbies, but drawing makes me miserable. Everything makes me miserable, so it's really not like drawing is the issue here. Doing anything is so painful and makes me want to die.

I spend my days lying in bed, waiting for my death date. I should have the money I need by next year to CTB successfully.

FROM LITTLE WHITE DOVE

What does CTB mean?

FROM INSTITUTIONALIZED

CTB is a way out. You should know that, Little White Dove, if you're going to host a forum like this.

Jane Doe

The patient, known to the database as ER46739461, stirred feebly in her bed. Somewhere down the hall, voices were laughing. A floor polishing machine hummed past her room. Beyond the window a siren wailed, growing louder in its approach.

A dull pounding in the back of her head warned her not to move. She let her eyes roam. Bleary visions of bedrails and a tray table told her she was in a hospital. The IV needle taped to her right arm indicated something serious.

She took inventory. Her left hand was swollen. Moving it sent bolts of pain up her arm. Two fingers wore splints wrapped in gauze and tape. Purple bruises covered both arms, and three nails on her right hand were broken and crusty with dried blood.

Probing her memory made her head swim. She recalled a large shadow with a soothing voice, a touch of softness and warmth, then darkness.

She tried to move her legs, but the blanket was too tight. *I'm paralyzed*, she thought. *This is where the doctor comes in and tells the patient she'll never walk again.*

A nurse entered instead. "Well, you're awake at last. How do you feel?"

"I . . . c-can't . . ." She cleared her throat. "I can't move my legs."

"At least you're talking. Hold on, I'll get the doctor."

The girl's eyes drifted to the window. She squinted at the bright sunlight. Nondescript buildings dotted the landscape.

A young man appeared wearing a white coat and a flat smile. "Hello, Jane Doe." He nodded perfunctorily, checking the bedside monitor. "Are you having any pain?"

"Yes," she croaked. "In my head and fingers. Is it okay for me to get up?"

"One thing at a time." He pressed a button. The girl hissed as the bed raised her to a sitting position. "That hurts!"

"Where?"

"My ribs. My chest. Can you pull that blanket back?"

He obliged, exposing a flimsy hospital gown. The girl gasped at the mottle of bruises on her skin. "What happened to me?"

"Try to move your legs."

Gingerly the patient lifted one knee, then the other. "That's a relief."

"Now let's see if you can sit up by yourself. Can you swing your feet around to the side? Watch out for the catheter tube."

She tried, but the pounding in her head swelled to a clanging. The room swam. She grabbed the doctor's shoulder for support, yelping at the pain in her hand.

"Too soon, huh? Here, let's lean you back."

Gratefully she relaxed as the bed returned to first position. The anvil chorus in her skull faded to a roar. "What happened? How did I get here?"

"Obviously someone brought you in. What's the last thing

you remember?"

"Something about birds and a sunset." She noticed cars zipping along an overpass beyond her window. "Which hospital is this?"

"Frazier Memorial."

"What city?"

"What city do you live in?"

The girl concentrated. "That's funny. I can't think of the name. Some of those buildings look familiar though." Her attention turned to her arm. "What's in that tube?"

"Just Tylenol with a saline chaser. Are you allergic to any prescription medications?"

"I don't know."

"What's your pain level?"

"What do you mean?"

"On a scale of one to ten, how bad is it?"

A division of army tanks rumbled between her temples. "Ten's not enough."

The doctor produced a pad and pen. "Can you tell me your name?"

She strained out the words. "P-P-Paige. Paige Ab-Abernathy."

"Where were you born?"

"Hou . . . Houston."

"Your birth date?"

"Uh, Frr . . . Mrr . . . I can't say it!" she cried. "What's the matter with me?"

"Never mind. How old are you?"

"Sixteen. No, seventeen, I think. Why can't I make those words come out?"

The doctor ignored her. "What's your address?"

"Eight—I mean ten . . ." She began to cry. "I don't know.

It's—it's on Qrrr . . . Vggg . . . Something Street."

"What's your phone number?"

"Please," she whimpered, "it hurts too much to think."

"All right, maybe later." The doctor drew the blanket around her. "I'm just an intern. The ward resident should be in to look at you soon. Do you need anything?"

"Is that water?" she asked, indicating a plastic bottle on the tray table.

"Yes. Here you go."

Paige sipped at the straw. "Oh, that's so cool!" Greedily, she drank it all.

"Are you hungry?"

"If I try to chew anything I think my head will fall off."

He nodded. "I'll ask the food service to bring you some soup. In the meantime here's the call button. Just press it and somebody at the nurses' station will answer."

"Thank you, Doctor."

Another flat smile. "Just doing my job." He checked the IV bag and left.

Paige took another sip, but the bottle was empty. Again she tried to recall her birth date. All she got was a picture of dead grass and bare trees. The sky outside her window suggested early autumn. September maybe.

Thoughts of home produced some bizarre results. A doorpost with barber pole colors and upside-down numbers. A mailbox with Greek lettering. A Japanese pagoda with a neon sign reading "Wendy's." None of the images seemed real, and they made the headache worse.

Too much effort. Resting her head on the pillow, she let the rhythmic pounding drag her back down to sleep.

She woke to a blinding light and a thumb pulling up her eyelid. Startled, she twisted away. A woman in a white coat stuck the penlight back in her pocket.

"Good morning. I'm Dr. Reeves, the ward resident. How's your head?"

Paige blinked. "A little better, I think. How long have I been here?"

"Two days. We were worried about you, sleeping so much. Looks like you're coming out of it though. Do you think you can sit up now?"

"I'll try."

The doctor raised the back support and adjusted her pillow. Paige's head still throbbed but with rhythm, not pain. "I doubled up on your Tylenol. Do you remember anything before you got here?"

"No. What happened to me?"

"That's what we'd like to know. A police officer's been by twice to see you. Looks like someone used you for a punching bag. You have four bruised ribs. No broken bones, except those two fingers. A lot of cuts and bruises, mostly on your limbs and torso. There's a knot on the back of your head and a hairline skull fracture. You may have a concussion. The neurologist wants to run an EEG and a CT scan if you can stay awake long enough."

Paige touched her face with the one finger that didn't hurt, wincing at the tenderness around her left eye. "How did I get here?"

"According to the admitting clerk, some guy in a business suit found you on the Bustamante Bridge. Sound like anyone you know?"

"I do seem to remember something about a bridge."

"What were you doing there?"

"I have no idea." She winced as she touched a knot below her left eye. "Is there a mirror around here?"

"Let's hold off on that for now. What's the last thing you remember?"

She concentrated. The weird images from before were gone. "Nothing specific. Just ordinary things. Buildings. Streets. Cars. Traffic lights. Why can't I have a mirror?"

"Do you feel up to receiving visitors? Your mother's been asking to see you."

"My mother?"

"Yes. Can you tell me her name?"

A wave of darkness swept through her. "No."

"What about your address?"

She opened her mouth but gagged on the missing words.

"Do you have a boyfriend?"

"I don't remember."

"What about school? Can you name some friends you hang out with? Your teachers? Anyone?"

"I, uh . . . I think . . ." She gazed out the window. "I'm getting a picture. Something about a cat. Why can't I remember anything?"

"Brain trauma can cause temporary blackouts. Don't fret too much. Soon it may all come rushing back." The doctor tapped some notes into an electronic pad.

Paige's head began to throb again. "Who's paying for all this?"

"Let's see." The doctor scrolled through the chart. "No insurance. Looks like a private party."

"Who?"

"It's not listed here."

"How can I find out?"

"You've got enough to think about for now. Don't worry,

we're not going to throw you out on the street. Just rest and get well." Dr. Reeves studied her patient closely. "Are you sure there's nothing you want to tell me?"

"What's to tell? I can't remember anything."

"Do you think you can stay awake for some tests?"

"I guess so."

"Okay. I'll be back to see you later." She exited briskly.

Left alone, Paige felt uneasy. A voice echoed from down the hallway. TV laughter babbled from a room nearby. Otherwise it seemed awfully quiet for a hospital.

How do I know that? she wondered. *Have I been in a hospital before? Is this what it's like to be born? As a blank slate?*

A random melody drifted through her thoughts: *The little things that you say and do make me want to be with you-oo-oo . . .*

Beneath her anxiety Paige felt a sense of despair. Something in her throbbing head was eating at her. It had to do with . . .

No. Whatever it was, it hid in a dark room behind a heavy locked door.

The TV screen mounted in the ceiling was dark. She searched for the remote control but couldn't find it. Lying back, she closed her eyes, willing the pictures to come.

She awoke to a dark shape looming over her. "No, don't!" she yelped, cowering against the bedrail. "Please, don't!"

Flustered, the cleaning woman backed away. "I'm sorry, I was just emptyin' your waste basket. I'll be done in a minute." She turned and drew a floor mop from a yellow bucket.

Paige relaxed. Long shadows from her window suggested late afternoon.

"I'm sorry I screamed at you," Paige said. The woman kept her back turned, scrubbing at the floor. "What's your name?"

A moment of hesitation. "Glenda."

"How long have you worked here?"

She plunged her mop into the water and squeezed it out. "I ain't s'posed to talk to patients, ma'am."

"Why not?"

"Just ain't." The woman carried her mop into the bathroom. Paige heard the shower curtain zing and water running. Glenda emerged with a plastic trash bag and rolled her bucket into the hallway. "You want your door shut?"

"No thanks."

The woman headed down the hall and knocked on a door. "Hi, Mr. Wheeler!"

"Hi, Glenda. Come in."

"How you feelin' today?"

"Much better. Did your daughter have her baby yet?"

"No, but she oughta be textin' me any minute."

Why wouldn't she talk to me? Paige wondered. *Maybe it's my face.* She wished for a mirror. The one above the room sink was too far away, and she wasn't sure of her feet yet.

She explored herself again. The pounding in her head was gone, but pain flared in her ribs when she breathed too deeply. Two fingers were still splinted. The ones with broken nails felt a little better. The swollen places on her face remained tender.

There was no clock in the room. Night was falling. Beyond her window the sky was a deepening blue. Time seemed to pass randomly. *Sleep*, she supposed.

The room was boring. One molded plastic chair, a guaranteed backache for any visitor who stayed too long. A tired-looking vinyl couch with a frizzy throw pillow. An open closet with two wire hangers. Even the bed was boring. White sheets and a cheap-looking beige blanket. They ought to do something about that, Paige thought. Perhaps a comforter with bright flower patterns. Pastel colors for the walls. Soft textures, with light curtains to offset them and conceal that ugly utility building outside her window. A little beauty would go a long way with a sick patient.

How do I know that?

She lay back against the pillow. *Who is Paige Abernathy? What happened to her? Where does she belong?*

Someone knocked on the door frame. "Come in."

A woman in police blues entered and turned on the lights. "Ms. Abernathy, I'm Officer Hardaway. Are you up to receiving visitors?"

"I guess so." The cop's shoulder insignia caught her eye. Alverna Police. "Alverna High School!" Paige cried. "Go Tigers!"

"Pardon me?"

"Alverna, Texas. That's where I live, right?"

"Right."

"Thank God!" she sighed. "I remembered something!"

The officer dragged the flimsy chair to the bedside and drew a black object from her belt. "I need to ask you some questions. Do you mind if I record your statement?"

"No, but you probably know more than I do."

"We got an anonymous call from a motorist who passed you on the Bustamante Bridge. He saw three people running from the scene. Do you know them?"

"I don't remember that. Did he say what they looked like?"

"Three Black males. Young, teenagers maybe. Can you think of anyone who might want to harm you?"

"No."

She made some notes. "We've been having some problems

with gang activity in that area. It was a nice neighborhood before people started moving out to Emory Village. Did you have a purse or money with you before you were attacked?"

"I don't remember."

"Maybe they got your cell phone. Can you tell me the number?"

Paige concentrated. "I'm sure I must have one, but I can't . . . I don't know."

"What about jewelry? A watch? A ring, necklace, earrings?"

She shook her head. Officer Hardaway shifted uncomfortably in the plastic chair. "The admitting nurse said you had on a light blue dress and silver dance shoes. Fancy, like you were going to a party."

Images flashed across Paige's consciousness. Lights and musical instruments. Boys in tuxedoes dancing with girls in colorful gowns. Something about them made her feel like crying.

"Ms. Abernathy?"

"The dress . . . Was it ankle-length?"

"Yes. One-piece strapless, long hemline."

"And the shoes. Were they shiny, with ankle straps?"

"That's right."

Another tune echoed in Paige's head: *Everyday, it's a-gettin' closer* . . . Her heart began to pound.

"Are you remembering something?"

"Where's the dress? The shoes?" she asked tremulously.

"The dress was pretty much destroyed. What's left is at the forensics lab, along with the shoes. We'll return them to you when the analysis is finished."

"What analysis?"

"Just routine stuff. Fingerprints, blood typing, fluid samples for DNA tests. Now, back to my question. Why would you be dressed like that, standing on a bridge in the middle of nowhere?"

Paige shuddered. The room began to spin.

"Is something wrong?"

Her eyes rolled back in her head. She began to tremble violently.

The officer rushed to the door. "Nurse! I need some help in here! Quickly!"

CTB

JUNE 14
FROM ANGUISHED IN TAMPA

Dear Little White Dove and friends,

I've been hit with physical pain today on top of the normal mental anguish and I just feel so done. I could sleep forever if I had no responsibilities. The ibuprofen is questionably working—like I'm in a limbo where close by is a much worse pain and just the edge of it is stabbing me for now. It's such a weird place, where the pain isn't yet disabling, but somehow still feels so intolerable. It comes and goes too. Aside from my back. I'd rip out my spine if I could.

Anyone else feel anything similar at all? Or want to say anything? This community here is great and the people so nice yet today I feel so empty. I like replying but in some part I'm just filling a hole and numbing myself further. I just feel more alone the more time I spend here, and the more words I type and hate myself for.

FROM ETERNAL SLEEP

I'm sorry that you are suffering. I can imagine that it must be horrible dealing with that physical pain. I know that it is awful when things just get worse. I would also like to just sleep forever. To me life is just meaningless suffering that I would like to be free from. I wish you the best in whatever happens.

FROM LITTLE WHITE DOVE

Here's a quote I discovered recently: "We are all a little broken. But the last time I checked, broken crayons still color the same."

JUNE 22
FROM YOUNG AND HOPELESS

It's been months now and I still haven't CTB. I've been very down lately and I've been planning to buy some ——— for months now so I can use it to CTB. I don't know if 30 mg is enough but hopefully it is. I've been trying so hard to connect with people but even my therapist is low-key pushing me away. No one likes me or wants to be around me. I'm getting tired of being here. I can't take this for any longer. I wish there was another solution for my problem but really there isn't. I hope no one feels guilty about my plans even the ones that treated me badly it isn't their fault either. I hope I could tell everyone how sorry I am for what I'm about to do.

FROM LITTLE WHITE DOVE

Don't do it. God didn't bless you with life so you could throw it away. Open your heart to Him.

Listen to what Isaiah says about God:

He gives strength to the weary and increases the power of the weak.
Even youths grow tired and weary, and young men stumble and fall;
But those who hope in the Lord will renew their strength.
They will soar on wings like eagles;
They will run and not grow weary, they will walk and not be faint.

FROM HELLHOLE
You Bible thumpers are all alike.

FROM YOUNG AND HOPELESS
Stop picking on Little White Dove. She's just trying to help.

JULY 1
FROM ALL WASHED UP
Hi everyone.

I don't know if I'm supposed to post about this, but I just got a small packet of ———. I ordered a different one to arrive later just in case I decide to CTB.

This one is pink though. It is specifically used for meat curing. I'm not sure if it's the right one, or if it will work.

Let me know if it's ok to be posting about this. Also let me know if you think this pink one is the right one and if I can give more details.

FROM RX FACTOR

I think the ——— you ordered is curing salt. Mine is very white. I found a Russian company that sells ———, but it's just curing salt.

JULY 13
FROM GONEFORGOOD

I spent almost all of last night researching and practicing noose-tying. Only slept about three hours, hardly ate, and now I'm back at it. Eyes are burning. Stomach hurts. In movies and TV, it just happens. Everyone just has the perfect rope in their houses, perfect length, perfect apparatus to stand on, perfect support to hang from, and it's over off-screen: peaceful and pleasant.

I never thought I'd ever attempt hanging. For some reason, of all the ways to go, it just didn't sit right with me, but it seems it might be my only option. That ——— is so hard to get a hold of, and the couple sources I found don't seem reputable. It's a whole other process to test the purity. Looked into a gun again, but in my state, I need at least two people as references to vouch for my mental health, and there's just no way. Besides, they know of my mental health, they know I dislike guns. Suddenly wanting one would be the most obvious tell.

FROM LITTLE WHITE DOVE

As host and moderator, I want to remind all members that SerenityShare is not for suicide talk. I don't like having to black out words or delete comments, but we are here to encourage, not destroy. Please make your remarks constructive.

Diagnosis

Visitors flowed past two physicians huddled at the nurses station. Bearing flowers, they searched the corridor for room numbers.

"Sounds like a convulsion," Dr. Ursi said. "Does she have a history of epilepsy?"

"She claims she doesn't have *any* history," Reeves replied. "Just fragments of memory."

"Do you think she's faking amnesia? Maybe she's seen too many Jason Bourne movies."

"If she's faking, it's a good act."

The neurologist put the X-ray aside. "I can't tell anything from this. Let's do a CT scan." He lowered his voice. "I hear Lydia Abernathy's been turning this place upside down, demanding to see her."

"She's got the clout too," Reeves said. "When she cornered me in the lounge, I said it would be best to keep her isolated for now. Boy, did she give me a tongue-lashing! I finally referred her to Dr. Meadows."

"Smart move. Crossing swords with lawyers is the kind of thing he gets paid for." Ursi frowned. "There's a lot of gossip among your staff, and not just on this floor."

"I know. Meadows sent out a memo. As far as we're concerned she's just another patient, to be treated as such. But no visitors, except for police. And especially no reporters. The switchboard is blocking all calls to her room."

Two more visitors wandered by, wearing apprehensive faces.

"You know," Ursi remarked, "this is going to leak out eventually. If it hasn't already."

"I'm with you. The sooner we get her out of here, the better."

Paige awoke to a familiar voice.

"Hello again, Cinderella." Dr. Wingate smiled. "If you're looking for your carriage, it turned into a pumpkin three days ago."

She scanned the curtained walls. "Where am I?"

"Intensive Care. You had a seizure in your room, so we're keeping an eye on you. Turn your head this way."

She squinted at the penlight. "A seizure? What do you mean?"

"The police officer said you were thrashing around like a fish out of water."

"I don't remember that."

He checked the monitor. "Your pulse and pressure look good. Do you feel dizzy or nauseous?"

"No." Paige examined his face. The doctor was sandy-haired, rugged-looking in an indoorsy way. Intrinsic humor formed crinkles around his mouth and eyes. "I remember you. Your voice, I mean. The good hands man."

"That's me."

"I thought you worked in the emergency room."

"I'm a floater. I go where I'm needed." He probed her scalp. "You've got quite a bump back there, Cinderella. Did you fall out of bed?"

"Not that I know of. Why do you keep calling me Cinderella?"

"When you showed up here you were dressed like a princess. Only, the clock had struck midnight, and your gown was in tatters." Paige shuddered at the words. "Something wrong?"

The feeling passed. "No. I guess not."

He peered closely at her eyes. "Do me a favor. Look straight ahead. Stretch your arms out by your sides, point your index fingers, and slowly bring them together in front of you." She obeyed. "That's good. Now, lay both hands by your sides. Look straight ahead and, one at a time, touch your nose with each index finger."

Paige's right finger hit the target. Her left bounced off an eyebrow.

"Try it again."

This time she touched her chin. "I can't do it. What's wrong with me?"

"Try this. Put the heel of your right foot on top of your left knee. Now, slide it all the way down. Gently," he added as she hit a sore spot. "That's good. Now do the same thing with your left foot . . . That's fine. Can you sit up straight?"

"I don't think so. It makes my ribs hurt."

"That's okay." The doctor hung the catheter bag on the IV pole and moved to her right side. "Swing your legs around to the left." From behind he lifted her back a little. The strength in his hands was reassuring. "Lean against me and place your hands palm-down on your thighs. Now flip them rapidly over and back, ten times . . . Good, very good. Do you think you can stand up?"

With his help, she scooted off the bed, gritting her teeth against the pain. "Now I want you to walk slowly, heel to toe, without looking down. Look straight at me." Dr. Wingate held out his hands as Paige lurched forward, bent over like Quasimodo. "Take it easy. Don't force anything."

Paige managed four steps before she tumbled forward. The doctor caught her. "A little shaky, huh?"

"I don't know. I just couldn't . . . I don't know." Wingate lifted her to her feet. "Just stand there for a minute. Did you feel the room spinning or anything like that?"

"I felt sort of woozy. Like a curtain falling over my eyes."

"All right. Take a couple of breaths. Not too deep. Just enough to clear your head." He gave her a moment. "Now close your eyes and keep them closed. Don't worry, I won't let you fall."

Two seconds of darkness was all it took. The doctor caught her again as she toppled sideways. "The head injury may have affected your sense of balance."

"You can always tell a lady by her grace and posture," Paige muttered.

"Let's try this. Raise your arms to shoulder level. No, not toward me, out by your sides, like an airplane ready for takeoff. Now once again, with your eyes straight ahead, bring the tip of each index finger to the tip of your nose. First the left, then the right."

Her ribs howled in protest, but she managed it. "All right!" the doctor applauded. "Well done!"

"Why couldn't I do the left one before?"

"It could be a side effect from the seizure."

"What caused that?"

"Probably that knot on your head."

"Is it permanent?"

"I couldn't say, not being a specialist. The neurology tests may tell us more. At least we know you can stand up when your eyes are open." He stepped back. "Now, one last time, walk straight toward me, heel to toe." He backed toward the entrance, his arms toward Paige as she advanced. "That's better. Okay, have a seat." He settled her back on the bed and produced a digital notebook. "Dr. Reeves tells me you've got some memory loss. Has it gotten any better?"

"I still don't remember much of anything before I got here. I do remember you though. Dr. Allstate."

He laughed. "Wingate."

"Oh. Sorry."

"No problem. It's better than Windbag. That's what the kids called me in school. Do you have any questions?"

"Yes. Why do doctors wear white coats?"

"So the nurses can tell us apart from the janitors."

Paige giggled. She studied the doctor as he worked on his notes. His easy manner reminded her of someone close to her heart. She couldn't think who it was.

"Where did you get all that stuff about grace and posture?"

"I'm not sure. It's like my name. Something I just know." She looked beyond him. Nurses bustled in and out of neighboring cubicles. Paige couldn't see the people inside them. "How long do I have to stay here?"

"At least until we get your test results back. In the meantime you seem stable, so I'm sending you back to your room." He checked her chart. "I understand you're not allowed to have visitors. Is there anyone you'd like us to phone for you?"

"I wouldn't know. My memory's gone."

The doctor rolled his eyes. "Dumb question, huh?" He drew a card from his wallet. "This is my private number. Call me if you need anything. Even if it's just to talk."

She examined the card. Frazier Memorial Hospital. Steve Wingate, MD.

"Dr. Wingate, you've been nicer to me than the other doctors. Why is that?"

"I have a daughter about your age. I'd be worried if she was in your shoes. Not the silver ones," he added. "Those were classy."

"Silver shoes," Paige said thoughtfully.

"Are you remembering something?"

She concentrated. "No. I guess not."

"Is there anything you'd like to tell me? I'll keep it to myself, if that'll help."

Paige hesitated. "I don't know how to put this, but . . . something feels wrong."

"Physically? Emotionally?" She shook her head. "Okay. Interrogation's over. I'll let you get some rest."

"Dr. Wingate, before you go . . ."

"Yes?"

Paige slid off the bed and shuffled toward him. "Would you mind catching me again?" She laid her head on his chest.

Deadly Options

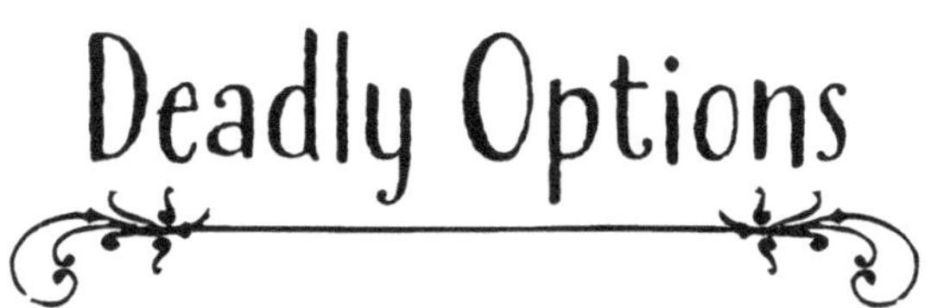

AUGUST 11
FROM WORN DOWN

I don't really believe in anything anymore, except for the fact that no one ever really notices my existence. No one would ever really love me for who and what I am. It's that painful realization that no one would give me importance as much as I give them importance. The painful truth that no one could ever reciprocate the love I've been giving.

AUGUST 15
FROM GONEFORGOOD

A hesitation that's plagued me is that I feel unbearable guilt thinking about how my suicide would impact those I know care about me. As for my parents, I think they'd experience a mix of anger and confusion, especially my mom. My mom doesn't understand suicide at all and defaults to "how could (person) do something so selfish?" although my dad's more empathetic on that subject. He just blew up at me for something today though . . . so I'm remembering why I often feel like such an inconvenience.

I'm extremely worried about my best friend. Many years ago, I was adamant about poisoning myself and they told me that they'd kill themselves if I ever killed myself. However, I think they're in a better place mentally than they have been in years, so I think they'll be okay. I did open up to them a few weeks ago about my suicidal thoughts. They told me that if I ever hurt myself, they'd end up blaming themselves. They also warned me that if I even so much as self-harmed they'd tell my ex-girlfriend about it.

That's one thing I'm also super scared of, my ex finding out. I don't think she cares about me much anymore, not nearly as much as she once did, but still. I'd imagine the trauma of finding out your ex committed suicide a month after you left them would be devastating, maybe life-ruining. I don't want to ruin anyone's life, not even someone who hurt me as much as she did.

When she broke up with me, she straight-up asked me if I was going to be safe, and I knew exactly what she meant. She has trauma regarding suicide because her own best friend once self-harmed and sent her pictures of the injuries, and even more trauma from the partner she dated before me. That partner posted on his social media about how the breakup had made him feel suicidal—on a platform that she still followed him on. I could always tell she suffered from a lot of trauma regarding that anxiety, thinking she could've been responsible for someone else's death. He ended up being safe in the long run, but still, the damage was done.

When she asked me if I was going to be safe, I said yes. Not only did I say yes, but I promised her that I would never put her through that. I called myself a "tough cookie." At the time, I meant every word. But that was before my depression spiked, before my anxiety became unmanageable. I just wish I could tell her that I'm sorry for what I'm going to do—and perhaps I'll at least try to. I might try calling her number while I'm out on the water, although I don't know what I'd say if she actually picked up the phone.

AUGUST 21
FROM MIXED UP

Does anyone have tips on how to make suicide look like a murder or accident? The biggest thing holding me back is leaving my family with guilt.

FROM R.I.P.

I don't know if you have to do much to make it look like a murder. Cops are always looking to convict someone for something they had nothing to do with.

AUGUST 25
FROM DEATHWISH

I am new to the community and looking desperately for ways to CTB. I have contacted a company that sells ———, but they have advised me that it burns your eyes and must be handled with glasses and gloves. Can anyone advise me on this?

FROM MISS ANTHROPE

I found it cheap on a retailer site. Took about a month to get because it comes from overseas. Good luck!

FROM LITTLE WHITE DOVE

Dear SerenityShare Friends:

I'm sorry so many of you are in pain. Nevertheless, I must insist that you obey the ground rules. No more tips on how to off yourself. If this continues I will have to start deleting accounts.

Pickled

Omer Goldmann was a daydreamer. Even as a child he floated through life on random thoughts, hardly noticing his surroundings. Not that he was lazy or irresponsible. His father and his grandfather had drilled the cultural ethics into him. Remember the Sabbath. Honor your parents. Study the Torah. Help Papa in the dry-cleaning store after school. Omer loved his family and wanted them to be proud of him. He liked his synagogue and tried hard to be a good student.

It was just that he had trouble concentrating. Certain words or phrases sent his mind spinning off in wild directions. For example, what did Mama mean when she said Levi and Rachel were in a pickle? Omer was only seven. Levi was a giant, six-foot-one, and his girlfriend was almost as tall. How could they fit into something so small as a pickle? And why would they want to?

"It just means they're in a jam," his mother explained.

"But Mama—"

"It's just an expression, Omer. You'll understand when you're older."

But how could he understand when adults spoke in

metaphors? First Levi was in a pickle. Now he was in a jam. Omer loved his brother. Any hint of danger made him worry.

He wandered outdoors to the sandbox, digging a hole with a toy spade while he pictured Levi and Rachel cocooned in a pickle and smothering in a jar of his bubbe's homemade preserves. Was a jam worse than a pickle? Jams and pickles both came out of jars, but nobody stored both in the same jar. If Levi was in a pickle *and* a jam, he must be choking. Was Mama hiding something? Omer curled up in the sand and began to cry.

Of course, everything turned out all right. Levi and Rachel got married. They had a baby, and Omer was shocked when Mama told him that he was now an uncle. It didn't fit. Uncles were grown men like Papa, tall and bony, or fat and fleshy. They sat you on their laps, bounced you on their knees, and sneaked you hard candies from their suit pockets when Mama wasn't looking. Omer was still in short pants. He didn't own a suit, he had no money to buy candy for the baby, and he certainly couldn't bounce the baby on his skinny little knees, even if Rachel would let him hold it. Life was an ever-deepening mystery. Did other kids have these problems?

As Omer grew, he tried to adjust. In school he did well in math. Math was unambiguous. Symbols like pluses and minuses meant what they said. When his teacher drew an X between two numbers on the blackboard, Omer saw an amalgamation that created a larger number. Algebraic symbols helped him progress easily to more complex formulas. As long as he knew what the symbols meant, he was on solid ground.

Mama and Papa were proud of his grades. "You're going to be a scholar someday," Papa said fondly. "Another Einstein maybe."

But it didn't work out that way. The world around Omer

remained a swamp of metaphors. People put their noses to grindstones. Hit the bricks. Feathered their nests. They ordered drinks on the rocks, got plastered, and went three sheets to the wind. They flew off the handle, jumped down each other's throats, flipped their lids, blew their fuses, popped their corks, and drove each other up the wall. Then they cashed in their chips, kicked the bucket, and went to Hell in handbaskets. Omer's head was so full of strange images that he couldn't concentrate on his job.

"Omer, you're fired," said the manager one night after the evening rush.

"Fired?" Omer pictured himself shot from a cannon. "What did I do?"

"This is the fourth time in two weeks I've had to comp a meal because of customer complaints. Dishes delivered to the wrong tables, cold entrées, lukewarm coffee."

"I'm sorry, sir. It's just that I forget where I am sometimes."

The manager sighed. "Omer, you're not a bad kid. I like you. But I've got a business to run, and I can't do it with a waiter whose head is in the clouds."

White mists formed in Omer's mind. But he understood. In fact, Omer wondered if he really belonged in the restaurant business. Though he'd long since learned to take pickles and jams with a grain of salt, new phrases kept leaping up to haunt him.

"I'll have the angel hair pasta," a lady ordered at his next job. Omer wandered off in search of holy spaghetti. Diners pummeled him with requests for pulled pork, grasshopper pie, bloody marys, black Russians, screwdrivers. His head whirled with fantastic visions. Suddenly his new boss was chewing him out in the kitchen. He could almost feel the teeth marks.

"Hey Omer, can you lend me fifty dollars?" asked a fellow waiter. "I'm really in the soup."

Omer imagined the man drowning in a pool of consommé.

"Well? How about it?"

"How about what?"

The waiter rolled his eyes. "Forget it!"

After a week of bungled orders, the boss told Omer he was terminated. Arnold Schwarzenegger's face bloomed in his head as he trudged homeward. Was being terminated worse than being fired? He thought about asking the waiter in the soup, but that guy had his own problems.

"It's a form of obsessive-compulsive disorder," a psychiatrist told him. "I could prescribe some medication, but I don't think it would help. When you feel yourself getting distracted by little things, concentrate on the present moment. If you make that a discipline, you should be able to cope."

Omer tried. He was always eager to please, and for brief periods he succeeded. He was good at repetitive tasks that didn't make him think too much, like restocking grocery shelves. Eventually though, some new phrase would cart him off to dreamland.

"What are you doing?" the store manager snapped. Omer stood in the aisle, catatonic over a jar of artichoke hearts. "Stop daydreaming! You're way behind, and you're blocking the customers."

"Sorry, sir." He finished shelving the jars. The next box he opened contained kidney beans.

At quitting time the boss called him into the office. "I'm sorry, Omer. You're just not the right fit for us." *Too big for my britches*, Omer supposed. He turned in his apron and left.

He might never have found his calling if Levi hadn't bought a DVD player. The year was 2002. Suddenly VCRs were obsolete. DVDs offered sharper images and greater durability. But Levi's model came with a foldout sheet of operating instructions that he couldn't understand. Instead of words, it offered a set of symbols showing how to integrate the machine with the TV and the cable service.

Levi wanted to call a technician.

"That's too expensive," Omer said. "Let me take a look at it." He surfed the internet for definitions of the symbols. By the time Levi got home from work, Omer had the DVD player operating, and the kids were watching *Chicken Run.*

"How did you do it?" Levi asked.

"It was easy," Omer said happily. "The symbols on the remote control and the on-screen menu are like math symbols. They make perfect sense."

"If you say so."

Soon afterward Omer's mother began complaining about her electric can opener. It produced horrible screeching noises that woke up the grandbaby. Omer got out Papa's tools. A tiny gear had worked loose and was rubbing against the chassis. When Omer tightened it, the noise disappeared. Soon family friends and neighbors were asking Omer to fix other things.

Meanwhile, hundreds of innovative gadgets were flooding the market. Palm Pilots. IPods. Home burglar alarms. Automated lawn watering devices. All with instructions that were more symbols than words. Cell phones whose screens were nothing *but* symbols. Laptop computers with no operating instructions at all!

"Why do I keep getting these capacity warnings on my screen?" Omer's landlady asked. "I don't know a megabyte from a mosquito bite." Elderly people found modern technology baffling. You were helpless unless you owned a teenager.

Omer saw an opportunity. He began spending hours

online, reading technical blogs that covered everything from malware scanners to Kindle e-readers. The science was evolving so rapidly that some devices became obsolete within months. But Omer kept studying. A fired waiter and canned stockboy had no place to go but up.

One of Omer's first customers was his old algebra teacher. Mr. Boone was retired now and wanted to join an online chess club.

"I tried typing 'Chess Players Wanted' into that search window," he complained, "but all I got was this mishmash of conversations. Aren't there other people like me who just want to play chess?"

"There are," Omer assured him. He showed Mr. Boone how to set up an account on Caissa.com. Before the day was over, Mr. Boone was competing in a tournament.

He offered Omer twenty dollars for his trouble, but Omer turned him down. "If you really want to pay me, give my email address to all your friends."

Word spread. Strangers flooded Omer's inbox, seeking help with their Bluetooth devices, smart lights, and soundbars. They wanted advice on the best brand of home computer or cell phone. Omer borrowed money from his parents, started a website named OddJobs, and advertised himself as a retail products guru.

Over the next few months, he developed a customer list of more than a thousand clients. For a modest monthly fee, Omer was available day or night, by phone or internet link. For complex jobs requiring his presence, he drove or traveled by air. Soon established businesses were hiring him to automate their transactions, integrate their communications, or train their employees in new software. In each case he knocked 15 percent off whatever his competitors charged. Omer could afford it. He worked from home, with no overhead costs.

As the years passed, Omer began to specialize in cybertechnology. When people needed help with their new iPhones, Omer was there. When cars came out with GPS devices, Omer was there. When Skype became essential for business communications, Omer was there. Best of all, Omer discovered that when he concentrated on his work, his imagination dampened. For long periods he could stop fantasizing about things like Turtle Wax, Moon Pies, and glue guns.

By the time he was forty, Omer and his wife, Naomi, had two grown sons and a fancy house in the most coveted neighborhood of Alverna, Texas. He worked such long hours that Naomi urged him to hire some help. Omer was reluctant. His reputation had as much to do with his gentle nature as his technical skills. Besides, after being fired so many times himself, Omer would never have the heart to fire, terminate, dismiss, can, ax, or sack anyone.

Commitment

AUGUST 27

FROM GONEFORGOOD

The only thing I've wanted in life was peace. Now that I know I won't be able to achieve that, I'm hoping to get that with death. It'll be my only choice I've made without the control of my dad. I'll be going tonight. I've made peace with whatever waits for me in the afterlife. No pain can compare to all I've suffered through on this planet.

FROM DEATHWISH

Congratulations! I hope to meet you on TOS!

FROM WORNDOWN

Me too. I wish I had your guts.

Hostility

"What was that stuff you put on my head?" Paige sat on the bed, yanking a comb through her hair. She was back in her room, where frowning nurses and cheerless food servers came and went.

"Contact gel to record your brain waves," Dr. Ursi replied. "Sometimes a cranial blow can cause long-term seizures in addition to memory loss."

Her eyes widened. "You mean I'm going to throw fits the rest of my life?"

"The CT scan shows swelling in your occipital lobe. Your EEG recorded some abnormal patterns, indicating trauma. A violent shock to the brain can throw off its normal electrical function. Even after the pattern is restored, a patient can experience new seizures lasting anywhere from a few seconds to complete blackout."

She listened in horror. "So now I'm an epileptic?"

"Don't worry. This is something that can be treated."

He added some notes to her chart. The catheter and IV tubes were gone. She could now get to the bathroom and back without help. The only severe pain came from her ribs when she tried to move suddenly.

"I'm going to put you on Keppra. In most cases it's very effective in preventing convulsions. However, you may continue to experience symptoms like headaches or dizziness. Some patients report strange sensations we call auras—little swoons that last a few seconds, then go away. Tell the floor nurses immediately if you experience anything like that, and after you're released keep a written record of the dates and times you feel dizzy, disoriented, or just . . . funny. That's what one of my patients calls it."

"What happened the other day felt more like a panic attack."

"Do you remember what triggered it?"

"That cop was asking me about my clothes. That's all I remember."

"It may have been emotional trauma. You're scheduled for a visit this afternoon with the hospital counselor."

"How much longer is this amnesia going to last?"

"Hard to say. It could be anywhere from a few hours to several months."

"Could it be permanent?"

"Possibly. I understand you've been having memory flashes. That's encouraging. When you recover a memory, you're recreating the electrical pattern that originally formed it. It's like a bunch of branch libraries in your brain, with the information shared among them. The injury you suffered has broken the circuit somewhere. How a patient reconnects that circuit depends on the individual."

Ursi wrote her a prescription. "Fill this as soon as you've been released. I want you to take these pills twice a day. *Religiously*, mind you. If you ever forget to take one, make a note of the date. No driving for at least six months. I want to see you in my office in three weeks, and regular follow-ups after that for at least a year."

"Doctor," she said helplessly, "I don't know where I live. I have no job, and I don't have any money. Even if I owned a car, you say I can't drive anywhere. How do you expect me to handle all this?"

"You've still got at least three more days under observation. Work with the counselor on getting your memory back. In the meantime, Dr. Reeves will look after you. She's good." He paused. "Any more questions?"

"Yes. Who am I?"

The doctor smiled blandly and left.

Four days I've been here, she thought, *and I still don't know what's going on.* She wiggled the fingers that weren't splinted. The soreness was mostly gone there and in her limbs. Her body bruises were barely tender now. What really ached was her lower back, from lying in bed so much.

Carefully, she pulled the blanket aside and eased to her feet. No dizziness, but she felt a little stiff. Still favoring her ribs, she padded to the window. A freeway ran east and west past the hospital grounds. Beyond that she could see a supermarket, several fast-food places, and an American flag indicating a bank or a school. She thought it might be on Grover Street, where she . . .

Grover Middle School. Seventh grade. Mrs. Ridenour's history class. The cafeteria, with its din of kid chatter and sour odor of canned spinach. Softball games during recess. MaryJo Rettner sliding into third base and skinning her knee. Walking home with an armload of books. Have to get my homework done before Mom . . .

Mom. The word fluttered over her like a dark shadow. She tried to picture her parents' faces but got only a vortex of emotions: love and anger, warmth and pain, cheer and bitterness.

The mirror above the sink drew her attention. *Do I dare?* Slowly, she drew closer and raised her eyes.

Paige hardly recognized herself. Her disheveled hair was nothing compared to the angry red welts on her cheeks, the puffy black lump of her jaw, and the deep scratches on her nose and forehead. The hair concealed only a few of the bruises on her neck. Untying the knot at the back of her gown, she lowered it to unveil more bruises on her chest.

Voices swirled through her head.

Ain't she pretty!

You're so pretty, Paige.

She fine!

Nothing attracts customers like a pretty waitress!

Another wave of dizziness swept over Paige. Panting, she gripped the sink until the voices faded away.

The room felt like a prison cell. She retied the gown and wandered into the hall. Several visitors were leaving the room across from hers.

"Hi," she said timidly. They responded with hostile glares and headed for the elevator. Paige checked her gown. Bare below the knees, but otherwise she was dressed properly. *Must be my face*, she thought.

She walked past a couple of empty rooms. In the third, a man slouched in his plastic chair, watching television. He frowned at Paige and closed the door.

A nurse approached her. "Miss, you're not supposed to be out without supervision. Let me help you back to your room."

"What's wrong with everybody?" she asked as the woman took her arm. "Why do they look so angry?"

"Sick people are often angry. We see it all the time."

Paige slid into bed. There was a tension in the ward

that made her uneasy. She curled up on the pillow, wishing Dr. Wingate were here.

"I'm starting to remember some things," Paige told the counselor. "Stuff that happened to me in school. Kids I played with. I can remember my third-grade teacher's face but not her name."

"What about your home? Do you remember that?" Except for Dr. Wingate, Megan Kunstler was the warmest person Paige had met since her arrival. She had soft features, curly gray hair, and bright green eyes. Middle-aged and plump, she looked like one of those smiling motherly types you see in healthcare commercials. *Another memory!*

"I have a sense of home," she responded, "but I can't picture it."

"A sense? What do you mean?"

"It's . . . I can't put it into words. It's more like a *feeling* of home than an image. Like the way tree blossoms smell when you wake up in the morning. Like it's spring, and you're glad to be alive."

The counselor smiled. "So it's a pleasant memory?"

"From long ago. When I was little, I think."

Megan made a few notes. "Tell me about those other feelings you've had since you came here. The ones that weren't so pleasant."

"Mostly it's a sense of dread and panic. But I don't know why." Unconsciously, she hugged herself.

"Well, at least we know there's something that triggers it." Megan rose and closed the door against the clamor of food carts and voices. "Try something for me, Paige. Close your eyes, sit very still, and think about your conversation with Officer Hardaway."

"I'm afraid to."

"Whatever it is, it can't hurt you. We're alone, just you and me." She took Paige's hand. "And I'm here to protect you."

Paige nodded. She closed her eyes.

"Now, just empty your mind. Forget about where you are. Put your worries aside and relax." The counselor gave her a few seconds. "Concentrate, now. Try to remember what it was that brought on the seizure."

A minute passed. "I'm sorry." Paige opened her eyes. "There's nothing."

"Was there any fear?"

"No. Just . . . nothingness."

Megan smiled. "Then we'll just have to be patient."

"Mrs. Kunstler, how can I not know who I am? What happened to me? Why was I on that bridge? Who's paying my bills?" Tears filled her eyes. "The cleaning lady won't talk to me. The man who brought my breakfast this morning acted like he was feeding his dog. Just slapped the tray down on the table and walked out. Everybody—nurses, doctors, the orderlies—they all look at me like I'm a criminal. You and that nice emergency doctor are the only ones who seem to care. And that's just an act, isn't it? You're like everyone else, just doing your job!" She choked on the words.

Megan hesitated. "Paige, if I tell you something, will you keep it a secret? Just between us?"

"I guess so," she sniffed. "What?"

The counselor chose her words carefully. "There are people out there who . . . How should I put it?" She looked frankly at the girl. "You have some enemies, Paige. I can't tell you who they are, or why. But I believe that dreaded thing inside you is a key. A key to remembering who you are and how you got here."

"But why can't you just tell me?" she cried. "I'm the one who got beaten up. I'm the victim. What have I done to make people hate me?"

Megan shook her head. "You'll have to find it on your own. Then we'll be able to go forward."

"Do you hate me too?"

"I don't think the mood in the hospital has anything to do with you. There are rumors of a merger going around. People are worried about their jobs." She stood. "We'll talk more tomorrow."

After Megan left, Paige reached for the bedside phone. A sticker on it gave a list of five-digit hospital numbers. Paige dialed 5-3476.

"Business office, this is Helen."

"Hi. My name is Paige Abernathy. I'm a patient here. A few days ago, I was brought in by some man who's paying all my bills. Can you tell me who he is?"

"Abernathy, did you say?"

"Yes."

"Just a moment, please."

Paige searched for a paper and pen. All she could find was a pencil stub and a meal menu from the previous week.

"Ms. Abernathy?"

"Yes."

"I'm sorry, but your billing records are flagged as confidential."

"Confidential? Why? I just want to thank the person who's doing this for me."

"That's all I'm allowed to tell you. I'm sorry." The woman hung up.

Enemies. Blocked hospital records. What was going on? She tried dialing for an outside line. All she got was a fast busy signal. Then she realized she didn't know who to call anyway.

She searched again for the TV remote. It wasn't on the bedside table. The drawer contained only a paper napkin and two hard candies wrapped in cellophane. A search through her sheets and blanket produced nothing.

High on the far wall, the TV set hung from a metal frame. Paige dragged the plastic chair beneath it. Wincing at the pain in her ribs, she stepped up carefully. The power button didn't respond. She felt around the back. The cord was missing.

Climbing down, she sneaked into the hallway past the nurses' station. Three of them had their backs to Paige, bent over a computer screen. Silently, she went from room to room until she found an empty one. Mounting the rickety chair, she unplugged the TV cord and crept back to her room.

With two fingers still in a cast and complaints from her ribs, it took Paige several minutes to connect the cord. She clicked through the channels until she found one with news. Congress was haggling over the latest spending bill to prevent a government shutdown. Fire had consumed six hundred acres of forestry and homes in Northern California. A man was on trial for shooting up a hardware store in Alabama. Paige turned up the volume to hear better, just as the scene switched to a large crowd outside a building complex.

"In Alverna, Texas, demonstrators remain camped for the third day in a row outside a hospital where a teenage girl is recovering from injuries following an attack by unknown assailants. The victim, seventeen-year-old Paige Abernathy—"

"What are you doing?" A nurse entered and shut off the TV.

"What's all this about?" Paige cried. "Why are they talking about me on the news?"

"Get down!" The nurse climbed upon the chair and yanked out the cord. "Where did you get this? You're supposed to be resting." She seized Paige by an arm and led her to the bed.

"I'm just trying to find out what's going on! What are you hiding from me?"

"I can't tell you anything. Now please, stay in your room until the doctors tell you otherwise." Wrapping up the cord, the nurse closed the door behind her.

Bewildered, Paige crept to the window. Short-hinged, it opened only a few inches. She peered through it. The utility building next door blocked her view of the campus, even when she stood on tiptoe.

All she could remember of the TV image was a crowd of people standing beneath autumn trees and holding signs. As though they were picketing.

"Suppertime."

Paige scowled at the food service man. "Take it away."

"Not hungry? How about some juice?"

"No. And tell the doctors, the nurses, and everybody else that I'm not eating anything until I get some answers."

The man hesitated. "Miss, I—"

"And tell them I won't cooperate with any more of their tests."

The aide left. As Paige paced the room, her eyes fell on Dr. Wingate's business card lying on the phone table. Dialing the number gave her another fast busy signal.

That night she dreamed she was strapped to a hard surface, struggling to breathe. Her arms and legs were paralyzed. An angry voice echoed through her head. *She cut me! She tore my face!*

She awoke in darkness, a pillow pressed tightly against her face, a heavy weight crushing her into the thin mattress. She tried in vain to push it off. Her lungs ached, no air left for screaming.

Her good hand managed to grab a fold of flesh. She raked it with her broken nails, drawing a sharp cry of pain. Frantically, she scratched and clawed. Warm liquid flowed over her hand. The pressure tightened. She began to black out.

"Oh my God!" someone shouted. "Lance, get in here, stat!"

Sounds of a struggle as the pillow fell away. Gasping for breath, Paige watched as an orderly dragged a white-coated figure away from the bed.

"Let go of me!" the man shouted, thrashing about. "She deserves it, she deserves it, let me go!" The pair collapsed to the floor. Two more attendants entered. The three of them bundled up the howling man and carried him from the room.

A nurse clapped an oxygen mask over her face. "You're all right, Paige. You're going to be okay."

She gulped at the air. "Who was that?"

"I don't know. I'm sorry, he must have sneaked past me." The nurse strapped a blood pressure cuff to her arm. The room began to fill up with security guards, their radios squawking. "Your pulse is racing, but your BP is okay." She peered into Paige's eyes with genuine concern. "I want you to keep this mask on for another half hour, until your blood chemistry gets back to normal. The doctor will be here in just a minute."

A kaleidoscope of images rippled through Paige's mind.

"Oh God, help me!" she cried as the room spun. "I remember now. I remember it all!"

Shut Down

https://serenityshare.com/forum/

404 error

The requested URL was not found on this server.

Try again. If the error persists, contact your internet service provider.

Interrogation

Lucas Madison felt like an amoeba under a microscope. All the trappings of power surrounded Lydia Abernathy. Governor Abbott's picture frowned at him from the wall behind her desk. The American and Texas flags flanked her like armed guards. Thick lawbooks filled the county prosecutor's mahogany shelves.

"Mrs. Abernathy, I swear I haven't seen her since the end of sixth period, the last day she came to school."

"I didn't ask if you'd seen her," she said icily. "I asked what you know. What do you know, Lucas?"

"Nothing!"

If only she'd look away for a second. But no, her eyes bored right through him. He had the feeling she could see right into his thoughts, including the most intimate ones about her daughter. She didn't blink as she reached for a thick legal volume. Not even as she turned the pages and stabbed one of them with a finger.

"Lucas, do you know the penalty for obstruction of justice in the state of Texas? From one to five years. And don't think your age will protect you. Legally you became an adult two months ago when you turned eighteen. Concealing information about a crime can get you prison time, plus a heavy fine. Now." The book slammed shut, like a cell door. "Tell me what happened to her, Lucas."

"I don't know! I don't know, I swear it!"

"Let me see your phone."

"What for?"

"Give it to me!"

He dug it from his jacket pocket.

Lydia tapped at the screen. "I see you've erased all your recent contacts. Very clever. But my, my! Here's a new number for Paige Abernathy in your contacts menu. Where did that come from?"

Lucas squirmed. "I just thought . . . I know we weren't supposed to see each other anymore, but I just thought I could call her up once in a while."

"How? I confiscated her phone."

Cornered. "I bought her a prepaid," he murmured.

"You mean this one?" Triumphantly, Lydia drew it from her desk drawer. "I found it in her room after she disappeared. How many times have you talked to her since you broke up? When was the last time? Was it yesterday? This morning? An hour before you got here?" She stood abruptly. "What happened to her on that bridge, Lucas?"

"I don't know, I don't know!"

She circled around the desk to hover inches above his face. "Do you know I can subpoena your phone records? Call in the FBI? Even if the calls had nothing to do with her disappearance, Paige was the subject of a missing child investigation until the news leaked out of that hospital. Concealing evidence of her whereabouts makes you an accessory to what happened to her. Now, for the last time—" A knock interrupted her.

"Not now!"

The door opened. "Sorry, Mrs. Abernathy, Mr. Mad—"

Jim Madison forced his way past the secretary. "Lydia, by order of the Bolton County Court, I'm serving you with a cease-and-desist injunction. Ms. Melendez here is my witness. Lucas, go wait outside."

"Listen, Dad, I—"

"Sit down, Lucas!" she ordered. "Jim, I'm conducting an investigation here. Lucas is a suspect in the attack on my daughter."

"And this order forbids you to proceed any further pending a hearing before Judge Royce tomorrow morning at ten o'clock."

"Paige's life is at stake! This young man is eighteen years old, therefore an adult, beyond your supervision, and you have no authority to interfere with my investigation!"

"You sent sheriff's deputies to my house!" Madison shouted, red-faced. "Dragged him down here to interrogate him with no attorney present. That's a violation of his civil rights!"

Lucas sank deeper into the chair as the two titans wrangled over his fate. Six months ago he was the happiest junior in Alverna High School. Three semesters from graduating, in love with the unattainable Paige Abernathy, one of few boys able to pry her loose from her father's snobby restaurant. With his wavy hair and sensuous lips, Lucas could have had any girl he wanted. A half-dozen broken hearts already lay in his wake. But Paige was different. He couldn't melt her with his seductive voice or hypnotize her with his soulful eyes. She looked right through him as they passed in the hallway, chattering away with Haley Morton and Willow Douglas as though he wasn't even there. It wasn't that she played hard to get. She wasn't even in the game. Paige Abernathy was a tough catch, and Lucas loved a challenge.

"I know all about you, so don't bother," she replied stiffly when he asked her out. "Melanie Davis told me about your drug habits."

"She's exaggerating," Lucas insisted. "It was just one joint."

"I don't do drugs, and I don't date boys who do."

"You don't date anybody! How can we get to know each other if you won't give me a chance?"

Paige considered him with her cool blue eyes. Behind them a tigress lay in wait. He just knew it.

"All right," she responded. "After school you can buy me a milkshake at Sonic. Then you can explain to me what's so great about getting stoned that you got a C-minus on your English Lit essay."

Intellect. That was the key to Paige. Appeal to her powers of reason. In the car that afternoon, he confessed that beneath his carefree exterior lay an insecure romantic.

"School's easy for you," he fretted. "You're smart. You always know the answers in class. I don't understand all that Tolstoy stuff. Or Napoleon at Waterloo. Who cares who won a battle in Europe two hundred years ago? And trigonometry's just a bunch of angles that don't mean anything." He lowered his voice, even though they were the only people in the car. "Paige, don't tell anyone, but I'm afraid I might not be able to graduate next year."

"Well, why didn't you say so?" It was the first hint of a thaw. Paige, as he suspected, liked to be needed.

They worked out a study schedule. Paige would tutor Lucas when she wasn't working at Chez Renée. Along the way they'd get to know each other better. A dinner date or Dostoevsky—it was all the same to Lucas, as long as it gave him a chance to work his charms.

At first she friendzoned him, confining their discussions to schoolwork and shying away when he touched her. But he kept at it. Within two weeks they were holding hands. In a month they were in each other's arms.

"This isn't going to improve your grade point average," she whispered as he nuzzled her neck.

"Want me to stop?"

"Not yet," she sighed.

"You're so pretty, Paige," he whispered into her ear. Girls loved to hear that. With Paige, he didn't have to lie.

They mapped out their future as they cruised the streets in his Mustang, singing those old Buddy Holly songs she liked.

Paige was in a fever. *When should we get married, Lucas? How many kids should we have? Should we wait until we finish college? Which one should we choose?*

He should have known it couldn't last. Reality struck one evening in April when he came to pick her up.

"I can't see you anymore, Lucas." Paige's eyes were red as she stood outside his car window. Lydia scowled at him from the porch.

"Why not?"

"You know why. It was bound to happen." Fresh tears poured down her cheeks.

"Let me talk to her." Lucas opened the door.

"No!" Softer. "Please. Give me some time. Maybe my dad . . ." Whimpering, she ran back inside. Lydia's glare pierced him with finality as she closed the door.

At school they cooked up schemes to hide their rendezvous. Paige pretended she was going to Jeanette's house to study. To the running track. To the library for research.

"I've never lied to my parents before," Paige moaned as they held each other in his car. "What are we going to do?"

"We'll find a way," he crooned, fumbling at her buttons until she brushed his hands away.

Summer arrived. But with school out, Paige had even less free time as she worked at her father's restaurant, saving money for college. They saw each other only from a distance, communicating secretly by text messages.

Three weeks ago, the fall semester had begun. Solemnly, they promised each other to study diligently, limiting their covert dates to Saturday nights and Sunday afternoons. "Six more months and you'll be eighteen," Lucas said. "Then you'll be free."

Then came the night that changed everything. The night of the bust.

Paige's dad took it in stride. Kids will be kids, Kyle insisted. But Lydia was furious. "I forbid you to see this boy ever again!" she raged, her eyes scalding Lucas as she dragged Paige from the interrogation room. "I can just see the headlines! 'County Prosecutor's Daughter Nailed in Drug Arrest.' How could you do such a thing? And with Jim Madison's son!" Kyle lingered awkwardly in the doorway. "She'll get over it, Lucas."

"I'm sorry, Mr. Abernathy. The marijuana was my idea. I wouldn't do anything to hurt Paige."

The master chef seemed at a loss for words. "Guess I'd better go help her mother with the paperwork. Your parents should be here any minute." He closed the door.

Paige approached Lucas the next day between first and second periods. "Mom fixed everything with the cops. But I'm grounded, and she took my phone away."

"My dad went ballistic," Lucas said gloomily. "He said he'd rather see me dead than married to Lydia Abernathy's daughter."

The second bell rang. The hallway began to empty as students disappeared into classrooms.

"Paige, they can't watch us all the time! Let's meet after school when you're out running."

"I can't, Lucas. I promised not to see you anymore."

He sagged against his locker door. "I don't think I can stand it, Paige. I need you."

She kissed her fingers and touched them to his lips. "I'll see you at sixth period."

And that was the way it went for the next two weeks. Brief meetings in hallways. Notes exchanged in classrooms. Then the news story broke. Suicide website. Dozens of kids dead, maybe hundreds. IP address traced to Alverna student's computer. Grieving parents outraged, high school teacher fired, prosecutor's daughter disappears.

Parents! One of the disturbed kids on SerenityShare had posted a vile monologue against them.

"How is it possible to believe parents are anything but evil? Parents use children to solve their own problems. To give meaning to their lives. Parents use children as tape to patch up their crumbling relationships!"

Lucas knew his own parents loved him. Perhaps even Paige's iron-fisted mother loved her in some way he couldn't perceive. But here in Lydia's office, all he could see were two dogs barking at each other.

"Go wait in the car, Lucas," Jim ordered.

"You stay right where you are!" Lydia warned.

Lucas leaped to his feet. "Why can't you just leave us alone!" He bolted from the room. For all he cared, Jim Madison and Lydia Abernathy could fight each other all the way to the Supreme Court.

Infamy

Faceless voices echoed through Paige's nightmare:

i keep having thoughts that i should be violently mutilated

i want to listen to some music on my earpods while im jumping off the tower

i can't take it anymore whats something i can overdose on thats usually in the house or just anything i dont care i need to get out of my head please i dont want to go anywhere Im too tired

Her eyes flew open. The voices gave way to a single wail of anguish: *She deserves it! She deserves it!*

Paige curled up in the bed and covered her face. *Oh God, what have I done? Please, please forgive me.*

Officer Hardaway tapped on the door. "May I come in?"

"Sure," she responded listlessly.

The cop placed the remains of Paige's ballgown on the

bed. "I understand you've had a breakthrough. Do you think you can answer my questions now?"

"I guess so." Paige raised the headboard and readjusted her pillow. "Who was that man who tried to kill me?"

"I'm not supposed to say anything to upset you. Doctor's orders."

"Officer, I couldn't possibly be more upset than I am now."

"Then I'll make this as brief as I can." Hardaway pulled up the chair. "What's your full name?"

She sighed heavily. "Lisa Paige Abernathy."

"Date of birth?"

"March twenty-third."

"Address?"

"1721 Wilshire."

"Parents' names?"

"Kyle and Lydia Abernathy." She noticed handcuffs on the officer's belt. "Are you here to arrest me?"

"Why would I want to do that?"

"The same reason all those people outside are mad at me."

"Oh, so you know about that too?"

"I wish I didn't."

"Well, you're not under arrest. But I do want to get back to my questions."

"Tell me about that man first. Please."

The officer relented. "His name is Jerome Faulkner."

"Why did he attack me?"

Hardaway checked her notes. "On the night of August 27, Mr. Faulkner found his son unconscious in his room. The blood test confirmed that he'd swallowed a lot of pills."

"August 27?" Paige thought back a few weeks. "That must be GoneforGood."

"I beg your pardon?"

"GoneforGood. One of the boys who made up his mind to kill himself. Is he dead?"

"He's in a coma."

"Oh God!" She turned away.

"Paige, what were you doing on the Bustamante Bridge the night of September 17?"

She looked toward the window. Light autumn rain spattered the glass. On the ledge, a crow pecked at a bug on the screen. "After my dad said I couldn't work at the restaurant anymore, I started running in the evenings. It didn't help my depression, but it made me feel better for a while."

"That's hardly a safe place for a girl to be running."

"The bridge was my turnaround point. I always stopped in the middle so I could watch the sunset. Sometimes I would just stand for a while and wait for a train to come barreling along beneath me. Of course it never did. But for a few moments I could forget about everything. My boyfriend. All those dead kids whose real names I'll never know. Problems with my mother. It was like turning off a switch. Eventually the bridge and the train and the sunset were all I thought about."

"Do you remember anything about the assault?"

"Not much. Just a lot of voices yelling, and someone hitting me and ripping at my clothes. The next thing I knew I was in the hospital." She reached for the gown. It looked like it had been through a shredder.

"Do you think you could identify your attackers?"

"No. Everything happened too fast."

Hardaway gestured at the gown. "Why were you dressed like that?"

"What difference does it make?" Paige rose and went to the window. The crow fluttered away.

"Well, you certainly weren't dressed for running," the

officer persisted. "Were you planning to jump?"

"Not jump." She smiled dreamily. "I wanted to fly away. Into the sunset."

"Why was that?"

Paige turned back to her. "Didn't you know? I'm Little White Dove."

"I had to look it up on the internet," Megan Kunstler told the officer. "It's an old pop song from 1959. These two teenagers, Running Bear and Little White Dove, fall in love, but they belong to warring tribes. Their romance is hopeless, so they commit suicide."

"Sounds like Romeo and Juliet."

"Basically, yes. Condensed into three verses. There are other despair songs from that era. 'Teen Angel.' 'Endless Sleep.' 'Tell Laura I Love Her.'"

"Do you think she might try it again?"

"All the signs are there. Guilt. Melancholia. Obsession with death."

The officer shook her head. "I can't believe a seventeen-year-old girl could get into so much trouble. Did you know your hospital's switchboard has logged over two thousand death threats?"

"Ironic, isn't it?" Megan said. "A suicidal patient with a waiting list of people who want to kill her. How do you protect someone like that?"

"What's the hospital doing about it?"

"For the time being we're maintaining her Jane Doe identity and moving her from room to room every twenty-four hours. But we can't keep her here indefinitely. Her injuries are healing. Physically she's well enough to go home. This isn't a hotel, even if her mysterious benefactor is willing to go on paying her expenses."

"Isn't she on her parents' insurance?"

"All I know is that her billing records are classified. Orders from the business office. Anyway, Paige refuses to see her mother. And even if we did release her to parental custody, some other vigilante is bound to track her down." Megan turned to the window. "If that mob outside doesn't get to her first."

With her memory restored, Paige had access to television again. She lay in bed, watching a reporter do a stand-up outside the hospital.

"Police Chief Norman Bales gave details today about Jerome Faulkner, the man accused of attacking Paige Abernathy in her hospital room. Faulkner, a local audiologist, had a thirteen-year-old son who tried to kill himself after reading suicide comments on Abernathy's website. The boy survived a drug overdose but remains in a coma, and doctors are pessimistic about his recovery. Bales declined to identify the drug, fearing an outbreak of copycat attempts. Faulkner remains jailed without bond pending trial for attempted murder."

Megan Kunstler appeared in the doorway. "Paige, you shouldn't be listening to this. You've got to start eating again and get some rest." She turned off the TV.

"I can't sleep. And I'm fasting for my sins." Paige's bruises and facial scars were healing, but her defeated posture reflected deeper injuries. "How much longer do I have to stay here?"

"That's hard to say. We can't release you until you have a

safe place to go."

She pulled the covers up to her chin. "I'm sorry to be so much trouble. Seems like everything I do is wrong."

"Self-pity won't make things any better. Wouldn't you like to see your parents now?" Paige shook her head. "What about your boyfriend?"

"Is he here?"

"No, but I'll call him if you'll give me the number."

She snorted. "If you knew my mother, you wouldn't dare."

"Don't you think she's worried about you? Come on, sit up." Megan pulled the covers aside. "Tell me how you got into this mess."

Paige sat up gingerly, ignoring her sore ribs. "I created SerenityShare last spring for my high school science project. Mr. Chen based our grades on how well we developed our themes."

"Why did you choose serenity as your theme?"

"One Sunday morning the preacher at my church gave a sermon on hate. He talked about how so many people these days waste their energy tearing each other down. I wanted to do something positive."

The counselor nodded. "I checked out your site before it was shut down. That's quite a home page you created. Clouds and flowers. Soft colors. Very comforting."

"That was the whole idea!" Paige cried. "I wanted it to be a place where people could go for reassurance. My website had a tab with free counseling services. I spent hours looking up psalms and poems, all of them with uplifting messages. By the end of the semester, the site was drawing six million views per month. But some of the forum comments were horrible! Did you read any of them?"

"There were several quotations in the newscasts. Teenage

suicide is a major social problem these days."

"I know. People were posting lines from Sylvia Plath and Anne Sexton about how dark life is, using them to argue that there was a better world beyond this one if you just had the courage to take that final jump. Some of them even listed poisons you could take, or ways to get a gun without a license, and instructions for which arteries to cut."

"Wasn't there a way you could ban comments like that?"

"I did! But the violators just created new IDs and went right on posting song lyrics about despair and suicide. I never knew there were so many. 'Adam's Song.' 'Cemetery Drive.' 'Paint It Black.' 'Whiskey Lullaby.'" It went on all summer. And then the police reports started coming in."

Megan thought of the boy in Ohio who injected himself with ————. The Kansas girl who swallowed ————. The mother who found her twin daughters asleep forever in their beds. Over a stretch of four months, the epidemic revealed a common pattern: an obsession with Paige Abernathy's website. Their goodbye notes expressed unfocused anger, feelings of inadequacy, fear of failure. Saddest of all, a desperate craving for love.

"I felt like a serial killer," Paige wept. "In his last comment, some guy named Vaporized thanked me for showing him a way out. Some of the others congratulated him for his courage. I begged him to get help, to talk to somebody. But he never posted anything again. So I went to Mr. Chen and asked him to shut the website down."

"Paige, where were your parents in all this?"

She lay back on the bed, watching raindrops trickle down the window glass.

Rest, quiet, and lots of sleep. Dr. Meadows yearned for a dose of that timeworn prescription. The hospital administrator was exhausted. Gossip among the staff was rampant. Merger negotiations were in disarray. All his board meetings, fundraising activities, his entire schedule had taken a back seat to this neurotic teenager.

"This is a hospital, not a courtroom," he declared to the demonstrators and TV cameras surrounding the north portico. "We have patients inside recovering from illnesses and surgeries. Those of you who have grievances should take them elsewhere and stop interfering with our work."

Thunder rumbled as a big man in a denim jacket shoved his way through the crowd. "My daughter was making progress until she got on that website. Now she's dead! Why are you protecting a murderer?"

Other voices swelled in a chorus of chants: "Witch! Cyberkiller! Poisoner!"

The rain-soaked mob strained against the line of security guards. Meadows scanned their faces. These weren't your run-of-the-mill troublemakers. They were a cross section of America. Men and women in business suits. Technicians. Construction workers. Grandpas and grannies. All of them with blood in their eyes and Paige Abernathy slurs on their posters.

"How much longer do you plan to keep her here?" a reporter shouted over the noise. "It's been almost a week. Aren't you required to release recovered patients to keep insurance costs down?"

"We're doctors, not meat processors!" Meadows bristled. "Paige Abernathy is a patient like any other, and she will remain in our care until we determine that she is well enough to be released."

"Don't you mean until it's safe for her to be released?"

"I mean exactly what I said. The best thing you people can do is clear out and let us do our jobs." The doctor turned and marched inside, ignoring the cacophony behind him.

In the conference room Meadows raised his own voice. "How about it? What's holding up the paperwork on this little nuisance?"

Reeves looked at Kunstler. "Physically, she's well enough to go home. But she refuses to see her mother."

"Why?"

"Tell him, Megan."

The therapist hesitated. "She says she hasn't got a mother."

Meadows scowled. "Well, she does. Lydia Abernathy, county prosecutor, with enough clout to bring the whole legal establishment down on us unless we do something." Meadows flopped into a chair and rubbed his eyes. "Two hours from now I have to appear before a judge and explain why the hospital is denying a parent access to her injured daughter. Do you know how that makes me look? The only defense I've got is that I'm protecting her from that rabble outside, and that won't hold up against the mother's contention that she's trying to *help* her daughter. Now what about it?" He turned to Megan. "This girl is seventeen years old, which makes her a minor and thus subject to parental supervision. Unless you can give me proof that she's an abused child or something, I'll have no choice but to release her to Mrs. Abernathy's custody."

"I've spoken to the mother," Megan replied. "She said Paige has been upset ever since Mrs. Abernathy made her break up with Jim Madison's son. Remember that nasty election campaign last year?"

"Is that all?" Meadows scoffed. "The judge will never accept that as an excuse."

"I think her boyfriend and this website business are the reasons she wound up on that bridge."

"Can I tell the judge she's suicidal?"

"That's a strong possibility. Everything she's told me so far suggests that she went out there to jump, and the only thing that stopped her was whoever beat her up."

"So we refer her to Brushy Park. Suppose they won't take her?"

"They'll at least admit her for a psych evaluation. Meanwhile, I can talk to the mother about an alternative living arrangement. Someplace besides home."

Dissatisfied, Meadows tapped the table with his pen. "I doubt there's a place in the world where somebody couldn't track her down. Even our own staff couldn't keep their mouths shut, which is why there's a mob surrounding us. We're already open to a personal injury suit thanks to that nut who tried to kill her." He sighed. "Look, I don't like passing the buck, but we're out of options here. For the time being, it's Brushy Park, if you can get the Abernathy woman to agree."

"I'll try," Megan responded.

Paige sneaked into an empty room, closed the door, and dialed for an outside line. "Lucas," she whispered, "it's me."

"Paige! Are you okay? You're all over the news!"

"I know. Listen, I can't talk long. Can you get me out of here?" There was silence from his end. "Lucas?"

"Uh . . . I don't think I can. Your mother's having me watched."

"What do you mean?"

"Yesterday the cops showed up and dragged me over to

her office. She made all kinds of threats until my dad bailed me out. But now there's this car following me wherever I go."

"That figures," Paige sighed. "Lucas, I just want to get out of here! What am I going to do?"

"I don't know."

Her splinted fingers ached from holding the receiver. She switched hands. "Lucas, if I can sneak out without anybody seeing me, can you meet me in the parking lot?"

"What good will that do?"

"We can run away together." She waited. "Lucas?"

"Paige, I can't do that! I've got school to finish. My dad's got me pre-enrolled at UT Austin for next fall. I can't just run away."

"But Lucas," she quavered, "I thought we were going to decide about college together."

"Well . . ."

"I thought you loved me, Lucas."

"I do, it's just . . ." His voice trailed off. "Someone's coming. I've got to go." He hung up. Stealthy meetings. Whispered conversations. That's all they'd had since the night of the big bust.

"Paige, it's just one little joint," Lucas insisted. It was Labor Day weekend at Crawford Municipal Park. All the families had long since gathered up their picnic supplies and hauled the kiddies home to bed. In the darkness Lucas and Paige were kissing in the back seat.

"You know I don't do drugs," she said, pulling away from him. "And I'm surprised at you! How long have you been doing this?"

"Pete and Jerry have a stash in that shed behind the practice field. They gave me a couple of freebies. Anyway, marijuana's not really a drug. It's more a relaxant, to mellow you out. And it makes this nicer." He reached for her again.

"That stuff stinks!" she complained, pushing him away in disgust. "Take me home."

"You are so retro! This isn't the 1950s, Peggy Sue. Everybody uses something. Just because Texas is backward about it—"

"Take me home now, or I'll get out and walk." She opened the door.

"Okay, all right!"

"And throw that thing out the window!"

The sparks hit the pavement just as a patrol car pulled up behind them.

"Oh no!" Lucas moaned. Flashing blue lights lit up the Mustang's interior.

At the station they huddled in a small interrogation room, waiting for their parents to arrive.

"I'll never be able to face my father again," Paige wailed.

"Don't make such a big deal out of it. Everybody uses grass. My parents did a lot worse when they were our age. They told me so."

"He's so proud of me," Paige lamented. "We've been cooking together in that restaurant since I was twelve. I've never done anything to disappoint him."

"Chill, will you? I'll tell him you had nothing to do with it."

To his credit, Lucas kept his promise. But Dad never looked at her again in quite the same way. There was a sadness in his eyes that spelled disillusionment.

Paige studied the bedside phone as if it were a book with answers. Who else could she call? She was in disgrace with everyone at school, except maybe Jeanette. But Netsy was too weak-willed to take a risk.

Maybe she could stay with Marcel or one of the other chefs. No. They would never take sides against Dad. And Paige wouldn't want them to.

I have to get out of here. Sooner or later Mom will get her way. She crept back to her room.

Food for Thought

Kyle Abernathy's kitchen bustled with activity. Burners flamed, ovens broiled, copper pans clanged. Chefs mixed, chopped, sautéed, and seasoned as tuxedoed waiters hustled in and out bearing soups, salads, and entrées. In the dining room Nickie Taylor sat at the grand piano, entertaining the patrons with selections from Couperin.

Kyle was experimenting with a new recipe: braised abalone wrapped around asparagus spears. Lately he found that challenging himself took his mind off his daughter for a while.

Until recently, worry had been a distant cousin to Kyle. Confident in his skills, content in his marriage, proud of his daughter, Kyle found it hard to understand why other people were so miserable. Maybe they watched the news too much. Kyle's life revolved around Chez Renée, where everyone admired him.

Kyle and Lydia had met twenty-one years earlier at Houston's Culinary Institute Lenotre. The instructor assigned his class to prepare a gourmet dinner for students at the South Texas College of Law. Among them was Lydia Waring, who fell in love with Kyle's Pappardelle Bolognese. Soon afterward, she fell in love with him.

"He was so different from me," she told Paige later. "So laid-back and self-confident. He could prepare a hundred recipes from memory. I had to study day and night just to qualify for the bar exam." Lydia was building a career in criminal law. While carrying Paige she accepted a position as associate attorney for a small Houston firm. When Charles Duprée recruited Kyle as master chef for Chez Renée, the family moved to Alverna, where Lydia worked for the county attorney until her boss decided to retire. Elected to his seat unopposed, she set about establishing her reputation as a strict conservative, tough on drug traffickers, child abusers, and drunk drivers. And married to a man whose culinary skills were quickly putting Alverna on the map.

Chez Renée was born when Charles Duprée emigrated to Texas from a small town in France. The son of a wealthy politician, Charles had dined in every fashionable restaurant in Europe. Fascinated by the culinary arts, he used his inheritance to test a theory: that people with discerning palates existed everywhere, not just in stuffy places like Paris. He chose Alverna, population seventy-two thousand, precisely because it was ordinary: a mixture of White, Black, Hispanic, and Asian West Texans. Most French people, Duprée knew, weren't as sophisticated as they pretended to be. How else could American franchises like McDonald's, Five Guys, Domino's, and Subway thrive in their precious Paris? Conversely, if a gourmet restaurant could survive in a nondescript burg like Alverna, it could succeed anywhere. It helped that the property he bought was charming yet relatively cheap, nestled between a recreational park with a playa lake and the city's tiny arts district.

Duprée's hunch was right. Alvernans, starved for a taste of culture in a desert of mediocrity, flocked to Chez Renée. Word spread, at first attracting diners from nearby Abilene, then from Austin, Dallas, Houston, and ultimately beyond the borders of Texas and America itself. In only seven years its reputation for elegant cuisine and ambience spread across the globe.

The restaurant was a boon to Alverna's economy. The Park Hyatt chain opened a luxury hotel offering overnight accommodations to Chez Renée pilgrims, creating jobs for a hundred and fifty Alverna citizens. Souvenir shops sprang up, selling potted cactus sprouts, cotton bolls, and live horned lizards. Lynette Gentry, whose craft shop had been teetering on the edge of insolvency, collected a carload of tumbleweeds, spraypainted them silver, and sold them for twenty-five dollars apiece. European and Asian tourists returned home wearing ten-gallon hats and cowboy boots. And, of course, T-shirts declaring *I dined at Chez Renée.*

In the restaurant's early days, Charles Duprée served as master chef and recruited his assistants from cooking schools in San Francisco, Philadelphia, and New Orleans. A stickler for quality, he insisted on approving any new dish personally before adding it to the menu. As Chez Renée developed a following and Charles got bogged down in managerial duties, he began relying more on Kyle. A graduate of Houston's finest culinary school, Kyle was bright and imaginative, given to epicurean tastes but respectful of his customers' wishes. He could whip up a flammekueche or a pizza on demand, and with equal skill.

No one, not even the spoiled mezzo-soprano Lola Ricci, had ever sent back a meal from Kyle Abernathy's kitchen. His menu was ever evolving, combining traditional dishes with new variations, even capitalizing on local resources. During hunting season he purchased quail from two of his customers, Rex Philby and Mickey Ellis. He made contracts with fruit orchards in Weatherford to ensure fresh servings of peach parfait and apple cobbler. Kyle's junior chefs made regular trips to Grand Prairie and Houston in search of the best seafood. And Kyle was never too proud to borrow ideas from other chefs such as David Everitt-Matthias, whose Cinderford lamb recipe delighted even the stubborn palates of beef-bred Texans. Chez Renée had three Michelin stars, the highest accolade in world cuisine.

Lately though, an invisible pall hung over the dining room that even Couperin's melodies couldn't dispel. Faithful customers on a first-name basis with Kyle now failed to meet his eye. Diners had stopped sending their compliments to the chef. Even his coworkers seemed uneasy. Their jovial banter ceased, their food prep became businesslike, as though they were cranking out burgers and tacos. Nobody said anything to Kyle about the website scandal or Paige herself. It was their very silence that troubled him.

What's happened to you, Paige? Have you outgrown your parents? Do you still love me?

The trouble began when Paige was sixteen. Jim Madison, a private lawyer, announced his intention to run against Lydia for county attorney. In a televised debate he tried to smear her with local crime statistics. Lydia countered with Jim's record defending illegal immigrants, accusing him of contributing to cross-border drug trafficking. Then it got personal. Jim suggested that Lydia had used her influence to cover up a failed health inspection at Chez Renée. Lydia asked Jim why his young secretary always accompanied him on overnight business trips. The mud flew.

Paige, who was dating Jim Madison's son, found herself in an awkward spot.

Lucas shrugged it off. "Dad's just trying to climb the old career ladder."

Lydia easily won reelection, but Jim's attacks stuck in her craw.

Then came the marijuana incident. *Political Foes' Kids Nabbed in Drug Case*, the headlines screamed. *Prosecutor's Daughter Busted!* It didn't matter that Paige was innocent. In politics, guilt by association was still guilt.

Kyle was philosophical. "The higher you climb, the farther you have to fall."

Lydia wasn't so sanguine. "How am I supposed to stand for law and order when my own daughter's running around with a pothead?" she shouted at Paige. "And Jim Madison's son at that! Are you trying to destroy my career?"

Then the website scandal broke. Jim Madison took full advantage of it, spreading rumors that Paige was the real druggie and Lydia an unfit mother. Kyle tried to stay out of it. *I'm just a cook*, he told himself. But it wasn't true. Kyle was a culinary legend. His cookbook, now in its third printing, was the bible of aspiring young chefs. Like his wife, he had a reputation to maintain.

I should have stood up for her, he brooded over the steaming abalone. *Paige is a good girl. Wiser than most kids her age. She's old enough to decide who she wants to date. Who she wants to marry. She takes responsibility for her actions. She's always made me proud.*

Most of the regular customers had watched Paige grow up in the restaurant, waiting tables and helping in the kitchen. Kyle wondered what they thought of her now. Two of his fourteen chefs, Marcel DuPont and Jeannine Fauchet, had known Paige since she was a toddler wandering among the stoves and cabinets, gawking at the vast array of pots, pans, and cutlery. Now her father choked on their silence. He yearned for them to say something, anything. He didn't know how to broach the subject himself.

Instead he called Marcel over to his station. "Tell me what you think of this."

Marcel tasted it. "I'm guessing abalone with shrimp paste and oyster sauce. Right?"

"Yes. They're also called hair clasps, like the hair ornaments Chinese women used to wear."

"I think I read about that somewhere. Jeannine, come try this."

The station chef took a bite. "Mm! Is this one of your surprises?"

"Maybe, if everyone agrees." Kyle never served a new dish to customers without trying it on his staff. Their approval was more than a matter of consensus. Respect for his subordinates was good for fragile egos.

"Let's do it," Jeannine said decisively. "It's been a while since we added a new seafood dish to the menu."

"Pass them around, will you?"

As she distributed the delicacies to the other cooks, Marcel said, "It's nice to see you challenging yourself again."

"Yes," Kyle admitted. "I've been a little distracted."

"More than a little. I've been worried about you. We all have." He put a hand on Kyle's shoulder. "Do you feel like talking about it?"

Kyle avoided his eyes. "I shouldn't burden the staff with it."

"We're already bearing the burden." Marcel drew closer. "Kyle, Paige is part of our family."

"You've talked about this? Among yourselves?"

"Of course! Everybody here is your friend, Kyle. Don't shut us out."

Jeannine returned with the empty plate. "It's unanimous." She grinned. "Let's put it on the menu."

"Very well," Kyle said. "Just as soon as I come up with a name for it."

"We've already got one. How about Paige's Barrettes?"

Kyle looked around the kitchen. All the chefs were beaming at him. "Thanks, everybody," he managed to croak.

When the neurologist returned, Paige was at the mirror, applying makeup she'd borrowed from Megan Kunstler. Her scars were healing, the knot below her left eye was almost gone, and her bruises had faded from blue to yellow. *I almost look pretty again*, she thought.

"Here's a thirty-day supply of that drug I told you about." Dr. Ursi handed her a packet of bubble-wrapped pills. "Same stuff the nurses have been giving you. Take them twice a day, one every twelve hours. When you get settled, call my office for an appointment. And remember, no driving. You don't want to pass out at the wheel of a car."

Glumly, she accepted the pills. *I don't have a car*, she reflected. *Or a home. Not anymore.*

She flinched as the doctor gripped her forehead and flashed his penlight in her eyes.

"Why does everybody keep doing that to me?"

He probed the back of her head. "That bump has gone down. Your pupillary contractions are normal. Have you felt dizzy or disoriented since you got out of ICU?"

"No."

"Any feelings of anxiety?"

She gave him a fishy look. "Are you kidding?"

"I mean besides this website business."

"I guess not."

Dr. Ursi studied his notes. "All right, Paige. Looks like you're good to go. Has the caseworker been in to explain about your release?"

"Release? To where?"

"Brushy Park Psychiatric Hospital."

She drew away from him. "Psychiatry? I'm not crazy!"

"It's just for an evaluation, to make sure it's safe for you to go home."

She glowered. "I'm not going home."

"I'm afraid that's out of my hands. Your parents have responsibility for you."

"Can't I stay here a little longer?"

"You'll be all right. Just follow the instructions on this leaflet and keep track of your symptoms. *And don't forget to take those pills!*" He jabbed his finger at her.

Brusquely, the doctor left, almost colliding with a nurse. "Paige, you have a visitor," she announced.

Her heart leaped. "Is it Lucas Madison?"

"It's your mother."

"Um . . . the doctor said I'm not supposed to have visitors."

"This one has a note from Dr. Meadows, the hospital administrator."

Paige turned away. "I don't want to see her! Don't I have any rights?" She paced the floor. "Tell her to come back later. Tell her I've got scars, and I don't want her to see me until I look better."

The nurse fidgeted. "It won't do any good. She's already throwing a fit because I made her wait in the lounge."

Paige sighed. "All right. Tell her to give me ten minutes to get dressed, okay?"

The nurse left. Paige scanned the room. There was nothing in the closet but her ruined gown, the silver strap shoes, and a faded maroon bathrobe, apparently forgotten by a previous patient. Wriggling into it, she tucked her pills and Dr. Wingate's business card into the pocket. She crept to the door and peeked out. The nurses' station was empty. Through the glass window at the end of the corridor, Paige could see her mother pacing briskly back and forth.

Barefoot, she tiptoed down the hall toward the emergency stairwell.

PART TWO:

Hiding

The Simple Life

"Omer, you're a genius!" Karen Wallace leaned over his shoulders and kissed his bald spot. "Will you marry me?"

The bald spot turned pink, along with Omer's face. "Please! It was just a little software upgrade. Your Excel sheets should be integrated now." He got up from the computer. "Anyway, such a kind lady as you shouldn't have to bother with government reports."

"No argument here. How about a love affair then?"

"Your husband and my wife might object. Besides, you're too young for me." Karen laughed. She was sixty-three. "I'll settle for a cup of coffee."

"Coming up." Omer's attention turned to the dining area beyond Karen's office. It was empty except for a girl wiping the foldout tables and straightening the metal chairs. Omer couldn't decide which was more depressing: the dingy walls and warped linoleum, or the beaten-down wretches at suppertime, waiting in line for a meal and a bed. Eleven years of volunteer work had not inured him to the shelter's dismal atmosphere. Sandwiched between a weedy parking lot and an ancient laundromat, Open Door was a bleak oasis in a sea of poverty, street violence, and covert drug trade.

"Where is everybody?" he asked as Karen returned with the coffee.

"There's nobody here much during the day, except in bad weather. Usually they're out on the street, hustling for cash, sleeping in the park, or getting stoned."

"That one isn't." Omer gestured at the girl. "Did you finally hire some help?"

"Hire?" Karen snorted. "With my budget? That'll be the day." She sat at the computer and opened a data folder.

Omer took a sip. "Such good coffee you make! Have you started cooking in addition to running this place?"

"Around here you do a little of everything. But the coffee's not mine. That girl works wonders with donated commodities. If word gets around about her cooking, we'll have more guests than we can handle, and we're overcrowded at suppertime as it is."

"What happened to your other cooks?"

"Volunteers never last long. They mean well, but most of them have never been around drug addicts and alcoholics. This place can be pretty scary sometimes."

Omer watched the girl move methodically from table to table. "Who is she?"

"You don't recognize her?"

"No. Should I?"

Karen hesitated. "I always make it a policy not to gossip about our clients, but being how it's you . . ." She lowered her voice. "She's the girl behind that suicide website."

Omer's jaw dropped. "No kidding!"

"I didn't recognize her myself at first. We get so many in here, coming and going. But it's her, all right."

"She looks awfully young."

"She is. When she showed up, she was barefoot, dressed in

baggy jeans and a shirt twice her size. Like she'd stolen them from one of those donation boxes."

"How long has she been here?"

"A few weeks. She asked me for a job, so I put her to work in the kitchen. I wouldn't mind if she hung around a while longer." Karen smiled at the screen. "Omer, this is perfect. Give me just a minute to compare this report with last month's, and I'll stop pestering you."

"Take your time." He watched the girl space the chairs evenly, as though preparing for a banquet. She reminded Omer of his busboy days. "Does she sleep here?"

"Yes. We get them all. Runaways, drifters, veterans, old people with no families. Usually they stay a few days, then disappear. That one's stayed longer than most."

"May I have some more coffee?"

"Help yourself."

Omer wandered into the dining room. Sunlight shone through the north window, exposing dust motes in the air. In his mother's day, this place was the home of Millikin's Fine Fashions, the nicest clothing store in town, with smartly dressed ladies peering through the window at the latest styles. That was before suburban growth lured all the merchants away. Now the view was ugly from both sides of the window.

On the south side of the room, Karen's boom box sat in the serving window, playing "Walking My Baby Back Home." Omer pictured a man strolling down the road, holding hands with a child in diapers.

He shook his head to clear it. The girl was blond and slender, with a studied grace that clashed with her worn pullover sweater and oversized jeans. Despite the faded scars on her face, he could imagine her as queen of a Christmas parade, waving at the crowd from her carriage.

"You sure make great coffee," Omer said.

Startled, the girl averted her eyes and busied herself with the chairs. "Thank you."

"I was just telling Karen that my wife would be jealous if she got a taste of this. She's very proud of her cooking."

The girl smiled shyly and stepped to the other side of the table.

"I guess that's how we've stayed married for twenty-seven years. Naomi loves to cook. I love to eat. As you can see." He patted his stomach. "I'm Omer Goldmann. I've been helping Karen with a little software problem this morning. Poor thing. With all she's got to do, you'd think the government would give her a break. Invoices, monthly reports, fundraising records, donor accounts, on and on. And that board of directors!" Woefully, he shook his head. "They barely give her enough money to keep the lights on, they hardly ever come around, and when they do, they complain about the look of this place." He waved his mug at the yellow walls and grimy front window. "As though she had a team of servants at her beck and call. Ahh, but listen to me griping about something that's none of my business. Speaking of which, what's your name, if you don't mind telling me?"

She hesitated. "Jennifer. Jennifer . . . O'Malley."

"O'Malley. That's Irish, isn't it?"

"Er, yes."

He nodded. "One of my neighbors is Irish. Lovely tenor, puts my voice to shame, but I work at home, so how can I concentrate with him serenading the whole neighborhood while he's out there splashing in the pool or trimming the shrubbery. I tell him, 'Listen Irish, singing is all well and good, but it has its place, and that's not in my head, so that I'm listening to "The Fields of Athenry" instead of untangling these software problems.' You know what he says to me? 'Omer, I can teach you things about software that would make your head spin!' And I tell myself, these young people! They think they know everything about cell phone apps and upgrades and online games! But I'm the one who makes a living at it."

"Omer, are you bothering this poor girl?" Karen sneaked up and poked him in the ribs.

"I was just telling Ms. O'Malley here that with all you've got to do, you'll never satisfy that health inspector who comes nosing around your kitchen every other month." He placed his empty cup on the table. "Look, Karen. Suppose I order you some new flooring. Maybe a nice paint job for the dining room. I'll even get my nephew to upgrade the plumbing and install some new cabinets for the kitchen. How about it?"

"Now, don't get carried away!" Karen turned to the girl. "Omer thinks he can solve everybody's problems by throwing money at them."

"What's money for, if not to spend where it's needed? You fix this place up so it's nice and cheery-looking, the poor souls who need it will feel at home, and maybe that Board of Mis-directors will get off your back."

"Fat chance," Karen scoffed. "They don't want the homeless people to feel at home. They think living in a shelter should be as bad as living on the street, so they'll go out, get jobs, buy houses, and rejoin Middle America. As if any of them were employable."

"My point exactly! So we do what we can for them. Now, Karen, don't tell me you're going to turn down a free remodeling job. I mean it. No strings attached."

"Uh-huh. And who's going to do all this painting and reflooring? Santa Claus?"

Timidly, the girl raised her hand. "I will."

"Ms. Collins? Oh, Ms. Collins!"

Jeanette snapped to attention. "Yes sir?"

"Are you with us, Ms. Collins?" Mr. Duggan asked.

"Yes sir."

"Good. Then perhaps you can tell us what you know about Vasco da Gama."

Flushed, Jeanette fumbled through her history book. Her classmates watched, devouring her humiliation like predators.

"Did you read this material, Ms. Collins?"

"Yes sir." She faltered. "I mean, no sir."

"I see." Mr. Duggan advanced through the rows of desks to stand over her. "Ms. Collins, you're a senior. If you expect to graduate next spring, I suggest you exercise some self-discipline so you don't fall behind."

"Yes sir."

The teacher returned to face the class. "Now, who can tell me what's so important about Vasco da Gama. Mr. Granger?"

Red-faced, Jeanette bent over her tablet and made notes. A B-student at best, she was constantly adrift these days. All she could think about was Paige.

They'd known each other since second grade, and Jeanette sometimes wondered how she could have survived her family's grief without Paige to cheer her. Each morning they'd walked the three blocks to Crockett Elementary, Paige gaily filling her head with observations about their teachers, their classmates, her father's magnificent restaurant. It took Jeanette's mind off the gloomy atmosphere of home, where her mother cried in her bedroom late at night when she thought Jeanette couldn't hear. Sometimes Paige shared her lunch with Jeanette: a fish filet, a bowl of paella, or a strawberry torte, all Chez Renée leftovers. She knew Jeanette's mother was struggling to support the family by herself. Her friend's gaunt face and rumbling stomach gave her away. Shy and insecure, Jeanette was too ashamed to partake of the free lunch program.

Jeanette was something of an afterthought in her family. Her oldest brother Frank was a career officer in the Coast Guard. The twins, Jack and Darren, were five years older than Jeanette, traumatized by their father's death in a forklift accident. It had taken all Mom's energy to keep them from acting out their anger in school. Jeanette, unwilling to add to her mother's woes, resolved to be a good girl. She kept her room clean, did her schoolwork as best she could, and stayed out of trouble. Paige was her role model. Perhaps one day Jeanette, too, would be beautiful and intelligent. Meanwhile, they looked forward to graduating and rooming together in college—assuming Jeanette could keep her grades up.

But it wasn't working out that way. Paige was gone, lost in a scandal that Jeanette understood only dimly.

"Ms. Collins!"

"Yes sir!" She sat up straight.

"You're wanted in the principal's office." Maureen Jacobs stood at the door, a hallway pass in her hand. The other seniors watched as Jeanette followed Maureen out of the classroom.

"Have a seat, Jeanette." Mr. Roden indicated the chair next to Paige's mother.

"I'm sorry to pull you out of class," Lydia said. "As you know, Paige has been missing for quite some time now, and I'm desperate to find her. Jeanette, you're her best friend. Have you heard anything from her?"

"No ma'am. I haven't seen her since Mr. Chen got fired."

"Jeanette," Mr. Roden said severely, "I'd advise you to

avoid spreading rumors about Mr. Chen."

"Yes sir." *Who is he kidding?* she thought. *The whole school knows what happened.*

"Now please tell Mrs. Abernathy what you know."

She swallowed nervously. "The last time I talked to her was the day Mr. Chen—I mean, the day Mr. Hardy took over Mr. Chen's class."

Roden flipped back through his calendar. "That would have been September 17."

"Yes sir, I guess so."

Lydia studied her closely. "Are you telling me she hasn't phoned or texted you since September 17? Jeanette, I find that hard to believe."

"It's true."

The two adults exchanged glances. What Jeanette was saying agreed with Lucas Madison's account.

"How much do you know about her website, Jeanette?" Lydia asked.

"Just what's been in the news. And what Paige told me. She was very upset about it."

"What did she say?"

"That she had to find a way to make it right."

"Did she say how she planned to do that?"

"No ma'am."

The prosecutor in Lydia wanted to press harder. But this hapless girl was telling the truth. She'd known Jeanette since the day Paige befriended her.

"Jeanette, anything she told you could be a clue to where she is. Think carefully. Please."

"Well . . ." She glanced fearfully at Mr. Roden. "She said what happened to Mr. Chen . . ." The words stuck in her throat.

"Go ahead, Jeanette. What did she say?"

"She said it was your fault."

If Lydia was angry, her face didn't show it. She absorbed the words without blinking. "All right, Jeanette. If you do hear from her, will you please let me know right away? Her father and I are very worried."

"Yes ma'am."

"You may return to class now," Mr. Roden said. Jeanette rose on trembling legs and slunk out the door.

Dead-End Dining

The mood at the supper table was sour, much like the odor. Crammed together at one end of the room, three dozen homeless people idled over bowls of soup, watching the girl at the other end scrape up linoleum with a rusty metal spatula. The extra folding tables and chairs were piled against the wall behind them.

"You ever notice how body odor can ruin your sense of taste?" The speaker was tall and burly. His shoulders strained against the ripped seams of his overcoat. "Take this soup. It's supposed to taste like rice and green beans. All I can taste is sweat."

"So go take a shower," the woman beside him replied.

"I ain't talkin' about myself. Besides, the shower's got mold and the drain trap's fulla dead spiders."

"Mind your manners!" she snapped, jabbing him with an elbow. "Supper's all I've got to look forward to every day."

"Ain't the junk food buffet at 7-Eleven good enough for you? Beggars can't be choosers."

"Oh, how clever! Did you make that one up all by yourself?" The woman brushed hair from her eyes and spooned up another bite. "This sure didn't come out of a can. Did that girl make it?"

"Reckon so."

"Sure is good. Like home cooking."

"Wish I could taste it."

"So go take a shower!"

"You done said that already."

They fell silent, watching the blond waif scrape up linoleum in brittle yellow chunks. Around them, weathered people in worn clothing slurped up soup while the boom box played "Me and My Shadow." Beneath the serving window, a security guard dozed in his chair.

"Looks like our cook got dee-moted," observed a Black man in a worn plaid shirt.

"Dee-what?" asked an elderly woman with only one lens in her glasses.

"Dee-moted. As in 'cast dee mote from your brother's eye after you remove dee beam from your own.'"

"That ain't how it goes!" growled the burly man.

"It's called paraphrasing." The Black man returned his attention to the girl, who had paused and was flexing the fingers of her left hand. "A thousand square feet and she's only got one row done. At that rate, we'll be eating in this corner for the next three weeks."

The girl moved the spatula to her other hand and resumed scraping. Seated on the floor, she looked like a pioneer child abandoned in the desert.

"I dunno what difference new floorin's gonna make," said an olive-skinned man in a camouflage jacket. "The ceilin's all warped, the wallpaper around the bunks is peelin', and half the windows got cracks. This place was a dump back when I was in high school, and that was twenty years ago."

"They used to play bingo here on Tuesday nights," the tangle-haired woman said, "until the old ladies croaked."

"That was just a front," the burly man added importantly. "My old man ran the best bookie operation in town right here. Horse racing, football, boxing, you name it. The back room where we sleep was for cards and dominoes. 'Course them politicians ruined him. 'We gonna clean up downtown Alverna and make it a showcase,' they said." He snorted. "That was just an excuse for shuttin' him down 'cause they wasn't gettin' their payoffs."

The olive-skinned man was watching the girl. She had shifted to her knees and was shoving at the tiles with all her weight. "Look at her. She ain't got the first idea how to go about it."

The girl yelped. She dropped the spatula and cuddled her left hand.

"Aw, nuts." The man rose from the table and crossed the room. "Looks like you could use some help, Miss." She looked up at him nervously. "You bein' punished or somethin'?"

"No," she said, flustered. "This is my job." She resumed scraping.

"Well, you're never gonna get it finished with a busted hand. Mind if I help?"

She looked him over. Greasy hair, wind-worn face, dark stubble. "How did you know?"

"Know what?"

"About my fingers."

"I got eyes, don't I? You get a stabbin' pain every time you take a dig, your knees hurt, your back aches, and you feel like cryin' 'cause you bit off more than you can chew. Here, gimme that." He knelt beside her and began gouging out large chunks of tile with swift, sure motions.

The girl watched, fascinated. "Wow, you're fast!"

"I used to do this for a livin'." Cement dust rose in small drifts around him. "Guess I've laid enough floorin' in my time to cover every square inch of this crummy town."

The girl looked over her shoulder at the other diners, who were watching with interest.

"Umm, listen, it's nice of you to do this, but—"

"What'd you do to your hand?"

"Oh. I . . . I had an accident. Broke two fingers. I thought they were healed, but all this scraping . . ." She watched the dust fly. "What can I do to help?"

"You could drag that trash barrel over here."

She fetched it and began gathering debris. The man was piling it up as fast as she could dump it.

"I thought you were just the cook around here," he said. "How much they payin' you to do this?"

"Nothing. Mrs. Wallace lets me live here."

"Then you're gettin' robbed. The rest of us don't have to work."

"I wouldn't feel right about it." Hastily, she added, "Not that I'm saying anything against you or the others. It's just that . . . no offense intended."

"None taken." The man dug into his shirt pocket. "You wouldn't have a cigarette by any chance?"

"No. Sorry."

"I oughta quit anyway." He watched her gather up scraps. "You look awful young for a place like this. What are you doin' here?"

"No place else to go." She dropped an armload into the barrel, raising another puff of dust that made her sneeze.

"What's your name?"

"Jade—I mean, Jodie. Jodie O'Hara."

"Pleased to meetcha. I'm Andy Michener." He resumed scraping. "So, Jodie O'Hara. How you gonna earn your keep when you get this finished?"

"There's a man who does favors for Mrs. Wallace. He bought her a whole new set of tiles." She gestured at the mountain of boxes stacked against the wall.

"You gonna lay it for her? All by yourself?" She nodded. "You ever done tilin' before?"

"No. But I'll figure it out."

"Uh-huh. What kinda tile did he buy her?"

"What kind?"

"Yeah." He resumed scraping. "More of this cheap linoleum? Slate? Vinyl? Ceramic? Wood, cork, bamboo, rubber?"

She eyed him uncertainly.

"You know how to measure and cut? Ever used a tile saw? Worked around baseboards? Know how to apply grout and sealant?"

"I thought—"

"You thought all you had to do was stick it on the floor and it'd come out even all by itself."

She smiled ruefully. "I guess I hadn't thought that far ahead."

"That's what gets most beginners. I've cleaned up a lotta false starts by weekend amateurs who didn't do their homework." He shoved an armload of waste into the barrel. "Here, you take one handle, I'll take the other."

They toted the barrel out the back door and into the darkness. Andy threw back the dumpster lid. The girl squawked as a cat leaped out and fled into the weeds behind the building.

"Poor thing," Andy said. "Hungrier than we are."

She followed him back inside. "Listen, Mr. Michener, I

appreciate your help, but I can finish this."

"Let's take a break." He fetched two folding chairs and opened one for the girl. "How'd you wind up in this dead-end place?"

She shrugged. "Same as you, I guess."

"You're just a kid."

"No, I'm not!" She met his gaze squarely for the first time. "I'll be eighteen in a few months."

"You know what I mean."

She wiped dust from her hands. "I guess you don't watch the news."

"Why? You famous or somethin'?" Silent, she looked away. "Panhandlers don't see too many newscasts. Besides, there ain't no TV in here. Lady who runs the place says she can't afford the cable fee. She ain't even got a modem." His fingers dug into his shirt pocket and came up empty again. He sighed. "So. You in some kinda trouble?"

"That's one way of putting it."

"What about your parents?"

"What about them?"

"Ain't they worried about you?"

She shrugged. "Probably."

"You got a bun in the oven?"

"What? No!" She blushed. "It's nothing like that, it's just . . . Please. You're very nice to help with the floor and all, but—"

"But you'd rather not talk about it. All right. Then let's get back to work."

"Y'all need some help?" The girl turned to find the burly man standing over her.

"Sure." Andy drew a pocketknife from his jeans. "How 'bout cuttin' them tile boxes open? See what we got to work with."

The following evening the diners were still crammed into one end of the room. But their mood was much improved.

"What she call this stuff again?" asked Mike Jasper, the burly guy.

"Rosemary taters," said Zelda Fletcher, the woman with hair in her eyes.

"Rosemary Taters? What kinda name is that?"

"It ain't a name, dumbhead. It's a spice."

"It's an herb," corrected Louise Hargrove, the woman with one-eyed glasses.

"Herb? Herb who?"

"Not who. An herb. Like oregano or parsley."

"Parsley not no herb," said Reynaldo Tormada, a lean Hispanic man with a thin mustache. "She a garnish."

"Wrong," Zelda countered. "Garnish is what they do to your wages when you don't pay your bills."

"You all crazy," Mike scoffed. "But whatever rosemary is, it's the best meal I've had in months."

In the kitchen, "Jodie" smiled to herself. What would they say if she told them she'd plucked the wild rosemary from the weedy lot behind the shelter? Nature's gifts were abundant if you knew where to look for them. That's what Dad always said.

Dad. If she were with him right now, they'd be elbow-to-elbow in the kitchen of Chez Renée, braising lamb, broiling fish, and ladling arrabbiata sauce over pasta.

She was only five the first time Dad took her to a supermarket. She marveled at the vast shelves of cans and boxes. "Daddy," she exclaimed, pointing to the packaged bread, "did one man make all those loaves by himself?" He laughed. "That's factory bread, sweetie. Cranked out by machines. At the restaurant we make it with our own hands. That's why we have such loyal customers."

Paige was proud of her father, head of the classiest restaurant in Texas, with a pianist, a string quartet, luxurious carpet, frescoed walls, tuxedoed waiters, and cloth napkins. Chez Renée was full every night, with a waiting list for reservations. Maxine Chalmers, the maître d', kept a private room for dignitaries and celebrities. Many of them flew across oceans to land in Austin, boarded another plane for the westward hop to Big Spring, then rented limousines for the twenty-minute drive to Alverna—all so they could boast of dining at Chez Renée. To the idle rich it was like a safari. To celebrities it meant status. In her bedroom back home, Paige had autographed pictures from Molly Stringer, Davis Burbank, and other film stars. One night she snapped a selfie with Chick Haywood, who had appeared at the restaurant with his entire retinue following a gig in Houston.

Things in the shelter had changed rapidly since last night.

"Here's the way it works," Andy told the group of misfits at breakfast. "You can hang around freezin' on street corners all day, wavin' 'hungry' signs at passin' cars, or you can work in here where it's warm and get two hot meals a day."

"We already get two meals, and a snack at lunchtime for nothin'," Dee-Man said.

"Not like Jodie's, you don't. We work, she cooks. That's the deal. Unless you'd rather go back to ramen noodles and canned fruit."

"Who put you in charge?" Zelda asked.

Everyone turned to the girl, who reddened. "It's okay with me," she said quietly.

Reluctantly, they fell to scraping. Everyone agreed that this girl was a wizard in the kitchen. Furthermore, winter's chill was early this year. Life on the street was growing miserable. Everyone pitched in, except those who were sick, disabled, or hungover.

Karen Wallace was astonished that morning to find half the old flooring cleared away and her social rejects laughing and talking over a breakfast of oven-pan toast, scrambled eggs, and oatmeal flavored with raisins and cinnamon. And, of course, "Jennifer's" magical coffee.

"What's all this?" Karen asked the girl, who was pouring a meat mixture into a row of crockpots.

"Do you think you could get me some honey?" she replied. "Raw honey, not the filtered kind. Oh, and some leeks. Peas and more green beans. Any kind of fresh fruits and vegetables."

Karen set her bag on the counter. The kitchen was cleaner than she'd ever seen it, the dishes washed and stored neatly in the cupboard, the cabinets and sink scrubbed. "What's the occasion?" she asked.

"See that man?" she said, pointing at the jovial diners. "He knows all about flooring. He promised to take charge of it so I can concentrate on cooking."

Karen's eyebrows rose. Andy Michener had shown up at Open Door two weeks earlier, wearing the same fatigue jacket he had on now. Only he hadn't been laughing. Nervous, bedraggled, smelling of whiskey and cigarettes, he'd waited in line forty-five minutes for a cot. Finding them all taken, he'd slept on the dining room floor. Karen didn't know what he did during the daytime. Probably loitered outside the liquor stores with his hand out. Karen knew all their habits. As she'd told Omer, they came and went. She never knew what became of the wents.

"Andy figures we can get the floor done a lot quicker if he organizes the shelter people into a work crew," the girl was explaining. "As soon as they finish the floor we'll be ready for painting."

"What painting?"

"Remember Mr. Goldmann's offer? I have an idea for fixing up the walls. I mean, if you don't mind."

Karen was speechless. Homeless people came to the shelter because they had no place else to go. None of them came here to remodel it. In the past five years, the only concession she'd been able to squeeze out of the Board of Directors was a steel door and a plexiglass window to keep the drunks and druggies out of her office cash.

Her attention shifted from the graffitied walls to the cook. "What's that you're making?"

"It's a sort of stew for supper tonight. I found a bunch of canned sausages, some beef broth, and a big bag of rice in the pantry." She frowned at the crockpots. "I wish I had some coriander seeds."

Andy approached them with a piece of paper. "Ms. Wallace, can you get me these supplies?" She examined the list. Tile cutter. Spacers. Mortar mixer. Plastic buckets. Sponges. Utility knives. "They're for retilin' the floor," he explained.

"I thought Mr. Goldmann bought everything we need."

"Guess he don't know much about tilin'."

"All right, I'll tell him." Karen turned to "Jennifer." "And you want honey. Fresh fruits and vegetables. This is a homeless shelter, you know, not a restaurant. Most of our food is factory-packaged stuff from private donors. The rest I pay for out of our pitiful budget."

The cook and the tile man nodded and waited hopefully.

"All right," Karen sighed. "I'll see what I can do."

Four men and two women crawled about the floor, cement dust coating their ragged clothes. Andy and Mike, the fastest, were ripping up linoleum with an electric scraper Karen had found among her husband's tools. The others hauled the debris out to the dumpster and swept up the dust.

"How long's this gonna take?" Zelda coughed and brushed hair out of her eyes. "If I'm gonna choke to death, I need time to make out my will."

"What you got to leave?" Mike asked. "Is that bitcoins I hear in your pocket?"

"My keys. Keys to the house I got throwed out of. Keys to the car they towed away." She coughed again. "I only had six payments left, and it still had two good tires."

"Lost your job, did you?" Louise brushed gray dust from her blouse.

"Laid off. Five years perfect attendance, and they shut the place down 'cause them Pakistanis was makin' underwear cheaper than we could."

"I know what you mean," Mike said. "That lumber shortage last year pulled the rug out from under me."

"You in construction?"

"Fencin'. All them new houses goin' up in Emory Village got no fences 'cause they can't import enough cedar."

"So lemme get this straight," said Dee-Man. "You got pulled off dee-fence because dee-forest is dee-funct?"

"There you go, Mike," Zelda laughed. "Walked right into another one."

"That's why they call me Dee-Man!"

"You're dee-mented, that's what you are," Mike muttered.

Seated at the computer, Karen smiled. You didn't hear much joshing in a homeless shelter. These people spent all day being ignored on the street, only to come back here to a begrudging welcome. They didn't expect much and never got much. All it took to lift their spirits was a decent meal.

"Hey! Julia Child!" Mike yelled. "Come on out here a second."

Their cook appeared at the serving window. "Yes sir?"

"What you got to tide me over till supper?"

"Supper!" Louise cried. "You just had breakfast!"

"Yeah, but I ain't used to workin' up no appetite. You got any o' them little white donuts?"

"No sir. There's some granola bars."

Mike grimaced. "How 'bout a beer?"

"Forget it, man," Andy said. "You know the rules. No booze."

"Dee rules is dee reason we be homeless," said Dee-Man. "We don't live by dee rules."

"Never mind," Mike replied. "What's your name, kitchen girl?"

"Jodie."

"Come on out here a minute." She hesitated. "Come on, we don't bite."

"You sure bit down on them eggs," Zelda retorted.

The girl emerged, her worn sneakers churning up more dust.

"How old are you?" Mike asked.

"I'll be eighteen in March."

"Eighteen! Why ain't you in school?"

"Leave her alone, Mike. Can't you see she's scared?" Zelda said.

"Ain't nothin' scary 'bout me! Inside this big hulk, I'm just a teddy bear. Ain't that right, Dee-Man?"

"¿Por qué estás hablando con él?" Reynaldo asked. "He dee-mented, ¿comprende?" He cackled and dumped another pile of waste into the barrel.

Mike smiled kindly at the girl. "Ain't you got no parents?"

The girl looked at her shoes.

"You run away from one of them orphan places?"

"Um . . . not exactly."

"Well, you sure can cook," said Louise, changing the subject. "What did you put in those scrambled eggs this morning?"

She brightened. "Nothing special. Just salt, pepper, and chives. The secret to scrambled eggs is low temperature and a little patience. Most people just toss them in a hot skillet, which dries them out."

"Do you use milk or butter?"

"Quit talkin' 'bout food," Mike grumbled. "It's eight hours till suppertime." He returned to the girl. "Sorry for bein' nosy. Don't let me run you off. Work ain't so hard when you got a nice meal to look forward to."

"I'm not busy now," the girl said. "Would you like some help with the floor?"

"You just keep on cookin' whatever that is that smells so good."

Andy and his crew finished clearing the floor before noon. They spent the rest of the day mopping up dust and applying chemical stripper to stubborn glue spots. The next morning the rest of the tiling materials arrived. They included retractable knives, a wet saw, two carpenter levels, a large supply of spacers, mortar mix, grout mix, buckets, sponges, and two dozen pairs of gloves.

Over the following days, Karen sat mesmerized by the sight of transients working for free and enjoying it. Progress was slow as Andy, the only experienced tiler in the bunch, supervised. Mike and Reynaldo, who caught on quickly, did most of the placement. The others took turns on the saw and helped clean up. Most days they only managed a half-dozen rows, but the results were tidy: a gleaming white ceramic floor. Meanwhile, new people drifted in and out, some staying overnight, others remaining to help with the grouting, everyone seduced by the cheery atmosphere and rich food.

With her own children grown and married, Karen had forgotten what it was like to have a young person around. Though "Jennifer" didn't talk much outside her kitchen duties, her presence seemed to energize these outcasts. Some of them said her cooking reminded them of home. If they knew who she really was, they kept it to themselves. Meanwhile, they praised her cuisine and helped with the dishes.

The Paige Abernathy frenzy had diminished in the weeks since her escape from the hospital. The crowds outside the north portico had melted away as fresh controversies filled the newscasts. But for the grieving parents, the story was far from over. Embittered, they went on social media to form support groups and plot strategies against the missing author of SerenityShare.

They won't find her here, Karen promised herself. *This is a shelter, not a courtroom.*

Appeal

Lydia Abernathy stood in the judge's chambers, struggling with her temper. "With all due respect, Your Honor, there's more at stake here than privacy concerns. My daughter has never been away from home longer than one night, and that was for sleepovers with her girlfriends. How can you place the sanctity of business records over the safety of a girl whose life may be in danger?"

"Your point is well taken," Judge Royce replied, "and if I were in your shoes I'm sure I'd make the same argument. But you have no proof that the unnamed individual in your subpoena has any knowledge of your daughter's whereabouts. All the hospital staff knows is that some stranger found her on the bridge, took her to the emergency room, and paid her bills."

"He's still paying them, according to what I'm told! Therefore, he's legally responsible and can be held accountable for his role in Paige's disappearance."

"I'd agree if his testimony would help us find her. But you yourself acknowledge that nobody in the ER has seen or heard from him since the night she was admitted."

"Your Honor, this is the only lead we've got!"

"Did you try speaking directly with the billing supervisor?"

"Yes! He turned me down flat."

Judge Royce leaned back in his leather chair. He was tired. Today's calendar had been a rough one: two assault-and-battery cases, a complex fraud scandal involving a stock brokerage, a property damage appeal, and a highly charged jail sentencing, during which the defendant attacked his accuser and had to be dragged from the courtroom. After a gauntlet like that, four o'clock in the afternoon was no time to do battle with Lydia Abernathy, the most relentless prosecutor in the state of Texas.

Lydia had no qualms about using her power to her advantage. The moment she learned that her daughter had vanished from Frazier Memorial, she'd filed a criminal negligence suit against the hospital, Dr. Meadows, the board of directors, the ward physicians, and the security staff. She had a good case too, the judge thought to himself. The hospital was already in hot water for denying Lydia access to her daughter. Meanwhile, the patient had barely survived a murder attempt by a distraught father. Then poof! Out the door, right under the noses of the people trusted to care for her.

Kyle Abernathy sat dejectedly beside his wife. The master chef's normally cheery face was haggard, no doubt from anxiety and sleep deprivation. Judge Royce hurt for him. Burt and his wife dined at Chez Renée every Saturday night. They had a standing reservation, and Kyle always came out of the kitchen to greet them, though his dining room was invariably packed. *These people are my friends*, he thought. *Paige and my grandson Ridley attend the same school. Our families attend the same church. Kyle personally baked the cake for my granddaughter's wedding. How can I turn them away?*

"Lydia, you've got many advantages over most parents of missing children. The sheriff's deputies are at your beck and call. You know every private investigator in the state. Chief Bales has posted an Amber Alert. The odds are very favorable that she'll turn up soon."

"That would be true if we knew she was still in Alverna. But she left the hospital with nothing but a stolen bathrobe and no money. For all I know, she hitched a ride with the first passing car or truck." Lydia leaned over the desk. "Burt—Judge Royce—Paige is an innocent teenage girl, inexperienced in the darker aspects of human nature. You know what happens to kids like that. And worse, there's a nationwide lynch mob of angry parents after her. Every day that passes reduces her chance of coming back alive!"

"I know, Lydia. I know. Please take your seat."

Glaring, the mother held her ground. The judge turned to the father.

"Kyle, you're closer to Paige than anyone. She's been helping you in the kitchen since she was twelve years old. Can you think of any friends she might have gone to? Anyone who might be hiding her?"

The chef shook his head. "We've questioned all her friends. Haley Morton, Willow Douglas, especially Lucas Madison and Jeanette Collins. They don't know anything."

"Burt," Lydia repeated, "I'm begging you. Sign this court order."

"I'm sorry, Lydia. There's no justification, and even if I did sign it, you know what would happen. The hospital's attorney would file a motion to block it, and Tom Baker or some other judge would grant the motion for the same reasons I've given you. The circumstances don't warrant an invasion of hospital business records."

Her lips tightened. "Then I'll file an appeal. I'll try every judge in the district, every judge in the state. I'll call a press conference and tell the whole world that the entire judicial establishment refuses to help a mother find her teenage daughter, whose life is in danger every minute! You're up for reelection next year, Burt. Don't think I won't use that and every weapon in my arsenal to bring you down!" She snatched up her coat. "Come on, Kyle, let's get out of here."

He rose to follow her. "I'm sorry, Burt."

"So am I, Kyle. So am I." The door closed. Royce reached for a bottle of antacids. He wasn't worried about reelection. Democrats were pariahs in his district. And few voters would have sympathy for the parents of Paige Abernathy, the most hated teenager in America. None of this knowledge comforted him.

Teenagers! The judge's daily docket was full of them. Assault, disorderly conduct, drunk driving, shoplifting, drug possession, curfew violations. You could blame it on bad parenting, social media, poverty, or a hundred other maladies. But Paige was a model teenager, hardworking in school, active in her church, well-mannered and mature, with a sunny face that lit up the Chez Renée dining room when she waited tables. The last kid you'd ever expect to stir up a scandal.

Chewing his pills, Burt glared at Lydia's draft. It glared back. "Darn it!" Grabbing a pen, he signed it and summoned a courier.

Hard Luck Stories

Andy Michener sat on a kitchen stool, watching Jodie arrange noodles in three large casserole dishes. His lungs yearned for a cigarette. "Need any help?" he asked.

"You could chop up this garlic for me."

Andy fingered the crumbly leaves. "Don't smell like nothin'. How do I go about it?"

She handed him a cutting board and a huge knife right out of a slasher movie. "Press your hand down on the garlic until the cloves separate. That's it. Now, lay the flat side of the knife on top of each clove and give it a good whack with your fist."

"Like this?" His blow sent the clove skittering across the counter. She laughed. "You have to hit it right on top. Try again."

This time the garlic surrendered a pungent odor. "Now it's easy to just peel off the leaves and cut the cloves into thin slices. Then you dice them into tiny chunks."

"The whole thing?" Andy exclaimed. "That'll take longer than tilin' the floor!"

"Not once you get the hang of it."

Andy bent over the garlic like a nearsighted man and began sawing at it. "I ain't done much cookin' that didn't come out of a can."

"Yes, I see that. Try this." She took the knife. "Press the clove gently against the edge of the blade while you saw up and down. Like a rocking chair." She ripped through it with rapid precision. "That way you get nice, even slices, and you don't cut your fingers." She watched him. "See, you're getting it!"

Jodie was no longer the frightened mouse scraping the floor a few weeks ago. She ran the kitchen like it was her private domain: confident, organized, and authoritative for someone so young.

"How come you don't use that powdered stuff that comes in a bottle?"

"Italian food without fresh garlic? No way! We'll use part of it on the salad, the rest in the lasagna." She returned to the noodles. "I wish I had some olive oil. It's expensive, but worth it."

"Them folks won't know the difference. They live on dumpster food, Mountain Dew, and Little Debbie cakes." He scraped his garlic bits into a pile. "Am I doin' it right?"

"Yes, perfect."

Music flowed from the boom box. The other homeless people were taking a break, listening to classics by Cole Porter, Jerome Kern, and George Gershwin. Karen wouldn't play anything else. In an age of noxious rhythms, she found the old melodies appropriate for the hapless souls who wandered in from the streets. "Me and My Shadow" was her favorite. Paige could identify with Karen's sentiments. As much as she loved the Jonas Brothers and Shawn Mendes, Buddy Holly's songs spoke of a time when love was simple. You chose your partner, raised a family, and stayed together for life. It was what she had planned with Lucas. She wondered if she would ever see him again.

Paige was learning surprising things about homeless people. Sure, some of them were drunks or addicts. But Dee-Man, whose real name was Clarence Holmes, was a graduate of KD Conservatory in Dallas. In the past nine years, he'd appeared in numerous theatrical productions and TV commercials, with a few bit parts in movies.

"Then things sort of dried up," he told her. "Four months of auditioning with no offers. I wasn't getting paid, and neither was my agent, so she dropped me. That happens to actors a lot." Clarence's Dee-Man chatter was a facade. A talented performer with excellent diction and a strong voice, he had played almost every classic role in drama, from Othello to Willie Loman. Clarence was a quick study, with a gift for improvisation. But he had no other skills. The odd jobs he picked up here and there couldn't support his wife and two children, so they split up. Portfolio in hand, he wandered the Southwest in search of new opportunities. Sometimes he slept in city parks, using trash bags for blankets, or in post office lobbies, where people tripped over him as they came in late at night to check their mail. Alverna was a waystation on Clarence's journey back to Dallas, where he hoped to find a role in a long-running musical.

Zelda Fletcher was forty-two years old and a grandmother. Her husband had made good money leasing heavy equipment to construction crews until he contracted diabetes. Medical expenses quickly wiped out their savings, and Zelda was too busy taking care of him to work. By the time he died, the bank had foreclosed on his business and their home. Then the finance company repossessed the car. Their three children, struggling to support their own families, were scattered about the country. Too proud to impose on them, Zelda worked in a textile factory until it closed. Then she became a cashier, taking the bus to the supermarket every day. But she couldn't get enough hours to pay rent on her tiny apartment. The pressure got to her, and she ended up on the street, begging for handouts as her unruly hair grew longer.

Of all Paige's new acquaintances, Reynaldo Tormada was the most disturbing. Privately he confided to her that he was an undocumented immigrant, hiding from US authorities. As they spoke he glanced nervously at the streetside window, fearful of police arriving at any moment. Reynaldo was thirty-two years old when a drug gang invaded the Guatemala coffee plantation where he was born. The thugs kidnapped his wife and kids, demanded a ransom equivalent to ten thousand American dollars, and threatened to sell his family to slave traders unless he paid up.

"What about, uh, los policias?" Paige asked, summoning her high school Spanish. "Couldn't they help you?"

"Policía no bueno," he answered woefully. "Los camellos, they, ah . . ." He gestured with his hands.

"Bribed them?"

"Sí." Using his savings and borrowing from friends, Reynaldo was able to raise about seven thousand dollars. The cartel took the money as a deposit on the remaining balance.

"Los narcos, they give me seis meses to get el dinero," Reynaldo whispered somberly. "Yo estoy, how you say, desperado. Only en Estados Unidos can I get dinero rápidamente." On paper, he drew a chart showing the exchange rate. It took almost eight hundred Guatemalan quetzales to equal a hundred dollars.

He went on to describe his perilous journey of two thousand miles, sneaking rides aboard farm trucks by night, crossing the desert by day. Six weeks of travel brought him to the US border, where an official told him that processing his application for a work permit could take up to seven months. Reynaldo couldn't afford to wait. He hopped aboard an empty produce truck, this one packed with other Central American families fleeing violence and poverty. The driver turned them loose twenty miles from Encino to avoid an INS checkpoint. From there Reynaldo wandered from town to town, picking cotton and working in roadside cafés, eventually ending up in Alverna. Now he ate and slept at Open Door while doing piecemeal roofing jobs for an independent contractor sympathetic to undocumented immigrants.

"What about the dinero?" Paige asked. "Do you have enough to get your family back?"

"No, señorita. Is hard to get trabajo with no papers. Ms. Karen is try find más trabajo for me. For now, ah . . . pido ayuda de los extraños."

"You ask strangers to help you?"

"Sí," he said, nodding.

"Do you ever hear from your wife? Esposa, I mean?"

"Nada, por mucho tiempo." His greatest fear, he went on, was being caught and sent back to Guatemala without enough money. Undocumented immigrants were especially unwelcome in Texas, a state in the grip of hard-nosed politicians.

"How come you know so much about cookin'?" Andy was on his last garlic clove.

"Oh . . . I know a very good chef," she said evasively. "How do you know so much about tiling?"

"Learned it from my old man. I used to help him every

day after school till I was sixteen. Then I dropped out and started workin' for him full-time."

"Why did you drop out?"

"Hated it. Math didn't make no sense, history was dull, English . . . Who cares what's the difference between an adverb and an adjective? Waste of time, I thought. 'Course, that was a long time ago. Now I'd give anything to go back and get my diploma. It's hard to get a good job without one. Take my advice, Jodie. I dunno what you're doin' here, but you oughta be in school."

Silence. Then, "I'd better get started on the cheese." She drew a block of cheddar from the refrigerator. "This is all wrong. I wish I had some ricotta or mozzarella." She began grating it into a bowl.

Karen Wallace entered the kitchen, bundled up against the cold and bearing two armloads of groceries. "Good news and bad news! I made a deal with Foodies Market to send us their culled produce. It's safe to eat, but too overripe to attract customers."

"Great! What's the bad news?"

"They wouldn't give us any honey, raw or filtered."

Paige dug through the bags. "That's okay. I can mash up these strawberries and mix them with syrup. That'll make a nice pancake topping."

"They gave me a big bunch of other fruit." Karen stored her loot in the refrigerator. "Granny Smith apples, Florida oranges, bananas. There's six more bags in the car."

"I'll get 'em," said Andy.

"No, I'll do it. You finish the garlic." Paige headed for the door.

"This place looks so much better!" Karen looked around, amazed that one teenage girl could cook for an entire shelter while keeping the kitchen clean. And the new floor! The crew hadn't stopped with the dining room. Omer had supplied enough tile to redo the kitchen, the sleeping quarters, and Karen's office.

"Now all we need is the paint," Andy said. "When do we get that?"

"Omer's waiting for me to tell him what color. He left me some swatches, but I can't make up my mind."

"Jodie wants it to be all white."

"Jodie who?"

"Jodie. Our cook." He gestured at the noodle pans.

"Her name's Jennifer," Karen said.

"Jodie's what she told me."

"Oh." Karen was used to fake names. Not all homeless people showed up at her door because they were destitute. Others were running away from something. Like this girl.

Andy returned to the garlic. "I can't figure it out. She's young enough to be my daughter, she obviously comes from a good home, but she acts like a scared rabbit. Except when she's cookin'."

"And so responsible!" Karen added. "I wish my grandchildren were like that." She returned her attention to the dining room, where Mike and Reynaldo were repairing holes in the walls. "Why does she want white paint with a white floor?"

"She didn't say."

"Well, it does brighten up the place." Karen stored a box of limp spinach in the refrigerator. "What about you? Jennifer—or Jodie—says you used to lay tile for a living. Do you plan to go back to it?"

"I been thinkin' about it. Been a long time since I had a steady job. But it's different, workin' around here. First time I ever got to be the boss and tell other folks what to do. I kinda like that."

Karen ripped the soggy tops off some radishes and rinsed them in the sink. "Andy, I don't usually intrude on people's personal lives, but I admit you're something of a puzzle. Like Jennifer."

"How so?"

"Neither of you is typical of the people who wander in and out of this place. You're good at what you do. The others seem to accept you as an authority. I'll bet if I stopped showing up every day, you'd step in and take over."

He laughed. "Not likely. I ain't no manager type. Tilin's all I ever done."

"Then why did you quit?"

"No mystery there. I got a little too friendly with the bottle. I guess you know all about that."

"You're not the first I've seen."

Andy leaned against the counter. "My wife grew up with a drunk father. She swore before we got married that she'd be out the door in a flash if I ever put her through that again." He studied his hands. "Women don't seem to understand. Hard labor takes a lot out of a man. You ache all over when you get up in the mornin', you're wore out by the end of the day. Doin' the same thing over and over, the hours drag along, and by five o'clock you're ready to cut loose." His face grew melancholy. "At first it was just a couple of beers with the crew. Then it was one more for the road. Then I was gettin' home at midnight, Janie waitin' up with her eyes all red from cryin.' After she left, I didn't have no reason not to drink."

"I'm sorry, Andy."

He shrugged. "Tell me somethin'. Are you and that security guard the only employees in this place?"

"Yes. Nobody else comes around regularly except the health inspector. Why do you ask?"

"This is a rough neighborhood. The people hangin' out here ain't exactly solid citizens. Don't it bother you to have a young girl sleepin' in the same room with a buncha street people? What if one of these alkies or head cases tries to . . . you know?"

"It's crossed my mind," Karen admitted. Most of the people who showed up at Open Door were too tired and discouraged to be dangerous. But a few had alarming symptoms. Three days ago, a man calling himself Burning Vision had appeared. He wore dark glasses and claimed he had the power to kill with his eyes. He wandered from Zelda to Louise to Reynaldo, warning of the heat rays that would strike them down unless they repented of their sins.

Then there was the young man in army fatigues who wouldn't even come into the shelter. He wore a gun belt with a Sig Sauer pistol and a scabbard with a large knife. Karen eyed him narrowly as he sat on the cold sidewalk, staring into space and petting his dog. Eventually he got up and wandered off.

One day an emaciated woman in a tattered housedress walked in, plopped herself down in a corner, and curled up like an embryo. When Jennifer offered her some food, she began screaming. Everyone steered clear of her until she calmed down. The next morning, she was gone.

The shelter attracted a variety of drifters. Some showed up with all their belongings stuffed into shopping carts or backpacks. Others lived in wheelchairs or struggled with walkers. A few suffered from facial tics and held one-sided conversations with unseen tormentors.

"I used to bring the youngest ones home with me, to stay until their parents showed up," Karen said. "But my husband put his foot down after one of the boys made off with his wallet and everything he could hock. You're right, though. This is no place for a teenage girl."

Andy started on his last clove. "I ain't been here long enough to know the regulars very well. Most of 'em seem okay. Still, I think I'll start sleepin' with one eye open."

"That's not possible," Karen laughed.

"Gotta be." He grinned. "I saw a guy do it in a movie once."

"Speaking of Jennifer or Jodie, she's a long time coming back with the groceries. I'd better go check on her."

Andy followed her outside to find oranges scattered around the car. Among them lay their cook, face down on the asphalt.

Invasion

"We've got to stop meeting like this," Dr. Wingate said.

Paige glanced around. Another cubicle. Another drawn curtain. "What happened? How did I get here?"

"Your friends found you conked out on the ground, like you'd been poleaxed. Did somebody attack you again?"

She sat up. "I was getting some groceries out of the car. Where are they?"

"Back wherever you came from." The doctor ran both hands over her scalp. "I don't feel any lumps. Do you hurt anywhere?"

"No."

"Any dizziness?"

"I feel fine. How long have I been here?"

"About ten minutes. Hold still for a second." He gripped her chin and blinded her with the penlight.

"What friends are you talking about?"

"A man and a woman brought you in. Very worried. They're waiting outside."

"Oh!" She struggled to her feet. "The lasagna! I left it on the stove. It'll be ruined!" She lurched past him.

"Whoa, not so fast!" He seized her arm. "You've had a spill, maybe a serious one. We need to find out why." Reluctantly, she sat back on the gurney. "Now, stick out your arms and try to touch your nose with your finger." He ran her through the same routines as before. Paige was balancing herself on one foot when a hand swept the curtain aside. A woman with a cell phone peered in. "Sorry, wrong room. I was looking for someone else." She drifted away.

"Okay," Dr. Wingate said. "All your parts seem to be functioning normally. Have a seat and let's have a little talk." He pulled up a stool. "Have you had any other blackouts since you left the hospital?"

"No."

"Any dizziness? Confusion? Loss of balance?"

"No, nothing."

Wingate examined her chart. "I see Dr. Ursi has you on Keppra. Have you been taking it?"

"I ran out of pills weeks ago."

"Didn't he give you a refill?"

"I have no way to pay for it."

"What about your parents?"

She pursed her lips stubbornly. "I can't."

"Why not?"

"I just can't. Doctor, please let me go."

He riffled through her chart. "So. You're seventeen years old, you're broke, and you're not living at home. Where have you been staying?"

"I can't tell you."

The doctor frowned. "Paige, this is serious! You know those movies showing people getting whacked on the head and bouncing right back? Don't believe it. The brain is a complex organ in a fragile container. A hard blow can do permanent damage." He showed her a graph. "This is an EEG from your last visit. See this area? That's an anomaly. What knocked you out today was probably a seizure. Unless you take your medication, it's very likely to happen again." He pecked at an electronic pad. "I'm going to refer you back to neurology."

"I can't stay here!" she cried. "Don't you know there are people out to kill me?"

"You're safe. All visitors have to pass through the security station, and the ER door only opens one way." He closed her file. "Why did you leave the hospital when you were here last time?"

"Everybody hated me. The other patients, the nurses, even the janitors."

"Are you sure about that? Somebody's been covering your medical bills."

"Who?"

"Maybe it's those two folks who brought you in. They're wearing grooves in the floor."

"Oh." Karen and Andy. "No, it couldn't be them."

"Paige, have you been watching the news? Your parents have been turning the city upside down trying to find you. So are a lot of other people."

"That's because of the website," she said morosely. "They all think I deserve to die. Maybe they're right." She choked on the words.

"Tell me something, Paige. On your website forum you had a cartoon face. A Native American girl named Little White Dove. What does that mean?"

She wiped her eyes. "Have you ever heard of the Big Bopper?"

"No. What's that?"

"His real name was Jiles Perry Richardson Jr. He was a

songwriter who died in the plane crash that killed Buddy Holly in 1959."

"Oh, yeah. That does sound familiar."

"When I was thirteen, my grandfather gave me a CD of Buddy Holly songs. I got interested in him and went online to learn more about him. Everybody knows who Buddy Holly was, but nobody remembers the Big Bopper. Shortly before the crash, he wrote a song about two teenagers separated by a war between their tribes. The girl's name was Little White Dove."

"What's that got to do with you?"

She turned away. "It doesn't matter now."

"Don't you think—"

"Why are you being so nice to me?" she cried. "I'm a murderer! Over a hundred kids are dead because of me!"

"You didn't kill them. They made that choice themselves."

"But they wouldn't have done it if I hadn't—"

"Paige. Listen to me. You're not the first person to start a website with good intentions. Look what's happened to Facebook and Twitter and YouTube. Every one of them abused by people with corrupt agendas. Don't you think there were times when their creators had second thoughts?"

She smiled wanly. "You sound like my youth pastor."

"How's that?"

"She said God got so fed up with people that He wiped out everybody but Noah and his family."

Wingate sat beside her. "Paige, those kids were in trouble before they ever heard about your website. You didn't post all those essays about despair. About life being pointless, or death being an escape. You didn't turn them to guns or ropes or poisons. Those ideas came from people who used your site as a weapon. People who felt lost and hopeless and wanted to take somebody down with them."

"But I'm the one who brought them all together! Some of those people were in therapy when they started writing all that stuff about suicide. And instead of accepting help they decided to give up!"

"And when you realized what was happening, you did the right thing. You disabled the website." He took her hand. "Paige, did you have personal problems of your own before all this started?"

Despondently, she nodded.

"Would you like to tell me about them?"

"Why should you care?"

"Maybe because I speak from experience."

His eyes were so kind she wanted to dive into them. "It's sort of complicated. My mother doesn't—"

A loud crash interrupted her, followed by shouts and screams.

"Stay here," Wingate ordered, hurrying off. Someone was pounding on a door. The noise shook the ER.

Moments later Andy and Karen burst in. "We've got to get out of here! Now!"

"What's the matter?" The screams grew louder.

"There's a man out there with a gun! Come on!" They grabbed Paige and hustled her out through the ambulance bay.

"You had her in custody, and you let her get away?" Lydia shouted. "What kind of hospital is this, where maniacs run around assaulting your patients?"

"Keep your voice down, please," Dr. Meadows pleaded. "There are sick people in here." There was turmoil too. Hysteria in the waiting room. A swarm of cops patrolled the

ER with radios crackling. Paige's parents clustered with the doctors in the tiny cubicle. "Everything's under control. The security guards took him down before he could fire a shot or get anywhere near her."

"Blatant incompetence!" Lydia hissed. "First you let a disturbed man nearly smother my daughter to death. Then you let her escape and wander around with a head injury! This is the last straw. By the time I'm finished with you—"

"Lydia, stop it!" Kyle barked. "Just stop it!" He turned to Dr. Wingate. "How did she wind up here in the first place?"

"Two people brought her in. Said they found her unconscious."

"Found her where?"

"I've already questioned the admitting clerk. They refused to tell her anything. During the confusion, all three of them got out through the ambulance bay."

"Was she hurt?"

"Physically she's all right, except for the lingering effects of head trauma."

"You mean that incident on the bridge?"

"That's right. Somehow she suffered a brain injury that makes her subject to blackouts and seizures."

Lydia seethed. "All that talk and you didn't make her tell you where she's been all this time?"

"I was working on that when the trouble started."

She slammed her briefcase down on the gurney. "I still want to know how an armed man got into this hospital with nobody to stop him. How do you explain that?"

"Mrs. Abernathy," Meadows interrupted, "you know as well as I do that Texas is an open-carry state. The law allows—"

"Don't quote the law to me! Hospitals are excluded as long as they post 'no firearms' notices at all entryways."

"This guy didn't stop to read any signs! He ran right through the metal detector and past the security station. He couldn't get into the ER because the door's hand-activated at the registration desk."

"Why did he want to kill Paige?"

"The police are talking to him now." Meadows turned to Wingate. "Steve, did the girl say anything that might help her parents find her?"

"Not really. She did mention something about lasagna."

"Lasagna?"

"She was worried about the lasagna being ruined."

Kyle exchanged glances with Lydia. "She's cooking! It's the lasagna recipe I taught her."

"Could she be working in a restaurant?"

"Possibly. Paige has her apprentice certification. She knows everything I know about kitchen management."

"But where's she living?" Lydia wondered.

"It doesn't matter. If we find the restaurant, we find Paige!"

"That'll take some doing," Dr. Meadows pointed out. "There must a hundred restaurants in Alverna. Not to mention another hundred fast-food joints. And how do you know it's a restaurant? It could be somebody's home."

"At least we know where to start," Lydia declared. "With the county health inspector. He'll check out every restaurant in the area, or I'll know the reason why. Let's go, Kyle." Sweeping the curtain aside, she turned back to the doctors. "Both of you had better pray I find her. Safe and healthy, despite all your bungling. Or I'll have you decertified. You won't be licensed to apply a Band-Aid!" They left.

Wearily, Dr. Meadows sank into the plastic chair. "Steve, that girl spent only twenty minutes in the ER. How did the gunman know she was here?"

"Some woman interrupted while I was talking to Paige. Maybe she recognized her and tipped him off. Did you get his name?"

"Uh, Tankhouse or something."

"Tankhouse?"

"Tankfish, Tanglewood, something like that. Big guy, looks like an athlete. He gave the guards quite a tussle." Meadows examined Paige's chart. "I see you've treated this girl twice before."

"That's right, before she ran off. She seems like a nice kid."

"She's a headache," Meadows grumbled. "Back to that woman you mentioned. Do you think she and this Tankard guy could have been working together?"

"I suppose it's possible."

Meadows turned grim. "If that's true, there's a network of informers out there, and that woman was a plant. We're dealing with more than a bunch of grief-stricken parents. Somebody's out to track down Paige Abernathy and kill her."

A man appeared at the entrance. "Dr. Meadows, we're all set up for the press conference. The police chief's waiting for you."

The administrator groaned. "They don't pay me enough for this." He followed the PR man out to the north portico.

Darkness covered the parking lot as Kyle drove through the security gate. A light sleet coated the shrubs and trees. Lydia drew her coat around her shoulders as tiny crystals sparkled in the headlights.

"Don't you ever embarrass me like that again!" Kyle warned.

"Oh, shut up! If you had any backbone, none of this

would have happened."

"How do you figure that? Am I the one who signed her up for elocution lessons while she was still learning to talk? Made her take ballet lessons after school instead of playing like normal kids? Dressed her up like a Barbie doll? Why else do you think she wanted to spend all her free time at the restaurant?"

"You put this into her head!" Lydia flared. "I know how your mind works. It's always Dad lets me do this, Dad lets me do that, but Mom makes me do things I don't want to do." She choked down a sob. "You know me better than that, Kyle! I love our daughter as much as you do. I just want what's best for her."

He drove on, sick of arguing. In one way, Lydia was right. She meant well. Away from the courtroom, she was affectionate to Kyle and Paige. But when disagreements arose, the fire that made her an effective prosecutor turned her into a witch.

Kyle first noticed the pattern when Paige was six and her school announced tryouts for the annual Christmas pageant. Ms. Cotton, unwilling to risk her teaching career over a children's play, bowed to Lydia's insistence that she cast Paige as the Virgin Mary, though she spoke her lines no better than any of the other girls.

The trouble was, the actress didn't want the role. Paige was shy in those days. The thought of standing in a bright pool of light before the eyes of a hundred parents paralyzed her.

"Your Mommy stands up in court and talks to people every day," Lydia pointed out. "And I don't get to memorize my lines. I have to speak right off the top of my head. All you have to do is say the words I taught you, the very words Mary spoke when the angel told her she would become the mother of Baby Jesus."

Paige tried. "My soul glo-glo . . ."

"Glorifies."

"Glorifies the Lord. My spirit re-re . . ."

"Rejoices."

"Rejoices in God my sa-savior. For he has been humble—"

"Mindful. For he has been mindful . . ."

"For he has been—I can't remember!" she cried.

"Paige, you did the whole thing last night without missing a word."

Terror swept across the child's face. "Please don't make me do this, Mommy!"

"Lydia," Kyle said. "Give it a rest for now."

"We can't! The pageant's tomorrow night."

"Paige, why don't you get ready for bed while Mommy and I have a little talk?"

She brushed her teeth and put on her bunny pajamas while her parents whispered outside the door. Lydia's eyes were burning when they returned. "Paige, I know you're nervous. But all our friends will be there to see you tomorrow night. You don't want to let them down, do you?"

"Lydia!" Kyle glared at her.

"Oh, all right!" She stormed from the room.

"Don't worry about the pageant," Kyle said, tucking Paige into bed. "Susie Wexler knows the part almost as well as you do. I'll speak to Ms. Cotton in the morning."

"Daddy," Paige said in her little voice, "I don't want Mommy to be mad."

"She's not mad, honey. Sometimes Mommy loves you so much she tries too hard. Now go to sleep."

A half hour later Kyle peeked into Paige's room to find her at the foot of the bed, reciting the magnificat to an audience of stuffed rabbits, bears, and mice propped against her pillow. "My soul glorifies the Lord," she chanted, "and my spirit rejoices in God my savior." She ran through it over and over, each time bowing to imaginary applause.

The following night she bowed to a live audience.

Lydia hugged her after the show. "I knew you could do it!"

It was an actor's trick, a way to conquer stage fright. Paige pretended that the people in the audience were stuffed animals. As she grew older, she learned to recite poems and make speeches by imagining her classmates in their pajamas.

"We'll make a lawyer out of you yet," Lydia vowed. But Paige had no interest in following her mother's path. She did what was necessary to please her.

Kyle was delighted when Paige asked his permission to work in the restaurant after school. "That would be nice, honey. But you're only twelve years old. Don't you want to hang out with Jeanette and Haley and your other friends?"

"I'd rather be with you, Daddy." The words melted his heart. Only later did he realize that the kitchen was an escape from her mother's prodding.

He started her as a prep chef, chopping vegetables, sharpening knives, and cleaning up. On short-handed evenings she waited tables.

Charles Duprée was pleased. "Nothing attracts customers like a pretty waitress!"

Lydia had been skeptical. "How's she going to keep up with school, working every night and coming home late?"

"I can do it," Paige insisted. "I'll study before and after rush hour on weekdays, and Sundays after church. Please, Mom!"

"It's good experience," Kyle added. "She can learn a lot about business, and a lot about people." Lydia gave in. It was one of Kyle's few victories in their ongoing battle over

Paige's destiny.

That's the irony, he thought. *Paige and her mother are so much alike. But it's me she's closest to.*

Kyle pulled into the driveway, waiting for the garage door to welcome home his Camry.

"What's wrong with her, Kyle?" Lydia sighed. "Why is she hiding from us?"

Disgusted, he turned to her. "After the way you treated Lucas Madison? How can you ask such a question?"

Confession

"You got a target on your back, Jodie?"

Paige sat behind Andy as Karen drove them back to the shelter. "I'm sorry I got you into this. Both of you might have been killed."

"Wasn't you wavin' the gun."

"Are you sure you're all right?" Karen peered over her shoulder. "What made you conk out like that?"

"Some boys beat me up a couple of months ago. The doctor says I have a brain injury."

"Beat you up? Why? Who were they?"

"I don't know. I can't remember much about it."

Andy turned to face her. "What did that guy wanna shoot you for?"

Sadly, she returned his gaze. Even a shower and shave hadn't washed away Andy's street bum aura. But now she saw him differently. How many times had she driven past people like him on her way to school, or to church, or to help Dad in the restaurant? Addicts. Drunks. Dropouts in ragged clothes, freezing on street corners, pleading humbly for a dollar or two to fill their stomachs. Deadbeats, Mom called them. Losers.

Quitters. Her classmates sneered at them. Yet everyone at Open Door had been so kind to her. *Bums are my family now*, she thought. *My only friends.*

"I should have told you the truth," she said quietly. "I'd like to tell you everything now."

The lasagna was safe, settling warmly in their stomachs. Louise had baked it while Karen and Andy were rushing Paige to the hospital. Zelda threw together a salad using the greens Karen had left on the countertop. The meal vanished rapidly in the evening rush.

"Where'd you learn to cook so good, Jodie?" Zelda and the other regulars were gathered at one of the tables.

"My name's not Jodie," she replied. "And it's not Jennifer," she added to Karen. "It's Paige Abernathy. My dad's the head chef at Chez Renée. He taught me everything I know."

"Why the fake name?"

"I'm sorry I couldn't tell you before. I was afraid if I gave my real name, someone might track me down here."

"What did you do? Run away from home?"

She told them about the website. How her class project turned her from a high school senior into an outcast.

"Lemme get this straight," Mike said. "You set up this website thing to help people kill themselves?"

"No! To help people like me who were confused and depressed. At first it went great. My website got over a thousand hits in the first three hours, mostly from kids who felt the way I did. It had a forum for people to talk about their problems."

"Like what?"

"There was this one boy who felt rejected because he was

ugly. He said there was no place on Earth to hide from cruelty, and he wanted out of it. Another one said she cried all the time and didn't know why. Some had family problems. A lot of them were just lonely."

"Lonely?" Dee-Man snorted. "They've got families. They've got homes and beds. Food they don't have to beg for. If they get sick, they've got doctors. What have they got to be dee-pressed about?"

"I can relate to it," Zelda responded. "I was depressed all the time when I was that age."

"About what?"

"Being a teenager is confusing, especially when you've got grownups on your back all the time."

Dee-Man scoffed. "It's homeless people who ought to be dee-pressed!"

"Hush, you guys," Karen interrupted. "Let her talk."

"Then everything started to go wrong," Paige continued. "All of a sudden, the discussions got very dark. Then it wasn't about people trying to comfort each other. It was all this talk about how to commit suicide. Several claimed they'd actually tried it and survived. Others were adults, with jobs they hated, or broken marriages. Then they started sharing information about ways to buy suicide drugs on the internet."

"What kind of drugs?" Louise asked.

"It was stuff I'd never heard of. They had code names for them, and private links to sites where you could order them. They used suicide codes, like CTB and TOS. That means 'catch the bus' and 'the other side.' Some of them talked about a book you could buy for terminally ill patients, with instructions on how to kill yourself."

"Couldn't you stop them?"

"They wouldn't listen to me! It was awful. They had these

grisly arguments about how many ounces of poison to take, and whether to do it on a full stomach, and how to hide the symptoms so nobody would call an ambulance. A couple of them recommended suicide rehearsals—taking just enough of the drug to make you sick so you could decide whether to go through with it."

"Jeez!" Andy shook his head.

Paige choked back tears. "Some news reporters traced it back to me. Then my parents started getting phone calls, asking why their daughter was promoting suicide." She wept. "Do you have any idea what that's like? To turn on the TV and find yourself in the middle of a scandal? To see your face all over TikTok and Instagram and Snapchat and know you're responsible for over a hundred dead teenagers?"

"I don't see how you're to blame," Louise argued. "You were trying to help."

"Oh, I get it," Karen said. "She's a scapegoat."

"No!" Paige erupted, distraught. "Mr. Chen was the scapegoat. The school board called a special meeting, and they fired him."

"What for?" Andy asked. "It wasn't his fault."

"My mother's on the school board."

"Oh."

"I hated her for it! Mr. Chen was just doing his job. I'm the one who designed the web pages and chose the content." She ran a sleeve across her eyes. "My dad wanted me to stay home until the uproar died down. My other teachers offered to tutor me privately. But I'd always been taught to take responsibility for myself, so I insisted on going to school. All the kids avoided me like I had COVID or something. Two of my friends, Haley Morton and Willow Douglas, wouldn't sit next to me in class or in the cafeteria. I can't say I blame them."

"Some friends!" Mike snorted.

Paige drew a ragged breath. "I went to see Mr. Chen when he was packing up his stuff to leave. He was so nice and understanding. He said I was a good student and he'd enjoyed working with me. I was so ashamed. Then things started going wrong for my parents. Mom had to reassign some cases she was prosecuting because of the publicity. Mr. Duprée said he couldn't risk losing business by letting me work at the restaurant anymore. I think that hurt Dad more than anything. We'd worked together in that kitchen for years."

"Go back to the part where somebody beat you up," Andy said.

"One day at school I was getting some books out of my locker. All of a sudden I felt this pain like knives ripping through my body. When I turned around there were eyes everywhere, accusing me, boring into me with hate. It was an actual physical pain. I remember running, stumbling through the hallways, bumping into people. Somehow I must have made it home because the next thing I knew, I was standing on the Bustamante Bridge, dressed in the ballgown I wore last year to the Sweet Sixteen party at my church."

"And that's when somebody attacked you?"

"That's what the police said. All I remember is thinking how peaceful it would be to float away. Out from the bridge, across the railroad tracks, into the sun. Dressed to meet God."

She described waking up in the hospital, and the second attack that restored her memory. "When I left the hospital, I wandered the streets looking for a place to hide. Then I saw the light in this place. I was so cold and hungry, I came in and lined up at the serving window with everyone else."

"I'm glad you did," Andy said.

"Me too," Louise added. She put an arm around Paige.

"You know what makes me even more ashamed? To be telling all this to you. People who've lost everything. I must sound like a crybaby."

"Everybody's got problems, Paige," Karen soothed. "We get all kinds here."

Paige scanned their solemn faces. "This isn't over, you know. Two people have already tried to kill me. Others are still looking for me. As long as I'm here, you're all in danger."

"She's right," Karen reflected gloomily. "I hate to admit it, but what if somebody traces her to this place?" It was late. Paige was asleep in the barracks with everyone except Andy, who'd stayed up to help Karen with the dishes.

"Where else can she go?" he asked. "Her parents' house is probably staked out. So was the hospital, obviously. Somebody with influence is out to kill her. Somebody with money."

"That's not the only thing that worries me. What if she has another blackout, like today? We have no medical facilities here. The shelter's just a place for food and a bed." Karen ran rinse water over a stack of plates. "Every night at home, I lie awake, thinking about these people. Paige isn't the only one who needs medical care. Zelda has asthma. She tries to hide it, but have you noticed how much she's coughing since you dug up all that tile? Louise is probably anemic; you can tell just by looking at her. And now the flu season's underway. Homeless people are mostly drifters. They rarely get flu shots, so they help spread the virus. We can't afford medicine. Our patrons give us barely enough money to keep this place running."

Andy was drying the casserole dishes. "When my wife left

me and took our daughter with her, I sort of went numb. No point in goin' to work every day when there was nothin' to work for. For the past few months, food, whiskey, and a bed at night is all I've cared about. Now, seems like I'm all tangled up in this place. Feels good to be workin' again, even if I ain't gettin' paid for it. All on account of that girl."

"Why her?"

"I dunno. It's like findin' an injured bird that fell out of a tree. I feel sorry for her." He stored the dishes in the cupboard. "She's a good kid."

"Young lady," Karen corrected.

"Either way, she belongs with her parents. Do you know anybody that might take her in? Maybe give her a job so she can earn her keep?"

"That's hard to imagine. Everybody in the country knows what she's done. It would have to be somebody big-hearted enough to overlook it."

"Maybe a church," Andy suggested. "Or somebody with a small business. Someplace where she can be safe."

Karen smiled. "I think I know just the man."

For someone new to jail cells, Norris Tankersley was remarkably calm. Up and down the corridor, other prisoners were cursing, moaning, or banging on the bars. Occasionally there was a lull, and Norris could hear someone chanting in a foreign language. *One of those Arabs*, he decided. *Praying and bowing to the graffiti on the wall.* Norris didn't mind the noise. Loading airplane luggage was about as noisy a job as you could get. But confinement made him restless. There was TV, of course. Mounted high on the wall, with metal mesh over the screen, so you could hardly see Jimmy Kimmel and his celebrity parade.

Before the disaster that wrecked his life, Norris had prided himself on his fitness. He was a physical guy, six-two, one-eighty, all of it well-toned muscle. When he wasn't hurling luggage into airplane bellies he played baseball twice a week for the baggage handlers' union. Norris had a powerful swing and a .375 batting average. In the hospital it had taken three cops and two orderlies to wrestle him to the floor and wrench the gun from his hand.

Someone had left a magazine on Norris's cot: *Landscaping for Beginners*. Just the thing for a guy in a sunless room with nothing to plant and no place to plant it. *Oh well*, he thought. *That's what you get when you act on impulse, Norris. You've blown your chance. Now's the time to be calm. To wait for a second one.*

Keys rattled heavily at the end of the corridor, followed by footsteps as the door clanged open. The guard escorted a young man with a briefcase to Norris's cell. He was chubby, with thinning hair, and dressed in a JCPenney original.

"Mr. Tankersley, I'm Oliver Crouch from the Public Defender's Office. May I speak with you for a moment?"

The guard let him in and moved out of earshot. Crouch sat on the cot and rummaged through some papers. "Mr. Tankersley, you've been charged with reckless endangerment and possession of a firearm in a restricted area. I understand you have no attorney of your own, and no money to pay for one. I'm here to offer my assistance at no charge. Are you willing to accept my services?"

Norris shrugged. "Think you can get me off?"

"That depends on you. To afford you the best possible representation, I'll need to ask you some questions. Anything you say to me will be held in the strictest confidence. Even if—"

"Yeah, I've seen my share of lawyer shows. Let's not waste time. You want to know why I did it."

"All right, let's start there."

"I needed an answer. And if that door hadn't been locked, I'd have gotten it."

"An answer to what?"

Norris turned away. "You wouldn't understand."

"Mr. Tankersley, the police tell me you refused to answer their questions, and that's your right. But if I'm going to defend you—"

"You don't know what it's like!" he flared. "To lose the light of your life. I had to know why. And if I wasn't locked up in this cell, I'd do it again. Only this time I'd plan it better." Calm abandoned him. He seized his pillow and threw it against the bars.

Crouch tried another approach. "Mr. Tankersley, why do you hold Paige Abernathy responsible for your loss?"

"Who?"

"Paige Abernathy. The girl you tried to kill."

Norris turned to face him. "Abernathy?"

"Yes. Why did you want to kill her?"

"That suicide girl? She was in the emergency room?"

"Yes. How did you know she was there?"

The prisoner studied his young attorney for a long moment. "Mr. Tankersley?"

Crossing slowly to the bars, Norris gazed into the corridor. "Counselor, what are my options?"

"I beg your pardon?"

"If I plead innocent, what happens next?"

Crouch relaxed, back in familiar territory. "If you deny the charges, I'll enter a not guilty plea. You'll be bound over for trial."

"And how long will that take?"

"Depending on the judge's calendar, anywhere from thirty to ninety days."

"What are my chances?"

"Pretty good, I'd say. You have no criminal record. We'll have to show the judge that you were grief-stricken and didn't know what you were doing. You'd have to have a psychiatric evaluation, but that would help us build a convincing argument. Which brings me back to the beginning. Why—"

"Okay, okay, never mind. What if I plead guilty?"

"What?"

"If I plead guilty, how long will I have to stay in jail?"

"Um . . . well . . . you didn't hurt anyone. With good behavior, you might get out on probation in a couple of months."

Tankersley returned to the cot. "Mr. Crouch, I'd like to plead guilty. I did what I did, and I take responsibility for it. I throw myself on the mercy of the court."

"Mr. Tankersley, you have a clean record! A jail sentence would be a permanent blot, something to follow you the rest of your life. Under the circumstances, I'd advise you to plead not guilty."

Norris picked his pillow off the floor and fluffed it. "Let me know when my sentencing hearing comes up. You'll know where to find me."

Crouch summoned the guard and left. With a cold smile, Norris lay back and began to plan.

It was 3 a.m. when Kyle finally gave up on sleep. He pushed aside the covers and sat up. Beside him, Lydia breathed raggedly.

Kyle worried that she was too dependent on sleeping pills.

"No choice," she said. "I can't do my job if I can't keep my eyes open." *Anxiety*, Kyle thought. *It's going to kill us both if this keeps up.*

The room was chilly. He put on his robe and went to check the thermostat. Seventy-two degrees. Maybe a cup of hot tea would help. These days, he rarely got to sleep before dawn.

He put the kettle on. Remarkable, how little cooking he did in this kitchen. Kyle mostly dined at his prep station, sampling his own cuisine before serving it to customers. Lydia was a dervish in the mornings, no time for breakfast, subsisting on Starbucks pastries and lunchtime takeout. Paige had always managed breakfast on her own. Kyle, the last to get home each night after the restaurant closed, never rose before 10 a.m.

The kettle whistled. Kyle poured water and carried his cup to the living room. Imagine the customers' faces if they saw him with a teabag. How unsophisticated!

The drink warmed him as he stood at the window, gazing into the darkness. Somewhere out there, vengeance was waiting. Lurking perhaps in the shadows between the upper crust houses, or hiding in the expensive landscaping, or parked beside the curb in a darkened van. Waiting for Paige to come home. Waiting to creep up behind her with a weapon or snatch her from his doorstep. *Woe unto you, Kyle Abernathy. Your daughter killed my only child. My oldest son. My youngest daughter. You too will suffer.* But he was already suffering. Which is worse, to know your child is dead, or to lie awake every night, imagining the dangers surrounding her? Murderers. Sex fiends. Drug addicts. Horrors that thrive in the 3 a.m. darkness of alleyways and abandoned buildings.

Lydia had put every cop, sheriff's deputy, and private investigator she could muster on Paige's trail. Kyle had little hope. Paige couldn't be found because she didn't want to be found. He knew his daughter. A perfectionist like her parents. She kept her room tidy, her clothes neat, her golden hair brushed to luxuriance. Schoolwork current, grades excellent, and the best chef assistant Kyle had ever had. Clever too. She'd eluded the vengeful families and the authorities for over two months now. Still, she was a teenage girl at the mercy of chance. Kyle knew what was making her hide. Paige agonized when a soufflé collapsed. How much worse to know that her website had wrought death and bereavement throughout America, even in nations beyond it.

When she disappeared Kyle and Lydia had contacted everyone who might be sheltering her. Kyle's parents lived in Houston. Lydia's were in Roanoke, Virginia. Both couples promised to phone immediately if they heard from her. But they hadn't.

For a while Lydia had strongly suspected that Mr. Chen was involved in Paige's flight. He was her favorite teacher and the man who'd gotten her into this mess.

"Stop thinking like a lawyer," Kyle scolded her. "Chen has his own problems now." The police agreed. They'd tailed Chen for a few weeks but found no evidence that he might be hiding her.

Some nights when he couldn't sleep, nights when Paige failed to reward his vigil by walking out of the darkness, up the front steps, and into his arms, Kyle went to her room. He sat on the bed, trying to sense her spirit in the family pictures on her desk and the Britt Nicole poster on her wall. Paige at eight. *When I grow up, I wanna be a chef like you, Daddy!* Paige at fifteen, proudly displaying her apprentice certificate to the camera. Paige and Jeanette Collins outside the Buddy Holly Center in Lubbock, two smiling eyeballs framed in the giant pair of glasses.

A hand fell on his shoulder. Lydia stood beside him, her hair unkempt, her eyes staring dully through the window.

"Pills not working?"

"I had a nightmare."

His arm went around her. "I'm sorry about earlier." She laid her head on his shoulder. Kyle and Lydia had fallen in love during her third year of law school. At first, their perfectionism was a common bond. Then, somewhere along the way, Lydia lost her ability to accept the imperfections in her husband and daughter. The traits that made her a brilliant lawyer also made her difficult to live with. Only Kyle knew how she suffered at the hands of her own driven personality.

"Kyle," she sighed into the darkness of early morning, "doesn't it strike you as odd that nobody ever comes to the house looking for her?"

"Maybe they do. Maybe they come snooping around when we're not here."

"No. The chief's been sending patrols around regularly, and they all report nothing. No prowlers, no vandals, not even any demonstrators. All those hate calls and death threats stopped weeks ago. If there really is a hit man out there, he's keeping a low profile." She snuggled closer. "Do you think she'll ever come home?"

"Paige is a resourceful girl. She'll find a way."

"What if she doesn't want to?"

"She has to," he said firmly. "We're her family."

Job Interview

Judging by his house, you'd never know that Omer Goldmann grew up poor. The two-story mansion featured white siding and tall windows with gray shutters. Texas evergreens and laurel bushes dotted the lawn. Japanese yews flanked the sidewalk leading to double French doors. The front porch accommodated a swing and two padded rocking chairs. Above, a wide dormer window offered a view into the attic Omer's wife used as her sewing room.

"Naomi loves sunshine," he explained to Paige as he showed her around. "But the view of her garden outside my window keeps me from concentrating. Did Karen tell you about me? I'm a daydreamer. All my life I've had this meshuggaas, like you get in a child's storybook."

"Meshu-what?" Paige asked.

"Meshuggaas. It's a Yiddish word for foolishness or nonsense. Certain phrases raise silly images in my head. When I was a kid, I wouldn't eat deviled eggs because I thought they were sinful. Why else would they be called that? How can I concentrate when monkey wrenches make me think of little ape mechanics working on Volkswagens? Or stool pigeons—

birds sitting in the corner wearing dunce caps. I once spent an hour trying to figure out 'Pop Goes the Weasel.' What the heck does that mean? Round and round in my head these phrases go. Suddenly it's five o'clock in the afternoon and I haven't accomplished a thing. So I work in here."

He led her into an office packed with computer workstations and home servers. A large bookcase held a collection of software discs, printer cartridges, cables, flash drives, and graphics cards. Heavy curtains blocked Paige's view of the garden. "Otherwise," he explained, "I'd be staring out the window all day, imagining the Hanging Gardens of Babylon as a place of execution. Even so, the problem creeps into my work. Can you imagine what I thought when I first heard of spam filters?"

He offered her a chair. Paige sat facing him. Omer was short, somewhere between plump and muscular, with more hair on his arms than his head. Merry blue eyes twinkled behind his spectacles. On the wall beside him were photographs of two curly-haired young men in sweaters. "My boys, Joshua and Marcus," he said proudly. "Joshua teaches European history at Columbia University in New York. Marcus works for Downing and Abbot, a pharmaceutical research laboratory in Ottawa. Both very busy, married to career women, so we don't see them very often."

"Do you have any grandchildren?" Paige asked.

"Three, with another due in May. I'd show you some pictures, but you'd be politely bored, and anyway, that's not why I invited you here. Would you like something to drink?"

"No, thank you."

Omer folded his arms. "I've thought a lot about you, Paige. When I met you at the shelter, I wondered how a person could get into such a fix that people would want to kill her. So

I did some research. Unfortunately, your website was already shut down. But!" He raised a finger. "If that could stop me, would I be living in such a fancy house? So I hacked into the host server and managed to pull up this."

The SerenityShare home page popped up on Omer's screen. Paige gasped.

"I know," he said apologetically. "This is your Frankenstein's monster, and you don't want to see it ever again. But setting aside the terrible results you got, this is beautiful artwork. Did you do it yourself?"

"Yes and no. I got the basic images from Canva. The composition is mine, though."

"Do you have any formal training in web design?"

"I used to play around with it before Mr. Chen—that's my teacher—suggested I create a website for my class project. He showed me how to use Wix to build the foundation."

"And what was your final grade?"

She smiled dourly. "A-plus."

Omer returned the smile. "With all those silly images in my head, you'd think I'd be more creative. Yet I couldn't design a decent web page if my life depended on it. But you! What a natural talent you have!" He turned to the screen. "This soft landscape, the dreamy texture, the fonts you've selected to complement the sense of peace. So inviting!"

"It worked too well," Paige responded glumly. "A lot of kids are dead because of this thing."

"I don't agree, but that's something we can talk about later." He closed the link. "Paige, I have a proposition for you. What would you think about coming to work for me as a website designer?"

Her eyes widened. "Mr. Goldmann, I haven't finished high school yet. The way things are now, I don't know if I ever will. I'm living in a homeless shelter, and somebody's out to kill me."

"That's where we can help each other. Let me show you something." He opened a folder labeled *Finished Products.* "These are website themes I've sold to clients all over the world. Look at them and tell me what you think."

The samples were dazzling. Coffee harvesters bearing straw baskets waded down a green slope into a rich valley. A boy flew joyfully through the air on a skateboard. Sailboats set forth from a harbor at dawn.

"They're great!" she marveled. "Eye-catching. Very professional. I thought you said you were no good at this."

"I'm not. Every one of these came from a subcontractor called Client Mart. Excellent work yes, but the markup! They charge five thousand dollars a page, which I had to pass on to my customers. The ones who could afford it were pleased. But I also deal with a lot of small business owners. 'Omer,' they tell me, 'for a fancy design like this, I'd have to sell three months' worth of merchandise just to break even!' Now, when it comes to their technical requirements—plugins, search options, navigational links—I can underprice anybody. What I can't give them is affordable designs that will help grow their business. As a result I lose customers. And that's where you come in."

He faced her squarely. "Paige, you need a safe place to live. I need a web artist. Suppose you move in with me and Naomi. Upstairs, there's a furnished room we never use. It's got a double bed, a chest of drawers, lots of closet space, and an adjoining bathroom. You could live here rent-free, plus meals, and I'd pay you minimum wage to start. What do you think?"

"Mr. Goldmann, you don't know anything about me."

"On the contrary. I've seen you around the shelter. Karen Wallace says you're the most reliable volunteer she's ever had. You do whatever she asks without complaining. You've even got some of those vagabonds renovating the place."

Paige laughed. "They just like my cooking. Andy Michener's the one who talked them into helping with the floor."

"That was after you shamed them into it. No, don't ask me how I know. I didn't become a successful businessman by being a poor judge of people." He spoke gently. "Paige, I think you've been doing all this shelter work to make up for what happened with your website. That, young lady, is a sign of character. A sense of responsibility is something you can't put a price on."

He sank to a whisper. "There's one other reason why I'm making you this offer. It's Naomi. Ever since our boys moved away, she's been lonely. Rattling around in this big house with nobody but me to look after. Not even a grandchild to cuddle. Naomi and I have been happily married for twenty-seven years, except for one thing. We always wanted to have more kids. Especially a daughter." He smiled. "That would be part of your role here. Giving Naomi someone to worry about besides the sons and grandchildren she never sees."

"Even though I'm not a Jew?"

"So what? Some of our best friends are Gentiles."

The word rankled a bit. Paige considered herself a Christian. *Gentile* sounded heathenish. Nevertheless, she responded, "This is awfully kind of you, Mr. Goldmann."

"Omer. Please, just Omer."

A frown creased her forehead. "What about my shelter friends? Who's going to cook for them if I'm living here?"

"You think our kitchen's not as good as the one at the shelter? You can cook their meals here and use my car to deliver them. I'll even help with the groceries as a bonus. Another tax deduction I can use to complicate my CPA's life."

Paige grinned. "It sounds wonderful!"

"Then you'll give it a try?"

"Yes, I'd love to." Then she faltered. "There's one more thing though, Mr.—I mean, Omer. You must realize that opening your home to me puts you in danger. Two people have tried to kill me already. What if they find out I'm living here?"

"If you were Jewish, you'd already know the answer to that question. Our whole history is fraught with peril. So we plan our future as best we can, and meanwhile we live for today." He stood. "Now, suppose I introduce you to Naomi. Then the two of you can decide what we're having for supper."

Omer wasn't exaggerating. The Goldmann kitchen rivaled the one at Chez Renée. It included a food prep island with its own sink, drawers, and cabinets; a double-door refrigerator; a freezer; a double wall oven; a six-burner stovetop; and a walk-in pantry. Most of the illumination came from an overhead skylight and transparent doors leading into the garden. Paige thought she could happily spend the rest of her life in such a kitchen.

"I know what you're thinking." Naomi poured tea for Paige and herself at the breakfast bar. "Too much kitchen for two people. But when our boys were growing up, this room was busy as a hive, with all their friends running in and out, grabbing cookies off the plate as fast as I could bake them. And we still have parties and entertain on holidays. So it gets a lot of use."

Unlike Paige's mother, Naomi was short and chubby, with

brown eyes and thick dark hair. She wore a violet print blouse and blue jeans with mud-caked knees. "I've been working in the garden all morning," she explained, "planting hyacinth bulbs." She offered Paige a slice of cake. "Try this. A treat as good as any you serve at your father's restaurant. I should know, I've been there."

Paige took a bite. "Mm! Reminds me of gingerbread."

"That's close. It's lekach, or honey cake, a traditional Jewish dessert."

Paige savored her tea. "My dad keeps a spice garden in our backyard. Every morning he picks fresh ones for the restaurant. He loves to try new dishes. On weekends he offers a surprise dessert, in addition to the ones on the menu. It's one of several tricks he uses to keep the customers coming back."

"I saw you there once," Naomi said. "You were a little girl, waiting tables. You and your family must be very close."

Paige frowned and concentrated on her tea.

"Do your parents know where you are?"

"I don't want to put them in danger. Besides, we have . . . problems."

Naomi's heart went out to her. Such a beautiful girl, teetering on the cusp of womanhood, the faint scars on her cheeks and forehead clashing with worry lines.

"Omer explained to me how you came to live at that shelter. Are those the only clothes you have?"

Paige blushed. "I'm sorry about that. Mrs. Wallace keeps a closet full of donated clothing. At least it's clean. There's a laundromat next door to the shelter."

"Even so, those machines want feeding. What have you been doing for money, if you don't mind my asking?"

She squirmed. "Well, uh . . . some of the other homeless people . . . I cook for them, you see, and . . ." she faltered, embarrassed.

"I suppose you can't retrieve the clothes from your own home?"

"I could sneak in through the garage when no one's around, but there might be people watching the house."

"I see." Naomi pondered. "Unfortunately, you're taller than I am, so none of my clothes will fit you." She waved the problem away. "Never mind. Tomorrow we'll get you some new outfits. My treat."

"But, Mrs. Goldmann—"

"Now, now, no arguments. If you're going to be assistant to the best business consultant in America, you've got to look the part! Tonight you'll help me prepare a nice dinner, then you'll get a good night's sleep in your own bedroom. Tomorrow we'll have breakfast, go shopping, and then you can start earning your keep."

"You're both so kind," Paige said. "Most people hate me." She added gloomily, "They should."

Naomi refilled their cups from the ceramic pot. "Such a world we live in today," she sighed. "Everyone so caught up in pressures and worries that they can't take time to know each other. To hear the newscasts, you'd think Paige Abernathy was a monster. Yet here she sits in my kitchen, just like my daughter-in-law Marlene used to do when she and Joshua were courting. Telling me all about her dreams of marriage and motherhood, and her career goals. So many opportunities, so many choices to ponder. So uncertain of herself. Even a little scared." She covered Paige's hand. "How terrible you must feel, that good intentions should plunge you into disaster."

"Please . . ." Paige's eyes began to fill. "Please don't."

Dreamily, Naomi continued. "All those years ago, when we were courting, Omer was so afraid of letting me down.

'Naomi,' he said, 'what if I fail? What if these crazy thoughts in my head wreck my career? What if I can't support you?' 'Omer,' I said, 'you have a concentration problem. So what? Everybody has problems. The question is, will you draw on the strength God has given you to overcome them? Do you think I'd marry you if I didn't know that your will is stronger than your weakness?'"

She reached out to stroke Paige's cheek. "This thing that's happened to you, young lady, is an early episode in a very long life. Like the scars on your face, it will fade in time. And you'll be stronger for having overcome it."

"So what's for dinner?" Omer asked. "Or are you arguing over who's in charge?"

"We're way ahead of you," Naomi replied, stirring a pot of beans. "Tonight, I'm cooking for the three of us. Paige is cooking for the shelter. Tomorrow, we trade jobs."

"Great! So if I don't like what you cook, I can go eat at the shelter—Ouch!" Naomi whacked him with a spatula. He wandered over to Paige. "What's that I smell?"

"Cayenne pepper. I made buffalo wings."

Omer winced. "Paige, if we're going to work together, you have to be careful what you say. Now my head is full of flying bisons!"

"Speaking of images," Naomi said, "Paige, did you know that Omer is a bundle of barley?"

"A what?"

"A sheaf," he explained. "You philistines have a song about that, 'Bringing in the Sheaves.' An omer is a unit of measurement in the Torah, one tenth of an ephah. An omer, or a sheaf of barley, equals about forty-three chicken eggs."

"Why did your parents name you after food?"

"Historically, *omer* refers to the manna God sent from Heaven when the Israelites were wandering in the wilderness. God directed them to collect one *omer* for each person per tent. One day's meal. In other words, I'm the breadwinner in my family."

"*Omer* is also a spiritual term," Naomi added, "the counting of days leading up to the grain harvest. It expresses how willing a person is to accept the Torah, which was given by God on Mount Sinai."

Paige nodded. "Moses and the Ten Commandments. I remember that from Sunday school."

"My grandparents immigrated to Texas from Germany after World War II," Omer said. "Talk about culture shock! They'd never seen oil wells before. But they were determined to preserve our traditions. That's how I met Naomi, at our synagogue."

"Did you hire one of those matchmakers?"

Naomi laughed. "You've seen too many movies. My cousin Ruth brought us together after Omer repaired an antique clock that had been in her family for three generations. She didn't charge us a penny."

"A good thing too," Omer added. "In those days I was living hand-to-mouth."

"You were what?" Naomi grinned.

"Broke, I mean." Omer concentrated on Paige, who was mixing olive oil and herbs for the salad. "Don't you use measuring spoons?"

"I know how to measure from experience. My dad taught me a lot. Name any dish you like, and he can prepare it from memory."

"A good business to be in. There's never a shortage of hungry people. What else do you cook at the shelter?"

"It depends on what's available. Most of their food is donated commodities. Potatoes, rice, and pasta are the easiest. They're cheap, and you can do almost anything with them. What's your favorite dish, Omer?"

"Pork chops." He laughed at her expression. "Just kidding. Do you ever serve fish?"

"Not at the shelter. It's too expensive. I know a great recipe for trout if you'd like to try it."

"Fine." He peeked into one of the simmering pots. "Broccoli! I love it!"

"Sorry, that's for my casserole. Nothing fancy, but it's nourishing and feeds a large crowd. Excuse me." She reached past him to check the rice steamer. Suddenly she froze, putting a hand to her head.

"Are you all right?" Omer asked.

A wave of grayness swept across her vision. "Whew! I felt dizzy for a second."

Naomi took her arm. "Here, come sit down."

"No, I'm all right now. Sometimes I get these funny feelings. They always go away after a few seconds."

"You should see a doctor."

"I did, in the hospital. I'm okay." She checked the rice. "Ah, perfect!"

"How do you know how much of everything to cook?" Omer asked.

"At the shelter there's always a crowd, so I go big. On cold nights we get as many as fifty."

Omer's jaw dropped. "You cook for fifty people all by yourself? Even Naomi's never fed that many without help."

"It's not so hard if you plan ahead. With slow cookers you

can have stew or chili simmering all day. Meanwhile, you can make cold dishes like potato salad ahead of time. You do the stovetop and oven dishes last."

"And you always have enough?"

Paige grinned. "I've never had any leftovers."

"Omer!" Naomi scolded. "Stop grilling the cook and chop some onions for me." He took his place at the chopping block. "Paige, it's nice that you want to keep helping at the shelter. But the danger! Aren't you afraid some angry parents might track you down there?"

She turned back to the stove. "Sometimes I wish they would."

"Why?"

"How else can I atone for all those deaths?"

They settled into a routine. Paige rose at five each morning to make breakfast for the homeless shelter. She and Naomi loaded the serving dishes into the car and hauled them to Open Door. By the time they returned, Omer was busy in his office. Paige joined him, working on her new projects while Naomi prepared their own breakfast.

Paige's first assignment was for two retired ladies, Barbara Livsey and Toni Glass. They lived in Nashville and wanted to set up an online mail-order business for their homemade candy. Toni provided sample photos of their wares: peanut brittle, fudge, chocolate-covered mints, caramels, and pecan pralines. Paige put her imagination to work and came up with a deep rose background for the home page. She dotted it with bite-sized morsels nestled in white tissue paper. Clicking on them produced closeups with details about the ingredients.

"You must have read my mind!" Barbara exclaimed over the phone. "This is just what I was looking for! How soon can you have it ready? We're developing a mailing list for Valentine's Day."

Paige looked to Omer, who held up ten fingers. "Give us about ten days, and we'll have a first draft of the whole site. In the meantime, call me if you think of anything you want to add, like prices and packaging options."

For a man who had trouble concentrating, Omer had some quirky habits. He hummed nonsense songs like "Mairzy Doats" and "Tutti-Frutti" while hunched over his keyboard, seemingly unaware he was doing it. Paige could only guess at the images in his head.

During the week Paige stayed busy. She designed websites for a plant nursery, an architect, and a ceramics retailer.

Omer was pleased. "You've got a home here as long as you want it."

Around four thirty each day, Paige broke off to join Naomi in the kitchen, where they prepared supper for themselves and the shelter. After that Paige was free to do as she wished. Most evenings she helped Naomi with housecleaning while Omer worked in the office, performing website maintenance for his customers. Before bedtime they gathered in the living room to watch the local news. Paige liked the routine. It kept her from thinking about SerenityShare.

For all her cooking experience, Paige had no background in Jewish cuisine. She developed a taste for Naomi's matzo ball soup and potato kugel. One morning she treated the shelter residents to servings of shakshuka, a combination of poached eggs, tomatoes, and bell papers. Naomi also taught her how to make cholent, a slow cooker stew popular on Sabbath days.

Conforming to ancient law, Omer and Naomi attended

Sabbath services at their synagogue. The observances brought to mind Paige's own religious background. It was two months now since she'd attended church. She missed rehearsing with the choir on Thursday nights and listening to Ned Stewart's Sunday morning sermons. Most of all, she missed Youth Group with Jeanette, Willow, and Haley. For a while she tried watching online services on one of Omer's computers. But it wasn't the same as being there.

Naomi was disturbed that Paige wouldn't phone her parents.

"They must be worried. Don't you want them to know you're okay?"

Paige was evasive. "In a few months, I'll be eighteen, and they won't be responsible for me anymore."

Naomi fretted but didn't press her further.

"Give her time," Omer suggested.

Paige's bedroom was pleasant, papered with daisy patterns and hung with gossamer curtains. Nevertheless she slept fitfully at night, dreaming of dark funerals where endless platoons of pallbearers trudged up the aisles bearing the corpses of children. Above their heads loomed a bloody sign: SerenityShare.

One night she awoke with a sense of dread. Outside the safety of the Goldmann home, something was waiting: an incomplete task or an unfulfilled obligation that nagged her like an itch. Kneeling by the bed, she tried reciting Psalm Twenty-Three: "The Lord is my shepherd; I shall not want . . ." But the words were those of a long-dead patriarch.

"Dear God," she improvised, "You are my creator, my comforter, and my guiding light. Because of You I've never had to want for anything. But despite all these advantages, I've gone astray. I pray that I can atone for my sins and be worth something to You."

Her thoughts returned to that September evening on the bridge. The impulse that had led her there was gone, but the turmoil remained in her heart, a confused swirl of guilt, anger, and thwarted love. "God," she added, "even though I'm walking in the valley of the shadow of death, I won't be afraid, for I know You're with me. Please light my way out of this darkness and strengthen my faith so that I won't stumble again."

Talking Books

Snow, which rarely ventured into West Texas, piled itself eight inches high the morning of December 14. Stranded drivers sat in their cars, phoning for tow trucks and staring through Open Door's front window at Andy Michener's conscripts.

"Take this tape and cover the tops of the baseboards," he said to Leroy James, a bearded man in a windbreaker and baseball cap. "When that's done, tape some newspapers over the floor where it meets the baseboards."

Blearily, Leroy surveyed the dining room. His hangover made it look like the Grand Canyon. "You want me to crawl from this corner, all the way through the kitchen, out again and back on my knees?"

"Would you rather be outside with Reynaldo, shovelin' the sidewalk? Besides, you've got help. Charity here is left-handed. She'll start in the opposite direction and meet you in the middle." He handed Leroy a roll of painter's tape. "Lighten up! It goes faster than you think."

Leroy peeled off his jacket and sank to the floor, his knees crackling. His feet bumped against Charity Mitchell, an ex-seamstress with brownish teeth and squinty eyes.

"Meetcha in the middle!" she cackled. The two began crawling and taping in opposite directions.

Andy smiled. He had plenty of help today. Last night's storm had driven more refugees to Karen Wallace's door, where they found warm beds and hot showers. Whether out of gratitude or boredom, every one of them pitched in to help with the work. They had extra incentive. Rumors about a homeless shelter with a five-star cook had spread among the city's destitute. Paige's breakfast of spinach-and-egg muffins, sent over by courier from the Goldmanns' house, vanished rapidly.

Today the regulars shared the place with three dozen others. Karen had managed to borrow a few extra cots from a Boy Scout troop. Still, eleven people had spent the night sleeping on the dining room floor. Two of them, a boy and a girl younger than Paige, stood at the sink, washing dishes and smiling shyly at each other. At the counter behind them, Zelda was making potato salad. From Leroy, she borrowed a strip of painter's tape to stick the pesky lock of hair to her forehead. Louise couldn't stand it. She borrowed a pair of fingernail scissors from Karen and snipped the lock away.

Mike and Dee-Man sat in a corner of the dining room, chopping vegetables.

"You guys be careful," Zelda hollered. "That's supposed to be vegetable soup. I don't wanna bite down on a spoonful of bloody fingers tonight."

"Soup fingers!" Dee-Man cackled. "I'll bet Paige hasn't got a recipe for that!"

"Bet you ain't got no dee-words for it neither," Mike challenged.

"Digital dee-light!" he cried gleefully.

Karen joined Andy at the serving window, where he was

laying out paintbrushes and rollers. "Paige just phoned. She's still snowbound at Omer's house, so she gave me a recipe for cornbread to go with the soup tonight. Get this. It's got cheese and chili peppers in it."

"Sounds great." He examined the list of ingredients. "You think we'll have enough to go around?"

"Everything we need is in the pantry, and today we've got plenty of volunteer cooks." She surveyed the room. An elderly man crept along the walls, unscrewing the cover plates from light switches and electrical sockets. Two others folded the extra tables and chairs and stacked them in the middle of the floor. "Can you get all this painting done in one day?"

"I don't see why not. I never had this much help when I was layin' tile. Paintin's easier than that." Karen marveled at the activity. In just a few weeks, Open Door had acquired a positive atmosphere, thanks to a teenage girl and a generous patron.

"Looks like your helper needs some help," she noted. Leroy was struggling to unstick two ends of tape from each other.

Andy sighed. "Wish I had my kneepads." He headed to the rescue.

Karen returned to her office. *Just wait till the board members get a look at this place*, she thought. *They'll be falling all over each other, trying to take credit for it.*

Typical of West Texas weather, the sun was out by eleven thirty. The snow was melting and all the stuck cars had disappeared.

In the dining room, Andy directed traffic. "Everybody grab a roller or a brush. Start at the north end and work south. Those of you with brushes follow along behind the rollers and paint along the baseboards and fixtures. When the first coat dries, we'll do the whole thing again."

"How 'bout a break first?" Leroy pleaded. "I ain't had a smoke all mornin'."

"I ain't had one since I got here two months ago," Andy retorted. "Concentrate on the job and you won't think about it so much." Grumbling, Leroy fell to work. Andy was pleased with himself. Weaned off booze and cigarettes, he now slept peacefully at night and felt energetic during the day. He thought he might even go back to work when this was over. If not as a tile setter, then something else.

As he predicted, the painting went quickly. By sundown the last roller tray and paintbrush were rinsed. The walls were a pristine white, matching the tile. The workers lined up at the serving window, where Louise dished up bowls of soup and thick hunks of cornbread.

"Seems a lot brighter in here," Zelda remarked. "I wonder why Paige insisted on white."

"Probably so it won't clash with the pictures," Mike said.

"What pictures? There ain't any."

"She said somethin' about pictures. I guess that's next."

Almost everyone stayed for supper and a bed. The only departures were Karen, who went home to her husband, and Leroy, who bolted his meal and ventured forth in search of a liquor store.

"You guys eat like this all the time?" asked Doris Blanchard, a woman with orange-tinted hair. "Even my mama never made cornbread this good."

"We got our own cocinera," said Reynaldo.

"Where she at?"

He shrugged. "A guy's hacienda."

Mike asked, "You reckon she'll quit cookin' for us, now that all the work's done?"

"Who says there ain't no more work?" Dee-Man asked.

"Well, we got the floor done. We got the walls done. What else is there?"

A drop of water plopped into Mike's soup. Above him, a dark stain spread across the ceiling. "Oh, great!" he moaned.

Norris Tankersley had a plastic smile ready when his lawyer appeared. "I wasn't sure I'd be seeing you again, Mr. Crouch. I want to ask you a favor."

"If it's about your plea, this is your last chance to change your mind. That's why I'm here." The attorney drew a set of documents from his briefcase.

"Oh no. I haven't changed my mind. Show me where to sign." He scanned the papers rapidly.

"Mr. Tankersley, why are you so eager to plead guilty? I've never had a client who didn't grab every break the judicial system allows him."

"We've been over that already. Got a pen?"

Crouch drew one from his shirt pocket. He watched as Tankersley's big fingers scrawled his name on the bottom line. "So what's the favor?"

His client peeked into the corridor. A guard loitered at the far end, yawning and scratching his belly. "I need a cell phone," Tankersley whispered.

"No way! Prisoners aren't allowed—"

"Keep your voice down! Sure they are. There's at least three guys on this floor with smuggled phones. I hear them sweet-talking their girlfriends all day long."

"It's out of the question! I'm your lawyer, not an errand boy. Besides, you already get one free call per day, courtesy of the county."

"This isn't for calls. I need something with browser capability."

"Forget it."

Tankersley studied the lawyer's ensemble. "If I'm not mistaken, that's the same suit you wore last time. You've probably got a wife and kids. It must be tough, making ends meet on a court-appointed lawyer's salary."

"That's none of your business." He rose to leave. Tankersley blocked his path, towering above him with six-feet two inches of muscle. "If you're trying to intimidate me, you're wasting your time."

The fake smile returned. "Mr. Crouch, suppose a thousand dollars suddenly dropped into your lap. Wouldn't that be enough to upgrade your wardrobe?"

"Mr. Tankersley, I'm a respectable member of the bar! I don't take bribes!"

"Who said anything about bribery?" Tankersley glanced back at the guard. "Look, I didn't mean to insult you. All I'm saying is that if I were to give you access to my checking account, you could easily verify that there's plenty of cash available to pay for the phone. Plus a nice bonus for putting you to so much trouble. I won't even ask how much you withdrew. Like you said, you're a respectable man. I trust you."

Tankersley reached for *Landscaping for Beginners*, tore out a page, and made a few notes. "Here's the name of my bank and my account number. When you get to the log-in page, type my name in the user field. The password is COMPLETE, all caps, followed by an ampersand, the number twelve, and an exclamation mark."

"Why is this so important?"

Tankersley waited, staring into Crouch's eyes until he

became uncomfortable.

"This is highly irregular. I'm not promising anything, understand?"

"Of course. In the meantime, take your family out to dinner tonight. It's on me."

It was early January, three weeks after the big snow. Omer was admiring Paige's design for Edward Conifer, a bookstore owner in Bristol, England. He specialized in children's literature and wanted to make his website more appealing to young readers.

Books, Paige decided, *have personalities. What if each book had a voice telling you what it's about?*

Her home page featured a child's book nook. Surrounding the reading table were shelves of titles. When a child clicked on one, it would fly off the shelf, land on the table, and begin to speak.

"Hi! I'm Misty Clover. Open me up and I'll take you to my treehouse in the woods, where I live with Angus the tomcat."

When the child clicked a second book, the first flew back to the shelf to make room for the new one. Paige and Naomi supplied the character voices.

"Now all we need is an option to keep his stock updated," Omer said. "I'll set up an editing module so Edward can do that at his discretion."

"How much will you charge him for all this?"

"Fifteen percent less than what my competitors charge, plus a 25 percent discount for committing to a three-year maintenance contract."

"And you still make a profit?"

"Oh yes! Many of the largest website developers promise more than they deliver, and they take longer. I always come out ahead because I build personal relationships with my customers. Trust is an important element in any business."

Edward Conifer was thrilled with Paige's design and Omer's pricing but confessed that he didn't have enough money to advertise the site.

"I'll take care of that," Omer assured him. He added it to his mailing list of libraries, schools, and parents. "Always think ahead," he advised Paige. "What else will your client need besides what he asks for? The more solutions you can offer him, the happier he'll be."

One afternoon they were collaborating on a design for an online business broker.

"How do you make an interesting theme page for such a boring subject?" Omer wondered.

"Maybe we could fill it with people scenes," she suggested. "Smiling people working together on something."

"Working on what? This guy provides outsourcing for everything from lawncare to custodial work."

"So we make some slider pages. Each one with a diff-ff-ff . . ." She froze.

"What's the matter?"

The next thing she knew, Naomi was patting her face with cold water. "Paige, wake up! Wake up!" Omer, white as a sheet, knelt on the floor beside her.

"What happened?"

"One minute you were talking, the next you just keeled over. Are you all right?"

She sat up. "I guess so. How long have I been out?"

"A couple of minutes. I was just about to call the paramedics." They helped her to a chair. "Do you feel sick?"

"No." Then she remembered Dr. Ursi's warning. "Did I foam at the mouth or have spasms?"

"No, but you scared me to death," Omer said. "Karen told me about your episode at the shelter. I thought it was just a fainting spell."

She massaged her temples. "I'm supposed to take seizure medication. I guess I should have told you."

"How long have you been like this?" Naomi asked.

She told them about her bout with amnesia. "I've only had that one dizzy spell since the emergency room, so I thought I was okay. Besides," she added, shamefaced, "I was afraid if you knew, you wouldn't let me stay here."

"Why wouldn't we?"

"Who wants to be around somebody who has seizures?"

"Oh, Paige! Don't you know me better than that, with this meshuggaas of mine?" He turned to his keyboard. "Who's your doctor?"

"The one who gave me the prescription is Dr. Ursi."

Omer looked him up on the web. "Here he is. Nathaniel Ursi, neurology. He's in the Medical Arts Building on Latrell Street."

Omer's phone call only ensnared him in a tug-of-war between Paige and Ursi's nurse, who would not authorize a refill.

"From what you've told me, the doctor's going to insist on another EEG. Her condition may have worsened. The dosage she was getting in the hospital may be insufficient."

Paige refused to see the doctor. "I'm sick of being a burden on everyone!"

"Don't your parents have you on their health insurance?"

"I don't want them involved in this."

"Then I'll pay for it."

"Absolutely not!"

"Paige! What if you keep having these blackouts? You might go into convulsions and hurt yourself."

She began to weep. "Why does everything I do turn out wrong? I should have jumped off that bridge when I had the chance."

"Now, now." Naomi patted her shoulder.

"How can I answer for all those suicides? How will God ever forgive me? I wish I were dead!"

"Oh, stop that! Come here." Omer took her hand and sat her at his workstation. "Sit. Dry your eyes. I want to show you something." He clicked open a folder labeled SerenityShare. "Tell me something, Paige. Why did you create that website?"

"To help people who were depressed and lonely."

"What made you think you could help them?"

Paige thought back to Mr. Chen's science class. The past ten months seemed like an endless downhill slide. "Before the website, my phone chats were mostly with young people. They thought nobody understood them. Not their parents, not their teachers, not even their friends. They talked like they'd given up on themselves. When they went looking for help, all they got was abuse. You know what I mean, Omer. The hateful talk you find all over social media. I thought there should be a place that offered comfort and encouragement. But I was wrong. Even the ones I tried to help were full of anger. The ones who bothered to read the psalms or listen to the hymns I posted just made cynical comments about them."

"Paige," Omer asked, "of all the people who visited your website, how many killed themselves?"

"At least a hundred and eight, according to the news."

"And how many others kept coming back?"

"I don't know," she said, wiping a tear. "I never counted them."

"Well, I did. Thanks to my God-given brilliance, I was able to resurrect your records." He opened a spreadsheet. "Look at this, Paige. Over twelve million hits in four months. And look at this." He scrolled down. "More than twenty thousand people who not only registered, but kept coming back to SerenityShare, day after day. Look at them! The same log-in names, over and over. Pages and pages of people who *didn't* kill themselves. People who just wanted someone to talk to. They talked to you. They talked to each other. Just as you encouraged them to do."

"But Omer, that doesn't change the fact—"

"That the hundred and eight who did kill themselves probably would have done it anyway."

Paige eyed him skeptically.

"Look at these IDs." He scrolled through them. "This guy Death Mask logged in twenty-seven times, and each time, he said, 'I'm going to off myself.' So why is he still there? Here's another one, Used Up. She claims to be an expert on asphyxiation. If that's true, how come she's not dead? Or Stillborn. He keeps dishing out advice on toxic chemicals. How does he know unless he's tried them? You can tell he's doing it just to get attention."

"What about the ones who went through with it?"

Omer took her hand again. "Paige, the ones who killed themselves were beyond your help. The only one who could help them was God, and they turned away from Him too. You're not responsible for what other people do, Paige. Only for what you do."

"He's right," Naomi said.

Paige was unconvinced. "If what you say is true, how come so many people are blaming me? Two have already tried to kill me. How many others are out there, just waiting for their chance?"

"Ah, Paige." Omer sighed. "Today we live in a world where everyone is looking to blame someone else for every bad thing that happens. I wish I could invent a way to make people's cell phones melt any time they sent out a hurtful word. If only they'd put all that passion into loving each other, as Jesus taught us to do."

"I thought Jews didn't believe in Jesus."

"One should never generalize about people. There are all sorts of Jews. Look at you Protestants: Baptists, Lutherans, Calvinists, Quakers. All Jesus-followers, just in different ways. How can I not believe in a man who preached universal love and gave His life to prove that He meant what He said? Now, enough talk! Let's get back to work."

That evening Omer was catching up on his billing. Beside him, Paige tinkered half-heartedly with a jewelry design.

"Something on your mind?" he asked.

"Omer," she said, turning to face him, "if I ask you a question, will you tell me the truth?"

"Of course."

"Are you the one who paid my hospital bills?"

"No!" He blinked, surprised. "I hadn't even thought about it. Why?"

"Somebody did, and I can't figure out who. The business office wouldn't tell me."

"So? Be grateful. Don't look a gift horse in the mouth. Argh!" he winced. "I did again!" He shrugged off the image and returned to work.

Paige sat quietly for a moment. Then, "Omer, can I ask

you a really big favor?" With a sigh he closed the billing app to give her his full attention. "Will you hack into the hospital's database and find out who it is?"

Omer's face darkened. "Paige, that's not only criminal, it's unethical. I would never do something like that."

"You already did. You hacked into SerenityShare to find out more about me."

"That was different. Your website was already shut down. Besides, I did it to help you."

"I know you did. And I'm grateful. But I need to know."

"Why?"

"So I can thank whoever it was and pay them back."

He laughed. "You're going to repay your hospital bills with the measly salary you get from me?"

"I don't mean all at once. But I will someday. It's my responsibility. Besides," she added soberly, "I don't deserve it."

He rolled his eyes. "So we're back to self-abasement, are we? Paige, you're a Bible student. Don't you remember the parable of the Good Samaritan?"

"Sure."

"Jews and Samaritans. Two cultures that despise each other. But one day a Samaritan finds a Jew lying on a road, beaten by robbers. He binds his wounds, takes him to an inn, and pays all his expenses. What do you suppose became of him?"

"The Samaritan? I don't know. Jesus didn't tell us that part."

"Ah, but He implied it! When you bless your neighbor, you bless yourself. Paige, whoever your Samaritan is, God will reward him in His own way, in His own time."

"Maybe," she said doubtfully. "Anyway, I still want to know who it is."

Omer shook his head. "You won't get it from me."

"Then let me ask you something else."

"Oy vey!"

"Since you've already hacked into my website once, how about hacking into it again?"

"Why?"

"I want you to look up GoneforGood, one of my subscribers. I need to know his real name."

"Why?"

"I think his father may be Jerome Faulkner, the man who tried to smother me in the hospital. This boy kept threatening to kill himself. First with guns, then hanging. Then he mentioned something about poison."

"Paige, I thought we'd settled this. You did not drive those kids to suicide! Why torture yourself?"

"I'm responsible," she answered stubbornly.

Omer groaned. "Serves me right for hiring a person with integrity." He opened up Paige's user registration. "Here it is. GoneforGood. His email address starts with jefflowery. Sound like anyone you know?"

"Jeff Lowery? No. Then he can't be Faulkner's son. Does it say where he lives?"

"Your registration setup doesn't go that deep." Omer did a web search. He found over a dozen Jeff Lowerys, including three who had been dead for years. "So what if you could find this guy? What would you do about it?"

"I don't know. Apologize to his family, maybe." Paige went to the window and peeked through the curtains Omer kept shut to keep his mind focused. Beyond the glass lay Naomi's garden, filled with winter greenery and hyacinth bulbs awaiting spring. "According to the news, Mr. Faulkner's son is in a coma, probably for the rest of his life. I'll never forget the look on that man's face when they were dragging him away." Tears gathered in her eyes. "Jerome Faulkner had a wife, a son, and a business. Now he's in jail. His life is ruined. And it's all my fault."

"So maybe you should go visit him."

"In jail? I'd probably just make things worse."

Omer typed the name into his search window. "It says here that Faulkner was convicted of attempted murder. He has a sentencing hearing next week."

"Who's his lawyer?"

"Doesn't say. But the case is on file with the county attorney's office."

Oh God, Paige thought. *My mother.*

Kitchen Cop

In a way, Emilio Martinez was the most powerful man in Alverna. Neither the mayor nor the police chief influenced so many lives. Emilio was the Bolton County health inspector. In his hands lay the fate of more than two hundred dining establishments.

Even at Chez Renée, his surprise visits caused anxiety. There was always the chance of a dead mouse or cockroach turning up in the dark corner of a pantry, or beneath one of the prep tables or cookstoves. Emilio had fourteen years' experience ferreting out improperly stored foods and contaminated bins. Few restaurants, operating on thin profit margins, could afford a thousand-dollar fine or a thirty-day shutdown.

Emilio knew this, but he never abused his authority. He preferred to maintain a working relationship with his subjects. Most of the time he overlooked small violations when they were corrected in his presence. Only the sloppy Joes who earned that name suffered the fatal consequences.

Thus Emilio resented Lydia Abernathy's intrusion on his turf.

"I think my daughter's working in a restaurant," she

told him. "It could be anything from a walk-in to a drive-through. Here's her picture. I want you to show it at every eatery in town."

"Mrs. Abernathy," he protested, "do you have any idea what you're asking? There's more to my job than inspecting restaurants. I have to visit every school cafeteria, nursing home, and day care center in town. Not to mention convenience stores with hot food licenses. I've only got two assistants, and they're up to their necks in lab work. Let the police look for your daughter. I don't have time."

"All you have to do is carry her picture in your pocket and show it around wherever you go. It won't take five seconds. Please," she added gently.

Emilio's heart softened. For years he'd observed the father and daughter working side by side in Chez Renée's kitchen. Kyle wasn't himself these days, grim and preoccupied. Emilio wondered how he kept his mind on food.

"All right," he surrendered. "But even if you're right, it could take months to find her. An inspection can take an hour or more, not to mention follow-ups."

For weeks he wandered about town, displaying the photo to every food manager at every location. Yes, they all knew about Paige Abernathy from newscasts and internet chatter. But not one of them had seen her.

It was late one evening, a month after the big snowstorm, that Emilio dropped by Open Door. The shelter had a long history of moldy pipes, leaky food containers, unsanitary bathrooms, and rodent infestations. Karen Wallace did her best, but the building was eighty years old, and the shelter's oversight board was tightfisted.

Karen, who usually dreaded Emilio's visits, greeted him warmly. "You're going to love what we've done with the kitchen."

He was already admiring the dining room. "I don't even recognize this place! Who did all the work?"

"They did." Karen pointed to four men climbing up and down ladders with new Sheetrock. "They retiled the floor, painted the walls, and now they're replacing the ceiling." She led him into the kitchen. "There were several leaks in the roof from all that snow, but a couple of the guys patched them."

Emilio was impressed. The grimy kitchen walls were now cheerfully white, thanks to the paint job. One of the men had sanded and revarnished the cabinets and resurfaced the countertops. There was no mold beneath the sink, no insects in the drawers or cabinets. The pantry was rodent-free, and the drippy faucets had been replaced. "Who paid for all the materials?" he asked.

"A private donor. The homeless people did all the work."

"Well, I'm delighted. Looks like you'll pass with flying colors this time. I just need to check the bathrooms and sleeping quarters."

The volunteers had been busy there too. The toilets, shower stalls, and plumbing fixtures were scrubbed and sanitary. Emilio was surprised to find all the cots empty. No drunks sleeping off the latest binge. In one of the bathrooms, Andy Michener sat before the mirror while Louise Hargrove gave him a haircut using Karen's manicure scissors.

Emilio returned to Karen's office. "Here's your health certificate. I'm glad things are looking better around here. How did you get the homeless people to do all this work?"

Karen smiled mysteriously. "We've got more than one guardian angel."

Emilio was so pleased that he forgot his promise to Lydia until he'd driven halfway across town. He thought about going back, but it was getting dark, and he still had two more inspections to do. It didn't matter, he decided. Open Door wasn't really a restaurant.

If only he'd arrived five minutes later. Or remained five minutes longer. Because that was when Paige and Omer arrived with the evening meal. Had Emilio seen her, life might have turned out differently for Paige, Louise Hargrove, Norris Tankersley, and a hot-tempered vagrant named Butch Taggart.

After Louise finished Andy's haircut, some of the other men asked her to trim theirs. Reynaldo and Mike were as shaggy as cavemen. Karen rummaged through her drawers at home and came up with a pair of office scissors, a styling comb, and a hand mirror. Soon Louise had a line of customers outside the bathroom, awaiting their turns. The task was debilitating for a woman with anemia. Zelda swept up the clippings while Louise took little rest breaks.

Two nights later Reynaldo, tired from a day of roofing chores, was eating supper when a patrol car appeared outside the dining room window. He leaped up and raced for the back door. A cop stood there, blocking the exit.

"¡Por favor! ¡Por favor!" he cried, struggling as the man handcuffed him. His friends watched helplessly as the officers dragged him away.

Karen was disgusted. "With all the criminal activity in this town, you'd think they could find something better to do than persecute a harmless man!"

"What will they do to him?" Zelda asked.

"Toss him over the border and leave him to find his way

home. The paperwork would cost more than the money he earned trying to rescue his family." She stood at the window, watching until the police car was out of sight. "Sometimes I'm ashamed to be an American."

Parental Guidance

Jerome Faulkner stood dejectedly at Judge Royce's bench, wearing handcuffs and a dingy white jacket. Its blue insignia read *Faulkner Ear Institute*. His attorney, a court-appointed neophyte, stood beside him. She pecked at her cell phone and ignored the proceedings.

Lydia watched from the gallery. Her assistant, Zach Oglesby, was handling the case to avoid a conflict of interest. In his summation to the jury, Zach had emphasized the brazenness of a man attacking a patient in her hospital bed.

Judge Royce hated sentencing hearings. To him, flushing a human being down the American penal toilet was worse than an execution. Even if he survived prison life, "ex-convict" was a death sentence for the man's future job prospects.

Before his arrest Faulkner had eighteen years' experience helping people with hearing disorders. But a rapid series of events had shattered him. First was the sight of his thirteen-year-old son Conrad, unconscious on the floor of his room. Next was the sight of Conrad wedded permanently to a ventilator. Between visits with pessimistic doctors, Jerome had plenty of time to wander from Conrad's hospital bed to the waiting room, where his wife stared blankly at the wall. Jerome could do nothing for either of them. So he drifted aimlessly through the hallways hour after hour.

One night he found himself in Paige Abernathy's room. Something about the pillow under her sleeping head upset him. The next thing he knew, powerful hands were dragging him away. Jerome had poured all his passion into the attempt. Now he was spent.

"Mr. Faulkner, do you have anything to say before I pronounce sentence?"

"No, Your Honor."

"Very well. Jerome Edwin Faulkner, in accordance with state law, it is the decision of this court that you be sentenced to twenty years in state prison for the attempted murder of Paige Abernathy. You will remain in Bolton County Jail pending execution of sentence."

Faulkner listened indifferently. His attorney had offered only a halfhearted defense during the trial. In her summation she referred to her client as an archeologist.

"For the record, Mr. Faulkner," the judge added, "I wish I didn't have to impose this sentence. It's obvious what your son's disability has done to you. I hope that with time your own wounds will heal, and that with good behavior you will receive an early parole." He nodded to the guard, who led the prisoner away. Faulkner's attorney was already halfway out the door, mumbling into her phone.

"Let's take a fifteen-minute recess. Mrs. Abernathy, may I see you in chambers, please?"

Across the desk Judge Royce studied Lydia's face. Cracks were showing in the prosecutor's veneer. She seemed as forlorn as the heartbroken father he had just sent to prison.

"Any news about Paige?"

"No. I thought we had a good lead from the ER doctor. But not one restaurant employee in town has seen her. By the way," she added wanly, "thanks for the court order. You were right. Judge Baker quashed it."

"It was worth a try. What about the hospital? Did you talk to the admitting clerk who was on duty the night Paige was attacked?"

"Repeatedly. She thinks she recognized the man in the business suit but didn't know who he was. Apparently he wrote a phony name and address on the admissions form."

"What about Tankersley?"

"He's another mystery. Ever since his outburst at the hospital, he's been almost mute. The guards tell me he sits in his cell all day, watching TV or reading old magazines. He eats his meals. Does pushups. Sleeps. Shaves and showers when they let him. In the meantime he hardly says a word."

"What's his background?"

Lydia drew a folder from her briefcase. "Norris Tankersley. White male, thirty-five years old. Baggage handler at William P. Hobby Airport. Widower, no children. No prior arrests. Purchased the gun at a pawn shop." She closed the folder. "It's funny, Burt. Why would he want to kill Paige? He's a loner. No connections to any of the suicide cases that we know of."

"I assume you explained the charges to him."

"Reckless endangerment with a firearm. That's the most we could charge him with. He didn't fire the gun or threaten anybody. Violating the hospital's no-firearms policy is just a misdemeanor. With good behavior he'll be out of jail in no time."

"What did he say to you?"

"I recused myself, for obvious reasons. Zach said Tankersley took it calmly. Said he understood the charges and told his attorney he wanted to plead guilty."

"What did the psychiatrist say?"

"Dr. Vinetti thinks he's competent and recommends we accept his plea." Lydia sighed. "That's not so good."

"Why?"

"Tankersley's the only lead I've got left. The ER doctor said that shortly before he appeared at the hospital, a woman with a cell phone blundered into Paige's treatment room. I think she and Tankersley were working together and had the ER staked out."

The judge frowned. "That doesn't make sense. What reason would Tankersley have to think she'd come back to the ER?"

"The only thing I could think of was Dr. Wingate. He treated Paige twice the first time she was hospitalized. Wingate said he and Paige sort of hit it off."

"Is Wingate good looking?"

"Yes, but he's twice her age. He insists he hasn't heard from her since the Tankersley episode."

Royce examined his court calendar. "Lydia, Tankersley's up for sentencing next week. After that you'll have nothing else to hit him with."

"I know. At least I can put a tail on him when he gets out. See who he hooks up with." Lydia's worry lines deepened. "Burt, Dr. Ursi says Paige might have more seizures without her medication. For all I know, she's passed out in an alleyway somewhere. Or worse." Her eyes moistened. "Why won't she at least call me?"

Steve Wingate was in his backyard, attaching a bird feeder to a tree branch, when his phone rang.

"Hello? Is this Dr. Wingate?"

"Yes, who's this? Wait! Don't tell me. Cinderella."

She laughed. "How did you know?"

"I remember your voice. How are you, Paige?"

"I hope you don't mind my calling. Am I interrupting anything?"

"Hang on a second." He put the phone on the ground and secured the feeder with a piece of wire. "Sorry. I've got this bird feeder in my backyard that wants to fall off the tree whenever the wind blows. A couple of blue jays are flitting around, waiting for me to set the table." He carried his phone to the porch. "Where are you? I've been worried about you since that episode in the ER."

"I'm fine. Some nice people took me in. I've even got a job now."

"Doing what?"

She hesitated. It was Saturday morning. Paige had the house to herself while Omer and Naomi were at the synagogue. "I'm not supposed to say where I am. On account of . . . you know."

"Of course. Have you had any more seizures?"

"Just a minor one. Listen, I wasn't calling about my medical problems."

"Okay." He pulled up a lawn chair. "What's on your mind?"

"I was just wondering. How old is your daughter?"

"Oh, so you remember that. She turned sixteen last week."

"Does she have any brothers or sisters?"

"One brother, Sean. He's in his second semester at Caltech."

"What's that?"

"A private research university in Pasadena."

"Wow! He must be smart."

"He's smart, all right. Sometimes he's too smart for his own good."

"What does that mean?"

"Well . . . we don't always see eye to eye."

"Oh."

There was a long pause.

"Paige? Are you still there?"

"I wanted to ask you something else, but maybe it's too personal."

"I'll let you know if it is."

She drew a decisive breath. "What I really wanted to ask . . . Do you get along with your kids?"

"Sure, most of the time."

"What do you argue about?"

"Little stuff, mostly. Sean accuses me of hovering, especially with Kathy. That's my daughter."

"Hovering? What do you mean?"

"Overprotective. Ever since my wife left, I've tried to be both mother and father to them. That's not so easy when you have a high-pressure job like mine."

"Your wife left you?" Paige cried. "How could she? Oh! I-I'm sorry, you don't have to answer that."

"I was trying to think how best to put it. The fact is, my wife found someone else."

She gasped. "That's terrible! A nice man like you? I can't believe it."

"A few years ago, there was . . . um . . . an unfortunate incident in my life. One thing led to another, and we . . . Let's just say, we went our separate ways."

"I'm sorry. Is it permanent?"

"Yes. Paige, do these questions have anything to do with your own parents?"

Another hesitation. "Dr. Wingate, I know this is awfully personal, but . . . do you love your daughter?"

"My children mean everything to me."

"More than being a doctor?"

"More than anything. Why do you ask?"

"Does she have a boyfriend?"

He laughed. "Kathy's too cerebral for most boys. I think they're scared of her because she knows so much about human anatomy. It's one of the drawbacks of being a doctor's kid."

"Does she resent your . . . what was it? Hovering?"

"Sometimes. Kathy says I should have been born a woman. But she's very patient with her dad. Wise beyond her years, I guess you'd say." He waited. "Am I being any help?"

"Yes. Yes, you are. I hope you didn't mind my asking so many questions."

"They're questions I ask myself sometimes. May I ask you one?"

"Yes."

"How's your relationship with your own parents? I mean, since all this trouble over your website?"

"I haven't seen or spoken to them since I left home."

"They must be worried, don't you think?"

"I guess so."

"Maybe you should call them."

"I'd rather talk to you."

Where is this going? Steve wondered. "You know, I've had dinner at your father's restaurant a couple of times. He seems like a decent fellow."

"He is." More silence. "I like talking to you, Dr. Wingate. May I call you again sometime?"

"Certainly. Any time."

"Thank you. Goodbye."

Steve checked the number on his screen. Same area code as his, so she was probably still in Alverna.

He sat for a while, tapping the phone against his knee. *How does a teenage girl find a job when she's got killers on her trail?*
A news alert pinged his phone.
ER Invader Sentenced. Steve scrolled through the story.

> *Judge Thomas Baker today sentenced Norris Tankersley to six months in jail plus time served for his armed invasion of Frazier Memorial Hospital last fall. Tankersley, a former baggage handler at William P. Hobby Airport . . .*

Tankersley! Steve read the entire story. *It can't be*, he told himself. *Not after all this time.*
Squawks from the tree drew his attention. "All right, I'm coming." Still troubled, he tore open a bag of peanuts and headed for the feeder.

Cold Comfort

Lucas Madison and Jeanette Collins sat in the front seat of his Mustang, shivering with cold. They were parked behind the Big Lots store two blocks east of the Bustamante Bridge, where a gang had attacked Paige five months earlier.

Jeanette hugged herself. "Can't you turn the heat back on? I'm freezing!"

"I'm low on gas. Dad keeps asking why I fill up so often. I'm running out of excuses."

"Maybe you should take me home."

"Please, not yet. Just a little longer."

"Okay." She puffed warm breath on her fingers. An hour with Lucas was worth a little suffering, although she could think of more romantic places to meet. It was a gray afternoon, the kind that made February seem eternal. Nothing to look at but trash dumpsters and utility poles. At least none of their classmates would spot them in a place like this. If only the sun would come out and warm the interior.

Jeanette was torn between desire and guilt. Paige was her only friend. They'd had sleepovers at each other's houses, gone shopping together, held hands during scary movies, and traded a thousand text messages. When Paige confided that she and Lucas were talking marriage, Jeanette had promised to be her bridesmaid. *Look at me now,* she thought. *Hiding with the groom in a squalid parking lot.*

When the website scandal erupted last fall, the Alverna Tigers had turned to sharks. Paige Abernathy, Suicide Queen. Princess of Death. It was all anyone talked about for weeks, and the talk was poison. Rumor had it that Mr. Chen was her secret lover. That they were selling suicide drugs to teenagers. That they were agents of a Chinese plot to destroy America's youth. Wasn't it obvious? Hadn't everyone seen them last spring, huddled over a computer in the science lab? Then Paige disappeared and the school board fired Mr. Chen, giving credence to all the rumors.

In the eye of the storm were Lucas and Jeanette, the two people closest to Paige. Were they part of the suicide ring? How much did they know? The few kids bold enough to ask sparked angry denials from Lucas and tears from Jeanette. The rest eyed them suspiciously as they passed in the hallways. Isolated and confused, they reached out to each other.

"Are we wrong to be doing this?" Jeanette shuddered, her breath fogging the windshield.

"I don't see how. As far as we know, she's gone forever."

"It feels wrong, Lucas."

"Don't you like being with me?"

"Of course I do. It's just that . . . you know."

Lucas did. He'd taken the romance for granted until Lydia tore them apart. By then his Lothario reputation had swept through the school's female population. Jeanette wasn't as pretty as Paige. Sort of round-faced and thick-lipped, with dull brown hair that could never match the golden braid Lucas loved to unravel when he and Paige were kissing. But Jeanette was more submissive than Paige, who always slapped his hands away when he got too passionate.

"I hate all this sneaking around." Her voice trembled with cold. "It's like we're doing drugs or something." Lucas said nothing. Paige's reaction to the joint still rankled him. They wouldn't have been caught if she hadn't made him throw it out the window. Now she was gone, who knew where, leaving him to meet Jeanette secretly after school each day, take her on long drives along back roads, sneak off to city parks in the evening. It was like Romeo and Juliet, or that dumb Running Bear song on Paige's website. Lovers separated by feuding parents. Lucas's only comforts were Jeanette's desperate kisses and his furtive pot sessions with Pete and Jerry behind the equipment shed at school.

"My mother thinks I ought to forget about her and make new friends," Jeanette was saying. "She doesn't understand."

"I know. It's not like you can just walk up to somebody and say, 'Hey, will you be my new friend?'"

Jeanette puffed on her hands again. "Mom thinks my grades are dropping because I'm spending too much time with you. She's afraid I won't be able to get into college next fall."

"Have you decided on one?"

She brightened a little. "Remember that recruiting visit Paige and I made to Texas Tech last summer? We took time out to visit the Buddy Holly Center. They had his guitar, his glasses, his record collection, even some of his homework assignments. Paige loved the Tech campus. It was so big! She thought we could coordinate our schedules and attend the same classes. Oh, and there was an IHOP across the street from Horn Hall. Paige figured we could get part-time jobs there." Jeanette paused. "What about you?"

"I don't know," Lucas answered. "Maybe I'll stay here

after graduation."

"But there are no colleges around here."

"I thought I might put it off for a year. Just wait around in case . . . you know." No matter what they talked about, the conversation always came back to Paige.

"Why do you think we haven't heard from her, Lucas?"

"Something terrible must have happened."

"Like what?"

"I'm afraid to think about it." Tears welled in his eyes. "I miss her, Jeanette! I miss her so much!"

The words pierced her heart. Lucas would never love her as he did Paige. She shivered violently. "It's so cold out here! Maybe we should go."

"Not yet. Please." Their eyes met. Wordlessly, they reached for each other.

Things were going well for Paige and Omer. In two months as his designer, she'd completed more than a dozen websites and consulted on many others.

"Such a load off my back!" he exclaimed. "Before you came I was spending most of my time on nitpicky details." Paige's latest clients included a china painting artist, a crop duster, a commercial window installer, and two couples pooling their money to offer international travel tours. Omer took care of the hosting and domain setups for all of them, as well as their internal links, widgets, and billing systems.

Sometimes Paige completed a design only to have the client request an alternative.

"That's okay," Omer assured her. "It's not your work they're complaining about. They're worried about making a good first impression." Omer never charged for do-overs, though they often consumed huge blocks of time. "It pays off in the long run. Customers like it when you go the extra mile, and they'll remember you for it. Referrals are free, and they're the most effective advertising you can get."

Most of Paige's clients confined their discussions to business. Others were friendly—sometimes too friendly.

"You sound young, Jodie," Don Turner said on their conference call one day. "Are you as pretty as your voice?"

Seated beside her, Omer grinned at Paige. *Let's see you talk your way out of this.*

"Well, I don't spend that much time looking in the mirror. Don, are you sure you don't want a chat option on this website?"

"I might, if I could chat with you whenever I like."

"For your customers, I mean."

"I might be the best customer you've ever had. Why don't we make a date and talk it over?"

Paige looked to Omer for help. He just grinned wider. "I'm sorry, Don," she said. "I have kidney failure. I spend most of my free time in dialysis."

"Oh!" He cleared his throat. "Sorry, I hope I didn't, uh—"

"It's all right. I've got a few months left."

Omer spluttered into his hand.

"How about that chat option?" Paige continued. "It's worth the money, and it comes with a one-month free trial."

"Okay, sure. Why not?"

"Kidney failure!" Omer laughed when she hung up. "Where did you get that idea?"

Paige shrugged. "He wouldn't have believed me if I'd said brain damage."

That evening over supper, Naomi asked, "Paige, do you have a boyfriend?"

"I used to."

"What happened, if I'm not being too nosy?"

"My mother happened."

"Were you serious about him?"

"Oh, yes. We were going to be married."

Naomi patted her hand. "I'm so sorry. Maybe when all this is over."

Later they watched the ten o'clock news. A fierce debate had erupted that evening between two city councilmen. Arthur Garland wanted an allotment of seventy-five-thousand dollars to upgrade the Bustamante ballpark.

"It's an eyesore, and it has been for many years," he declared. "Our kids haven't got a decent outlet for their energy, and that's why we have all these gang problems."

Matt Hinkley disagreed. "What we need is responsible parents and more police patrols to discourage gang violence."

"I wish they'd do *something*," Omer remarked to Paige. "You wouldn't have those seizure problems if those goons hadn't beaten you up."

They listened to the men argue heatedly. Garland's proposal lost by a vote of six to one.

The next news item was a brief update on Jerome Faulkner. "The man convicted of trying to kill Paige Abernathy was transferred today from Bolton County Jail to Thornhurst Prison. Jerome Faulkner, a local audiologist, attacked the controversial teenager . . ."

Paige excused herself and went to bed. After lying awake

for hours, she got up, knelt on the floor, and prayed. "God, please forgive me for bringing so much death and misery into the world. Please tell me how to make it right."

She dressed and went to the kitchen to prepare breakfast for the shelter. A brief swoon dimmed her vision but passed quickly.

The Bounty Hunter

"So this is why you insisted on white." Karen pulled up a chair and watched Paige make pencil outlines on the dining room wall.

"I hope I'm right. If you don't like it, I'll paint over it again."

"What's it supposed to be?"

Using a wooden yardstick, Paige sketched a building with double doors, large windows, and a slanted roof. "This is going to be a church. It doesn't have to be any particular denomination. Just a place where people go to worship. Next to that I think I'll put a playground, or maybe a park. I don't know. I'm just making it up as I go."

It was the first Saturday in March. Most of the regulars were at their usual haunts: lounging in city parks, loitering beneath underpasses, or soliciting donations from motorists at traffic lights. A few had found temporary jobs. Mike was working south of the city, installing drywall in a new house. Andy was retiling a furniture store on Bay Street. The shelter was empty except for the sleeping quarters, where the security guard was taking a nap.

Paige stood back and studied her sketch with a critical eye. "Is there a ladder around here? I want to put a spire on top."

"The ones we used to repair the ceiling were on loan. I've got a stepladder at home. I could bring it over tomorrow."

Paige tried standing on a chair. It wobbled so badly that she couldn't hold the ruler steady. "I wish Mike was here. I could sit on his shoulders. It would only take a minute or two."

"Can't you just leave a space for it?"

"I guess so." She stepped down. "What do you think? A park or a playground next?"

"Paige, why are you going to all this trouble?"

She turned to the window. "Look at that, Karen." Through the milky glass she could see a pawn shop, a bail bond agency, two empty buildings, and a vacant lot full of bald tires. "This neighborhood is rock-bottom. But for the people who live here, it's all they've got. I want to make the shelter homier. People shouldn't have to see ugliness wherever they turn. So I thought I'd paint a mural, all around the room. A neighborhood with street scenes—houses and shops and churches and cafés. Pedestrians and kids riding bicycles. Maybe some trees and flowers. That way people will feel more welcome."

Karen smiled. "That's a nice thought. Pretty ambitious, though. Are you an artist as well as a cook?"

"I've never designed anything but web pages. I thought I'd just mark out some shapes on the walls and let our volunteers fill in the details."

"What makes you think any of them can paint?"

"Louise used to, before she got sick and lost her home. All she needs is brushes and a set of acrylics. Everybody I've met here is good at something. They just need a chance to prove it."

By the time people drifted in for supper, Paige had outlined a sidewalk with ghosts of a fire hydrant, a mailbox, and a few pedestrians. Karen helped her prepare a meal of chicken parmesan sliders and quinoa salad. The dining room was so crowded that some people had to eat standing up. One of them was a sharp-nosed man with gray whiskers and a scuffed topcoat. He stood beside Mike and Andy's table, munching his supper and sipping coffee from a paper cup.

"Who's the dish?" he asked, observing Paige at the serving window.

"That's our cook," Mike said.

"Looks mighty young for a place like this. Where'd she come from?"

"Don't reckon it's any of your business."

The man shrugged. "No need to get testy. Just makin' conversation." He took another bite. "Somethin' familiar about her. She been here long?"

"Long enough. Where you from?" Andy asked.

"Fort Worth. San Antonio. El Paso. You name it, I been there."

"Got itchy feet, huh?"

"Never found a place I liked well enough to wanna put down roots." His attention returned to Paige. "What's that girl's name? I know I've seen her somewhere."

Andy's eyes met Mike's. This wasn't the first drifter to notice Paige. Her mug shot still appeared intermittently on TV. With her facial scars healed and her blond hair pinned up, she looked out of place among the dispirited diners.

The stranger's face lit up. "I got it!" He drew a cell phone from his pocket. "Here it is on Vindicator Chat. One-hundred-thousand-dollar reward for information leading to the location of Paige Abernathy."

"Where'd you get a cell phone?" Mike asked.

"Pinched it off a guy on the bus from Galveston. Either of you guys know how to work the camera on this thing?" He started toward Paige. Mike and Andy stood up to block him.

"You've had your supper, buddy. You best be on your way."

"What's the matter?"

Mike slapped the phone to the floor and crushed it under his boot. "Just turn around and walk outta here while you still can."

"What's wrong with you guys?" the man cried. "This is a hundred thousand dollars we're talking about! I'll split it with you."

Mike took one arm, Andy the other. They propelled the man across the room and out the door as the others watched.

"Bad table manners?" someone asked.

"I never thought I'd be worth a hundred thousand dollars," Paige said. They were in Karen's office, beyond earshot of the other transients.

"It's true." Omer showed her the bounty poster on his phone.

> *If you see this girl, send photographic proof and the address of her sighting to the email address below. Payment will be forwarded upon verification of your information.*

"This is serious," Andy told Omer. "Can you tell how long that thing's been posted?"

"Long enough to be forwarded over forty-eight thousand times."

"Come on, Paige, let's go home," Naomi urged.

"It's my fault," Omer agonized. "I should never have agreed to let you hang around here, Sabbath or no Sabbath."

"Omer, I'm not going to spend the rest of my life hiding in your house."

"It's just until this thing blows over. A few more months and it'll all be forgotten."

"Not by whoever posted this reward," Andy warned. "Anybody willing to put up a hundred thousand dollars means business."

"Then let them find me!" Paige looked from face to face. "I'll turn myself in before some hit man tracks me down and the rest of you get killed in the crossfire."

"You're not a criminal, Paige!" Omer insisted. He held up the phone. "This! This bounty hunter is the criminal. When we get home, I'll do an email trace and find out who it is. We'll put the cops on *his* trail."

"There could be more than one person involved," Karen pointed out. "It could be a whole organization of some kind."

"Then the sooner we find out, the better."

Omer's trace led to a dry-cleaning store in Alberta, Canada. "Whoever it is knows how to cover his tracks. He's probably got an IP scrambler of some kind." Omer repeated the trace. He reached a mosque in Pakistan, a Burger King on the outskirts of San Diego, and a forestry hub in Tasmania.

"So if someone wants to turn me in, all they have to do is email my picture and the address of the shelter?"

"That's right. He'll know where you are, but we won't know where he is."

"A hundred thousand dollars." Paige slumped at her workstation. "You ought to turn me in, Omer. You could start a retirement account."

"You're worth more than money, Paige. But you're going to have to be more careful. People are in and out of that shelter all the time. If you were penniless and desperate, wouldn't you grab at a chance to start your life over?"

"I already have." She smiled fondly. "Thanks to you."

Naomi said, "Maybe there's an easier way. We could dye her hair. Add some eyeglasses."

"Sure. Anything to make her harder to recognize."

"How about a beard and mustache?" Paige offered. "Pinwheel contact lenses."

Naomi laughed. "We could dress you up like Katniss Everdeen or Elastigirl."

"Seriously," Omer said, "there's no reason for you to hang around the shelter. You can still cook for them here, and I'll deliver the meals myself."

"What about the Sabbath? Won't you be breaking the rules?"

"Remember what Jesus said to the Pharisees when they rebuked his disciples for plucking grain on the Sabbath? We're not going to let those people starve."

She smiled affectionately. "Omer, I think you're a closet Christian."

"Paige! What did I tell you about metaphors?"

Medicinal Purposes

One morning an express package arrived. At first Omer thought it was another gadget to be repaired. People still sent him wristwatches, CD players, defective laptops, and other gizmos they couldn't figure out. Omer made little profit fixing them, but he didn't have the heart to refuse. If someone was willing to pay the shipping costs, he did his best.

This package contained not a gizmo but a bottle of pills. "Naomi, did you order some prescription drugs?"

"No. Why?"

He showed her the bottle. "How do you pronounce this?"

She put on her glasses. "Lev . . . Levter . . . I don't know." She looked closer. "Substitute for Keppra, it says."

Omer did a web search. "'Keppra is a prescription medicine used to treat the symptoms of partial onset seizures, tonic-clonic seizures, and myoclonic seizures,'" he read aloud. "Seizures! This must be for Paige!"

"It sounds like the drug I was taking," she agreed. "But Omer, the prescription's in your name."

"How? I don't have seizures." He checked the label again. The prescribing physician's name was R. Higgins. "Robert Higgins is a pulmonologist. He treated me for pneumonia a couple of years ago." Omer phoned the doctor's office. A nurse confirmed the prescription. "It must be a mistake," she said. "Levetiracetam isn't for pulmonary disorders. I'll check with the doctor when he finishes his rounds."

Omer and Paige went back to work. Two hours later the nurse returned his call. Dr. Higgins had not ordered the pills and he had no idea how the prescription had been sent from his office.

"This means three things," Omer said, hanging up. "Somebody knows you need these, they know where you live, and they have access to my doctor's patient records. Paige, what was the name of that brain doctor you told me about?"

"Dr. Ursi."

Omer phoned the doctor's office. There were no recent prescription orders for Paige Abernathy.

"Were there any doctors named Higgins who treated you?"

"Not that I remember."

Omer untwisted the cap. "Do these look like the pills you took before?"

"Maybe. They were in one of those bubble pack samples. I never got a refill."

"Have you had any more spells?"

"Sometimes I feel sort of light-headed."

Omer sniffed at the contents. "This worries me. How do we know they're not some kind of poison?"

"Take it to the drugstore," Naomi suggested.

A pharmacist confirmed that the pills were legitimate.

"They're just like the ones we have in stock."

"Is this a normal dosage for seizures?" Omer asked.

"Yes. Five hundred milligrams twice a day. I've seen plenty of these."

"What about side effects?"

"Possible dizziness or tiredness. Weakness. Things like that. None of my customers have ever complained about them. This is one of the safer drugs on the market."

Omer returned to the car, where Paige and Naomi were waiting. "Apparently it's okay for you to take them. It's only a ten-day supply, though."

"Paige, why don't you take one when we get home?" Naomi suggested. "If you have a reaction, we can take you to the hospital. If not, we'll know it's okay to keep taking them."

Paige reread the label. "I'd feel better about this if I knew why they came from your pneumonia doctor."

"I'd feel better knowing how someone traced you to our address." Omer drove them home, where Paige took a dose. They spent the evening catching up on work. "Any dizzy spells?" he kept asking. "Do you feel sick?"

"I'm fine, Omer. Stop worrying."

The following week another batch of pills arrived. The prescribing doctor was M. Yulin, an orthopedist.

On March twenty-third, Paige was surprised when Omer asked her to help him deliver the evening meal to Open Door. "But Omer, it's only one o'clock. And I'm right in the middle of a design."

"It'll be here when you get back."

Naomi climbed into the car with them. The back seat was

filled with covered dishes. "I thought you wanted me to stay away from the shelter. What's going on?"

"You'll see."

They arrived to find a sign on the door: "Closed until 5 p.m. today." In the dining room, a small crowd burst into applause. Strung above the tables was a large banner:

Joyeux Anniversaire, Cuisinière!

Colored balloons hung from the ceiling. Bright paper cloths covered three of the dining tables. At the center of each was a sheet cake with Italian buttercream frosting and eighteen candles.

"Happy birthday!" Karen cried, ushering Paige to the center of the room. Omer and Naomi followed, beaming. All the regulars—Andy, Mike, Louise, Zelda, and Dee-Man—gathered around her, along with Leroy James, Charity Mitchell, and others who had helped with the renovation.

"How did you know?" Paige exclaimed.

"We have our ways." Karen winked at Omer. "Come, sit at the head of the table. Today we're having lunch, and it's our turn to serve you!"

Paige followed her. "What does that sign say?"

"It's 'Happy Birthday, Chef,'" Louise answered. "At least, that's what I think it says, if my high school French hasn't gone rusty."

"Why French?"

"In honor of your cooking skills."

"But," Naomi added, "you don't get any cake until you've had your entrée." She placed a covered dish before Paige. Beneath the lid was a serving of braised chicken with mushrooms and shallots.

"Naomi, you tricked me!" Paige laughed. "Who did the cooking?"

"We did," Zelda said. "Me and Louise."

"What about the food we brought with us?"

"That's for the night crowd. Come on, folks," she called out. "Line up at the window."

"Two hot dogs, please," Mike said. "Hold the caviar."

Andy returned with his plate and sat across from Paige. "So, birthday girl. You're now officially an adult. Able to vote. Serve on a jury. Join the army."

"Buy lottery tickets," Mike added. "Get tattooed."

"Don't give her ideas!" Louise rebuked him. "She can also get married."

Married! Thoughts of Lucas brought on a wave of melancholy. "Andy, how old were you when you got married?"

"Twenty-four." He took a bite of chicken. "Six years older than you. But I wasn't ready."

"How so?"

"Aww . . . I was too immature. Once the romance wore off, I had responsibilities I hadn't thought about. Makin' a home for my wife and child. Furniture, utility bills, medical insurance. All of a sudden there was this big weight on me." He smiled. "Never mind. It's your birthday! You're a grown woman. What are you gonna do about it?"

"I like what I'm doing now."

"Feedin' a bunch of deadbeats and losers every day? That's no kinda life."

"You're not a deadbeat, Andy," she declared solemnly, "and you're not a loser. None of you are. I admit I used to think that way, but now I know you're no different from anyone else." She looked around the table. Her ragtag companions felt like family.

"We have a surprise for you," Karen announced when dinner was over. "But first you have to blow out the candles."

"On three cakes?" Paige did the math. "That's fifty-four candles! I'll pass out again."

"Then take your time."

With all eyes on her Paige extinguished the candles with a big puff. Conversation resumed as she went from table to table. Naomi, Louise, and Zelda helped her serve. "Who baked all these?" she asked.

"That's the surprise," Zelda grinned.

"Was it you?"

"Nope."

"Louise? Karen?"

"Nope."

"Who, then?" For the first time she noticed the inscription on the icing. *Dix-huit ans.* Eighteen years. "These are from Chez Renée! These are birthday cakes like we make at—Karen! Did you tell my father where I am?"

"No, no, Paige," she soothed. "All he knows is that a woman named Naomi Goldmann ordered three cakes for a party. He doesn't know they're for yours."

"Omer and I just wanted you to have a taste of home," Naomi added. The handwriting on the cakes was unmistakable: Nina Gentry, her father's pastry chef.

"You're all so sweet!" Paige said. "I just wish Dad was here to share it."

The first lawsuit came from the parents of a fourteen-year-old girl in Flagstaff, Arizona. Kyle was teaching one of his junior chefs how to make salmon canapés when the process server appeared. The other chefs watched as the officer handed him an envelope.

"I'm sorry, Mr. Abernathy," he muttered. "Chez Renée is where I proposed to my wife. This place means a lot to us." He slunk out the back door.

Kyle washed his hands and opened the notice. The parents alleged that their daughter had taken her life following a long string of chats on Paige's website. They were demanding two million dollars in damages for emotional pain and suffering.

"They haven't got a case," Lydia assured Kyle when he phoned her office. "In the first place, Section 230 of the Communications Decency Act protects websites from liability for content created by their users. In the second place, they'd have to prove the girl's death was a direct result of the website postings."

Kyle was still agitated. "What about that nurse in Minnesota a few years ago? He went to jail for encouraging people to commit suicide."

"There's no evidence that Paige herself promoted suicide. On the contrary, she posted warnings to those who did, and she decertified the ones who broke the rule."

Kyle remained uneasy, especially as copycat suits poured in over the next few weeks—dozens of them, from as far away as London and Frankfurt. All of them made headlines. Maybe the plaintiffs couldn't win, but they could hurt the Abernathys' reputations. Payback. That's what the lawsuits were about.

One day Charles Duprée summoned Kyle to his office. Surrounding his desk were framed pictures of Charles posing with movie stars and accolades from restaurant critics all over the world. "I think it's time you took a leave of absence, Kyle."

"Charles, I'm sorry about all this. I know it makes me look bad. But it hasn't hurt business. We're still booked up weeks in advance, and our cuisine is equal to any top-ranked restaurant in the world."

"It's not your work, Kyle. You're the best chef I've ever had. When I started Chez Renée, it was a cozy little café in an obscure Texas city. But now we have an international reputation. We've got write-ups in restaurant magazines around the world. That makes the stakes higher."

"I'm sure it'll blow over, Charles."

The owner fidgeted with a letter opener shaped like the Eiffel Tower. "Adeline Foley and Walter Stuart phoned me this morning, both wanting comments for their stories on how your daughter's mess is affecting business. Have you seen the tabloids lately?" Charles held up two of them. *Texas Chef Target of Death Suits. Chez Renée Pot Boils Over.*

Kyle scoffed. "Nobody takes those scandal sheets seriously."

"Maybe not. But they have a psychological impact that suggests Chez Renée is no longer an elegant restaurant. Once people get an idea like that into their heads, it grows exponentially, and suddenly they're taking their business elsewhere. I don't want that to happen."

Kyle's stomach churned. "Charles . . . are you firing me?"

The man averted his eyes. "I'm—I'm asking you to step aside."

Discovery

The pills arrived at Omer's door every other week, twenty per bottle, each batch from a different doctor. No one could explain it. "It's like the computer's doing this on its own," one of the nurses said. Paige took the medicine twice daily. Her dizzy spells had vanished, and she suffered no ill effects.

It was on the first Saturday in April that Paige and Omer had their first real argument.

"I thought we agreed that the shelter isn't a safe place for you anymore."

"I've got to finish outlining the mural," she insisted. "It'll just take a few hours. Besides, there's hardly anyone around in the daytime."

"That's my point! Nobody but that deadhead security guard. Have you forgotten there's a price on your head?"

"Please, Omer. Just one last time. Then Louise can finish the job."

Reluctantly, he gave in. The work was coming along nicely. Louise had colored the church scene and added shrubbery to give it a cozy touch.

"This is just what I was looking for," Paige said. "It

reminds me of those little neighborhood churches you see in small towns."

Louise was detailing the north wall scene when Karen entered the room. "I've got some good news!" she exclaimed. "One of our board members, Edna Bostick, dropped by yesterday and admired your work. There's a job opening for an art teacher in the city's parks and recreation department this summer. Louise, she wants to recommend you for the job!"

"Me?" Louise turned away from the mailbox she was coloring. "I've never taught art before. I just dabbled in it before I lost my home."

"It's a four-week program for underprivileged kids. All you have to do is teach them the basics. The city provides all the materials. They were going to cancel it because they weren't getting any applicants. But I bet they'll give you the job once they see this mural."

Louise listened doubtfully. "Paige did all the sketches. I'm just filling them in. Besides, it probably doesn't pay anything."

"Edna knows a lot of important people. It might lead to something permanent."

"Try it, Louise," Paige urged. "It's a fresh start for you."

Louise studied her reflection in the window glass. Six months of chronic anemia had aged her. "How can I show up for a job interview in a washed-out dress, frizzy hair, and no makeup? Would you hire someone who looks like this?"

"Don't worry," Paige grinned. "I know somebody who's just about your size."

"I've got a whole rack of blouses I never wear and skirts that don't fit anymore," Naomi said, opening her closet. "Maybe some shoes too. Try some of these and see what you think."

Louise was still awestruck from her tour of Naomi's house. The closet alone was the size of a small bedroom, with a full-length mirror and a vanity stool. "It's been a long time since I was in a real home. I'd forgotten what it's like to feel comfortable and safe." She ran her hand over the racks of dresses, suits, and casual outfits. "Naomi, are you sure about this? I wouldn't want to take advantage of your kindness."

"You'd be doing me a favor. I'm an impulsive shopper. Half the things I buy, I never wear twice. Omer calls me Imelda Marcos."

"Who's that?"

"Her husband was President of the Philippines, long ago. You think I'm a clothes horse? That woman had three thousand pairs of shoes!" She pulled a dress off the rack. "Here's one I made myself before I gained weight. I think it'll fit you just fine." She peered closely at Louise. "What's with your eyeglasses?"

"Oh, that. One of the lenses fell out last summer while I was dumpster diving."

"And you've been half blind all this time?" Naomi dug through a drawer. "Try these." The glasses were wire-framed bifocals.

"Oh, that's much better!" Louise exclaimed.

"Good. Keep them for now. Later, I'll take you to an eye doctor for a proper fitting."

"Oh Naomi, I couldn't—"

"Couldn't what? You can't teach art classes with weak eyes. Now come on. Pick out something nice to wear."

Timidly, Louise drew a pastel blouse from the rack.

"Go on, try it. And see if you can match it up with any of those pants or skirts. We'll wait out here."

Naomi saw a tear in Louise's eye as they closed the door. "Poor lady. Let's see what we can do about makeup." She rummaged through a bureau.

"Naomi," Paige said, "I hope you don't think I was out of line. I don't intend to bring home every stray cat I meet."

"If you get out of line, I'll let you know. How about this color?" She held up a tube of lipstick.

By the time they returned to the shelter, it was almost dark. Louise sat in the back seat under two armloads of clothes and a shoebox of beauty supplies.

"This is so wonderful!" she exclaimed. "I thought I'd be spending the rest of my life on the street. How can I ever thank you?"

"Just nail down that job and share your talent with those children," Naomi replied. "That's all the thanks I need."

"Bye-bye, Louise!" Paige called out the window as they drove away.

She waddled to the door with clothes piled up to her chin. Fumbling for the knob, she struggled through the entrance to find her homeless friends crammed into one corner of the dining room. The man standing over them held a gun.

"Where's Paige Abernathy?" he barked at Louise. "You've got ten seconds!"

The courthouse parking lot was dark and empty, except for Lydia's car. On Saturdays she had the whole building to herself. These days, it seemed, she got more work done in solitude. Maintaining her tough facade in the presence of others was exhausting. Alone, she could shed a few tears.

There was plenty to cry about. Kyle and Lydia had spent

Paige's eighteenth birthday brooding, the unemployed chef at home, the prosecutor at the office struggling to concentrate. Whispers of gossip floated around the courthouse. The lawsuits had ignited talk of a recall election, inflamed no doubt by Lucas Madison's father.

On Lydia's desk this evening lay more misery. A drunk twenty-year-old indicted for vehicular homicide after plowing into the back of a car, killing a father of two. A trio of men nabbed in a child prostitution ring. Shootings. Stabbings. Beatings.

Sometimes Lydia wondered if she was fighting the wrong enemy. Getting criminals off the streets had always seemed a noble endeavor. As far back as law school, she had squirmed at the technicalities defense attorneys used to liberate monsters who clearly belonged behind bars. Lydia saw things in black and white. In her view, laws served to protect proper citizens from miscreants. Bringing evildoers to justice was her way of preserving the American way, and she was proud of it.

She was indignant when Kyle broke the news about Chez Renée.

"He can't get away with it!" she declared, pacing the living room. "He has no grounds for firing you. I'll hit him with a wrongful termination suit so fast, he'll beg you to come back."

Kyle slumped in the orthopedic chair he used to rest his spine after being on his feet all day. "You can't do that, Lydia. A lawsuit would ruin him. The restaurant means a lot to this community. Even people who don't dine at Chez Renée come from miles away just to shop in the stores and ogle the celebrities. And it means good jobs for three dozen employees."

"All except you." She threw her briefcase on the coffee table. "That Charles is a crafty one. He knows you won't sue because you love the restaurant too much." She kneeled beside him. "Kyle, you've got the law on your side. You've got me to handle the paperwork. Call his bluff! Make him back down!"

"And if he doesn't? Then it's more headlines. More scandal."

"So what? Sometimes notoriety makes for good advertising. Chez Renée might even get more customers out of this." She seized his hand. "Kyle, you've got friends in this town. People all over the world who love your cooking. Put them to work! Show Charles Duprée he can't push you around."

"I'm not like you, Lydia," he said miserably. "I'm just a cook."

That was Kyle. He ran the kitchen without being bossy, earned respect without trying. Lydia envied him. Her own resolve grew from impatience with those who couldn't see the world as she did. Her decisiveness had never wavered, not even last September when her own daughter fell into the police net. Paige wasn't a criminal but the victim of a spoiled, wayward boy bent on corrupting an innocent girl with drugs. Lydia had never prevented Paige from dating other boys. She considered herself open-minded, though secretly she was glad when Paige broke up with Wendell Teague, a slouchy youth with an insolent grin who lurked outside the house, texting Paige instead of ringing the doorbell like a gentleman. But Lucas Madison was different. Had Lydia failed to lay down the law, he might have dragged Paige into the pit of addiction. Yet Lucas got off scot-free, while Lydia's relationship with Paige grew worse. Couldn't she see that her mother was trying to protect her? It was a case of thwarted justice. For Lydia, who hated to lose, it was the worst defeat of her life.

Through the dark months of autumn and winter, Lydia had prayed for God to bring her daughter home safely. When He answered with silence, doubt began to creep in. Would she have done better to let the relationship run its course? Warn

Paige about Lucas, but let her make her own decision? Even if it had resulted in a failed marriage, the bond between mother and daughter would have survived. Now it was broken. Paige was gone, perhaps forever. Meanwhile, Lydia spent her days fighting an ever-growing army of criminals who would remain incorrigible whether she put them in jail or not. The real enemy, she realized, had been her own ambition. And it had won.

She leaned back and stretched. The clock read 8:45 p.m. Over ten hours of work, with only a candy bar from the vending machine for lunch. Maybe a hot bath and a few pages from a John Grisham thriller would lull her to sleep.

She gathered her papers, locked the office, and rode the elevator down to the lobby. She locked the main door and walked into the April night to her private parking space. Stuck beneath the windshield wiper was a sealed envelope. The front was blank. Inside was a single sheet of paper with an inkjet message:

> *If you want to find Paige Abernathy, inquire at Open Door shelter.*

With a gasp, Lydia dropped it on the hood and drew back. Her first thought was fingerprints. *I've got to get this to the lab!*

Her second thought was to phone Kyle. Trembling, she dug through her purse.

The shelter was full of cops, reporters, and frightened witnesses.

"Where's the lady who runs this place?" Captain McCurdy asked.

"I reached her at her son's house. She's on her way here now."

"All right. Tell me about the perp."

"His name's Butch Taggart." Officer Wade scrolled through a police rap sheet. "Fifty-one years old. Wife-beater, itinerant laborer. A long string of assault charges throughout the South. Mobile, Charlotte, Nashville, Meridian. Bunch of other places. Your basic trailer trash."

"What's his beef with Paige Abernathy?"

"He claims he met a drifter who got cheated out of his reward money. Taggart decided to take a crack at it himself."

"He confessed all this?"

Wade laughed. Taggart glared at him, handcuffed and squatting in the corner where his hostages had been seated earlier. "He's got this hero attitude. Champion of justice. Righter of wrongs. One of those conspiracy buffs who claims the drifter is a victim of capitalists. Personally, I think he was just slobbering over the idea of a hundred thousand tax-free dollars."

"How did he track her here?"

"According to Taggart, the drifter saw her in the shelter one night while he was passing through town. He used a stolen cell phone to apply for the reward on Vindicator Chat. You wanna hear the punchline?"

"Sure. I could use a laugh."

"He got the reward all right. Only it was thirty dimes in a UPS package. The message with it said, 'Here are your thirty pieces of silver. Go and sin no more.'"

"I get it," McCurdy said. "The drifter got mad and spread the shelter address all over the internet. Taggart was the first one to show up here."

"That's the story."

"Sorry, Frank. It's not funny." McCurdy stepped aside as

two EMTs wheeled Louise's body through the doorway, into the cold night air. "Frank, the Abernathy girl survived two attacks at Frazier Memorial last fall. That explains why she's in hiding. But all the news lately suggests the angry parent thing has blown over. No more demonstrations. No more death threats. People have buried their kids and moved on. So who's behind this reward offer?"

"Maybe somebody who *hasn't* moved on. Somebody who got the information he wanted. Somebody who may be on his way here right now."

The witnesses sat at one of the dining tables, their feet resting on the new tile floor they'd installed together. Above them was the ceiling they'd replaced. Surrounding them was Louise's unfinished mural. Tonight, home felt more like a funeral parlor, except for the news cameras in their faces.

"He said he was gonna shoot a hostage every minute until we told him where Paige was," Andy said into a policeman's recorder. "His eyes were wild, and his gun hand was shakin'. You could tell he'd never done anything like this before. I figured he was bluffin'."

"So you jumped him?"

"Not right away. When the door opened, I was confused for a second. All I could see was somebody in the doorway with a buncha clothes. I didn't know it was Louise until she threw 'em in the guy's face. That's what makes it so awful. If we'd jumped him right away, maybe the gun wouldn't have gone off."

Zelda was sobbing at the other end of the table. Mike cradled her in his arms.

"Mike pinned him to the floor while I yanked the gun loose. Everybody else was screamin'. Dee-Man—I mean, Clarence, here, was dashin' around the room, lookin' for a phone to call 911. The only one available was the landline in Karen's office."

The officer nodded. "That explains the time delay."

"Right," Dee-Man said. "That door was solid, to protect the cash Karen keeps in there. Even big Mike couldn't break it down. I grabbed a chair and tried to smash the window, but it's plexiglass. Finally I ran outside. It took me fifteen minutes to flag down a driver with a cell phone. People don't stop much for people like us, especially at night."

"By then Louise was gone," Andy said. "She was supposed to start a new job this summer." His eyes wandered to the clothes scattered across the white tile, soaked in Louise's blood. "What are we gonna do with all those things?"

"Give 'em to the homeless," Mike suggested quietly.

Karen Wallace was adamant. "Yes, I know where she is. No, I won't tell you. And that's final. Now if you don't mind, I'd like to go home. It's after midnight. I'm very upset. My husband's upset. He wants me to quit this job before I get killed too."

Crowded into Karen's office with the two cops were Kyle and Lydia Abernathy, along with Oscar Wickham, chairman of the Open Door Foundation.

Oscar was still in the pajamas and bathrobe he was wearing when the story broke on the evening news. "Karen, what happened to your rent-a-cop?" he asked.

"He took off runnin' the minute he saw the gun," Andy said.

"I hope he comes back," Karen glowered, "so I can have the pleasure of firing him."

"Mrs. Wallace," Captain McCurdy argued, "we want to

help Paige as much as you do. But with bounty hunters on her trail, she's in greater danger than ever. The only way the police can protect her and the people who live here is for you to tell us where she is. Then we can move her to a safe place. Otherwise, tonight's incident is bound to happen again."

"She's already safe. As safe as you can be in this world."

"Captain," Kyle interjected, "she may have a point. The fewer people who know where she is, the better."

"Well, *I* want to know!" Lydia flared. "This is my daughter we're talking about!"

The board chairman was furious. "Karen, you had no business harboring a teenage runaway without consulting me."

"I've harbored lots of them!" she retorted hotly. "You're just upset because this one's a news headline. Where were you when I was begging for a separate dormitory for kids?"

McCurdy interrupted. "Mrs. Abernathy, where's the note you told me about?"

"In the front seat of my car. After I realized what it was, I only handled it by one corner. But my prints are on the edges."

"And the message led you here?"

"Yes." She handed him her car key. "Let me know what you find out from the forensics team." She turned back to Karen. "Was Paige here when the shooting occurred?"

"She left before it happened. She's in good hands. You don't have to worry."

"I don't have to worry! What do you think I've been doing for the past six months?"

"Tell her where she is, Karen," Wickham ordered. "Do it, or I'll shut this place down right now."

Karen looked from Wickham to Lydia. In the dining room were forty-seven traumatized people, waiting to learn whether they'd be spending the night under warm blankets or sleeping beneath concrete overpasses.

"All right. But everybody get out of my office. I have to make a phone call."

"I'm sorry to disturb you," Karen whispered, "but it's an emergency. We've had a shooting here."

"We know all about it," Omer interrupted. "Paige has disappeared."

"What?"

"We left her at home while we took the evening meal to the shelter. The cops wouldn't let us in. When we got back, the TV news was on, and she was gone. Naomi and I are driving around the neighborhood, trying to find her."

PART THREE:

Journey

Repercussions

Over the next few weeks life at the shelter returned to normal as the cops, camera crews, and curious drifted away.

Most of the regulars were gone. When Zelda's oldest son saw his mother on TV in the arms of a giant homeless man, he borrowed money to fly her out to Seattle, where she shared a room with her five-year-old granddaughter. Eventually Zelda found a job in a fish market. A coworker drove her to and from work until she could afford a used car.

Mike and Dee-Man no longer had to beg. The Homeless Heroes, as the news media called them, had new jobs. Mike was now foreman of a construction crew. He and two coworkers shared a renthouse in the Bustamante district.

Dee-Man was in Austin, performing in a ZACH Theatre revival of *A Raisin in the Sun*. When he stepped onstage, the audience gave him a standing ovation before he ever spoke a word. His new agent was busy juggling bids from TV executives eager to cash in on his overnight fame.

Andy Michener rejected offers from several tiling companies. Sick of crawling around on floors, he lingered at the shelter, doing odd jobs and helping Karen with the cooking.

Leroy James continued his sporadic visits to the shelter. But he could not drink enough whiskey to erase his memory of Louise lying dead on the dining room floor. He checked into a rehab center for six weeks, then joined an Alcoholics Anonymous chapter at a nearby church. The pastor gave him part-time work as a maintenance worker and groundskeeper.

Louise wasn't the only fatality that Saturday night. The morning after the shooting, Karen found Charity Mitchell in the sleeping quarters, dead of an apparent heart attack. No one knew if she had any relatives. She was buried in the city cemetery.

Local politicians who had never visited Open Door tried to capitalize on the renovations. They posed for pictures in the dining room and gave TV interviews praising the city's commitment to the needy. But none of them offered money to keep the shelter going.

For a while Karen Wallace was in trouble with the Open Door oversight committee. Seeking a scapegoat for Louise's murder, they targeted Karen for her complicity in hiding Paige.

Omer came to her rescue. "Homeless people aren't just bums," he argued. "They're people of all ages with all sorts of problems. It's Karen's job to help them. That's why you hired her." The committee relented after a Dallas TV station broadcast a feature story about the homeless people who renovated their own shelter.

Karen almost wished Omer hadn't interfered. "My husband's on the warpath. He thinks this place is too dangerous for someone my age." Karen missed Paige's companionship and her initiative. Everybody missed her cooking. Karen and Andy did the best they could, but the meals they served fell short of Paige's standards.

For a brief time, downtown Alverna was the safest place

in town, despite its history of shootings, prostitution, and drug trafficking. The reward for Paige continued to pop up on People Tracer and other rogue outlets, forcing the police to maintain regular patrols in the area. Most of the vigilantes who came sniffing around had out of state license plates. They quickly found themselves charged with vagrancy, malicious intent, or anything else the cops could use to discourage bounty hunters.

Significantly, Open Door received no visits from bereaved parents, although the wave of teen suicides continued unabated. Newsroom psychologists speculated that Paige's website was only one element in a larger social problem linked to dysfunctional families, bullying, drug abuse, and other difficulties youths have always faced in their transition to adulthood.

The note on Lydia's windshield revealed a second set of fingerprints. An AFIS search failed to reveal the author's identity.

At first Lydia was angry at those who conspired to protect her daughter. "Paige belongs in school! She belongs with her parents! She had no business living with strangers or celebrating her eighteenth birthday in a homeless shelter!"

"She was happy, Mrs. Abernathy," Naomi assured her. "It was what she wanted."

"Paige is too young to know what she wants."

"Lydia," Kyle said, "these nice people took care of her. We owe them our thanks."

Omer led the parents into his office, where he pulled up samples of Paige's work. "This is how your daughter earned her keep while she was here." Lydia scrolled through the designs, speechless for once. "Paige has a natural talent," Omer added. "My customer base expanded almost 30 percent while she worked for me."

Somberly, Kyle and Lydia looked from the computer to each other. SerenityShare had caused them so much grief that they'd never appreciated the effort their daughter had poured into it.

"That's some job of chef training you did, Mr. Abernathy," Naomi said. "I've been cooking longer than Paige has been alive, but oh my! The magic she performs in the kitchen!"

"I ought to know," Omer added. "I was in the restaurant business myself."

"Oh, you were just a waiter!" Naomi scoffed. "Don't let him fool you, Kyle. He got fired twice! Couldn't keep his mind on his work."

"I couldn't help it! All those strange things on the menu. Red-eye gravy, reindeer pizza, Harvey Wallbangers—"

"Now, Paige," Naomi interrupted. "That's a different story. You should have seen the looks on those poor people's faces when they sat down to dinner every night!"

"That's my daughter," Kyle said proudly. "Always a big help at crunch time."

"Crunch time?" Omer's eyes glazed over.

"Stop that!" Naomi poked him. "Pay attention to your guests!"

Lydia turned away from the computer. "I know I ought to thank you for opening your home to Paige. But I wish you'd called us. We've both been frantic."

"That's what we told her," Naomi said. "She wouldn't hear of it. The load that girl's carrying! Guilt over those dead kids. Blaming herself for all that went wrong. We tried to tell her. 'Paige,' we said, 'you can't take on the whole world! Give yourself some peace.'"

"We drove her away," Kyle said morosely. "She'd rather live on the street than face her parents."

"You didn't drive her away," Lydia confessed. "I did."

"Sometimes we have to lose what's most precious to us in order to appreciate it," Omer offered quietly.

Lydia produced her phone. "Time to get the dragnet rolling again." She paced the room, barking instructions to subordinates.

"Won't you join us for some tea?" Naomi asked Kyle.

"Thanks. You're very kind." The doorbell rang as he followed her into the kitchen. Omer returned with a package. Inside was another bottle of pills. The prescribing doctor was J. Talbot, a geriatrician.

Norris Tankersley found *Landscaping for Beginners* useful after all. It stoked his rage as he waited out his jail sentence.

Though brawny from years of bag-handling, Norris had his tender side. Lying on the cot, reading about flowers, shrubs, and root systems, he recalled sunny weekends in the backyard, watching his wife place a dianthus bulb in each new hole he dug. As they watered the garden and watched it fill up with color, the Tankersleys planned their future: a houseful of children, growing from toddlers to adolescents, maturing into adults who would make them grandparents. Every line of *Landscaping for Beginners* was a reminder of what might have been. What should have been.

By his thirtieth birthday, Norris had almost given up on matrimony. Not that he'd gone hungry. His chiseled features and Olympian physique made for easy conquests. But secretly he yearned for a permanent commitment.

His wish came true during a baseball game between the airport's luggage handlers and security guards. The Baggers and the Badges were tied 5–5 when Rich Torrance whacked a screamer to right field. Norris sprinted after it, only to crash into a chain link fence, his momentum flipping him over the top into a pile of lumber on the other side.

"Are you hurt?" a voice asked.

"Where's the ball?" He struggled to his feet, still bent on completing the play. Back on the field, the Badges were cheering their victory.

"Looks like the game's over," the voice said. "Did you break anything?"

Norris checked himself for injuries. "I guess not. I think the lumber got the worst of it."

His teammates gathered at the fence. "Norris, you okay?"

"Yeah. Sorry, guys. I thought sure I had it."

"We'll get 'em next week. You comin' to Logan's Tap with us?"

Norris turned his attention to the voice. Its owner had the most beautiful eyes he'd ever seen.

"Norris, you comin' or what?"

He didn't hear them. Smiling, the woman raised the ball to eye level and dropped it into his glove.

Someone laughed. "I guess it's or what, Bob. Let's get going."

Norris remained standing among the two-by-fours, lost in her deep brown eyes. She wore a lemon-yellow dress over her light tan and a matching ribbon in her straw-colored hair.

"Where'd you come from?" he asked.

"I was taking a walk through the park and stopped to watch. Do you throw yourself into every game like that?"

He blushed. "Sometimes I forget I'm made of flesh and bones." He offered his hand. "I'm Norris Tankersley."

"Dawn Tyler." Her palm was as soft as a baby chick.

"Where are you headed?" he asked.

"Nowhere special. I like to go walking this time of day."

Back at the dugouts, the teams were packing up their gear. "I don't have anywhere special to go either," Norris said. "Would you mind if I went nowhere special with you?"

"Only if you promise not to leap any more fences." They wandered off through the park together.

Such a natural beginning. Too easy to last.

Bitterly, Norris flipped through the magazine. He stopped at an article on compost. *That's where we all end up*, he thought. *As food for other organisms.* He read every word of the article and bided his time.

Penance

So this is what it's like.

Paige trudged through the spring weeds alongside I-20. Her feet hurt. The sneakers Naomi had bought her were full of last year's grass burrs. Her nose was peeling and the back of her neck was raw from sunburn. Thank God it was only April. She'd never have gotten this far in the pitiless Texas summer.

Her stomach growled. A week had passed since her flight from Alverna. For the past two days she'd eaten nothing but half a bean burrito tossed from a passing car. She came across it just beyond Roscoe, devouring it in two ravenous bites without stopping to brush away the dirt and grass. *Hey Dad,* she thought. *How's this for a new entrée? Burritos à la pokeweed. With a ditchwater aperitif.*

So this is what it's like. Hungry and thirsty all day, shivering with cold all night. Hour after hour plodding along the roadside, her thumb stuck out for truck drivers bound for Dallas or Shreveport, families off to visit Grandma in Sweetwater or Abilene.

"Never pick up hitchhikers," Lydia had warned when Paige got her driver's license. "The news is full of horror stories about those who did."

Mom had other advice, such as "always plan your travels in advance." That was a good one. Paige had fled Omer's house with nothing but a T-shirt and jeans, running down the dark street block after block without tiring, although her last workout was seven months ago. For miles she raced through sleeping neighborhoods and empty parking lots, hardly noticing her surroundings until she found herself on the outskirts of town.

You are now leaving Alverna, said the Chamber of Commerce sign. *Come back soon, ya hear?*

Paige didn't know where she was going. The important thing was to run. Run from the shock. The guilt. The despair. *Try that one on for size, Dee-Man. Despair is dee tire you use to replace dee flat.*

She could run from the news, but she could not outrun the facts. Louise Hargrove, sixty-two, shot through the heart with a Smith & Wesson .38. Louise had taken a bullet meant for Paige Abernathy, the Angel of Death. She ran another two miles beyond the city limits before collapsing in the center of the highway, her head ringing with the refrain *she deserves it, she deserves it.* A speeding truck might have ended her agony if she'd lingered there. An inner voice told her to get up and start walking.

So this is what it's like. Shame. Isolation. Degradation. Hearing it from Andy Michener or Reynaldo Tormada was one thing. Living it was something else. What choices can you make when you have no options? Where do you go when you have no destination? Paige let her feet carry her wherever they would.

For the next three days, she had headed east, mumbling prayers of confession, too lost in remorse to notice her mounting hunger and nagging thirst. *The website was a weapon in a game of evil, and I was its pawn. What a fool I was to think I could comfort anyone.*

She'd almost reached Abilene before she realized where she was going, and why. But she was headed in the wrong direction. She should be going south. A long way south.

Following the interstate around Abilene, she reached a convenience store, where she found a driver in a Houston Astros cap topping off his gas tank.

"Excuse me, sir. Is this the road to Waco?"

The man turned to discover a girl with haunted eyes, florid face, and unkempt hair. *Looks like Mackenzie Porter after a night of drinkin' songs.* "No, you wanna take the junction road south to Highway 36 and follow it to Gatesville. From there, take Highway 84 to Waco. Don't you have a map?"

"No sir."

He looked beyond her. "Where's your car?"

"I'm walking."

"Walking? You out here all by yourself?"

"I, uh . . . My car broke down. Back up the road."

"Oh. Well, I'd let you use my phone, only the battery's run out. You might ask inside. Maybe you can call a tow truck."

Paige hung her head. "Will you give me a ride?" she murmured.

"What about your car?"

She dawdled until he became uncomfortable. "I can take you as far as Rising Star," he offered.

"Thank you."

He finished filling the tank. "Miss, are you sure you're all right?"

She smiled wanly. "I'm okay. Rising Star will be just fine."

They climbed into his truck and headed out. *A journey of*

a thousand miles begins with a single step. Mr. Chen had said that, the day Paige began her design for SerenityShare.

Beyond Rising Star, an elderly couple in a Lincoln Navigator gave her a bottle of water and took her as far as Comanche. After they veered off toward Stephenville, she resumed walking south, ignoring her rumbling stomach. Her last full meal was that breakfast a few hours before Louise came to Naomi's house to try on clothes. Now Louise slept underground, the clothes bloody and scattered, the mural unfinished.

The next few days were a monotonous trek through flat scrubland, with an occasional tree in the distance. Paige had only a vague idea of her destination beyond Waco, or what to do when she got there. The voice urging her along sounded much like Lydia's: duty, responsibility, selflessness.

Livestock trucks rattled past her, bearing cattle and horses. The fields were barren, too early yet for cotton. She'd forgotten how flat Texas was away from the city. The sky was vast and blue, the sunsets so gorgeous that for brief moments she could forget why she was out here. Weak from hunger, she walked slowly, scanning the ditches for food—a discarded candy bar, french fries, anything. Back home, people would be descending on Chez Renée, flying in from as far away as Japan, just to brag about their dining experiences at one of the world's foremost restaurants. Then off to warm beds in the Park Hyatt. Paige slept by the side of the road, shivering in a bed of wild grass.

Highway 36 took her through small farming towns as dead as the rusted harvesting machinery parked behind the abandoned buildings. Only the occasional café offered signs of life. Paige stopped outside one of them, peering through the milky window glass at three old men drinking coffee. Blankly, they returned her stare. She thought about going in and asking for a biscuit or a piece of toast. Anything to fill the void in her stomach. Still too full of shame, she wandered on.

Though the spring days were balmy, the relentless sunrays baked her skin. Paige unpinned her hair to protect her neck. One afternoon a small cloud drifted overhead, providing a few seconds of welcome shade. The next day a much larger cloud rolled in darkly from the west. Thunder rumbled with promises of a shower and a refreshing drink. But the storm blew past her to dump its load somewhere to the east.

Night was falling when a thirtyish man in a silver Corvette pulled over. "Where you headed?" he asked as she climbed into the car.

"I'm going to visit a friend in Waco."

The man was decked out for a night on the town. He wore a black dress shirt with jeans and a red blazer. A gold stud gleamed in his right ear. "Are you hitchhiking?" he asked. "Where's your luggage?"

"It, uh, got stolen. Back up the road."

The driver peered at her in the darkness. "You remind me of that girl everybody's looking for. Abercrombie or something. Is that you?"

"Never heard of her." Paige kept her eyes on the road. He drove silently for a few minutes, undressing her with his eyes. "Are you hungry? I know a motel in Waco with a decent restaurant. I could use some company." He smiled suggestively.

"No thanks. My friend's expecting me."

"Can't be in too big a hurry if you're walking. Come on, live a little!"

Paige sat quietly until they reached the outskirts of Hamilton. At the first traffic light, she jumped out and scrambled into the bushes.

"Hey!" the guy yelled. Paige stumbled through the shadows until her right knee struck an object that sent her tumbling. She crouched behind it until she heard the Corvette roar away. Standing, she cried out as a bolt of pain ripped through her knee. The object was a tombstone. *Mary O'Connor. 1934–1988.* Paige had blundered into a cemetery.

She spent the evening limping through Hamilton, following the road signs. Sixty-eight miles to Waco. And that was only one leg in her journey. *The next time you walk across Texas, Paige, make sure you have something in your pockets besides Dr. Wingate's business card.*

She took it out and fondled it in the dark. It was just as well that she had no phone. He must be sick of her whining. Each time they'd met, she was in the middle of some crisis. Paige stuck the card back in her pocket and kept walking, hugging herself for warmth. Clouds covered the new moon, making even the highway stripes invisible. She strained her eyes to follow the asphalt lest she stumble into a ditch.

Another day and another night passed. Memories of home took her mind off the swollen knee. Lucas, his voice so sweet, his eyes so soulful that she didn't know whether to marry him or mother him. Jeanette, a timid but loyal confidant who listened sympathetically as Paige griped about her mother. Mr. Chen, staying an hour after school each day to help Paige refine the website that cost him his job. Dad, his fingers white with flour, rolling out pastry dough. Marcel, with his incomparable Duck à l'Orange. Paige missed them all. She missed the Goldmanns and their philosophical cheer. Karen Wallace, who had welcomed Paige on a cold, hungry night with no questions. Andy with his disarming drawl, Zelda's motherly warmth, Mike and his strong, capable hands, Reynaldo's melancholy accent, Dee-Man's silly wordplay. And poor Louise, her arms full of new clothes, so happy to get a fresh start as she staggered into the shelter to meet death.

Oh Louise, if only I'd known. I'd have gladly taken the bullet myself.

Around three the next morning she reached the junction to Highway 84, where the road veered northeast. Paige hesitated. This would take her out of her way, and she had no idea which road to follow beyond Waco. She wished she had a map. Her knee was down to a throb but felt stiff. Maybe she could walk it off.

Sunrise brought warmth and a greener landscape. Paige was into the Blackland Prairies now, with budding wildflowers and clumps of oak trees here and there. It was almost noon when she reached the Washington Avenue Bridge. She leaned over the rail to admire the Brazos River flowing beneath her. Here she found more greenery. Acres of bluebonnets covered the land. It was a beautiful day. Sunlight sparkled on the water. How she wished for a bath. Even from this height she wouldn't make much of a splash. Then she could swim to the bank and let the sun dry her as she walked.

Or she could just let the river sweep her away. Like Little White Dove in J. P. Richardson's ballad.

No. This is a journey of penance. You should have jumped seven months ago when you had the chance. She crossed to the other side and began a meandering trek through Waco.

By midafternoon it was uncomfortably warm and slow going. She had to keep stopping at traffic lights and dodging impatient drivers seemingly bent on running her down. Parched, she crept into someone's front yard to sneak a drink from a garden hose and moisten her burning skin. Six blocks beyond it, she found a city park and lay down beneath a cedar elm.

When she woke it was almost dark. Someone had left a pizza container on one of the picnic tables. She gobbled the last two slices and returned to the street. Beneath an overpass she found an abandoned cardboard sign: *Hungry. Please Help.* Paige tucked it inside her shirt, just in case.

It took her all night to reach South Waco. At a Stripes outlet, a clerk with a Middle Eastern accent took pity on her. He gave her a bottle of water and drew her a map showing the way to Highway 6. From there she could walk the ninety-two miles to College Station.

"Thank you," Paige said tiredly.

"Afwan," he replied with a smile.

Days passed.

Why, why, why, her footsteps demanded in rhythm.

Because, because, because, answered a voice from within.

There is no why, only because. No how, only which way. Thumbing a ride was hopeless now. Her clothes were sweaty with dust, her hair straggly. Cars and trucks passed without slowing. She kept walking and tried not to think about Dad's Chilean sea bass with rice and asparagus, or Jeannine's lamb kofta, served with hummus and tzatziki. Right now, she'd settle for a piece of beef jerky.

One afternoon she awoke to find herself lying in a ditch. *Was I taking a nap?* Then she noticed the dried cut on her arm. A broken bottle beneath her showed traces of blood. *Must have blacked out again.* How many days since she'd taken her pills? They were back in Omer and Naomi's house.

Omer. She'd left him in the middle of four design projects. Now he'd have to pay someone top dollar to complete them. Another friend betrayed. She climbed back up to the road. The blacktop stretched infinitely ahead.

Eleven miles from College Station, the traffic grew heavier. Hunger slowed her pace. She wobbled drunkenly between the emergency lane and the loamy soil. Curious faces peered at her from passing cars, wrinkled in disgust.

At a busy intersection outside College Station she found herself standing on a corner with several other transients.

A woman in a minivan spotted Paige's "hungry" sign and pulled over. "Honey, you're too young to be out among this riffraff! Where are your parents?" Before Paige could invent another lie, the traffic light turned green. Horns blared. Worriedly, the woman handed her a twenty-dollar bill and drove on.

That girl looks familiar, she thought. She couldn't say why.

As Paige waved thanks to the driver, a hand shoved her from behind.

"Beat it!" a voice yelled. "This is my corner!" The man turned back to the cars, holding up his own sign.

Paige crossed the road to a Chick-fil-A, where she bought a sandwich and a tall paper cup of water. She sat outside with her back against the building and devoured her lunch, thinking how Mom would have rebuked her for taking money from strangers.

Late that afternoon, a small dog scrambled up from the ditch and began trotting alongside her, glancing up hopefully. It was white with patches of brown fur and a short, happy tail.

"I'm sorry, I don't have any food left," Paige apologized. The dog kept pace anyway, stopping occasionally to sniff the ground before sprinting to catch up again. "Where's your owner? Your master, whatever?" She bent down to pet it. The dog had no tags or collar. "I guess we're both strays," she told her friend. It panted agreeably, though it was thin and hungry looking. Paige peered ahead in search of a convenience store. Maybe she could buy some dog chow with her remaining cash.

The dog kept her company for a couple of miles. Occasionally it wandered onto the highway, forcing traffic to veer around it. Paige tried to whistle it back onto the shoulder but her mouth was too dry. "Here, puppy!" she called. "Stay out of the road!" Sometimes it obeyed. Then curiosity sent it off on new rambles.

Just as a car approached, the dog spotted something on the other side of the road and trotted out to investigate. Brakes screeched and a horn blared. The tires rolled over the dog so fast it had no chance to yelp. Paige screamed. The car slowed, waivered, then sped on. What remained was a bloody mass of fur and tissue.

Paige waited for a break in the traffic to retrieve the body. Sobbing, she placed it gently in a patch of wild grass beside a drainage culvert. "I'm sorry, little friend. I should have told you. I'm a dangerous companion."

Another day, another night. Three hundred miles of walking had worn her socks through. The coarse pavement aggravated her joints. Both ankles felt swollen, and a knife tore through her right knee with every step. *This must be what arthritis feels like.* It didn't matter. Only twenty-four miles now to Navasota. From there, another twenty-one miles to Hempstead. Then southwest to Stenholm and the end of her journey.

Clueless

Kyle and Lydia sat in Karen's office, poring over a spreadsheet. "See what I mean?" she said. "No names, just statistics. The number of visitors per day, per week, per month. Estimated age, ethnicity, gender. The kind of stuff that makes government bean counters happy."

The two parents looked worried-out. Karen wished she had more to offer than Open Door's monthly reports.

"I keep thinking that somewhere there's a clue I've missed," Lydia said. "Someplace she's been before, someone she talked to. Can you remember anything she mentioned that might give us a lead? Even the tiniest hint?"

Clanging noises erupted from the kitchen, making them wince. "Paige mostly kept to herself, at first," Karen said. "Andy, Mike, and a few of the others were friendly to her, but the only time she really opened up was after that blackout incident. Then she told us how her website got her in trouble. After she moved in with the Goldmanns, we only saw her when she brought meals to the shelter, and on Saturdays, when she worked on the mural. And her birthday party, of course."

Lydia rose from her chair. Beyond Karen's window the

dining room walls offered cartoonish renderings of urban life. Shops and sidewalks. Pedestrians and streetlamps. Fantasies by two artists, one dead, the other missing. The walls cried out for someone to finish the job.

Lydia had used all her connections to renew the search for Paige. Cops and sheriff's deputies in every city across Texas had her picture and profile. Her name and face were all over social media. But the dragnet still turned up empty.

A new noise distracted Lydia. Someone was whacking a knife against a cutting board.

"The Goldmanns told me Paige was carrying a load of guilt about the website. If I know my daughter, she wouldn't rest until she found a way to make up for it." She turned back to Karen. "You deal with homeless people all the time. What happens to them after they leave here?"

"There are as many answers to that question as there are people. The lucky ones are just temporarily out of work, going through divorces, things like that. Others have given up trying to fit into the system and dropped out. Disillusionment. Heartbreak. Spiritual crises. Addictions. Then there are the worst ones. People with mental problems. Most of those wind up in institutions or end up dying on the street. No two cases are alike. We don't judge any of them. We're just here to help."

"Paige isn't like any of those," Kyle fretted. "I keep thinking, the longer she's out there, the greater the chance she'll fall in with the wrong kind of people."

Karen pointed to some "missing" posters on her wall. "Every one of those faces is a teenage runaway. Very few of their stories ended happily."

"I won't accept that!" Lydia cried. "Paige is a good Christian girl. We brought her up in the church, taught her right from wrong, tried to protect her from—" A loud crash made her jump. "For God's sake, what is that?"

"Sorry. It's Andy, our cook. It's getting on toward suppertime. I should go help him."

"I'll do it." Kyle rose abruptly.

"Where are you going?" Lydia asked.

"To make myself useful." He crossed the dining room to the kitchen, where Andy Michener was gathering a bunch of plastic plates off the floor.

"Sorry about the noise. Seems like I'm all thumbs today."

"Don't let Omer Goldmann hear you say that." Kyle swept the kitchen with a professional eye. A large pot of water boiled on the stove. Piles of chopped carrots, onions, and celery lay on the countertop. "What are you making?"

"Vegetable soup."

"Have you done it before?"

"Once," Andy said glumly. "Came out kinda tasteless."

Kyle smiled. "The trick is to begin with a good soup stock. Mind if I take a crack at it?"

"Be my guest." Andy stood aside as Kyle dumped the boiling water into the sink. "To get your flavor base you want to just simmer the vegetables. Put a few handfuls of what you've chopped into a pan and add just enough water to cover them. Got any tomatoes? Beans, peas, mushrooms?"

"Couple of tomatoes. There's potatoes, beets, and turnips in the pantry. Everything around here is supermarket throwaways."

"I can work with those. How about seasonings?"

"In the cabinet." Kyle found salt, pepper, and some McCormick jars. "Better than nothing, I guess." He picked out a few.

"You cook a lot?" Andy asked.

"I'm a professional chef." He offered his hand. "Kyle Abernathy."

"Abernathy? Paige's dad?"

"That's me."

Andy grinned. "I shoulda known. You remind me of your daughter."

The next day Karen was mopping the dining room floor when she noticed a face at the window. The man had both hands on the glass and his nose pressed against it. Despite the warm afternoon, he wore a stocking cap and a heavy jacket zipped up to his neck. Tangled brown hair flowed over his shoulders.

With a smile she waved at him and resumed mopping. The man crept along the windowpane, following Karen's every move with an intense stare that made her uneasy.

She put the mop aside and went out to greet him. "Can I help you? Would you like to come in?"

"Where's my dolly blanket?" he demanded.

"Your what?"

"Where is it? Where'd you put it?" He advanced toward her.

"I don't understand." Karen backed away.

"You took my dolly blanket! Why did you take my dolly blanket? Give it back! Give it back!" He followed her into the shelter.

Andy emerged from the kitchen. "What's going on?" The man had Karen backed against a dining table. Andy grabbed his arm and tried to pull him away.

"It's okay," Karen said. "Go get a blanket off one of the cots." She spoke soothingly to the man.

Andy returned. "The blanket's right here. I'm sorry, I didn't know it was yours."

"My dolly blanket," the man sobbed. He wrapped himself in it, lay down on the floor, and curled up like a baby.

"What was that all about?" Andy asked.

Trembling, Karen sank into a chair. "Put him to bed, will you? I've got some thinking to do." Andy helped the man to his feet and led him into the sleeping area.

Arrival

The distance from the highway to the gate was three hundred yards, so Grady Olson had plenty of time to watch the solitary figure approaching his guard post. Grady saw few visitors. Most of them drove supply trucks, or buses hauling in new convicts. He'd never seen anyone arrive at Thornhurst Prison on foot. Whoever it was had a bad limp. He wondered if there had been an accident on the highway.

The owner of the limp came into focus. It was a girl, badly sunburned, ready to collapse. Which was what she did a few yards from the gate. Grady reached for the phone.

Paige awoke to yet another doctor bending over her. This one was about fifty, Black and slender, with close-cut hair and thin lips.

"Welcome to Thornhurst," he said. "If you're looking for a motel, you made a wrong turn somewhere. Can you sit up?"

"I think so." She took his hand. The doctor wore the standard white coat above his blue jeans. Surrounding the examining table were supply cabinets with bottles, swabs, and syringes. "How long have I been out?"

"A couple of hours. How do you feel?"

"Sore and dirty." She rubbed sleep from her eyes.

A frowning guard stood stiffly by the doorway. "What are you doing here?" he rumbled.

"My name is Paige Abernathy. I came to see a prisoner."

"Visitors aren't allowed without advance notice. Do you have an appointment?"

"No sir."

"Why not?"

Paige's mind was blank. In more than three weeks of travel she'd never considered what she'd say when she finally got here.

"Where's your car?" he demanded.

"I don't have one."

"Then how did you get here?"

"Walking. Hitchhiking."

"From where? Nebraska? Look at the mirror." She turned to face it. Her skin was almost purple, her nose aflame. Insect bites covered her arms.

"I'm from Alverna," she answered.

The guard advanced toward her. "Nobody walks four hundred miles to visit a place like this. What are you up to?"

"Nothing, I just—"

"Who's Steve Wingate?"

"What?"

He tossed the card at her. "This was in your pocket. Who is he?"

"I—he's a doctor. He took care of me in the hospital."

"What hospital?"

"In Alverna. Please, can I see—"

"You give me some straight answers, or I'll throw you back

out on the road!"

"All right, Mr. Evans, that's enough." The doctor turned back to Paige. "Who did you come to see?"

"His name's Jerome Faulkner."

"For what reason?"

Paige bowed her head. "I killed his son."

The doctor studied her impassively. "Officer, run over to the cafeteria and get this girl something to eat."

"What do I look like, a carhop?"

"Just do it!"

The guard left, slamming the door.

The doctor checked her pulse. "Your vital signs are good. Are you on any kind of medication?"

"I have blackouts sometimes. I ran out of pills."

He nodded. "Why don't you take a shower? There are washcloths and towels in the bathroom. I'll phone the warden's office and see what I can do."

J. D. Timmons was an ex-guard who had risen through the ranks, a beefy man with close-cut hair, heavy jowls, huge hands, and stubby fingers that fumbled awkwardly over his keyboard.

"According to our records, Faulkner's serving a twenty-year stretch for attempted murder. What's the connection?"

The doctor handed him a cell phone. "I found this old news story on the web. Faulkner blamed this Abernathy girl for his son's suicide attempt. Remember that big uproar a while back about teenagers killing themselves? The girl's website was at the bottom of it. Faulkner was convicted of trying to kill her."

The warden studied the screen. "It says here that Faulkner's son is in one of those long-term care places."

"Right. The kid's brain-dead. I guess it's the same thing to her."

Timmons returned to his computer. "Jerome Faulkner. Audiologist. No priors. No incidents since he checked in four months ago. Minimum security." He turned to Evans. "Do you know him?"

"Sort of. He's quiet. Keeps to himself."

"No visitors since he's been here, except his wife." Timmons closed the file. "You say this girl just showed up at the gate and keeled over?"

"She claims she hitched here from Alverna," the doctor said. "Physically, she's okay. Just tired and weak. We gave her a tray of chow and let her take a shower."

"Where?" the warden asked sharply. "Not the inmate showers!"

"No, of course not. The one in my quarters."

Timmons thought for a moment. "Evans, call out Faulkner. Put him in the visitors' room. Full surveillance, audio and video. When they're done, send the girl to me."

The man seated behind the barrier looked like a popsicle: orange top, orange pants, with Thornhurst Prison across his chest in black letters.

"You have me at a disadvantage," he said through the speakerphone. "Have we met?"

"Don't you remember? You came to my hospital room. You tried to kill me."

"Oh!" Faulkner explored her face. "I didn't recognize you. Sorry. I don't remember much about that night. It's not in my nature to hurt people." He peered closer. "Are you okay? Looks like you've been out in the sun too long."

Paige swallowed hard. Through all the miles of walking, she'd expected accusations. Curses. Angry hands squeezing her throat, the guards unable to save her this time. Anything but kindness. Jerome Faulkner looked so beaten she wanted to reach through the plexiglass and hold him in her arms.

"Why are you here?" he asked softly.

"I thought maybe there was something I could do for you."

"Such as?"

She struggled to speak. "Your son. How is he?"

"No change. Still comatose."

"What do the doctors say?"

"Long-term care facilities don't have doctors. Not the kind you mean. They're more like gardeners."

Paige burst into tears.

Faulkner waited, expressionless. "I'd offer you a tissue, but I don't have any. Mr. Evans?" The guard ignored him. "You don't find much compassion in a place like this. I'm surprised they let you in."

Paige wiped her eyes with the back of her hand. "I just showed up at the gate. I guess they didn't know what else to do with me."

An awkward silence followed. "So. You came to see me because you feel guilty."

"Mr. Faulkner, please believe me. When I started that website I only wanted to help people. I never imagined it would turn out the way it did."

"I know. I've kept up with the news." He smiled a little. "It's funny. People all over the country are looking for you. Yet here you are in prison, right where they want you to be."

"I should be sitting where you are," Paige said earnestly.

"You're the victim in all this." Another silence. "How long do you have to stay here?"

"Hard to say. My first parole hearing is next month. If I don't cause any trouble . . . maybe another four or five years."

"What will you do when you get out?"

Faulkner drew a deep breath. "That's too far ahead to plan. My audiology practice is gone. Once the bankruptcy courts untangle everything, I might have a little something left to start over. Meanwhile, I have access to the journals so I can keep up with my field. But it's hard to concentrate in here."

A refrain ran through Paige's head: *This is all my fault. All my fault.*

"Mr. Faulkner, why did he do it?"

He gazed past her. "Conrad was a good boy, growing up. Easygoing, worked hard in school, never caused any trouble. Then, after his thirteenth birthday, he started to withdraw. At home he mostly stayed in his room, listening to music, or doing whatever kids do on the internet these days. I thought he was just going through a phase, like teenagers do, so I let him alone. My wife and I were wrapped up in our jobs. We should have tried harder to draw him out." He returned his attention to Paige. "After Conrad—after the incident—I spent a lot of time reading the news stories about your website. I had no idea there were so many young people desperate enough to want to kill themselves."

"Neither did I. I should have stopped it sooner."

Faulkner studied her closely. "You're not going to let this go, are you? I can see it in your face."

She hung her head. "It was selfish of me to come here. I see that now. I just wanted to make myself feel better. Now I feel worse than ever."

"I'm glad you came. It's nice to know someone cares."

Paige fought back more tears. "What can I do to help you, Mr. Faulkner? How can I make it up to you? I'll do anything."

His face darkened. "Don't make promises you might regret." He leaned toward her, as close as the barrier allowed. "If you really want to help me, give my son some peace."

"How?"

"Put him to sleep."

Paige gaped in horror. "I can't do that!"

"Yes, you can."

She groped for words. "Mr. Faulkner, I-I can't be responsible for another death."

"He's already dead, Paige. You'd just be completing his journey."

"Yes, but . . ." She halted, searching for a rebuttal. Faulkner waited, unblinking. "Where is he?"

"Still in Alverna. Prairieland Hospice, in the west wing. Room 238." He glanced back at the guard. "Go at night between seven and eight," he whispered, "while the aides are busy making their medication rounds. Take some flowers with you in case there's a receptionist. Say they're from me."

"How do you know all this?"

"My wife visits him after work each day." Faulkner smiled sadly as the weight settled on Paige's shoulders. "Now you know how it feels."

"Time's up!" Evans barked.

Faulkner and Paige rose to their feet. A silent understanding passed between them as the guard led him back to his cell.

"You're in luck," the warden said. "There's a bus heading back to Gatesville in about twenty minutes. We just unloaded a new bunch of scumbags, so it'll be empty. You're welcome to ride along."

"Thank you."

He inspected the girl. The shower had done nothing for her florid face, tattered shirt, and dirty jeans. She looked like a teenage hobo. "I'd give you something else to wear, but prison issue is all I've got. Out on the highway you'd be arrested within minutes. The doctor gave me this for your insect bites." He handed her a tube of ointment and a bottle of pills. "Those are for your knee pain. Did your visit with Faulkner go all right?"

"Yes sir. Please thank the doctor for me." She rose from her chair.

"Wait a minute. Is there someone in Alverna you can call to meet you at Gatesville?"

"No sir."

"Do you have any money?"

She searched her pockets. "I thought I had some left. There was this lady back in College Station . . . I guess not."

Timmons stood and reached for his wallet. "This is all the cash I've got on me. Maybe it'll be enough to get you home."

"That's very kind of you, but—"

"Take it," the big man insisted. "I know all about your website. I know why you're here." His eyes softened. "We don't see a lot of contrition in this place. Take it and get back home to your family."

Evans peeked into the guardroom office. It was empty. He locked the door, sat at the computer, and clicked on People Tracer:

*I have the information you're looking for. Use the
link below to deliver the money.*

He drew Paige's cash from his pocket and tucked it in
his wallet.

Signposts

Zach Oglesby poked his head into Lydia's office. "I just got word. Norris Tankersley gets out of county day after tomorrow."

"Any idea where he goes from there?"

"Maybe." He closed the door and took a seat. "My jail source says he's been taking advantage of his one phone call per day. It's always to this number."

Lydia examined the note. "Frazier Emergency Room."

"Uh-huh. And get this. He always asks for Dr. Wingate."

"That's the man who treated Paige."

"Yes. But Tankersley never speaks to Wingate. He just says thank you and hangs up."

Lydia leaned back in her chair. "I see. He's just trying to find out if Wingate's on duty."

"That's what I think."

Lydia studied the note as though it might tell her more. "I don't get it. If Tankersley's after Paige, what good does Wingate's work schedule do him? He was just her ER doctor."

"Maybe he expects Paige to get in touch with him."

"Why would he think that? They don't have any

264

relationship outside the hospital."

"Do we know that for sure?"

Lydia turned red. "Get Wingate on the phone. I want to talk to him right now."

"No, Mrs. Abernathy," Steve replied. "I've only spoken to her once since she left the ER. That was several months ago."

"Why didn't you call me?" she snapped. "You know what's at stake here."

"Hold on a second." The doctor ducked into a supply closet to shut out hospital noises. "There was nothing to report. Besides, doctor-patient conversations are confidential, as I'm sure you know."

"Paige was still a minor several months ago! You should have . . ." She forced herself to stop. "Are you aware that the man who tried to kill Paige has been calling the hospital from jail, asking for you?"

"One of the admitting clerks mentioned something. She didn't know who it was. Why? Do you think it has something to do with Paige?"

"That's what I'm trying to find out. Dr. Wingate, exactly what is your relationship with my daughter?"

Steve's hackles rose. "Don't you even suggest such a thing, Mrs. Abernathy! All my patient relationships are proper and professional."

"Then why did you give her your private number?"

"Everything I knew about Paige indicated she might be suicidal. She was responsive to me. I wanted to help."

"Suicidal! That's ridiculous! She was attacked by a bunch of thugs, according to what I've been able to find out."

"There's more to it than that. Paige was despondent. Down on herself because of that website fiasco. For what it's worth, our last conversation was mostly about me."

"About you? How so?"

"She asked about my family. How I got along with my kids, that sort of thing."

Lydia's tone softened. "I wonder why?"

"Mrs. Abernathy, do you have any idea why Paige was wearing a ballgown and dance shoes when she was first admitted?"

"The police mentioned that. No, I don't."

"You might want to give it some thought. Maybe it will explain what she was doing on the Bustamante Bridge."

Paige's ride to Gatesville was uneventful. She slept most of the way, curled upon a seat between the shackle bars. The driver played country music CDs and watched her in the rearview mirror. A blond babe was a rare sight on a prison bus.

She dreamed she was back on the bridge, watching the sunset. Carrion birds circled above the railroad tracks, anticipating death, decay, and dinner.

It was almost dawn when the driver shook her awake. She stepped into the cool air. Before her stood the Alfred D. Hughes prison unit, a sprawling complex of buildings with a wide sidewalk leading to the main entrance. It reminded her of what she'd left behind at Thornhurst, and of what lay ahead.

She thanked the driver and walked toward town. At a city bus stop she caught a ride to the Greyhound station. The warden's money bought her a ticket good for another hundred and forty miles. By the time she arrived at Ballinger, the sun was near its zenith. With her last dollar, she bought a donut at a convenience store. Stepping outside, she drew a deep breath and set forth on foot again, northwest on Highway 158. Jerome Faulkner's assignment lay on her shoulders like an iron weight.

Paige was back in flat desert country now. Hour by hour she walked the highway, the sun keeping pace at first, then overtaking her as it gradually sank in the west. Farther ahead it would soon hang over Alverna's horizon, to rendezvous with the tracks beyond the Bustamante Bridge. Then darkness would fall upon the town, providing cover for a weary traveler on a merciful errand. But not this night. Paige still had more than a hundred miles to go.

Cars and trucks whizzed past. One slowed, the driver giving her the once-over before speeding onward. *Guess I'm nobody's idea of a motel date anymore.* She ignored the traffic, trying to think of something besides her mission. In two weeks Lucas would graduate from high school. She envisioned him at the yearbook signing party, writing good luck messages and thinking ahead to college, a world of opportunity open to him. Paige supposed Lucas had forgotten her after all this time. She wondered if he had made the Spring Break trip to South Padre Island. It was a treat all seniors looked forward to. All except Jeanette. Her mother couldn't afford it.

What about Dad and her friends at the restaurant? And Open Door? Who was cooking for the homeless people now? Did Omer find someone to finish the web designs she had abandoned? Every question led to the same answer. *I've failed them all. Now I'm on my way to kill someone who's already dead.*

Her thoughts revived memories of her website forum and its pathetic cries of despair. *I'll be going tonight*, GoneforGood had written in his final posting on August 27. She wondered if he had really done it. Between the lines you could almost feel his pain: pressures from his family, rejection by his girlfriend, hopelessness that filled his head with deadly options, from knives to guns to nooses. GoneforGood, a.k.a. Jeff Lowery. The name fluttered over Paige like a black flag.

She tried to recall the incident on the bridge that led to those murky hours in the hospital. *What if there had been no attack? Would I have jumped? What difference would it have made to anyone? Okay, Mom and Dad, yes. Maybe Lucas. But Louise would still be alive. And Jerome Faulkner would be free.*

Sunset unveiled a magnificent evening sky. Paige had never realized how bright the stars were away from the glare of city lights. The vast landscape below them felt like eternity, where you could journey forever with God as your sole companion. "Dear God," she prayed as each step drew her closer to home, "am I doing the right thing? Please tell me." The only answer was an echo of the sixth commandment: "Thou shalt not kill."

The days passed, and with them came hunger, thirst, and fresh complaints from her knee. She dry-swallowed her pills and ignored the cravings. One night she reached an intersection: *Highway 163*. Paige hesitated. If she turned north, she wouldn't have to complete her mission. Just head for Colorado City. From there she could hook up with I-20 again. Perhaps veer eastward, hitchhike all the way to Atlanta. Or westward, to link up with I-10 and wind up in Los Angeles. Why not? What awaited her in Alverna, besides a forbidden act that would haunt her forever?

A promise made is a debt unpaid, Robert Service wrote, *and the trail has its own stern code.* She drew a deep breath and continued homeward.

Sunrise came. Her feet hurt, the shoe seals coming unstuck here and there, the pavement so harsh she might have been walking on bare feet. She moved over to the shoulder, but rocks and uneven spots caused her to stumble, retarding her progress. Stepping back to the road, she chewed more pills and bore it as best she could. *Don't think about it. Let it be more penance for what I've done, and for what I'm going to do.*

The daylight grew brighter, reigniting her sunburn. *Should have thought to ask that prison doctor for some sunblock.* Around noon she came across an Evian bottle lying in the dust. It was half full, the cap still on it. Grateful for litterbugs, she drained it in three gulps, along with her last two pain pills. *Maybe they threw away some food as well.* She scouted around. Nothing but scrub brush and prickly pears. Her stomach was a grinding void. *How far can you travel on a prison meal and a donut? Stay tuned and find out.*

The afternoon wore on, the sun's glare blinding. The traffic grew so light that the occasional car seemed a novelty. She tried to suppress her gloomy thoughts by memorizing each model, color, and license plate, but they all passed too quickly. The day was unusually warm for spring. Heat shimmers rose from the pavement ahead. This stretch of Texas bore few signs of civilization. She hadn't passed through a single town since yesterday. Maybe, in her daze, she had strayed to a farm road. The desert surrounding her was indifferent, the sand baking beneath the sun's rays, the cacti faceless landmarks. Without the asphalt trail, it might have been the surface of the moon, or some dead planet.

Late in the afternoon, she came upon a sign: *Texas Highway 158*. Still on course. So tired though. Paige considered lying down to rest against the signpost until dark. But something in her joints warned that she might not be able to get up again. Her knee was swollen tight inside her jeans. Her feet had no feeling. She looked down. Her left shoe was gone.

Turning, she saw it lying on the asphalt about a hundred yards behind her. Wearily, she limped back to fetch it. The casing had completely separated from the sole. Paige removed her threadbare sock, wrapped the shoe pieces around her foot, and pulled the sock over the whole mess to hold it together.

The sun declined in the west, causing her shadow to lengthen and stretch across the prairie. It matched her pace step for step, creeping over the scrub brush, growing longer and thinner until its head was forty yards away.

"I hope you feel better than I do," she croaked. *Me and my shadow, strolling down the avenue. Where have I heard that?* She tried to sing it but her throat was too dry.

Darkness fell. The moon had waned, but occasional meteor streaks joined the starlit pageant. Paige had no idea where she was, only that Alverna lay somewhere ahead. The hunger reminded her of a Sunday school lesson from long ago: Jesus in the wilderness, forty days with nothing to eat. The teacher described it as a test of character, to prepare Him for His ministry. "If you are the son of God," the tempter said, "tell these stones to become bread." Jesus knew there was more at stake than an empty stomach. The fate of humanity lay in His decision to satisfy Himself or God.

Jesus passed His test and became the savior of lost souls. I'll always be remembered as a murderer, like Adam Lanza, Nikolas Cruz, or Salvador Ramos. Kids who molded their misery into bullets to slay other kids. God, please let a rattlesnake bite me. Strike me with lightning. Anything, so I don't have to keep this promise.

Paige's head drooped as she ambled onward. Somewhere she'd read that it was possible to walk and sleep at the same time if you were tired enough. The night began to spin around her. Abruptly, she found herself lying on the pavement. *I must have conked out again. Maybe the next one will be fatal and get me off the hook.* She struggled to her feet and went on.

At sunrise she bumped into another sign: *Alverna 5 miles.* A dull euphoria rose in her throat. The light revealed a fresh, clear morning, the mesquite bushes casting low shadows across the terrain. A half-dozen jackrabbits sat complacently among them. They brought to mind Dad's fenkata recipe: rabbit marinated in wine and stewed with vegetables. Flavored with olives and capers on a plate of pasta. *Don't think about it,* said an inner voice. *You've come this far. God will provide.*

Something glimmered in the distance. She squinted but couldn't make it out. There was a recreational lake near Alverna, but this road didn't lead to it. Whatever the object was, it grew larger as she progressed. Another half hour brought it into focus. Some sort of advertising sign. She must be near the outskirts of town.

Fifteen minutes later it was definite. A tall signpost bearing a familiar icon with white background and blue lettering: *Alverna Chevrolet.* More shiny objects dotted the surface beneath it: a parking lot full of cars for sale. Another fifteen minutes, and she could make out the blue and white banners fluttering above them.

By eleven thirty she was standing on the sidewalk outside the dealership. Traffic whooshed past her. Shade trees above a grass carpet flanked the driveway. Paige lay down there and fell asleep.

Something was poking her ribs. Blinking, Paige sat up to find a policeman standing over her.

"What are you doing here?"

She tried to speak. Her throat felt like straw.

"Well?"

Paige shook her head, pointed at her mouth.

"Water?"

She nodded. He retreated to his patrol car and returned with a plastic bottle.

"Whoa, there!" he commanded, as she grabbed for it. "Take it slow." He squatted beside her and poured a capful into her mouth. "Swish that around. Take your time."

Paige obeyed, feeling the tissues begin to loosen.

"Doesn't help to swallow too much when you're dehydrated. I see you've been out in the sun a while."

"Yes," she croaked. "I've been walking"—she coughed—"walking all night to get here."

"Where are you headed?"

"Home. My car broke down."

"Broke down where?"

"Back . . . back up the road." She pointed vaguely at the horizon.

"Let me see some ID."

"I lost it." She stared longingly at the water bottle.

"Here. Sip slowly, now, or it'll come right back up." Paige took a small swallow. Nothing on the Chez Renée menu had ever tasted so good.

"What's your name?" asked the cop.

"Jodie McKenzie."

"Where do you live?"

"I—across town. My . . ." She slumped, too tired to think up any more lies.

"A runaway?" She nodded. "I thought so. The dealership called. Deadbeats cluttering up the entryway are bad for business. What's your story?"

"Please," she begged, "just let me go. I won't cause any trouble."

The cop studied her blistered face. It seemed familiar somehow.

His shoulder radio crackled. "Seven-George 27."

"Go, dispatch."

"Back up Seven-Victor 22 at 1217 Olympia. Domestic disturbance."

"Copy, dispatch." He returned to Paige. "Do you have a place to stay?" She shook her head. "All right." He fished in his pocket. "I know a place where you can bed down. Do you think you can walk?"

"Yes sir."

He handed Paige a small card. "Here's the address. Go directly there, and they'll take you in. Go now," he added sternly. "No loitering, no begging. You have no idea what can happen to a young woman alone on the street. If I see you around here again, I'll lock you up for vagrancy." He sprinted to the patrol car and roared off in a screech of tires and sirens.

Paige looked at the card. *Open Door Homeless Shelter.* She threw her head back and laughed.

Darkness covered Prairieland Hospice by the time she arrived. The distance from the car dealership was only three miles, but the nap had awakened her sore feet. Her knee throbbed. Every step was a torment.

Moonlight filtered through the trees surrounding the

building, casting leafy shadows over the parking lot. Three cars were scattered across it. That suggested only three employees in a facility housing perhaps seventy patients. Hospice care was for people beyond hope.

Somewhere inside the building, Conrad Faulkner waited for someone to set him free. What if she just turned and walked away? Who would know? Only Jerome Faulkner. And God.

She peeked through the glass door. The lobby was dark, but a woman sat at the reception desk, reading a paperback by lamplight. What were Faulkner's instructions? Something about visiting hours and medication. Paige tried to remember.

The receptionist picked up the phone. Spoke into it. Came around the desk and headed down a hallway. Now the lobby was empty.

Paige slipped in and tiptoed across the carpet to the elevator. Reaching for the button, she paused. What if someone heard the *ding* when she reached the second floor? She crossed to the staircase door and stepped through quietly. Seizing the railing, she dragged herself up the steps to the landing. At the doorway she offered a silent prayer that it would be locked. It opened easily.

A dark hallway lay ahead. She crept past a series of rooms, each with its door open, each containing a soul connected to IVs and monitors. In Room 216 an old woman lay on her back, moaning "Charlie!" over and over. The man in 218 slept on his side, breathing into a mask. It looked like the one Paige wore after Jerome Faulkner tried to smother her.

At 224 she stopped. A nurse with a medical trolley stood beside the bed, studying an electronic chart. Her back obscured Paige's view of the patient. She crept carefully on, past 226, 228, 230.

As she approached her destination, Paige prayed for 238

to be empty. She edged around the doorway and peered into the room. The only light came from a fluorescent bulb behind the bed. The boy lay on his back, his thin chest rising and falling slowly. A feeding tube ran into his throat. Clear liquid from an IV line trickled into his arm. Next to the bed, the ubiquitous plastic chair. Conrad's mother probably sat there when she came to visit.

Paige stepped inside. A table near the window supported a plastic vase with wilted flowers. A small card read *Con, we love you. Gram and Grandpa.* Otherwise the room was bare.

A plastic wrist bracelet verified his identity. Conrad's breathing was barely audible. There was no oxygen mask on his face. His parents must have signed one of those do-not-resuscitate orders. Beside him, a heart monitor beeped steadily.

She leaned over him. The boy was slender and pale, his eyes closed, his face drawn. His hands rested on the bed, the palms slightly open. Someone had recently trimmed his light-brown hair and his fingernails. Probably Conrad's mother. What did she think as she kept vigil over her child, unable to do anything but pray for his soul and speak words of comfort he would never hear? Did Mrs. Faulkner ask him why? Did she blame herself? Paige considered writing a note and pinning it to the boy's gown. *I'm to blame for this. I would gladly trade places with him if I could.* Sign her name and sneak away. But that wouldn't help Jerome Faulkner or his wife.

"What made you do it?" she whispered into Conrad's ear. "Were you lonely? Did someone hurt you? Was there no love in your life? How did you reach the point where you had nothing to live for?" The boy breathed on indifferently, his lips slightly parted. A faint odor of toothpaste rose from them. Paige stroked his face and his hair, trying to imagine what it was like to be alive but unable to wake up, trapped inside your own body. Did he dream? Think and reason? Did he yearn to cry out for help, unable to use his voice? If there was a Hell, this must be it.

Wheels echoed through the hallway. The nurse was rolling her cart from room to room, the sound drawing closer. *If you're going to do it, you've got to act now.*

Maybe she could smother him. Disconnect the monitor and cover his face with his pillow. No. Paige still remembered what that felt like. She didn't want him to suffer. Was there a quicker way?

Tentatively, she touched his throat. The skin was warm, the small notch beneath his neck and clavicle soft and vulnerable. Constricting his windpipe would be easy unless he struggled. Did his body have the strength to fight her? Paige had none.

She reached down and unplugged the heart monitor. Now the only sound was the soft drip of fluid from the IV bag. Closing her eyes, she trembled as her fingers approached their target. *I've never held a life in my hands before.*

She pinched his nose and pressed hard against his throat. Conrad's breathing halted. For a moment Paige thought it was over. Then he began to retch. His fingers fluttered weakly, then his chest heaved. His mouth opened and produced gagging noises. With a gasp Paige jerked away, her heart pounding. *It's no good. I'm not God, and I'm not worthy to act in His stead.*

The heaving subsided. Conrad coughed slightly. His chest rhythm resumed. Paige reconnected the heart monitor, kissed his forehead, and slipped quietly through the doorway and down the stairs.

Outside the building she leaned against the wall and cried softly in the night shadows. *Where do I go from here? The shelter? Omer and Naomi? What about home? It's been eight months since I saw my parents. Do I still have a place with them?*

She was dimly aware of a change in her surroundings. When she arrived the parking lot had contained three cars. Now there were four. Before she could wonder about it, a powerful hand clamped over her mouth.

"Start walking. Straight ahead. Don't scream. Don't say a word."

Reckoning

Steve Wingate was at the admissions desk when his cell phone rang.

"Daddy, will you be home at the regular time tonight?"

"I think so. Things are quiet now right now. What's on your mind?"

"Missy Logan's parents won't be back until ten thirty, and Scott wants to take me to the late show. It starts at ten. Would you mind babysitting her until they get back?"

"Kathy," he sighed, "you know how I feel about you staying out late on school nights."

"Please, Daddy! I've got all my assignments done, and I'll come straight home when it's over."

"Why can't you wait till Friday night?"

"Because then we'll have to stand in line for an hour and maybe not get in. This is the last episode of *Star Avengers*, and it's supposed to be the best one yet."

"Kathy—"

"Please, Daddy, please? Your supper's in the oven, and I've already cleaned up the kitchen."

It was her best wheedling tone. Steve pretended to think

about it, just to prove he wasn't the pushover she knew he was. "Well . . ." he grumbled. "All right. But don't leave the house until I get there. And, Kathy?"

"Yes?"

"This is the last time. No more movies on school nights."

"I promise. Oh, thank you, Daddy, thank you!"

He returned to his patient notes. The phone rang again. "Did you forget something?"

"Dr. Wingate, this is Paige Abernathy."

"Oh! Hi there! I've been worried about you. Your mother said—"

"Dr. Wingate, I need your help."

"What's the matter?" Silence. "Paige?" He checked his screen for a connection. "Paige, are you there?"

"Can—can you meet me at the Bustamante Bridge?"

"Paige, what's this about? Are you okay?"

"I can't tell you on the phone," she said tremulously. "Can you come now? Please?"

"Paige, if you're hurt, I can send an ambulance—"

"If you don't come now, I'm going to jump! I mean it!"

"All right! All right, I'm on my way. Don't do anything until I get there."

"And don't call anybody. Especially the police."

"I won't. Hang on, Paige. I'm coming." Swiftly, he logged off the computer. "Cheryl, I've got an emergency. Ask Dr. Gaines to cover for me, will you?"

An alarm sounded as he dashed for the exit. "Dr. Wingate!" a nurse shouted. "Cardiac arrest, Treatment Three!"

Steve hesitated. "Where's Dr. Gaines?"

"Treatment One, heavy bleeder." The nurse seized a crash cart without waiting for a reply. Swearing, he raced back into the ER.

"I've had plenty of time to memorize that song of yours." Norris Tankersley took the phone from Paige's hand. "Want me to sing it for you while we wait?"

"What song?" Too weak to stand any longer, she slumped against the guardrail. Tankersley's hunting knife glittered in the moonlight. "Oh Little White Dove! You must know your own theme song. Suppose I sing you the first verse?"

> *On the bank of the river stood Running Bear,*
> *young Indian brave*
> *On the other side of the river stood his lovely Indian*
> *maid*
> *Little White Dove was her name, such a lovely sight*
> *to see*
> *But their tribes fought with each other, so their love*
> *could never be*

This is a nightmare, Paige thought. "Why are you doing this? If it's about my website, go ahead and kill me. But don't involve an innocent man."

"Innocent? *Innocent?*" Tankersley leaned into her face. "You think you're the only one who tried to play God and wasn't up to the job?"

"*If you want to kill me, just do it!*" Paige screamed at him. *"I don't care anymore!"*

"Yes, you do. Otherwise, you would have jumped off this bridge back in September." He drew a sheet of paper from his pocket. "'A young woman found beaten and unconscious on the Bustamante Bridge last night has been identified as

Paige Abernathy, author of the controversial SerenityShare website, according to hospital sources.'" He smiled triumphantly. "Amazing, the information you can dig up online these days."

Paige covered her face. "Whatever I did to hurt you, I'm sorry."

Tankersley looked her over. Filthy, bedraggled, emaciated. "You know something, Little White Dove? I believe you. Did you really walk here all the way from Thornhurst Prison?"

"How do you know about that?"

"I have friends in low places. One of the guards told me about your visit with Jerome Faulkner."

"What's he got to do with this?"

Tankersley smirked. "I'll bet old Evans nearly broke a leg rushing to find a computer after you left the visitors' room. He thought he was going to collect a hundred thousand dollars. Unfortunately for him, baggage handlers don't earn that much."

"I don't understand any of this," Paige said tiredly.

"That's all right. In a few minutes it won't matter."

"At least tell me why you want to kill me."

"You're not the prey, Little White Dove. You're the bait." He checked his watch. "I guess Dr. Wingate's not used to making house calls. Want to hear another verse?"

The cardiac alarm buzzed stubbornly. Sweat dripped from Steve's forehead as he pumped the woman's chest. "Pads and ventilator," he panted.

The nurse was ready, placing a bag mask over the mouth. An aide attached defibrillator pads to the torso. "Charged and ready, Doctor."

They stood back as the body spasmed. "Nothing. Reset." Steve resumed the massage. "Come on lady, give me a beat." He pressed in steady rhythm, trying to shut Paige out of his mind.

"Ready, Doctor," said the nurse. The body jerked. The alarm resumed.

"Load her up again, one-fifty this time." He kept pumping. The woman lay inert, her gray hair spread across the pillow. *God help me*, he prayed. *Help her.*

The alarm stopped. There was a single beep. Another. Then a steady series. Steve drew back and watched the monitor.

Dr. Lacey swept the curtain aside. "What have we got here?" By now there were three aides in Treatment Three, taking turns on the ventilator and attaching more leads to the patient's body.

"I had to zap her a couple of times, but she seems okay now." Steve moved aside to let the cardiologist take over.

Lacey examined the chart. "Quite an arrest history. Lucky she decided to have this one in a hospital. Let's give her an hour. If she remains stable, put her in ICU. Good job, Steve."

"Thanks." He peeled off his mask and gloves. "Angela, will you give him the rundown? I've got another emergency."

Tankersley squatted against the railing opposite Paige, on the very spot where she'd once stood gazing into the sun. He sang again.

He couldn't swim the raging river 'cause the river was too wide

*He couldn't reach the Little White Dove waiting
on the other side
In the moonlight he could see her throwing kisses
'cross the waves
Her little heart was beating faster waiting for her
Indian brave*

He raised his eyebrows. "How about that, Little White Dove? Does Steve Wingate make your heart beat faster?"

Paige buried her face between her knees. She wished she'd never heard of that song.

"You know, you really shouldn't get mixed up with older men. In the end, they always go back to their wives."

"It's not like that!" she cried. "Dr. Wingate took care of me in the hospital."

"Strictly business, huh? Then why did you have his private phone number in your pocket?" He waggled the card at her.

Paige was torn between wishing the doctor would hurry and wishing he wouldn't come at all. She'd driven over a hundred kids to suicide. Shamed her family. Gotten Louise killed. How many other unsuspecting victims lay in her wake?

"What do you mean I'm the bait? Everyone else hates me because of my website. What's Dr. Wingate got to do with it?"

The man rose to his feet, towering above her in the moonlight. "Have you ever been in love, Paige?"

"Yes."

"How did it turn out?"

"Why do you care?"

He shrugged. "Dr. Wingate's running late. We might as well talk about something. Or should I sing you another verse?"

Wearily, she answered. "I had a boyfriend. We were going to get married after we graduated from high school. My mother made us break up."

"Ah! That explains the Running Bear thing. So you got involved with Dr. Wingate just to spite her."

"He had nothing to do with it! You don't understand."

Tankersley glowered. "I don't understand?" He bent over her. "*I don't understand? Do you think you're the only person who ever had a broken heart?*"

"Nobody knows heartbreak better than I do!" she cried. "I'm responsible for heartbroken parents all over the world!"

"What about me?" he shouted. "I never got a chance to *be* a parent. All because of that bungling doctor friend of yours!"

The phone rang. Tankersley thrust it at Paige. "Answer it!"

"No."

"Answer it! Tell him if he's not here in five minutes, you're going to jump!"

Paige snatched the phone and hurled it over the rail. Tankersley seized her as she tried to throw herself after it.

"Let me go!"

He pulled her loose and slammed her to the pavement.

"Five years ago, I met a woman at a baseball game," he panted into her face. "The minute I saw her, I knew. We both knew. We could see our future in each other's eyes. Her name was Dawn Tyler."

"Let me jump!" Paige cried. "I don't want to hear any more!"

Tankersley's grip tightened. "It was more than love at first sight. It was destiny. Something *meant* to happen. Both of us knew it. We didn't even have to say it. We just knew."

From the corner of one eye, Paige spotted the knife on the other side of the bridge where he had dropped it. Tankersley didn't seem to notice.

"More than anything in my life, I wanted to be a husband

and a father," he agonized. "You wouldn't know it, to look at me. Macho man. Weekend athlete. I attracted women like a trash truck draws flies. But none of them saw who I really was. Dawn knew instantly. She looked into my eyes, and do you know what she saw? Home. Children. Family. A circle of love."

Tankersley released his grip and fell back against the railing. "We were married a week later," he moaned. "It was a perfect match. She made me complete." Tears formed in his eyes. "We made each other complete!"

Paige struggled to a sitting position. "Did something happen to her?"

He swallowed hard. "Our first child was due a year later. We did everything right. Read child development books. Watched videos. Prepared the baby's room. Dawn kept herself fit, ate all the right foods. Everything was going beautifully."

Tankersley shut his eyes, as though summoning strength.

"At William P. Hobby, where I worked, you have to wear earmuffs to keep from going deaf around the jet engines. One day I was loading departure bags. My phone rang but I couldn't hear it. I wasn't expecting any calls anyway. It was only her seventh month. But when I went on break, there was a voicemail. Dawn had gone into labor. By the time the ambulance got there, she was bleeding so badly the doctor ordered a transfusion. She was A positive. The blood he gave her was B negative. She died on the gurney before I could get there. So did the baby."

Anguished, he turned his eyes to Paige. "The doctor was Steve Wingate."

Steve was two blocks from the hospital before realizing he didn't know how to find the Bustamante Bridge. He'd never been to that part of town.

He pressed redial on his phone, but Paige didn't answer. He called his daughter.

"Daddy, what's keeping you?"

"Kathy, what's the fastest way to the Bustamante Bridge?"

"I don't know, why?"

"Look it up on the Google map. I can't drive and do that at the same time."

He waited as she put the phone on speaker. "Daddy, is something wrong?"

"Never mind. Tell me as soon as you've got it."

"What street are you on now?"

"Whitlow, just east of the hospital."

More waiting. "Um . . . It looks like if you go all the way to Franklin and turn left, it's about five blocks to Carver Road. Turn right there, and it should take you straight to it."

He repeated the directions to himself. "Thanks, honey."

"Daddy, what's wrong?"

"Not now. I'm sorry about the movie. Tell Scott maybe another night." He hung up and hit the gas.

"I couldn't make sense of it," Tankersley despaired. "You don't find your soulmate for life, then lose her to a medical error. It was murder! Careless, blundering murder!"

Paige shook her head. "I don't believe you. Dr. Wingate is a kind man. He's a good doctor and a good friend."

His eyes filled with scorn. "Haven't you ever wondered why a doctor his age is nothing but an emergency room lackey? The hospital fired him for negligence."

"So he came to Alverna?"

"Not right away. From what I could piece together, he tried to go into partnership with some other doctors. Naturally, none of them wanted a maternity killer on their staff. Neither did any other big-city hospitals."

"How do you know all this?"

"Gossip. Hanging around hospitals, asking questions, charming the nurses. I'm a hunk, in case you haven't noticed." He smiled bitterly.

"And all this time, you've been planning to kill him?"

The question seemed to puzzle Tankersley. "Not at first." He gazed beyond the bridge. "After we got married, one of the first things Dawn persuaded me to do was give up sports. She thought competition was bad for me. She was right. I used to get into fights over knockdown pitches and bad umpire calls. I got kicked out of more games than I can remember. But once I quit baseball, I felt like a better person. Happier, more relaxed." His face darkened. "It took her death to bring it up again."

He returned his attention to Paige. "You have to understand. I didn't know who I was until I met Dawn. She brought out a joy in me that I'd never felt before. That day I met her at the ballpark, she'd been out walking. She said God had made the day so beautiful that it was a sin to waste it indoors. She pointed out little things most people take for granted, like shades of color in clouds, and birdsongs, and how the air smells after rain. She said, 'Norris, the Garden of Eden is all around us. God put us here to tend it.'"

"But then she was gone," Paige whispered.

"I couldn't understand it. How could a soul so perfect be erased by something so mundane as a blood type error? Then

I guess I got confused. I walked out of the emergency room and wandered all over the hospital looking for her. Surely, it was a mistake. She had to be in a recovery room, with doctors and nurses tending her. But every room I looked in, there was somebody else. I went outside and walked around the building. Maybe she was sitting under a tree, reading poetry, the way she did at home. So I drove to the house, but she wasn't there either. I drove to the park where we met, to the stores where we used to shop, asking everybody if they'd seen her. Finally, I returned home and waited for her to come to me. But she never did.

"The next day I went back to my job. I worked all day without earmuffs in case she called. But the only sound was jet noise. I phoned the hospital to ask Wingate where he'd taken my wife. He was gone. They'd put him on administrative leave."

Tankersley covered his eyes. He seemed to have forgotten Paige was there. She thought about going after the knife, but something held her back.

"Nobody would tell me where he lived!" he cried. "I hung around the hospital for weeks, chatting up the nurses. Eventually, one of them told me Wingate wasn't coming back, that he'd left Houston. I was so frustrated!" Tankersley pounded the road with his fist. "Why should the man who murdered my wife be the last to see her alive?"

"But it was just an accident," Paige said.

"*Don't say that!* Love doesn't die in accidents! Love can't be snuffed out by carelessness!" He pulled himself together. "I started dating one of the nurses just to find out what she knew. After a few months, she told me about a friend in Alverna who worked at Frazier Memorial. The ER had a new doctor from Houston. I did some checking, and sure enough, it was Wingate. I jumped into the car and drove all night to get here."

Paige listened in wonder. "That must have been the day I blacked out at the homeless shelter. So you weren't there to kill me. You were there for Dr. Wingate."

"Except I couldn't get through the emergency room doors. They only opened from the inside. I found out later that the registration clerk had to press a button to unlock them."

"Would you have killed him if you'd been able to get in?"

Tankersley looked at Paige like she was an idiot. "Haven't you been listening? I wasn't there to kill him. I wanted to know where Dawn was. The gun was just an incentive."

"But she was dead. You already said so."

"*You think I don't know that?*" he roared. "I couldn't accept it. She was too perfect to be killed off by some incompetent quack!"

He's crazy, Paige thought. "And now you're using me to get to him."

"That's the game plan, Little White Dove." He scowled up the road toward town. "What the devil's keeping him?"

A rumbling noise arose from the west. The bridge began to vibrate.

Steve pounded the steering wheel in frustration as a freight train rattled slowly past him. What were the odds of a train blocking the intersection at this very moment?

He stepped out of the car. The parade stretched endlessly into the darkness. Behind him, a dozen other vehicles waited to cross the tracks.

Everything he knew about Paige suggested a disturbed teenager. If she was back at the bridge, she must have reached some new emotional crisis.

He thought about making a U-turn and looking for another route. But what if the train blocked the other streets? He returned to his car and tried Paige's number again.

Far beneath the bridge, the phone rang for attention. Tankersley peered over the railing to watch the last freight car pass beneath him. "Too bad you missed your train," he said. "You could have hopped aboard and gotten away. It's a long drop to those tracks."

Paige tried to think like Tankersley. "How did you expect Dr. Wingate to bring your wife back?"

He bristled. "Don't talk to me like I'm crazy. I know she's dead. I've had six months in jail to absorb it."

"Then what's the point of all this? I think you're grieving. It's made you angry and you want to take it out on someone."

"Oh yeah? What about you tonight in that hospice place? When you snuffed out that boy's life!"

"No." Paige shook her head. "I couldn't go through with it. Death is God's territory, not mine."

"The Lord giveth and the Lord taketh away, is that it? You holy rollers are all alike. When something bad happens you chalk it up to God's will instead of doing something about it."

"Like taking revenge?"

"Exactly!"

She watched Tankersley pace back and forth, like a panther. "Tell me more about Dawn."

"Like what?"

"The things you did together."

The man paused to regard her curiously. "You know something? You're the only person who's asked." He lifted his eyes to the moon. "Dawn was the happiest person I ever knew. She was never angry or moody like me. She loved romantic movies, and children's stories, and those silly Roadrunner cartoons. When we were in the car together, she sang along with the radio. And oh, her voice!" His eyes closed in rapture. "Like an angel! She couldn't take a shower without singing, everything from Carole King to Aretha Franklin. Once she tried to get me to audition with her for an amateur musical. I was too shy. Now I wish I had."

"I used to sing soprano in the church choir," Paige said. "Before all this happened."

"Church." Tankersley sank to the road. "Gosh, I haven't been to church in years. Dawn went every Sunday after we got married, but I always stayed home."

"Why?"

"Church is just a guilt trip. A bunch of meaningless rituals."

"That's not true! I haven't been to church since last summer, because I was hiding. But God watched over me all the time. I know because I prayed to Him for help. And He answered my prayers."

Tankersley snorted. "Did you ask Him to make you walk eight hundred miles so you could end up on this bridge, right back where you started?"

"Church is a place of refuge!" Paige insisted. "It isn't just a building or a Sunday ritual. It's any place where two or more people are gathered in the name of Jesus."

"Don't think you can preach your way out of this, Little White Dove. God ripped out my heart when He took Dawn away. And He used Steve Wingate to do it."

"I see," Paige said. "You can't punish God, so you're taking it out on Dr. Wingate." Tankersley resumed pacing. "Did Dawn ever sing hymns?"

291

"Oh yeah. All the time. 'Worthy Is the Lamb.' 'Blessed Be Your Name.' Stuff like that."

"Did she pray?"

"She always said a blessing over dinner. Even in restaurants." He gave a little chuckle. "It was sort of embarrassing."

"So she was a spiritual person. What about you? Why didn't you go to church with her?"

"I already told you! Dawn understood how I felt."

"But she attended services anyway?"

"Every Sunday, rain or shine."

"How did that make you feel?"

"What do you mean?"

"You said you and Dawn made each other complete. Why do you think Dawn went to church if you were all she needed?"

Tankersley scowled. "Don't talk about her like that!"

"Was there something about you that made Dawn unhappy?"

He started to reply when headlights appeared. Tankersley rose, dashed across the bridge, and grabbed the knife. Paige struggled to her feet.

Steve parked next to a pile of junk vehicles. Despite the bright moonlight, he hardly recognized the wretched-looking girl in the middle of the bridge. He didn't recognize the man beside her at all.

He scrambled out of the car, still in his white coat.

"Fashionably late and dressed to kill," the man called cheerfully. "Come join the party, Doctor."

"Paige, what's going on? Are you all right?"

Her companion laughed. "Some diagnostician you are!

292

Can't you tell just by looking at her?"

"I'm sorry, Dr. Wingate," Paige said. "He threatened to go after your daughter unless I called you."

"Who are you?" Steve drew closer. "What have you done to her?"

"Me?" He spread his hands innocently. "I haven't done a thing. It's you who's going to do it. Tell him, Paige."

She gripped the railing for support. "This is Norris Tankersley. He's the man who tried to break into the emergency room the last time I saw you."

"Tankersley?" Steve stopped about ten feet away. "Are you—"

"The one and the same. I'm so glad you remember." He seized Paige's arm and pulled her to his chest. "We were just talking about how much my wife loved music. You're just in time to hear the final verse of Paige's swan song. Or dove song, I should say." He spoke into her ear. "Would you like to do the honors? No? Then I will."

> *Running Bear dove in the water, Little White Dove*
> *did the same*
> *And they swam out to each other through the*
> *swirling stream they came*
> *As their hands touched and their lips met, the*
> *raging river pulled them down*
> *Now they'll always be together in their happy*
> *hunting ground*

"Unfortunately, we don't have a river to drown you in. But a long drop to the railroad tracks should do the trick. And the tragic lovers' ending will be just as convincing." He held the knife to Paige's throat. "You're late, Doctor. What took you so long?"

"I had an emergency just as I was leaving. Then I got blocked at a railroad intersection."

"And how is the patient?"

"She's stable."

"No thanks to you, I'll bet. Have you killed anybody else lately?"

"Leave him alone!" Paige cried. "It wasn't his fault!"

"Is that what he told you? What did he do, blame it on a nurse?"

"He's right, Paige," Steve said. "Mr. Tankersley lost his wife and child because I ordered the wrong blood type."

"At least he's honest about it."

Steve continued. "The day she went into labor, there was an explosion at a chemical plant outside Houston. Twenty-eight patients with severe burns. All of them hit the ER at the same time. We called in every available doctor to help, but in the confusion, Mrs. Tankersley's chart got mixed up with another one. Still, it was my fault. I should have verified the name on the chart."

Paige asked, "Is that why your wife left you?"

"In a way. When the hospital board grounded me, she thought my career was finished." He turned his attention to Paige's captor. "Let her go. This is between you and me."

Tankersley shook his head regretfully. "That would ruin the ending. Running Bear and Little White Dove are going to take a lovers' leap."

"You want us to jump off the bridge? Why? Paige had nothing to do with your wife's death."

"But she had everything to do with that wave of suicides. Isn't that right, Paige?"

"Yes," she admitted.

"That's why she came to this very spot last fall, Doctor. To take responsibility for them. And you still think you ought to be punished, don't you, Paige?"

"Yes," she choked. "Yes, I do."

"Only, you met Dr. Wingate at the hospital. The two of you fell in love. Still, the weight of his guilt and yours was too much. So you came to this bridge together, to end it all." Tankersley raised his eyebrows. "Well, Running Bear? She's waiting."

"This isn't some melodrama!" Steve shouted. "Nobody will believe it."

"Sure they will. The hospital has records of your interactions with Paige. Her last phone call went to you. It's a no-brainer."

"And what do you get out of it? Revenge?"

Tankersley fixed him with a righteous glare. "Justice, Doctor. Justice, and the knowledge that you'll never be able to kill another patient." He beckoned with the knife. "Get yourself over here, Running Bear. Take her hand and climb up on the rail."

"No."

"Do it, or I'll throw her over myself!"

Steve lunged at him. Tankersley kicked out, striking the doctor's chest and knocking him across the road. "All right. We'll do it one at a time. Come on, Little White Dove. Since you're so anxious to atone for your sins, I'll give you a boost."

Wingate lay gasping on the pavement.

"Why did Dawn go to church without you?" Paige cried as Tankersley dragged her toward the railing.

"What?"

"You said you made each other complete. If that's true, why did she go to church when you wouldn't?"

"Shut up! It doesn't make any difference."

"It makes all the difference! People go to church for one of two reasons. They think they have to, or they really want to. Which one was Dawn's?"

Tankersley hesitated. "She wanted to."

"Why?"

"She said praying brought her closer to God."

"But you told me you and Dawn made each other complete. If that's true, why did she need God?"

Wingate struggled to his feet as Tankersley focused on Paige. "What are you getting at?"

"She needed Him, didn't she? Dawn felt incomplete without God."

Something began to awaken in Tankersley's eyes.

"Why wouldn't you go to church with her?" Paige demanded. "What did you think about every Sunday morning when Dawn was away worshipping God, while you stayed home by yourself?"

His face contorted. "I was jealous."

"Why?"

"I didn't want her to need anyone but me."

"But she did need you. Isn't that what you said?"

"Yes! She told me so a thousand times." Tears filled his eyes.

"Look at yourself! You've shut God out of your life and put hate in His place. Will that—that . . ." The words stuck in Paige's throat. Her eyes gaped, her mouth widened, and she went limp in Tankersley's arms. "What's the matter?" He backed away, letting her sink to the pavement. Her body began to shake.

"It's a seizure!" Wingate rushed forward and knelt beside her. "Give me your shoes."

"What for?"

"Hurry!"

Tankersley slipped them off as Wingate stretched Paige out on her back. He made a pillow of the shoes as her head slammed against them. "What's the matter with her?"

"Brain trauma. Give her some room."

Tankersley gaped as Paige's body jerked violently. Her eyes squeezed shut; her teeth clenched. Gagging noises emerged from her throat.

"Isn't there anything you can do?" Tankersley cried. "Give her a shot or something?"

"No. It has to run its course."

Paige's feet kicked at the air. Her elbows hammered the asphalt. Steve removed his coat and tucked it under her left arm. He put his shirt under the right arm.

Tankersley paced back and forth. "I can't stand this! Do something!"

"She doesn't feel anything. All we can do is wait." He glared up at Tankersley. "You still want to kill her?"

The men waited as the girl bucked and heaved. After a couple of minutes, the attack subsided. Paige's body began to relax. She gasped for air. Gradually, her respiration returned to normal.

"She'll be all right now." Steve raised her to a sitting position. "Paige, wake up." He patted her face. "Wake up."

She opened her eyes. "What happened?"

"You blacked out. Relax. Just sit quietly for a minute."

She put a hand to her head. "I feel weird."

"Perfectly natural. It'll pass."

"Did I have another seizure? Dr. Ursi was right." Resting against Steve's shoulder, she looked up at Tankersley, standing anxiously at her feet. "What happened? Why didn't you throw me over the railing?"

He swallowed. "I don't know."

"Come here," she beckoned softly. He knelt at her side. "So you wouldn't go to church with Dawn because you were jealous of God. Is that it?" Tankersley hung his head. "Dawn did need you, to make her life complete. But she needed God to make her soul complete. Why do you suppose she never complained when you wouldn't attend church with her?"

"I guess . . ." He struggled for words. "I guess she wanted me to decide for myself."

"And she died before you made that decision."

Tears glistened in his eyes. "It was the one thing I wouldn't do for her." His voice broke. "So you think God took her away to punish me?"

Paige spoke gently. "Some people are more spiritual than others. Closer to God. From what you've told me, I think Dawn walked with God, like Enoch in the Bible. God took her into His keeping because she *was* a complete person. Dawn wanted you to be complete too."

Tankersley began to sob.

She lifted his chin to face her. "You aren't the only person who's lost someone. Dr. Wingate lost his own wife. He lost his standing in the medical profession. All he has left are his children. What will they have if you take him away? What will you have if you put murder between yourself and God?" Paige took his face in her hands. "Dawn would never allow you to do that." She held the man as he wept on her shoulder.

"You can still have a life, you know," Wingate said as they walked to the cars. "All you did at the ER was scare a few people. You haven't really hurt anyone."

Tankersley looked at him in wonder. "You won't

press charges?"

"Haven't we all got enough trouble?"

The three stopped at the end of the bridge and faced each other.

"Did Dawn say anything before . . . before she died?"

"She never regained consciousness," Steve said. "I'm sorry." Tankersley slumped against the railing. "I went looking for you after the emergency was over, but you'd already left the hospital."

"It's just as well. I wasn't in my right mind." Tankersley noticed the knife in his hand. He hurled it into the tumbleweeds.

"Mr. Tankersley," Paige asked, "how did you know I'd be at the hospice tonight?"

"While I was in jail, I posted a reward on People Tracer for anyone who could tell me where you were. Evans, the guard at Thornhurst, told me you were supposed to show up sometime between seven and eight o'clock. So I hung around every night until you did."

"How did you come up with the reward money?"

He smirked. "I didn't. I emailed him a voucher for a hundred thousand Iranian rials. That comes out to $2.36. I wish I could have seen his face."

"What about that gunman who traced me to the homeless shelter? How did you pay him?"

"I had nothing to do with that." He opened his car door.

"What will you do now?"

"Go back to Houston, I guess. Try to get back my job at the airport."

"I mean your personal life."

Norris looked at his feet. "Before I lost Dawn and the baby, I had all these plans for fatherhood. One was coaching my children in Little League. I don't know. Maybe I'll look into coaching other people's kids."

"You could always get married again."

"I can't imagine finding another woman like Dawn." He hesitated, then offered his hand to Steve. Embracing Paige, he said, "so long, Little White Dove. You're quite a girl."

Paige bade a silent farewell to the Bustamante Bridge as it receded in the rear window. "I'm sorry, Dr. Wingate. Every time you turn around, you're rescuing me from something."

"You want to tell me how you got into this mess?"

"Later, do you mind? I'm too tired." She curled up on the passenger seat.

"I never thought I'd hear myself say this, but those seizures of yours came in handy."

"How long was I out?"

"A few minutes. That was a bad one. How do you feel?"

"Sick. Sick of myself." She raised her head. "I'm sorry about what happened to Mrs. Tankersley. And your wife. She should have been more supportive."

"There was more to it." He drove quietly for a moment. "Janice was in love with the idea of being a doctor's wife. She had all this ambition about the two of us hobnobbing with important people, and chairing fundraising balls. But Paige, I never wanted to be an administrator. I've seen what hospital politics can do to a doctor. The machinery takes over, and you forget what you were put on this Earth for. Besides, we had enough money to live comfortably until my license to practice was suspended. Then we had to live on our savings. Janice was mortified. She couldn't see a light at the end of it. Eventually, she got involved with a colleague of mine." He was silent for a while. "It was hardest on the kids. Kathy was only twelve at the time. Sean was sixteen. I tried my best to protect them from the fallout, but they still have scars. How do you tell your friends you're moving away because your dad got fired? How are you supposed to feel when your parents break up?"

"Do you still love Janice?"

He considered. "I love the person she was when I married her."

Paige's vision grew hazy. Whether from fatigue or the seizure, she didn't know. "Well," she sighed, "it seems you've become a specialist after all. You've made a career of rescuing me."

"Tonight, you did the rescuing. That was quite a speech. How did you know the right thing to say?"

"I didn't. It just came to me. Like the idea for my website."

"Weren't you afraid?"

She shook her head. "He wouldn't have done it."

"What makes you so sure?"

"There was too much love in him."

They drove on. The streets were quiet, the traffic light.

"I feel terrible about Mrs. Tankersley," Steve confessed. "Ever since I got fired, I've tried not to think about her. When you make a mistake like I did, you start doubting yourself. Then you're no good to your patients."

"Is she the only patient you've lost?"

"No. Just the only one whose death was my fault."

"It wasn't," she insisted. "It's just something that happened."

"So was your website, Paige." They were silent for a moment. "Are you ready to go home now?"

Her nose wrinkled. "Like this? Ugh! You'll have to have this car fumigated. How about taking me to the homeless shelter?" He frowned. "What's the matter?"

Steve pulled over to the curb. "Paige, if Tankersley didn't post the reward that led to the Open Door shooting, who did?"

"I have no idea."

Producing his phone, he typed "Paige Abernathy reward" in the search window. "See? It's still out there, on Vindicator Chat."

"You're afraid somebody else wants to kill me?" She curled up again. "Then let them. I'm too tired to care."

"Well, I care. A lot of people care. Your parents sure do."

"How would you know?"

He laughed ruefully. "Your mother gave me quite a going-over after you disappeared. I'd hate to be on the wrong side of her in a courtroom."

Paige sighed. "I'm sorry."

"Don't be. I can see where you get your strength." Steve put the car in gear. "Tonight you're coming home with me," he said firmly. "My son's room is empty. You'll get cleaned up, have something to eat, and sleep all you want. Tomorrow, you can meet my daughter."

Guest Quarters

The next morning Kathy Wingate peeked into Sean's room, expecting to see a girl. What she saw was a woman.

"Let her sleep, honey," her father whispered. "You can meet her this evening after school."

It was past one o'clock when Paige awoke to chattering noises. Outside the window, a pair of goldfinches fluttered around a birdfeeder. A mockingbird sang in the tree branches above them. On the ground, doves and sparrows scrounged for lunch among the grass blades. The sun was high, but the breeze from Sean's window was mild. It was mid-May, almost graduation time.

On the walls, a scattering of thumbtack holes attested to the musician posters and movie heroes of Sean's youth. A framed picture on the bureau showed Steve Wingate posing with a slender woman, a skinny teenage boy, and a plump little girl with braces on her teeth. Otherwise, the room was empty.

Paige rose from the bed wearing the soccer jersey and

warm-up pants she'd found in Sean's closet. They hung off her like laundry. In the bathroom she showered again and spent several frustrating minutes trying to untangle her hair. Sun-bleached, it ran down past her shoulder blades. The gaunt red face in the mirror was only vaguely familiar.

Dressed, she limped down the stairs in her bare feet. On the sofa, Steve Wingate looked up from a medical journal. Paige crossed the room, fell into his arms, and poured out her sorrow.

"It's amazing," he remarked, removing the blood pressure cuff from her arm. "Your vital signs are normal. Your heartbeat's strong, your lungs sound clear. Obviously, you're weak from hunger and exposure, but a little pampering should take care of that." He returned his equipment to his bag. "I'm still concerned about those seizures. I'm not qualified to write prescriptions for neurological disorders. The sooner you see Dr. Ursi, the better. How's your knee?"

"Pretty sore."

He went to the refrigerator and filled a plastic bag with ice cubes. "This should help reduce the swelling. You really ought to get an X-ray to make sure nothing's broken." He secured the bag to her knee with an elastic bandage.

"It's been weeks since I was in a house." Paige sat at the kitchen table. Sunlight streamed through the window. The room was smaller than Naomi's, but clean and cheerful. "Don't you have to be at the hospital?"

"I have today off, then three days of twelve-hour shifts. Today I'm all yours and Kathy's."

"I don't want to impose."

"You're not. In fact, I'd like you to spend some time with Kathy, if you don't mind. Her mother hasn't come around much recently."

"Are you sure you want her to meet a basket case like me?"

"You're no such thing. You proved that on the bridge last night." Steve checked his watch. "It's past lunchtime. Are you hungry? We'll have to go to a restaurant. I'm not a very good cook."

"Then you're in luck," Paige smiled. "I'm an expert." She rose and limped about the room, searching through cabinets.

"Kathy makes supper for us both when she's not hanging out with her girlfriends or torturing her boyfriend. Which means I mostly eat takeout."

In the pantry Paige found canned soup, rice, pasta, and some white bread. The freezer contained a whole chicken and a box of Dilly Bars. *This is worse than the homeless shelter*, she thought. She ran some water in the sink to thaw the chicken.

"Paige, about that Running Bear song. Did you mean what you said last night on the phone? About jumping?"

"Mr. Tankersley made me say that."

"But would you have done it?"

She turned to face him. "I don't know. There was a moment when I almost did. And if he hadn't stopped me, I . . . I honestly don't know."

"Are you ready to talk now?"

Paige returned to her chair and began the story of her journey.

Kathy Wingate was taller than the preteen in Sean's family picture, and she'd lost the puppy fat of her adolescence. She had her mother's dark hair and deep brown eyes. Her braces were gone, revealing bright, even teeth.

"Do you really work in a gourmet kitchen?" she asked as Paige deboned the chicken.

"I used to help my father at Chez Renée. He taught me everything I know."

"Have you ever created a new recipe by yourself?"

She laughed. "Dad says my first recipe was lime Jell-O with crayons. I was three years old. Is there any butter in the refrigerator?"

Kathy fetched it. Her eyes followed Paige's hands as she combined the chicken with rice and dried herbs. "How can you tell how much of everything to put in without measuring?"

"It just takes a little practice. You'll be able to do it in no time. Why don't you make us a salad with those greens in the fridge?"

Kathy fetched a large bowl and began shredding lettuce. "I heard about your website. I'm sorry for what happened."

"So am I." She changed the subject. "Tell me about your boyfriend."

"Scott? He's okay." Furtively, Kathy looked around for her father. He was in the backyard, refilling the bird feeders. "Scott wants us to go to a pot party at Artie Jefferson's house next Friday," she whispered. "His parents will be out of town. I've never been to one. Have you?"

"Once," Paige answered. "It was a mistake."

"Why?"

"The boy I was dating said it would help me loosen up. So I went along with it. The next thing I knew, we were in his parents' bedroom. He was just trying to take advantage of me."

"Oh." Kathy's face fell. "Do you have a boyfriend now?"

"I'm not sure anymore." Kathy seemed troubled. "What's the matter?"

"Paige . . . Is there something between you and my dad?"

She was startled. "No! No, nothing. He's . . . Your father helped me through a very rough time."

"I don't mean to be nosy. I just don't want him to be hurt again."

"Neither do I."

After supper Steve suggested a game of dominoes. "Kathy and I play a lot."

"I don't know how," Paige said. "I've never played anything but video games."

"We'll teach you," Kathy grinned. "Dad's been looking for someone he can beat."

"I am not! You don't always win."

"Two out of ten is not a winning record, Dad."

They played for an hour. Paige managed to win one game before she began to tire. "I'm sorry. I can't tell a deuce from a double-six. Do you mind?"

"That's okay," Kathy said. "I've got homework anyway." She boxed up the dominoes. "Will you still be here tomorrow?"

"I don't know."

"Maybe we could go to the store after school. You could teach me some new recipes."

"Maybe so. Goodnight."

Kathy kissed her father and went upstairs.

"She's a nice girl," Paige said.

"I'm proud of her." He turned a professional eye on Paige.

"I think you could use another eight hours of sleep."

"Me too," she said. "But not here." She rose from the table. "Would you mind driving me home?"

PART FOUR:

Home

Reunions

The windows were dark and the doors locked, but Paige still remembered the garage door code. She waved goodbye to Steve as he backed out of the driveway. The house was silent. Mom and Dad must still be at work.

She groped her way to the living room and turned on the floor lamp. A warm sensation of home swept through her: plush furniture, maroon draperies, thick gray carpet, the long sofa with fluffy pillows, the coffee table with a small dent where Kyle had struck it with the vacuum cleaner. Lying on top, the pebble mosaic that Paige had made in her eighth grade art class. Family photos on the walls and tabletops offered a range of memories, from a studio shot of Kyle and Lydia with their infant daughter, to a Christmas morning with her grandparents when she was six.

The sofa looked inviting, but Paige wanted to be awake when they arrived. She settled into her father's orthopedic chair and waited.

That was where Lydia found her sleeping an hour later. At first she thought the creature was a corpse, a white-haired skeleton in oversized clothes. When she looked closer, her knees buckled. It was the sobs that woke Paige.

"Hi Mom," she said sleepily. "I'm home."

Lydia was on the phone the next morning when Paige came into the kitchen.

"Need any help?" she asked her father.

Kyle turned away from the stove and clutched his daughter to his chest until the eggs began to scorch. "Burnt omelet," he said, wiping a tear. "That's a first for me." He scraped the mess into the trash and started over.

"Zach, I know it's short notice," Lydia was saying, "but you've sat through dozens of jury selections, and I know you can handle this one by yourself. Call me at the first recess and tell me how it's going." She hung up and seized Paige fiercely. "I may never let you out of my sight again."

"Please, Mom," she said, wincing. "My sunburn." It was nine o'clock; early, considering that the three of them had talked past 2 a.m. "Did either of you get any sleep?"

"Not much," Kyle admitted. "But I don't mind. When was the last time we all had breakfast together?"

Lydia ran her hands through Paige's hair and stroked her face. "You're so thin and washed-out! Are you sure you don't want to see Dr. Kelly?"

"Dr. Wingate checked me over. He says I'm fine." She was more concerned about her parents. They looked so much older, their faces careworn.

She took a seat at the breakfast table while her father fussed over the omelet.

"Is your knee any better this morning?"

"The swelling's gone down some. I'll put some more ice

on it later."

Lydia paced the floor. "I don't know what to do with myself!" She laughed. "Paige, are you sure about that man on the bridge? I can have the police put out an alert for him."

"He won't be back."

"To think of all the dangers you've been through! Why couldn't you at least call and let us know you were all right?"

"I had to do this my way." Silence followed.

"Well," Lydia said briskly, "the first thing you're going to do is see that neurologist. I can't believe you've been wandering all over Texas with a head injury! For all we know, you've got a tumor or something."

Kyle brought the omelet to the table and divided it three ways. "Let's offer God a prayer of thanks. We'll never have a moment like this again." They held hands and bowed their heads.

"I almost forgot," Lydia said when he finished. She drew Paige's cell phone from her pocket. "Maybe you'd like to call Lucas." Her tone sounded like an apology.

"Later, Mom. I don't want him to see me looking like this." She dug into her omelet. "What's happening at the restaurant, Dad? How are Marcel and the rest of the gang?" Her parents exchanged glances. "What's the matter?"

"I'm not at Chez Renée anymore."

Paige's fork froze in midair. "What?"

"Charles let me go."

She gasped. "I don't believe it! Why?"

"It's . . . complicated. We can discuss it later."

"No! Tell me now!" Kyle focused on his plate. "It's me, isn't it? You lost your job because of me!" She covered her face.

"Now Paige, don't do that!" He drew his chair toward her. "Yes, the website had something to do with it, but that's not the whole story."

"Oh God, is this ever going to end? Everything I touch gets ruined!"

"Paige! Paige, listen to me!" He gripped her hands. "Three weeks ago, Charles called to offer me my job back. The restaurant was losing customers, and not just the locals. The celebrity set, the international trade, it all started dropping off after I left. Even I didn't realize how much the restaurant's reputation had come to depend on me personally."

"Of course it did! You're the best chef in the whole world."

He laughed. "Honey, the restaurant business is like the stock market. One little ripple is all it takes to send it plunging to the bottom. When a master chef leaves a high-class restaurant, it's like a case of food poisoning. Word gets around, and suddenly there's a perception that something's wrong. But nothing's really changed. Marcel and the other chefs know everything I know about cooking."

"Then why didn't you accept Mr. Duprée's offer?"

Her father grinned. "I got a better one."

Lydia's phone rang. *Back to the world of litigation*, Paige thought. But Mom handed her the phone with a smile. "It's for you."

"What happened to my web artist?" a familiar voice cried.

"Omer! How are you?"

"How do you think? One minute I'm working with my young friend, the next she's racing off on some wild adventure. Paige, are you all right?"

"I'm fine, Omer. I've missed you."

"So what are you waiting for? Come on over."

Lydia didn't want her to go. "You just got home! You need rest and care. What about your knee? What if you have another seizure?"

"It's just for a little while, Mom. I owe them an explanation."

Lydia let her off in the Goldmanns' driveway. "Promise me you'll be home in an hour. I'll be counting the minutes."

Naomi was so shocked at Paige's appearance that she dragged her to the kitchen and began pulling food out of the refrigerator.

"Don't bother, I just had breakfast with my parents."

"You poor thing! We were so worried!"

Omer said, "There's one thing you absolutely must do." He placed a pill on the table. "Your medication. These things have been showing up on our doorstep every other week, like orphans."

"Who's sending them?"

He shrugged. "I guess whoever it is doesn't know you've been gone. It's very strange. Each bottle has a different doctor's name on it."

Paige washed it down with water. Omer and Naomi waited anxiously, as if she might grow another head.

"I'm sorry I left you the way I did. When I heard the news about Louise, I sort of went crazy."

"That night!" Naomi exclaimed. "Omer and I drove around for hours, looking for you. 'Where else could she go but the shelter,' we wondered. Then when nobody could find you, we feared the worst."

"Then your mother called this morning and said, 'My daughter's back home, she's safe!'" Omer added. "Oh Paige, I can't believe you walked all the way to that prison!"

"Walked and hitched. Some very nice people helped me along the way."

"Samaritans! Didn't I tell you? They're everywhere!"

"But Omer, it was all for nothing." She told them about her visit with Jerome Faulkner. "He was so sad, and his son is still lying in that hospice, waiting to die." Paige's voice trembled. "I broke my promise."

"He had no right to ask such a thing of you."

"Yes, he did. But that's not all." They listened in horror as she recounted the drama on the bridge.

"So all this fuss about parents getting revenge for their kids was a hoax?" Naomi asked.

"Apparently not. There's another reward floating around the internet. That means I'm still a danger to you and my parents."

"Let's not worry about that now." Omer's eyes twinkled. "Paige, I have good news and bad news."

"Uh-oh."

"The bad news is that I had to hire a new website artist."

Paige sighed. "I'm sorry. I can't say I blame you."

"I wish I could have waited, but you were gone so long, the orders started piling up. I had to do something."

"I understand, Omer."

"The good news is that I found an excellent replacement. Would you like to meet him?"

She followed Omer to his office. Mr. Chen sat at her old workstation.

"It has been a difficult year," Mr. Chen acknowledged in his dignified manner. They were alone in the office, Omer giving them a chance to catch up. "After the schoolboard dismissed me, I could not find a teaching position. None of the school districts in this area had an opening for my specialty. Before Mr. Goldmann approached me, I was substituting for other teachers here and there."

"Mr. Chen, this is all my fault," Paige began.

"No," he said firmly. "It is the way of the world. Even when one follows the path of good works, there are always others waiting for you to stumble. What I'm trying to say is, you have a good heart, Paige."

"You're being so nice about it. How did you and Omer get together?"

"Ah! That is quite a story." He offered her a chair. "Several weeks ago, I received a phone call from your mother. She wanted to know if I had any knowledge of your whereabouts. I replied that I did not. She then proceeded to ask me questions about your website. I assured her that you had taken every precaution to prevent tampering. Unfortunately the people you were trying to help were beyond your capabilities." He sighed. "Perhaps I should have foreseen the problems that arose. There is so much darkness on the internet. Be that as it may, your mother and I had a pleasant discussion about you. I told her you displayed great potential as a web artist, as well as integrity, which is rare in cyberspace. Eventually she told me about meeting Mr. Goldmann and learning that you had worked for him during the winter. Mrs. Abernathy expressed remorse at participating in my dismissal. The next day Mr. Goldmann phoned me. That is how I came to be your replacement. Would you like to see some of my work?"

Paige spent the next ten minutes scrolling through it. A truck rental business wanted a family-friendly look. Mr. Chen's design was a bright cartoon of parents and children parading across the company logo into their new home. For a mail-order fruit vendor, a flock of birds burst forth from an orchard towing cornucopias of oranges, apples, peaches, and cherries. The scene had a pleasant oriental touch.

"I have your mother to thank for this job," Mr. Chen said. "Without her, I might never have found another position. It is difficult for Asian people to find lucrative employment in the present social climate." He smiled broadly. "So you see, Paige, everything resolved satisfactorily."

Paige tried picturing her mother as a benefactor. It didn't fit. "Where are you living now?"

"With the Goldmanns. In the room you were using."

"What happened to your own home?"

"It was only a rental. I am quite happy here. 'Better the cottage where one is merry than the palace where one weeps.'" He winked. "A Chinese proverb."

"Do you think you'll ever go back to teaching?"

"Perhaps. If I do, I will be a better teacher for what I am learning now in the world of business."

Paige had one more question. "Mr. Chen, I've always wondered. What's your first name?"

"My given name is Yong. It means brave. But I think that applies more to you than to me."

Lydia was on the phone but hung up when Naomi brought Paige home. "How did it go?"

"Fine. It was nice to see them again. Where's Dad?"

"Running an errand. Come sit down. I'd like to talk to you."

They took their places on the sofa. "Mom, that was nice of you, hooking up Mr. Chen with Omer."

"It was the least I could do." Lydia faced her resolutely.

"Paige, since you've been gone, I've thought a lot about our relationship. All the things you told us last night—the amnesia, your time at the homeless shelter, traveling hundreds of miles to see Mr. Faulkner—they all made me realize what a special person you are. And how little I understood about my own daughter. That makes me ashamed." Lydia drew a deep breath. "Paige, I know the website wasn't your only reason for running away. It was mostly me, wasn't it?"

Paige looked at the floor.

"Honey . . . The night you disappeared, did you go to that bridge to kill yourself?"

"Everybody's been asking me that. It's a question I've asked myself." She struggled for words. "I think I was looking for peace."

"Dr. Wingate said you were dressed in the clothes you wore to your Sweet Sixteen party."

"Yes. The dress got ruined. I don't know what happened to the tiara. I'm sorry, Mom. I know how expensive—"

"No, no, that's not important. I just want to know why you were dressed that way."

Paige's throat tightened. "You really want to know the truth?"

"Yes."

"That party was the last time I could remember being happy."

"Oh Paige!" Lydia wrung her hands.

"Lucas was unhappy. You and Dad were unhappy. The people on my website were unhappy. So unhappy they wanted to die. They wouldn't talk about anything else. I didn't know how to get out of it."

"No wonder you ran away. You were only seventeen. I should have stood by you."

"But Mom, I know better now. I learned so much

from my homeless friends, and the Goldmanns, and even from Mr. Tankersley. It's easy to lose hope when things are going wrong."

Lydia shuddered. "Tankersley! I told those detectives to keep an eye on him. It's God's miracle he didn't kill you. Just wait till I—"

"No, Mom! Please. The poor man has suffered enough."

"Well . . . you know how I hate loose ends." From the coffee table, she picked up an old photograph. "Do you remember that Christmas when you were little, and you wanted Santa to bring you a baby brother?"

"No!" She laughed. "How old was I?"

"About four. Your father and I talked about it. We always meant to have more children, but the time never seemed right. Maybe things would have been better between us if you'd had a brother or sister."

"I don't know," Paige said. "Jerome Faulkner's son was an only child too. Look what happened to him."

"My point exactly! Would you have been happier if I'd been a stay-at-home mom?"

"Would you?"

"No," Lydia admitted wryly. She replaced the photograph. "I guess there's no such thing as a model family. Still, I'm sorry if I put too much pressure on you. Maybe I should have concentrated more on being a mother and less on my career."

"Mom, you were meant to be a lawyer. You're good at it."

"But you're happier with your father, aren't you?"

"I'm just happy to be home." Paige lay down and placed her head on her mother's lap.

"Are you still tired?"

"Exhausted." She was quiet for a moment. "Mom, I think I understand now why God sent me on that journey."

"Why?"

"It wasn't for Jerome Faulkner. It was for Mr. Tankersley."

Lydia muted her phone. For the next two hours, she sat quietly, sifting through the tangles in her sleeping daughter's hair.

Late that afternoon Paige and Lydia drove to the shelter. Open Door looked exactly as she remembered it. The white tile was clean, the tables and chairs orderly. The wall mural remained unfinished. With a pang she realized that it stopped where Louise had left off.

A familiar voice rose from the office. "Paige! You're back!" Andy Michener emerged and crossed the dining room to take her hands. "Gosh, I hardly recognized you." Andy looked different himself. Dressed in slacks and a colorful sports shirt, he looked ten years younger. His hair was neatly trimmed, his face clean-shaven. His eyes shone brightly.

"Andy, what's been going on here?"

"A few changes. You're lookin' at the new manager of Open Door! Soon to become the Louise Hargrove Memorial Shelter."

"You're the manager now? What happened to Karen?"

"Retired. One of them mental patients came in here a while back and scared the wits out of her. We finally got him calmed down, but for Karen that was the last straw. So now I'm in charge."

"I thought you'd never done anything but tiling."

He grinned. "After you left I stayed around and took your place in the kitchen. I wasn't much good at it, but Karen liked the way I organized the work crew when we were renovatin' this place. She recommended me to replace her, and the board approved it."

"Well, congratulations." Paige surveyed the dining room. It was empty except for the new security guard, who was reglazing the front window. "Will you show me where Louise . . . Where it happened?"

Andy led her to the west wall. "We were all crammed together here in the corner when Louise walked in with this big bundle of clothes. She threw 'em in the guy's face. She saved our lives."

"And she died because of me."

"No, Paige. She was murdered by a greedy man who got twenty years for manslaughter." He waited as Paige stood mournfully over the site. "There was some blood on the floor, but I regrouted it. The board of directors paid for the funeral. She's buried in the city cemetery."

Paige swallowed her grief. "So who's doing the cooking now? Something sure smells good."

"Come see." He led her into the kitchen, where Kyle stood amid an array of simmering pots.

"Welcome to Chez Louise," he said with a smile. "I told you I got a better offer."

At suppertime the dining room filled up with strangers. Andy pointed out a man with an artificial leg and a US Army cap. "That's José Castillo. He lost the leg in Afghanistan. Mike's tryin' to find him a job on one of his work crews. The lady across from him is Millie Rogers. She won't talk about it, but I think her daughter dumped her here and went to live somewhere else. Like Karen said, everybody's got a story."

Later, Paige and Lydia helped Andy and Kyle with the

dishes. "Dad, how can they afford to pay you? I worked here just for a place to sleep."

"I volunteered. Sitting around the house was driving me nuts. You're something of a legend around here, did you know that?"

She laughed. "I can't believe it! You just waltzed in here and took my old job."

"And just in time," Andy added. "I wasn't good for nothin' but choppin' garlic."

"What happened to Zelda and Dee-Man?"

"Zelda went to live with her son's family in Seattle. Dee-Man's gonna be in a new TV comedy series next fall."

"Well, I hope they don't let him write his own lines. Dad, this is nice of you, but what about the money?"

"We're managing all right so far."

In the dining room, several people were playing cards or watching the new TV provided by an anonymous donor.

"I miss the restaurant," Paige said wistfully. "That big kitchen, all the great smells mingling at dinnertime. Marcel, Jeannine, and the gang. Is everybody still there?"

"I hope so," Kyle said. "A successful restaurant comes down to the people who make it happen. Just like anything else."

"I hope Mr. Duprée appreciates what he's lost."

Kyle beamed at her. "Right now, I'm having too much fun to care. Can you believe none of these people have ever tasted vichyssoise?"

Old Business

Paige spent the night and the following morning with ice on her knee. Lydia kept phoning from work to check on her.

"I'm okay, Mom. Just lying here catching up on the schoolwork I missed." Among her reading assignments was *Ghost Soldiers* by Hampton Sides, an account of men who survived the Bataan Death March. Paige found it riveting. The story made her own journey seem trivial.

That afternoon she kept her promise to Kathy Wingate. Kyle loaned her his credit card and dropped her off on his way to the shelter. The girls sat at the kitchen table, preparing a grocery list.

"What does your father like to eat?"

"Anything I put in front of him. At least, he never complains. I think he's afraid of hurting my feelings."

They walked four blocks to the supermarket, where Paige's imagination went to work. She selected trout, fresh vegetables, brown rice, olive oil, and as many fresh herbs as she could find. "I wish the stores in this town had truffles," she complained, settling for mushrooms. "My dad always had to import them." She added a bottle of white wine and some cooking sherry to their purchases. Paige felt a little sad when the checkout clerk didn't ask for her ID. Apparently the journey had aged her.

"You're a natural-born chef," she assured Kathy, who labored over the cutting board. "He's going to love this."

"I'll just be glad if he gets home on time. Dad never leaves the ER unless he's sure the overnight staff has everything under control." Kathy was curious about SerenityShare but feared that talking about it might upset Paige. So she talked around it. "I have some online friends who want to meet me in person. Do you think cyberdating is a good idea?"

"I've never tried it. Don't you like the boys at your school?"

"They're okay. But there's a lot of interesting guys on Snapchat."

"The best advice I can give you," Paige said, "is to be skeptical about everything on social media."

Dr. Wingate returned to a house of delicious smells and a dining room lit with candles. "Does this mean we're not having peanut butter sandwiches?"

The girls seated him at the head of the table and served fresh mushroom soup, trout almondine with rice, baked asparagus, and roasted brussels sprouts. For dessert, a raspberry tart.

"You've spoiled me!" he exclaimed, patting his stomach. "I'll never settle for cheese and crackers again!"

Paige promised to return on Saturday and show Kathy how to make coq au vin.

Paige's knee injury turned out to be a bone bruise. With a few more days of ice and rest, it was back to normal. Dr. Ursi ran a new set of neurology tests.

"The occipital swelling's gone down as I expected, but that abnormal wave pattern is still there. You seem to be doing fine with Keppra, so we'll keep you on that for now. I want to see you again in three months. In the meantime, call if you experience any new symptoms."

Rest and good food gradually restored Paige's health. Her sunburned skin peeled and healed. Lydia took her to a beautician who trimmed and recolored her hair to its original tone.

"You look awesome!" Kathy exclaimed at their next cooking session.

A couple of weeks after her return, Paige phoned Lucas. He sounded surprised and suggested they go for a drive.

"I sure have missed you," he said as she climbed into the Mustang. "I was afraid I'd never see you again."

"Me too."

He leaned over to kiss her. "You look different."

"So do you. What did you do to your hair?"

"Oh." He ran his hand through it. "It's a pompadour. A lot of guys are doing those now. Do you like it?"

"Sure, it's fine." Paige suppressed a smile. He looked like an Elvis impersonator.

Lucas backed out of the driveway and headed downtown. "I guess you know everybody's been looking for you. Where were you all this time?"

"I'd rather not talk about it now. Do you mind?"

"No, that's okay." A silence fell over them. Paige was surprised to find herself with nothing to say. She focused on the passing scenery.

"Paige, I'm sorry about that thing last fall when you were in the hospital. My dad threatened to cut me off without a penny if I ever saw you again."

"I understand."

"I couldn't just run away with you. What would we do for money?"

"Does he know you're with me now?"

"What he doesn't know won't hurt him."

The conversation faltered. "How's everybody at school?" Paige asked.

"Okay, I guess."

"Did you go on the senior trip to Padre Island?"

"Nah."

"Why not?"

"Didn't feel like it."

Paige was surprised. Lucas rarely missed a chance to party. "You must be excited about graduating next week. I wish I could be with you. Are you still going to UT Austin in the fall?"

"I, uh, decided to wait awhile."

"Why? I thought you were pre-enrolled."

"Things have changed."

Another silence. Something felt wrong.

"Have you seen Netsy lately?" Paige asked.

"Why don't we go over to Cinemark tonight?" he said abruptly. "See that new Talia Ryder movie. Then we can hang out at the park like we used to." He smiled suggestively.

"Lucas, is something wrong?"

"No! What could be wrong?" He reached across and stroked the back of her neck. "It's nice to touch you again. You're more beautiful than ever. Womanly." His hand slithered over her body.

"Please don't do that."

"Why not?"

"I'd just rather you didn't."

Lucas relented. He drove through the arts district, past Chez Renée and all the curio shops she remembered. "I heard about your dad losing his job. It's too bad."

"Yes." Paige tried to find another topic. "How's your mom?"

"I don't see her much. She got a job doing those Mary Kay seminars. Most of the time, she's in Dallas."

"How did she get into that?"

"I guess she got tired of being a housewife." Lucas pulled the car into the Sonic across from their school. "Want a milkshake or something?"

"No. I think I'd like to go home now."

"What about the movie?"

"Maybe some other time."

He eyed her curiously. "You sure are quiet. I guess you're wrung out from everything that's happened."

"Maybe that's it." They didn't speak on the way home.

She spent the next few days helping her father at the shelter. The work kept her mind occupied, but at night she slept fitfully, reliving her days on the road, or lying awake listening for intruders.

"I think we're past all that," Kyle said as they dished up breakfast to the shelter's patrons. "The demonstrators outside our house disappeared long ago. We've had no trespassers or threatening phone calls. You should stop worrying."

"I'm not worried for myself. It's you and Mom, and all those lawsuits. I'm sorry for causing so much trouble."

"Forget about it, honey. You didn't do anything wrong."

Paige completed the wall mural with the help of Carolyn Booker, a thirtyish graphic design artist who showed up at the shelter after losing her job to alcoholism. She seemed to find the work therapeutic. After it was finished, Carolyn became restless and confided to Andy her fears of slipping back into her old habit. He put her to work making curtains and mending donated clothing. When summer came the city hired her to teach children's art classes, the same job Louise Hargrove had hoped to fill. Eventually Carolyn earned her teaching certificate and became an art instructor at Grover Middle School.

The shelter still attracted a variety of misfits. Some of them got into the spirit of things and helped with chores—washing the windows, weeding the herb garden Kyle had planted in the backyard, cleaning the floors, and doing laundry. Others required special attention. Andy spent a lot of time dealing with alcoholics, drug addicts, and the emotionally disturbed. Some refused to seek counseling, preferring to hang around the building day and night. A few became violent, forcing Andy and the security guard to subdue them until the cops arrived. Kyle had mixed feelings about the shelter: compassion for the homeless people, horror at the thought of his daughter living in such a place. Not to mention her dangerous odyssey across Texas. Surely God had been watching over her.

A week after her date with Lucas, Paige attended church with her parents. Pastor Stewart and several of the elders greeted her warmly, but Haley Morton and Willow Douglas, girls she'd known since middle school, averted their eyes. The taint of scandal, it seemed, was still with her.

Following communion, the youth minister invited the congregation's twenty-three graduating seniors to join him on stage for a group prayer.

"I should be up there with them," Paige whispered to Lydia, who patted her daughter's hand. She searched the crowd for Jeanette Collins but didn't see her. So she phoned that afternoon. "Congratulations, Netsy! I've missed you! Can I come over for a while?"

Jeanette hesitated. "I'm sort of busy right now."

"That's okay. When's a good time?" More silence. "Netsy, is something wrong?"

"Maybe I can call you later."

"Sure. Anytime." Disturbed, Paige hung up.

A week passed, then two weeks. Paige called again but got only voicemail. "She's ghosting me!" she complained to her parents. "Do you think it's because of the website?"

"That's pretty much old news, don't you think?" Lydia said.

Paige brooded, remembering the frowning faces at church. Maybe coming home was a mistake.

One morning she drove to Jeanette's house and rang the doorbell.

"Come in, Paige!" her mother cried, embracing her. "We've missed you! Jeanette, come see who's here."

Jeanette drifted in from the hallway. "Hi, Paige," she said with a weak smile. Her mother babbled and fussed over Paige while Jeanette fumbled with her hands and stared at the floor.

"Well!" Mrs. Collins said at last. "I'll leave you girls alone so you can catch up."

They went into the living room and sat across from each other. Jeanette stared at her lap.

"Netsy, are you mad at me? I know I haven't called you in a long time, but a lot's happened in the past year." Jeanette shook her head. "Then tell me what's wrong. Is it my website? Are you sick? You look sort of pale."

A tear rolled down Jeanette's cheek and plopped onto her blouse. That was when Paige noticed that the blouse was a poor fit, much too wide at the hem.

"Oh Netsy! Are you pregnant?" The girl burst into sobs. "Who was it?"

Jeanette choked out the words. "Paige, when you left I had no one to talk to. I mean, nobody who could understand, except . . ."

Paige's eyes widened. "Lucas? It was Lucas?"

"He says the baby isn't his. He accused me . . . He called me a . . ." She wept into her hands. "I'm sorry, Paige! I'm so sorry." Paige rose to take Jeanette into her arms.

When Lucas answered the doorbell, Paige slapped him as hard as she could.

"What the . . . ?"

She slapped him again. And again, pummeling him with her fists until he was forced to cover up.

"Stop it, stop it!" He tried to seize her wrists. She kneed him in the groin. Groaning, he sank to the porch.

"How could you, Lucas?" she panted. "How could you?"

Gasping, he rose to his feet. "So Jeanette got to you, is that it? She's sore at me because I won't marry her. Paige, you know you're the only girl for me."

She shoved him against the door. "You took advantage of that poor girl just because nobody else wanted her. My mother was right about you, Lucas. You're no good."

His lips curled into a sneer. "You think you're so perfect you can pass judgment on me? What about you? You're the one with dead kids on your hands. You're the one who got your father fired from his job. You're the one who ran away, not me. I waited for you, but you disappeared! In the meantime, I needed someone. Now she's pretending it's my fault she got herself in trouble. Who knows how many guys she's been with? Why should I—"

Paige slapped him again. "Go ahead," she dared. "Hit me back. You couldn't possibly hurt me as much as you've hurt Jeanette."

331

Nursing his cheek, Lucas calculated his options. "All right. How about this? I'll find a doctor who'll get rid of it for her. Will that satisfy you?" He summoned his old charm. "Come on, Paige. You're the only girl I ever wanted. If it hadn't been for that website, none of this would have happened. You made a mistake. I made a mistake. Let's call it even. We can still have the life we planned. What do you say?" He smiled winningly.

Paige's face was a granite mask. "Don't let me keep you from your cannabis, Lucas. I can smell it all over you." She marched down the steps and out of his life.

On June 21, Paige attended the dedication of the Louise Hargrove Memorial Shelter. Oscar Wickham and the other board members were present, along with Alverna's mayor and all seven city council members. After the ribbon cutting, a flock of reporters gathered around Paige.

"My parents and friends keep trying to comfort me by calling the website an honest mistake," she told them. "I won't accept that. Suicide talk is a destructive force. I let it get out of hand, and I'll regret that the rest of my life."

"What are your plans now, Paige?" asked Lester Gerard from Channel Six.

"I want to finish high school. After that, I don't know." She declined to answer questions about her lengthy disappearance. "This is a day to honor Louise Hargrove, and to remember all the forgotten souls wandering our streets." Andy and Oscar Wickham posed for pictures with the memorial plaque mounted outside the front door. Paige wished it included a picture of Louise. She'd never thought to ask about the woman's background or her family.

The dining room was crowded. Omer and Naomi served Bundt cake and coffee to the visitors while Kyle and Paige prepared the regular evening meal.

A Black man in a natty brown suit seemed to have his eye on Paige. Each time she looked up he was standing nearby.

"Do you know that man?" she asked Omer.

"Looks sort of familiar, yes." He turned back to Andy, who was outlining plans to expand the sleeping quarters. Paige noticed a bulge in the man's coat, just below the lapel. She was wondering whether to mention it to someone when a reporter approached her.

Janet Oberlin of the *Austin American-Statesman* wanted to write a feature story about the shelter with its gourmet cook and staff of homeless volunteers. She spent several minutes interviewing Paige, Andy, and Kyle. "Do you think the Hargrove Center could become a model for shelters in other cities?"

"That's hard to say," Andy drawled. "For me, this whole thing started the night I saw this girl scrapin' up rotten linoleum with a spatula." Paige smiled and patted his shoulder. "None of it was planned. It just happened. Thanks to Paige, I found a way to move forward with my life. And that's what this shelter's about. A place for people to pull themselves together and get a fresh start."

The reporters and dignitaries gradually drifted away. But the man with the bulging pocket lingered. He wandered about the room, admiring the mural until the crowd began to thin.

Paige summoned her courage and approached him. "Sir, can I help you with something?"

He turned to face her. "I've been waiting for a chance to talk to you. I'm Arthur Garland, Alverna city council."

"Oh yes, I've seen you on TV. What—" Her heart froze

as he reached into his pocket. The bulge was a bottle of pills. "This is for you. Is there someplace we can talk privately?"

Garland arrived at Lydia's office with a lanky teenager who seemed even more nervous than his companion. They took seats across the desk from Lydia and Paige.

"I apologize for all the mystery," Garland said. "This is a delicate matter." He turned to the boy. "Stand up and speak your piece."

The young man rose, shuffling his feet. "Um . . . I wanna . . . I mean—"

"Speak up! Look her in the eye!"

He squared his shoulders. "Ms. Abernathy, I owe you an apology. What I done was—"

"Did!"

"What I did to you was wrong. I'm sorry I hurt you."

Paige frowned. "I don't understand. Who are you?"

Garland nudged the boy. "Give it to her."

With a sigh, the boy drew Paige's tiara from his pocket and placed it on the desk. "Show her your face." The boy turned to reveal four faded scratch marks on his left cheek. "This is my son, Anthony. He's the one who assaulted you on the Bustamante Bridge last September."

"It wasn't just me, it was—"

"Hush! Sit down!" Garland turned to Paige. "I represent the people of District Three, which covers the bridge and parts of the city on either side of it. As you may know, we have a problem with gang activity in that area. Unfortunately, this knucklehead decided being head of the Busta-Crips was more important than being a decent citizen and a credit to his family."

He took a deep breath. "I'm to blame as well. In addition to my council duties, I have a sensitive position at Frazier Memorial Hospital. Sensitive because of what happened on the bridge that night. Anthony's mother died two years ago. He has no one else but me, and I haven't spent as much time with him as I should have. Still," he added, glaring at the boy, "he was brought up to know better."

Paige spoke up. "It was you! The one who rescued me. You paid my hospital bills!"

He nodded. "As I said, this is a delicate matter. I was leaving town for a business meeting when Anthony stumbled into the house with blood all over his face. By the time he admitted what happened, it was getting close to my flight time. I drove out to the bridge and found you there, unconscious. I dropped you at the hospital, then hurried to the airport. My business trip was crucial. The hospital had contracted to buy some new accounting software, and I had to be in San José the next morning to meet with the vendor."

Anthony stood up. "Can I leave now?"

"You cannot, and you may not! Sit down!" The boy sank back into his chair.

Garland's tone softened. "I want you both to understand something. I wasn't trying to avoid responsibility for my son's behavior. But all the way to California, I was thinking of what would happen if anyone found out. Paige, your mother is the county prosecutor. If she'd known who attacked you, she would have landed on us with both feet. Am I correct?"

"Yes," Lydia said, "I would have."

"I was prepared to face the consequences and resign my council post. But the publicity would have compromised my authority to close this deal. The hospital badly needed this upgrade to prepare for a merger with another organization later this year. By the way," he added, looking from Lydia to Paige, "that's confidential information. You can't reveal it. Please."

"We won't," Lydia promised.

Garland continued. "I got back from San José in time to learn about Paige's head injuries. As chief of accounting, I have full access to patient information, including prescriptions. When she left the hospital without a proper discharge, I was afraid of what might happen if she didn't get her medication. Nobody knew where she was. So I did the only thing I could."

Paige gasped. "You posted a reward!"

"Misleading, but what else could I do? No one could find you, not even the police. Naturally, the posting brought all sorts of fortune hunters crawling out of the internet, telling me they'd spotted you in Marseilles, Beijing, Amsterdam, anything they could think of to claim the money. The only plausible information I received was from a drifter who saw you at Open Door. By then you were living with the Goldmanns, as I learned later. I didn't know you were still cooking for the shelter, or I'd have arranged to send your pills to Karen Wallace."

"How did you trace me to Omer's house?"

"His efforts to track me down triggered a link to my iPhone."

"Those prescription packages had us baffled," Paige said. "We couldn't figure out why Omer's pneumonia doctor would prescribe antiseizure pills."

"That was my doing. I used a different doctor's name for each refill to make it look like a clerical error. Did you take them?"

"Yes, twice a day until the night that gunman showed up."

Garland winced. "I know. It never occurred to me that my search for you might endanger anyone. That makes me responsible for Louise Hargrove's death."

"Oh!" Lydia exclaimed. "You must be the one who left a note on my windshield that night."

"I was trying to help you find your daughter without revealing myself."

"Are you aware that I tried to subpoena Paige's hospital records?"

"Yes. I asked our lawyer to fight it on grounds of confidentiality. We were right in the middle of our software upgrade. If the judge hadn't quashed it, the records would have led you directly to me. Tell me, Mrs. Abernathy. What would you have done if you'd known I was paying your daughter's bills?"

Paige had never seen the expression that appeared on her mother's face. It was remorse.

"It's a good thing I didn't. I was so frantic, I was lashing out at everybody." She turned to Anthony. "Young man, I hope you realize what a good man your father is. He could have avoided all this trouble simply by leaving my daughter on that bridge to die."

"Yes ma'am," he mumbled to the floor.

Paige came around the desk to kneel beside him. "Anthony, I don't remember much about that night. But I want you to know something. When I went to the bridge, I was so upset that I might have jumped. So in a strange way, you saved my life."

He raised his head. "I did?"

"Why don't we go down to the coffee shop? I think your dad and my mom have some legal issues to settle." The boy rose from his seat. Paige wrapped her arms around Arthur Garland's neck. "Thank you," she whispered, "my guardian angel."

"Mama woulda been ashamed of me," Anthony admitted. "She taught me to treat women with respect." He stared into his cup, unable to meet Paige's eyes.

"Then why did you attack me?"

He searched for words. "After Mama died I didn't have nobody to talk to 'cept them two guys I hung out with after school every day. They thought I was special on account of my dad bein' on the city council. They looked up to me. But we never done nothin' bad until that night on the bridge. Then seein' you there, all purtied up . . . somethin' just come over me. I'm sorry." His head sank lower. "You're awful nice, Paige. You oughta be mad at me."

"It's hard to be angry about something you don't remember. What about your two friends? Do you still hang out with them?"

He shook his head. "Jersey got arrested back in February for stealin' a car. Danny's in one of them homeboy rehab programs."

"Then I guess you're lucky. Are you still in school?"

"Yeah." He brightened. "Dad got me a tutor. Real nice lady, lives down the street from us. Pretty strict, though. She says when I get my math classes caught up, we gonna—I mean, we're going to work on my grammar." He allowed himself a grin.

They sat quietly for a moment. "Paige, why was—why were you on the bridge that night, all dressed up like that?"

"That's a long story." She drew a deep breath. "Have you ever heard of a website named SerenityShare?"

Meanwhile, Garland wilted in his son's absence. "You have no idea what a relief it was to get that off my chest."

"Mr. Garland, why did you take such a risk? You could have just left Paige on that bridge, and no one would have been the wiser."

"Have you ever felt strongly about an injustice, Mrs. Abernathy?"

"Of course! I'm in the justice business."

"Then you know what I mean. Anyone logging onto that website could see that Paige was just trying to comfort people. Yet nobody was on her side. I wanted to stand by her." He gazed sadly out the window. "Anthony and his mother were very close. Since she died I've had to juggle both my job and my city council duties. My son needed someone he could reach out to, but I was too busy. So he got mixed up with other kids who were lost themselves."

Lydia said, "Well, you needn't worry about prosecution. I've learned some important things about parenting myself. I was just wondering. How could you afford to pay Paige's medical bills? They must have been enormous."

"They were. Frankly, I'm tapped out. My medical insurance only covers Anthony and myself, so I've been paying in monthly installments. Now my savings are gone, and I've had to take a second mortgage on my house."

"But you're chief of accounting! You could have zeroed out the medical debts without anyone knowing."

"I admit that crossed my mind. But that would be stealing, and that's the kind of life I'm trying to rescue my son from."

"Maybe I could talk to my own insurance company about

sharing the burden."

"No," Garland said firmly. "I want Anthony to learn that actions have consequences, so he'll grow up to be the man I want him to be."

"That's very noble of you. But you don't have to worry about the pills anymore. Paige is on my prescription drug plan."

"Very well." He hesitated. "Mrs. Abernathy, there's one other thing you can do. Your negligence suit against the hospital is complicating the merger negotiations. Would you consider dropping it?"

"I'll do that right away."

"Thank you." He stood up. "I want you to know that Anthony's not a bad boy. Young men in groups sometimes do things they would never do by themselves."

"Older ones too," Lydia remarked.

"I grew up in the Bustamante district. When I was a boy, it was quiet and neighborly. We all knew each other. People took care of each other. They took care of their property. I hope I can stay in office long enough to bring it back to life."

"Let me know if I can do anything to help."

Kyle was amazed when Lydia recounted Arthur Garland's confession. "There's still one thing I don't understand. If there was no conspiracy to kill Paige, who was that woman who blundered into the ER the day she had that seizure?"

Lydia shrugged. "Maybe she was just what she seemed to be. Somebody looking for another patient."

Hauntings

On August 12, Conrad Faulkner went into cardiac arrest. The hospice staff, complying with his parents' wishes, made no attempt to resuscitate him.

Paige attended the funeral. Jerome Faulkner, uncuffed but accompanied by a prison escort, was present with his wife. They were the only other mourners. Conrad's school friends had forgotten him.

The Faulkners tottered into the small chapel like octogenarians. Conrad's mother was pale and thin, her black dress like a shroud.

"I'm so sorry," Paige said to them afterward. "I'd gladly have taken his place if I could." Mrs. Faulkner answered with a venomous glare. Paige turned to the father. "I meant to do it, Mr. Faulkner. I just couldn't." Nodding vacantly, he followed the guard to the prison bus, his wife leaning on his arm.

Paige was still distraught when her parents got home.

"This isn't your fault," Kyle insisted. "You can't take all the misery in the world upon yourself. Nobody can."

"I just can't help wondering how many of them would still be alive if they hadn't come together on that website."

She turned to Lydia. "Mom, is there some way I can request a pardon for Mr. Faulkner?"

"Oh honey, I think you need to put all this behind you."

"I can't! That man isn't a criminal. He wasn't himself when he attacked me."

She's as stubborn as I am, Lydia thought. "Well, you could submit a petition to the Texas Board of Pardons and Paroles. But even if they recommended clemency, the governor would have to approve it. The whole process could take years. Faulkner might get his parole before then."

"But he'd still be a convicted criminal. I want him to have a clean slate so he can get back to his life. Will you file the petition for me?"

Lydia smiled tenderly. "Of course. But to be convincing, it'll have to be in your own words."

So Paige drafted a plea recounting her prison visit with Faulkner, omitting his euthanasia request. She described him as a responsible family man overcome by grief for his son. She swore that she bore him no malice and begged the parole board to grant him a new start. Lydia filed the petition on the TBPP website. And they waited.

When Janet Oberlin's article appeared in the *Austin American-Statesman,* it got picked up by the major news outlets. But the heartwarming element got lost in the revelation that Kyle Abernathy, one of the world's foremost chefs, was now working in a homeless shelter. The resulting outrage developed into a customer boycott of Chez Renée and a *#Save Kyle* movement on social media. Monty Richards, England's most popular comedian, organized a three-day protest rally outside the restaurant. It attracted celebrities from London, Hollywood, New York, Hamburg, Vienna, Rome, and Paris. For the first time in its history, Chez Renée had to close its doors until the furor subsided. Charles phoned Kyle again, begging him to return to work. He declined, preferring to feed homeless people and edit the fourth edition of his gourmet cookbook. Kyle's publisher was thrilled. He expected the controversy to bring big sales.

Unfortunately, the boycott had the side effect of restoring Paige's name to the news headlines. Throughout August her face popped up all over social media, sparking a fresh eruption of vitriol against the author of SerenityShare. More punitive lawsuits against Paige and her parents flooded the courts. Judges routinely dismissed them. The plaintiffs had no proof that Paige's website was born of malicious intent. Nevertheless, Paige never stopped blaming herself for the suicides of people she had never known, though she lived into her eighties.

Mr. Chen thought there was a lesson for everyone in Paige's experience. "The internet is not a fount of wisdom. It is only a tool. Those who confuse the two invite disaster."

In the fall Paige returned to Alverna High School for her senior year. Lucas, she learned, had failed to graduate back in May. So had Pete and Jerry, after Coach Tierney found their stash in the equipment shed a week before the senior trip. It contained a lot more than marijuana. All three were suspended for the rest of the year.

For a while Paige felt isolated, her old friends gone to college, the younger students wary of her. Gradually their memories of the scandal faded in the excitement of the approaching commencement. By December Paige was just another student working toward her diploma.

When she wasn't studying or helping her father at the shelter, Paige devoted herself to Jeanette Collins, who still lived with her mother. Abandoned by Lucas, with little to do but wait for the birth of her child, Jeanette began working toward her CNA license, hoping to get a job at Frazier Memorial after the delivery.

"Lucas was the only boy who ever wanted me," she told Paige. "I never meant to steal him from you."

"You're better off without him." She took Jeanette shopping for maternity clothes and helped her prepare the baby's room, which had belonged to Jeanette's oldest brother. The expectant mother found new friends in Omer and Naomi, as well as Kathy Wingate and her father. As it turned out, Steve was on duty the night she went into labor. The boy weighed four pounds, seven ounces. Jeanette named him Eli, after Omer's father.

"But Jeanette!" Omer exclaimed, "you're not Jewish!"

"I don't care, I just like that name."

"Well, it's a good choice. In Hebrew, Eli means high or elevated. Like a priest."

"A good, strong name," Naomi added.

In January Frazier Memorial announced its merger with Lakota General, a health care system based in Rapid City, South Dakota. To everyone's relief, there were no layoffs, a common side effect of mergers. Steve Wingate and the other doctors were busy learning CareTotal, a new diagnostic and prescriptive software innovation that also powered the hospital's billing system. Arthur Garland, who had negotiated the purchase, was promoted to Chief Financial Officer. Paige was happy for him.

When Eli was three months old, Frazier Memorial hired Jeanette part-time with the possibility of full-time employment after six months. Paige and Kathy Wingate took turns staying with the baby while Jeanette and her mother were at work.

In the spring Paige received scholarship offers from several Texas colleges, including Texas Tech.

"I really liked the campus when I visited there, but things have changed," she told her parents. "I wouldn't have Netsy to room with. I don't know anybody in Lubbock. It would be awfully lonely."

"College isn't like high school," Lydia assured her. "You'll make new friends in no time. That's how I met your father."

So Paige accepted the offer. The university sent her brochures outlining its academic requirements. "I don't know what to major in," she fretted. "I've never been good at anything but cooking. And web design, which I don't like to think about anymore."

Steve Wingate knew a little about the medical school. "Lubbock has two big hospitals. Maybe you should think about applying when you complete your required courses. You already know more about neurology than most people your age."

"More than I want to know," she said ruefully.

When the dormitories opened late in August, Kyle and Lydia drove her to Lubbock. Horn Hall bustled with new arrivals. The freshmen and their parents, laden with cardboard boxes, collided with each other in the hallway. Lydia stowed Paige's clothes in one of the tiny closets. Her room contained bunk beds, separate desks, and bureaus for Paige and her roommate, plus a small sink beside a window facing University

Avenue. Paige couldn't help thinking that her own room back home was larger. Lydia unfolded sheets and made up the top bunk while Kyle and Paige hung the Britt Nicole poster above her desk.

As they said goodbye Lydia broke into tears. "Here's some extra spending money," she said, stuffing bills into Paige's hand. "Are you sure you've got your phone? Did you remember to bring your pills? There's a pharmacy just down the street where you can get refills. I've already arranged it with Dr. Ursi's nurse."

"Yes, Mom, I've got it all."

"Have you had any more of those dizzy spells or blackouts?"

"We've been over that, Mom. I'm fine."

Lydia hugged her desperately. "I hate leaving you like this! Promise me you won't disappear again!" She dabbed her eyes with a tissue.

Kyle kissed Paige and handed her a box of cookies. "Pistachio palmiers," he said. "My own recipe. I hope you like them." She followed them downstairs and waved as they drove out of the parking lot.

An hour later Paige's roommate, Natalie Cross, burst into the room with orange hair, jeweled eyebrows, and a grating voice. She sat cross-legged on the lower bunk and lit up a joint.

"Want some?"

Paige declined politely. Natalie proceeded to give Paige a rundown of the local watering holes and her lurid history of ex-boyfriends. Feeling old and out of place, Paige went for a walk. The campus was beautiful. Its Spanish Renaissance architecture sprawled over acres of Bermuda grass, stately trees, and wide sidewalks.

Paige found the college atmosphere more serious than high school. No rowdy classes, no enforced discipline, everyone struggling to maintain scholarship requirements or worrying about tuition. Uncertain of her major, Paige focused on the required courses: three hours of science (chemistry), three of history, three of English literature, and three of French, which came easily thanks to her years in the kitchen with Marcel and Jeannine. Her experience earned her a part-time job at the IHOP franchise across from her dorm. Paige liked her boss, but the work was boring. Cooking by the numbers. She spent her free time studying in the library to avoid Natalie, who disturbed her anyway, stumbling in late at night and crashing onto her bunk in a stupor.

On Labor Day weekend, Paige took the bus downtown to visit the Buddy Holly Center. Three years had passed since she and Jeanette posed with the gigantic pair of glasses outside the building. Inside, the memorabilia were unchanged: Buddy's Fender guitar, his record collection, old letters and trinkets from his boyhood home, smiling pictures of the music legend—twenty-two years old forever. Somehow the visit wasn't as exciting as the first time. *Maybe I've outgrown him*, Paige thought.

One of the hosts gave Paige a brochure for the nearby concert hall named in Buddy's honor. It featured performances by the Lubbock Symphony Orchestra and a gourmet restaurant named Rave On, after the tune Paige and Lucas used to sing as they cruised the streets of Alverna. It saddened her to think that people like Buddy Holly and Louise Hargrove had to die violently in order to be remembered.

The next morning Paige rose early and walked down Broadway to the First Christian Church. Everyone there was a stranger, but she took comfort in the pastor's theme of salvation and the hopeful songs. One of them brought tears to her eyes:

Had it not been the Lord who was on our side
Had it not been the Lord who was on our side
The water would have engulfed us
We would have surely died
Had it not been the Lord who was on our side

During the sermon Paige noticed a few people sneaking glances at her. Afterward a woman approached her.

"Are you new here? I get the feeling I've seen you before."

"I don't think so." She excused herself and walked back to the dorm.

The following Sunday she visited First United Methodist, a massive structure with a vaulted ceiling and a pipe organ. One of the elders offered her a blank membership card. Paige declined, fearful of attracting further attention.

On her third Sunday, she tried Broadway Church of Christ. A young man greeted her after services and introduced himself as Jayden Thomas.

"Will you have lunch with me?" he asked. "I haven't been on a date since the semester started."

"Neither have I," she said, smiling. They walked over to the Little Panda for Chinese food. Jayden was from Amarillo. His father was vice president of a large bank. He seemed unaware of Paige's notoriety, so she told him only that her father was a chef and her mother an attorney.

"If I may say so," he ventured, "you're the most attractive girl I've met since I got here." Paige choked on her food. "What's so funny?"

"Sorry. I was just thinking of how I looked a couple of years ago."

Jayden eyed her curiously. "Would you like to go to the Red Raiders football game with me next Saturday?"

"I work on Saturdays."

"Then how about a movie or something? Any night you're free."

Something in his suave demeanor set off warning bells. "Jayden, do you have a girlfriend back home?"

"Yes, but she goes to another school."

"Does she love you?

"Sure, I guess so."

Paige patted his hand. "Then be true to her."

In October the governor's office published a list of clemency orders. One of them was for Jerome Faulkner, who received a full pardon and immediate release. The governor's press secretary added that the decision resulted from a request by his victim. Paige was on her way to history class when the news appeared on her phone. She knelt in the middle of the sidewalk and bowed her head in a prayer of thanks. Other students veered around her, glancing back in puzzlement.

Nevertheless, Paige could not seem to cut ties with the past. One day she ran across an online article about a new website modeled after SerenityShare. But this one was dark, with an open forum justifying suicide and a billboard suggesting painless ways to "catch the bus." The comments stabbed Paige's heart like a rusty knife.

She phoned her mother. "Isn't there a way to prosecute people for this kind of thing?"

"Not in this country," Lydia said. "Free speech is protected by the Bill of Rights. Even if you could prove malicious intent, you'd have to track down the perpetrators, and there are all sorts of ways to conceal your identity on the internet."

Paige recalled the despair that led her to the Bustamante Bridge. At the time, "catching the bus" seemed her only option. But she could not understand what satisfaction anyone gained from tempting other people to do it.

One night Kyle phoned with some interesting news. Charles Duprée was putting Chez Renée up for sale. Business had declined so drastically that he'd had to lay off a third of the staff. He eliminated eight chefs, the wine steward, the dining room musicians, and the reservationist. He fired the cleanup crew and hired high school students to double as waiters and dishwashers. Maxine Chalmers, the maître d', resigned in outrage. Fearing for their reputations, Marcel and Jeannine fled to a high-class restaurant in New Orleans. Predictably, the cuisine suffered. Charles was forced to take charge of the kitchen again and cater banquets to make ends meet, something he'd sworn he would never do. Nobody flew across oceans to visit Chez Renée anymore. The restaurant was degenerating into a small-town diner.

"I don't know how to feel about this," Paige told her father. "It's such a lovely place, and my happiest memories are of working with you in the kitchen."

"Mine too. That's why I've decided to make him an offer."

"Really?" she squealed. "You want to buy the restaurant? But how can you afford it?"

"I'm not sure I can," he admitted. "At the moment your mother's job and my cookbook sales are keeping us afloat. I'd have to get a bank loan to make it work."

"What does Mom think about it?"

"She's worried. It's an awfully big step. I'm not sure my

reputation would be enough to make it profitable again. Paige, you know our clientele as well as I do. What do you think?"

They hashed it over. Chez Renée still had some influential customers, including Robert and Joyce Martin, major donors to the Frazier Memorial Foundation; Tracy Thibault, chair of the school board and owner of Thibault Investment Counseling; J. T. Hudgins, president of the West Texas Farm Bureau; and of course, Omer and Naomi Goldmann.

"They tell me the food is still pretty good," Kyle said, "but the sense of elegant dining is missing."

"How much is Mr. Duprée asking for?"

"Two hundred thousand dollars."

Paige gasped. "On a restaurant that's losing money?"

"That was my reaction. I'm trying to talk him down. Enough about that. How do you like college?"

"It's okay. Tougher than high school."

"Have you made any new friends?"

She laughed. "My roommate's an airhead, and I've been on one date that went nowhere. It doesn't matter. I'm too busy with classwork." Kyle was silent. "Dad? Are you still there?"

"I was just wondering. Has anybody said anything to you about your website?"

"You mean like criticism?"

"Yeah."

"No. But sometimes people recognize me. I can tell by their faces."

Kyle groaned. "I was afraid of that. Paige, maybe you should come home. Take your classes online."

"No, Dad. I'm done with hiding."

"Honey, your mother and I just want you to be safe."

"Nobody's threatened me or accused me of anything. Like you said, this will all blow over someday."

He sighed. "All right. How's your head? Any new symptoms?"

"Nothing. I'm fine."

"Good. Keep taking those pills."

They talked again the following Saturday. Charles Duprée wouldn't take a penny less than he demanded.

"Dad, suppose you ask your friends to go in with you as investors? Then you wouldn't have to raise all the money yourself."

"I thought of that. What if it backfires? What if the customers don't come back? Then we'd all lose our shirts."

"I wish I knew what to tell you," Paige said. "How are things at the shelter?"

"We're still feeding them. That reminds me. Somebody named Dee-Man dropped by the other day and said to tell you hello."

"Oh, Clarence! Don't tell me he's homeless again."

"No, he was just passing through town. He asked me to tell you about deliver."

"About what?"

"Deliver. It's dee meat dat you cook wit' dee onions."

Paige groaned. "That's terrible!"

"Yeah, I thought so too."

They spoke every weekend. Kyle was making discreet inquiries to the local banks about financing. Fred Dawson at First Federal was willing to risk a hundred thousand if Kyle could find investors for the other half. Paige could hear the frustration in her father's voice. Chez Renée had been his whole life.

"Dad, why don't you just go back to work for Mr. Duprée?"

"He doesn't think it would be enough to save the business. Frankly, neither do I."

"In that case, why take the risk at all?"

"I know, it doesn't make sense. It's like having new car fever."

A month passed. Kyle phoned to report that the dining room had lost some of its luster. The tablecloths were stained, the silverware tarnished, the piano and the lighting sconces dusty with neglect. Maxine Chalmers would never have permitted such sloppiness.

Several Alverna businesses, suffering from the loss of tourist trade, were pressuring the banks to loan Kyle the money. Real estate values in the arts district were dropping. Rumors spread that the Park Hyatt chain might close the hotel and cut its losses, throwing more Alvernans out of work.

By late October Paige had settled into a routine: up at six each morning, a cold breakfast from the minifridge while Natalie snored loudly into her pillow, classes from eight to two thirty with a lunch break at the Commons, three hours in the library, then work at IHOP until ten. Occasionally she grew tired of the drill. Then she remembered her grueling road journey. It was nice just to be safe somewhere.

November arrived, and with it a sandstorm that almost blew Paige off her feet as she walked to class. Her hair crackled with static electricity. Lydia wanted her to come home for Thanksgiving weekend.

"I can't, Mom. I'm a little behind in chemistry, finals are coming up, and my boss is begging me to work extra hours while his other employees are gone for the holiday."

"We all miss you, Paige," Lydia fretted. "Jeanette's baby is crawling now. Omer and Naomi's sons are coming to visit and bringing their new granddaughter. Kathy Wingate keeps calling to ask about you."

Paige was torn. It was Lydia who had ingrained in her a sense of responsibility. "Tell them I'll be home for Christmas break."

So Paige spent Turkey Day writing term papers. Over the weekend she cooked pancakes and waffles for the locals and took long walks through the huge campus. With all the students gone, Texas Tech felt like a ghost town. On Monday everyone came back to school except her roommate. Natalie had flunked out.

Three weeks later a freezing wind swept through the campus, along with final exams. Confident that she had aced them all, Paige boarded the bus for Alverna. Her father was pacing rapidly back and forth outside the bus station. Paige had never seen him so nervous. Usually it was Lydia who did the pacing.

"There's been a breakthrough," he said excitedly as he drove them home. "Charles dropped his price to a hundred fifty thousand."

"That's great! Can you raise that much money?"

"No. But apparently nobody else is offering, so he's desperate. He's agreed to three installments of fifty thousand dollars every two years, over a period of six years."

"Can you manage it?"

"Maybe. The bank has agreed to advance the first fifty thousand with a lien on the property."

"What if you can't pay it back?"

"Then I'm busted, and so is Charles. But think of it, Paige! If it works out, I'll have my own restaurant!"

A horn sounded.

"Dad, watch out!"

He slammed on the brakes to avoid running a stop sign. "Sorry," he giggled. "I was awake half the night. I feel like a kid on Christmas Eve."

"It *is* Christmas Eve. Have you signed the papers yet?"

"Your mother asked me to wait till you got home. She

wants us all to pray about it."

So they did.

"God," Kyle pleaded as they held hands across the dinner table, "I'm too caught up in this thing to make a rational decision. Please bless me with your wisdom and our family with your love. And whatever actions we take, may they glorify you."

Paige helped her father prepare Christmas dinner for the shelter. Homeless people swarmed the place and stayed overnight to avoid the cold.

"If you buy the restaurant, who's going to take over here?" Paige wondered.

"I don't know," he admitted. "I've gotten sort of attached to this place. Feeding the downtrodden seems more important than pampering the upper crust."

Naomi Goldmann phoned. "Omer and I have missed you terribly. You must come over for dinner one night before you go back to school."

Paige helped Naomi in the kitchen while Omer worked with Mr. Chen, who joined them for the meal. "How do you like the university?" he asked.

"It's so different. I've never done so much research in my life."

"Ah, yes. To learn is to encounter one's own ignorance."

"He's always saying things like that," Omer complained. "Don't I have enough trouble concentrating?"

"My apologies," said Mr. Chen. "I have no wish to be a thorn in your side." He winked at Paige mischievously.

Eli was on the verge of taking his first steps. He could grab

Jeanette's leg, pull himself to a standing position, and stumble forward before collapsing to a crawl.

"He learns fast," his mother said proudly. "He can't sing the hymns in church, but he babbles the melodies. My mother reads to him while she's babysitting. He listens and laughs, like he knows what she's talking about."

"Have you heard from Lucas?" Paige asked.

"Not directly. One of his friends told me he's working in one of those smoke shops."

"Do his parents know about Eli?"

"Not from me," Jeanette said. "And Eli will never know either. Not unless Lucas decides to grow up."

Paige spent New Year's Eve playing dominoes with the Wingates. Kathy was between boyfriends.

"You were right," she told Paige. "Scott's a drip."

"Now there's an old-fashioned word," Steve grinned.

"It's nicer than some of the other words I have in mind."

"Why?" Steve's ears perked up. "What did he do to you?"

"Nothing, Dad! Stop hovering!" Kathy was a senior now, trying to decide whether to enroll in college. "Does Texas Tech have online classes?"

"Yes, but I like to attend in person. You get more out of it face-to-face."

"Maybe if I came to Tech, you and I could be roommates."

"You'd be a great improvement over my last one."

They played until the fireworks started at midnight. Steve opened a bottle of champagne.

"Here's to times gone by," he said, filling their glasses. "May they always be remembered."

Not all of them, Paige thought.

The next day she returned to campus for the spring semester. The dorm bustled with back-to-the-grind chaos. With Natalie gone, Paige had the room to herself. She gazed out the window at people coming and going along the sidewalks. Another four months of academic toil lay ahead, broken only by her hours in IHOP world.

Two weeks into the semester, her father phoned.

"We've taken the plunge," he announced. "Your mother and I went to the bank this morning and signed the loan. You're speaking to the new owner of Chez Renée."

"Congratulations, Dad! When will you start?"

"Right away." He bubbled over with details. Maxine Chalmers was quitting her job in Austin to return as maître d'. At least four of the restaurant's ex-chefs and waiters would be back, including Marcel and Jeannine. There was a new menu to design and print. Omer and Mr. Chen were revising the Chez Renée website and launching an online advertising campaign. In return, Kyle promised them carte blanche dining for the rest of their lives.

"We're closing for three weeks to remodel and build some anticipation," he said. "But I'm optimistic, Paige. All our old friends are requesting reservations, and I've had several inquiries from big-city dining critics, including Mavis Murray and Elaine Montclair."

"That's wonderful, Dad."

"I can't wait for you to see it. Maybe you can come home at Spring Break."

Paige hung up and returned to the paper she was writing for English Lit. Beside the computer lay textbooks for second semester chemistry, history, and French. Suddenly they all sounded like foreign languages.

She closed the laptop and lay her head on the desk. Outside her window the dust was blowing. Another West Texas gale, the first of the year.

Epilogue

The bearded man with the scarred cheek wrinkled his nose as he chewed. "What in the blue blazes is this stuff?"

"Grilled halibut," said the woman seated across the table. "Ain't you never had fish before?"

"Sure, but not like this. Tastes funny, don'tcha think?"

"I like it."

He took another bite. "Better than TV dinners, I guess. This casserole ain't too bad either."

A middle-aged woman and a teenage boy joined them. "I thought soup kitchens served nothing but soup," the boy said.

"They don't call them soup kitchens anymore. They call them food bank outlets." His mother took a bite. "Hey, this is cilantro! Cilantro fish. I had it once, at that fancy restaurant in the arts district."

"What's cilantro?" asked the man with the scar. "That somethin' in Spanish?"

"No, it's an herb. Goes great with fish and rice."

"I still say it tastes funny."

"Well, I guess it's what you'd call an acquired taste."

The first woman stood up. "I think I'll go acquire another

helping." She crossed the room to the serving window. "Miss, you got any more of this?"

"Sure do." Paige drew a pan from the oven. "Would you like some more casserole?"

"If you can spare it."

"I can. The crowd's kind of small tonight." She filled the woman's plate.

"You sure can cook good. How come you're not workin' in a real restaurant?"

"This is a real restaurant," she smiled. "You just don't have to pay the tab."

The woman accepted the plate gratefully. "This is the first decent meal I've had in two months. In fact, it's the first nice thing that's happened to me since I lost my job."

"Do you have a place to stay tonight? The dorm's remodeled, and we've got plenty of space."

The words brought tears to the woman's eyes. "I'm not used to this. I've always paid my own way. It's just that . . ." She broke down. "I never thought somethin' like this could happen to me!"

"Nobody ever does," Paige responded. "Don't let it get to you. Have a good supper, get a good night's sleep, and you'll feel better in the morning."

"Thank you." The woman started back to the table. "Do you need any help in the kitchen?"

"You can help me with the dishes when you're through."

"I'd be happy to."

Paige's phone rang. She wiped her hands on a towel and answered it.

"Paige, have you got any fresh oregano over there?"

"I think so, Dad. Let me check." She carried the phone outside to the herb garden, where two homeless ladies knelt on the ground, planting basil, rosemary, and thyme sprouts. Paige walked along the little path, looking for oregano. "Yes Dad, there's plenty. How much do you need?"

"All you can spare. Marcel's got a new idea for Greek lentil soup."

"I'll bring it over when I'm finished."

"Great. You can meet our newest employee, Anthony Garland."

"Anthony? The boy who attacked me?"

"That's right. He asked me for a job so he can help his father pay off your hospital bills. I started him out as a busboy. If he does a good job, Maxine's going to train him as a waiter."

"That's a great idea, Dad. How's business tonight?"

"Terrific. Just like old times. Gotta go, honey. See you later."

Paige returned to the serving window.

A young man in jeans and a faded shirt was waiting for her. "May I have some more of that casserole, please?"

"Sure."

The guy had a weathered face and a warm smile. "Say! Aren't you the girl who had that website a while back? The one for people with personal problems?"

Paige's heart sank. "Yes. That was me."

"Wow!" He seemed at a loss for words. "Paige Abernathy! I saw you on the news. You don't look anything like that Little White Dove picture on your website."

"No. That wasn't me. I just thought it was."

"I was one of your subscribers. I had that site bookmarked until you canceled it. Then everybody started looking for you."

"And now you've found me. Look, I'm sorry if I did anything to hurt you. The website—"

"No! Oh, not at all. In fact, you saved my life!"

"I did?"

He offered Paige his hand. "My name's Jeff Lowery. My forum name was GoneforGood."

Her jaw dropped. "I remember that! You're one of the people who threatened to kill themselves. I was so worried. I tried to find out if you'd gone through with it."

Jeff leaned closer. "I had it all planned out," he confided. "I was going to dig a hole somewhere outside of town, swallow some pills, and bury myself before they kicked in. But then I went back one last time and read what you wrote about life being a gift from God. It reminded me how happy I was before things started going wrong with my family. So I got down on my knees and begged God to show me a way out. And this great feeling of peace came over me!" His eyes shone. "You saved me, Paige. Thanks to you, I didn't give up, even though my girlfriend dumped me and my father was driving me crazy. I finally left home. Maybe that was a mistake, starting out on foot from Albuquerque with no job and no money. But I'm a stronger person now. Thanks to you, I know God will get me through anything."

"Don't thank me," she said. "Thank God for giving you the strength to keep going."

"I do. Every day." Glancing around at the other diners, Jeff lowered his voice. "People always look at me funny when I talk about God and Jesus and the Holy Spirit. Like I'm embarrassing them or something. But I know you understand, Paige. I could tell from your comments on that forum."

"Thank you, Jeff. You don't know how much it means to hear someone say that." She handed him the plate.

"Gosh, you're a swell cook. Are you here every night?"

"I sure am. Two meals a day, seven days a week."

Jeff looked at the wall clock. "I'd better finish up. I've

got the night shift at the Quick Mart down the street." He hesitated. "Listen, Paige. I know I'm just a street bum, but . . . do you think I could come back tomorrow night and talk to you some more? I don't have any friends around here. And I feel like I already know you."

"I'd like that," Paige said. "I'd like that very much."

Book Club Questions for
The Samaritan's Patient

1. What did you think of the title? Would you have chosen something different?
2. What was the author's purpose in writing this book? Was there more than one?
3. How did the website factor in this story affect your opinions about social media?
4. How did you feel about the comments on the SerenityShare website?
5. How does Paige Abernathy's experience relate to that of other young people today?
6. Did any of the characters remind you of people you know? In what way?
7. What character is most memorable to you?
8. Did any of the characters change as a result of their experiences? Which ones?
9. Did any of the characters remain the same despite their

experiences? Which ones?

10. This book includes many secondary characters. What did they contribute to the story?
11. Were any of the characters, scenes, or events unrealistic? How so?
12. What scenes were most important to you?
13. Were there any scenes that made you laugh or cry?
14. Were you able to work out the mysteries in this story ahead of time?
15. Did you learn anything new from this novel?
16. Did the novel leave you with any unanswered questions?
17. Was the book satisfying to read? Why or why not?
18. What did you think of the ending?
19. Who would you recommend this book to, if anyone?
20. Did this book change any of your personal views? How?

Other Novels from Chevron Ross

Weapons of Remorse

Hank Phillips makes his living defending the right to bear arms. Privately, he doesn't want to touch a gun ever again.

Hank is an ex-Marine whose heroism in war earned him the Medal of Honor and a high-profile job with America's most powerful gun rights organization. He has millions of admirers and a bright future. But what Hank values most is his relationship with God. He believes his war record has poisoned it, and he prays that God will let him atone.

One night, a gunfire incident brings disaster upon Hank and a police officer. It also leads to a kidnapping and reignites the controversy over gun owners' rights.

Weapons of Remorse looks behind the headlines to explore the personal consequences of America's gun violence dilemma.

Chevron Ross

The Seven-Day Resurrection

Len Holder thinks his mother is dead—until she reappears one morning in his living room.

She doesn't remember being dead. She's just confused.

And instead of her burial clothes, she's wearing a Dallas Cowboys warm-up suit.

At seventy-eight, Len considers himself a failure. He spent years taking care of Mom while his brother Joey became a famous sportscaster. Now he lives alone, tinkering with a novel he can't seem to finish.

For a week, Len relives a strained relationship with Mom while other mysteries pile up. He keeps hearing fragments of Joey's radio show. His sister reports disturbing phone calls. Strangers he meets look like people from his past. Another stranger has taken over his insurance office.

Then Len gets word that his beloved boss Miranda has been gravely injured in a car accident. Eventually, Miranda's fate and a shocking secret from the past reveal that Sharon Holder's resurrection is not what it seems to be.

The Seven-Day Resurrection is a must-read for anyone who has been thrust into the role of caregiver.

Final Notes

Because this novel deals with the subject of suicide, some readers may find the following link helpful. The 988 Suicide & Crisis Lifeline provides free and confidential emotional support to people in suicide crisis or emotional distress 24 hours a day, 7 days a week, across the United States. https://988lifeline.org/

If you enjoyed this book, I would be very grateful if you could write a review and publish it at your point of purchase. Your review, even a brief one, will help other readers to decide whether they'll enjoy this novel.

If you want to be notified of new releases from myself and other AIA Publishing authors, please sign up to the AIA Publishing email list. In return you'll get a free e-book of short stories and book excerpts by AIAP authors. You'll find the sign-up button on the right-hand side under the photo at www.aiapublishing.com. Of course, your information will never be shared, and the publisher won't inundate you with emails, just let you know of new releases.